ROBIN LEE HATCHER

LEISURE BOOKS **NEW YORK CITY**

To Aunt Marge, Mother, Polly and Annyta
because you believed in me enough
to make it come true.

A LEISURE BOOK®

February 1994

Published by

Dorchester Publishing Co., Inc.
276 Fifth Avenue
New York, NY 10001

Chapter 1

Morning burst upon the fields of Spring Haven with bright sunshine and blue skies. The singing of the field hands as they set about their tasks drifted up to the house. The flower gardens were ablaze with color and bees hummed busily about the bushes and vines. The manor house was already filled with activity even though it was still early. It wasn't every day that a Bellman got married.

Some of the house servants were already setting up chairs on the east lawn where the ceremony would take place. Their laughter and chatter flowed up to Taylor Bellman's room, waking her from her troubled sleep. She slipped out from under the light covers on her bed and crossed to the window. The scene below her was a merry one. For a brief moment she forgot the anxiety which had kept her awake most of the night.

Taylor leaned forward for a better view of the activities beneath her window. Her long raven-black hair fell forward into her face, and she pushed it back with an impatient gesture. Stormy blue eyes sparkled as she watched two small boys tumble over a chair as they tried to carry a table too large for young limbs to manage. Her night-gown clung to her lithe body, revealing high breasts, a tiny waist and long, slim legs. The door opened behind her and Jenny, Taylor's olive-skinned maid, entered, bringing her a cup of hot chocolate on a tray.

"Miss Taylor, I figured you'd prob'ly be up with so much goin's on round here," she said, setting the tray on a small bedside table. "You drink this here choc'late, Missy, and I'll get your bath ready."

Alone again, Taylor sat down and sipped the hot liquid. She leaned her head against the velvet material of the chair and closed her eyes. Visions of walking through the gardens in her mother's old wedding gown flitted through her mind. She envisioned the bridegroom standing in the distance. She strained to see his face, but like a phantom, he vanished. It was always the same. Fear gnawed at her heart.

"Oh, Papa," she whispered. "Why is this happening? Why must I face this alone?"

Taylor hadn't meant to eavesdrop. The door to

6

her father's study had been standing open, and Philip's angry words assailed her as she came down the hall.

"Mortgaged Spring Haven! How could you be so stupid?" he yelled.

"You watch what you're saying to me, Phillip. I'm still your father even if you are a grown man."

"Hell, you've never been a father to me. When my mother died and you married your precious Christina, I was just an unwelcome piece of baggage, shipped off to any boarding school that would have me," he spat out furiously.

Taylor peeked around the door in time to see Martin Bellman sit down, his face white with surprise. "I never meant for you to feel unwanted, Philip," he said.

Philip waved away his father's words. "Forget it."

"Philip, I . . ."

"Don't you understand?" Philip cut in. "Spring Haven is the only thing you had left to give me once *they* came into your life. It's mine! Nothing and no one is ever going to take it from me. Not even if I have to lie or cheat or steal . . . or even *kill* for it. This place is mine!"

Martin's head drooped forward in an air of hopelessness. "Yes. I guess I do understand," he said softly.

"Good. The point now is to save Spring Haven. Just how bad is it?" His voice shook with anger, his words uttered in a deathly calm.

"I don't know. I guess I haven't paid much

attention to those affairs lately. I . . . I've been. . .''

"You've been drunk," Philip growled.

"I'm sor . . . I'm sorry, Philip. Since Christina died, I haven't. . .''

"Oh, blast your Christina!" Philip shouted as he stormed from the room, nearly knocking Taylor down in his haste.

Taylor hurried to her father. Placing her arms around him, she pulled his head against her breast and waited while he sobbed out his pain and confusion.

"It's all right, Papa," she murmured, stroking his head, seeking to comfort him in some way.

"Nothing's right," he rasped, his words tearing at her heart. "Nothing will ever be right again."

Tears fell from her eyes to mingle with those of her father.

Two days later, Martin Bellman rode out on his spirited gray stallion and didn't return. They found him where he had fallen in a drunken stupor, his neck broken.

Taylor's heartache appeared to be neverending. The last two years had pummeled her spirit again and again. First her mother was taken from her and then her father. She was left in the care of an older half brother whose jealousy over her relationship with their father overshadowed any familial love which might have existed between them under other circumstances. Her father's heavy drinking and subsequent reckless gambling after his wife's death had forced the

8

mortgaging of the Bellman lands. Now Spring Haven was threatened with foreclosure.

The pain and loneliness caused by her father's death was still fresh within Taylor's heart when the next blow fell. She and Philip had sat down to another silent, strained supper, the long ebony table stretching out between them. Only the sound of knives and forks clinking against the plates broke the tomblike silence in the dining room. Taylor picked at her food, having little appetite. Her nerves warned her that something dreadful was about to happen. She could feel it in the air.

Philip cleared his throat. "Taylor, I received some unusual correspondence this last week. I think it might be of interest to you."

She looked up from her plate, her fork frozen in the air. Whatever this was about was bound to be unpleasant.

"David Lattimer, the gentleman whose bank holds our mortgage, has offered to release it . . . provided we can meet one small obligation." The smile he was wearing altered slightly. "He wants to marry you."

Taylor gasped. She stared, speechless, down the long table at her brother.

"Well," he said smugly, "don't you have anything to say?"

"Surely you're not considering this offer? Why, we don't even know who he is, do we?"

Philip gazed at her coldly. "My dear sister, we know the only thing that counts. He holds the mortgage to Spring Haven."

"But Philip. . ." Taylor rose swiftly in protest.

"Sit down," he said softly. His whispered words sent chills racing up her spine. She quickly obeyed him as he continued speaking. "I will remind you, Taylor, that I am your guardian and you must do as I say."

His eyes locked with hers, cold and void of emotion. Suddenly they were lit with a flame of passion. "You owe me, Taylor. You couldn't possibly understand just how much you owe me or even why. But owe me, you do. And this is how you can repay me. You will save Spring Haven from the hands of outsiders. You will keep it for Bellmans. You profess to love it as I do, as Father did. If that's true, this isn't too much to ask."

The color had drained from her face. She sought to keep the quiver from her voice as she replied, "I *do* love Spring Haven. But, Philip, I'm not going to marry someone I don't even know, let alone love."

"Then I will tell you about him. He is a widower with one son. He is the owner of a large bank in New York City. He was born in the South, but not to one of our *better* families, and he is eager to return here and settle down. He has purchased the old Dorcet plantation. It's where you will live after your wedding." He rubbed his temples as if they hurt. "Is there anything else you would like to know about your groom?"

"You can't make me do this. Papa would never have asked me to do it, not even for Spring

10

Haven. I . . . and I won't do it for you!"

She jumped up, knocking her chair over as she did so. She began to run from the room. Suddenly Philip grabbed her shoulders, arresting her flight as he spun her around. Fear spread its tentacles through her as he snarled his angry words.

"You will marry Mr. Lattimer if I tell you to."

"I won't!" she screamed at him.

She reeled backwards, her head snapping sideways as the back of his hand connected with her right cheek. Her shoulder smacked into the wall, and the air rushed from her lungs. Her fingers flew involuntarily to her face, covering the darkening angry welt his blow had left. Tears welled up in her dark blue eyes as she faced her tormenter.

Philip stepped closer, speaking in a false gentleness. "I have sent word to Mr. Lattimer that you have accepted his gracious proposal. Your engagement will be announced at once in the *Intelligencer.* You will be given the wedding of the year, of course. A wedding like every young girl wants. A June wedding." He reached forward and stroked the red mark on her cheek. "This is the only way, Taylor. Someday, perhaps, you will understand the importance of this decision. Once you are gone from here, Spring Haven will be truly mine." He was no longer speaking to her, only to himself. "You disrupted everything that should have been. He would have even left Spring Haven to you if he could. But he's gone now, and it's mine. This is what must be done to save it. It's

11

the only way." The hardness returned to his voice. "Taylor, I will be obeyed in this matter."

He stepped back, allowing her to escape. She fled to her room, closing the door safely behind her and leaning against it. She tried to still the rising panic. This wasn't happening to her. It couldn't be. Perhaps she and Philip weren't close, but he wasn't cruel. He wouldn't really force her to marry a stranger. Surely not!

Unbelieving, yet helpless to stop it, Taylor watched as preparations went on around her. She felt herself a prisoner, unable to break the bonds which were dragging her closer and closer to some unknown terror.

Today was that unknown terror—her wedding day. She would be seventeen next week. And today she was marrying a man she had never even met.

"Miss Taylor, your bath is hot an' waitin' fer you. Missy?"

Taylor opened her eyes, her memories scurrying back to their hiding places until they should be summoned again. For now, the present loomed much too real to be ignored for long.

She bathed quickly, her nervous anticipation not allowing her to linger in the perfumed water. She was sitting at her dressing table while Jenny brushed her ebony curls into order when the housekeeper, Susan, brought word that Mr. Lattimer had arrived. He and Master Philip were waiting for her in the library.

"I'll be down very shortly, Susan," Taylor told her. She glanced at Jenny's reflection in the mirror. "They say it's bad luck for the groom to see the bride before the wedding," she said wryly, "but I suppose it would be worse not to have ever seen one another. Don't you think so, Jenny?"

"Yes'm, Missy. I reckon you're right. That would seem even worse," Jenny replied. "There, we're done, Missy. You go along now, and I'll be gettin' your weddin' dress ready for you."

Taylor surveyed herself in the mirror. Her image was mute proof of her fright. Her complexion had lost the slightest hint of color, and her eyes seemed to sink behind her high cheekbones. Summoning up her courage, she lifted her chin and reminded herself that she was a Bellman. She would do what she had to do.

She took the backstairs down to the library, avoiding any guests who might have been wandering about. She knocked on the door before entering. Philip hurried to meet her and brought her over to where David Lattimer was rising from his chair. Taylor fought to keep the shock from revealing itself on her face as they were introduced. David Lattimer was a gray-haired old man!

"I'm glad to meet you at last, Miss Bellman. It's unfortunate that it couldn't have been earlier. Would you please join me on the settee?"

Taylor sat down obediently, still overwhelmed by this new twist. She glanced quickly at her brother. Had Philip known Mr. Lattimer's age?

Had he intentionally led her to believe she was marrying a young widower with a small son?

Mr. Lattimer turned to Philip. "May we be alone for a moment, Mr. Bellman?"

"Certainly. Please join me in the east drawing room at your convenience. The guests are arriving and will be looking forward to meeting you."

When the door had closed behind him, David cleared his throat and looked directly into Taylor's eyes. "Miss Bellman, I am sure you have been pressured into this marriage by your brother and your desire to save your ancestral plantation. There is no need for us to be anything but candid and honest with one another.

"I am an old man now, but I still have dreams for the future. I require a wife to accomplish those dreams. Not just any wife. I need a well-bred Southerner, a woman of the aristocracy. Not many are willing to marry an aging Yankee, even one who was actually born in the South not far from here. Not even one as wealthy as I am. Therefore, it was necessary to find a desperate one. You, Miss Bellman." He paused for her to speak. When she remained silent, he continued, "I was married before. My wife died after eighteen years of marriage. It was a good, solid relationship; we were quite fond of one another. We had one child, a son, who is abroad at this time."

He cleared his throat once again. "Miss Bellman, I am not such a fool as to think this is a pleasant arrangement for one so young and beautiful as yourself. I do think we can learn to be

14

comfortable together. I am not a hard taskmaster." He rose abruptly, drawing her up with him, and guided her to the door. "We get married in about an hour, Miss Bellman. I imagine you have some preparations."

"Yes," she whispered and left.

Her thoughts in much confusion, Taylor hurried up the stairs. She could hear the buzz of the guests as they mingled in the drawing rooms below and out on the lawn. The crunch of buggy wheels accompanied by the clip-clop of horses' hooves announced new arrivals in a continuous stream.

David watched her retreat—and retreat it was. She had taken him by surprise with her youth and beauty. To be sure, he was well informed of her age, but somehow, he had expected her to be homely, someone without a suitor or any possibility of making a good match. So his sources of information weren't as thorough as he had thought them to be. Well, he would tend to that later.

He sighed and moved to pour himself a drink. "What are you doing this for, you old fool?" he asked himself aloud.

But he knew the answer well enough. David Lattimer had planned carefully his return to the South. He had been slighted too often by the gentry. He was determined to pierce their closed ranks, and then Taylor Bellman had fallen into his hands like an answer to a prayer. Yes, he was old— old enough to be her grandfather. Was it fair to saddle her with such a husband, a girl so lovely?

He set the empty glass down with a crash, shattering its base. It didn't matter if it was fair or not. It was what he needed to do. He would be kind to her and would demand little from her other than to be called his wife. He had no intention of her really being a wife to him, just so long as she acted the part publicly. She would never be in want or mistreated. He need not concern himself with it. After all, she was gaining what she was after—someone to pay the bills on Spring Haven.

No, they had made their bargain. He must not worry over her happiness.

Jenny was waiting for Taylor. Christina's wedding gown, carefully preserved for just this day, was spread out on the bed.

" 'Bout time, Missy. We got t'hurry some if all's goin' t'run smooth now," Jenny said. She guided Taylor over near the bed and started to unbutton the dress, her fingers flying after years of practice. Jenny had been Taylor's personal maid since Taylor was ten years old. She had been married for two years to a big black field hand named Caesar. Taylor's marriage was taking her away from her husband since Philip refused to sell his hardest working slave, but Jenny remained stoically silent about this separation.

Taylor watched Jenny's administrations in the mirror. Often in the last few months, she had tried to ask Jenny what it was like to be married, to share a man's bed, but she never could manage to bring it up. Now it was too late.

After removing Taylor's dress and undergarments, Jenny slipped a silk chemise over her head. Taylor's figure needed no stiff corseting, so the next items were several petticoats of cream-colored taffeta. The wedding gown itself was made of old French lace and satin. The low neckline of the snug-fitting bodice was embroidered with pearls. The voluminous skirt contained yards and yards of rich satin covered by delicate lace and followed by a train nearly twelve feet long.

After all the tiny buttons up the back were fastened, Jenny placed on Taylor's head a crown of pearls, from which hung a finely woven veil. Then she brought her mistress a pair of satin slippers which had also belonged to the bride's mother.

"Mama must have been radiant when she married Father," Taylor said as she turned in front of her mirror. "They were so much in love. I wish I. . ." She stopped abruptly and turned with a whoosh of skirts. "Tell Philip the bride is ready whenever they are. Be quick about it," she snapped, her nerves stretched to their limits. "I can't even sit down."

Alone again, she went to the window and peered outside. The lawn was full of people, both friends and strangers. At last, Taylor caught sight of the groom. David Lattimer was a tall man with gray hair and a neatly trimmed gray beard.

Though slightly heavy, he cut a fine figure in his wedding attire. His manner was that of a man who expected to get what he wanted—and then went out and got it. He was ruggedly handsome and carried himself with a distinguished air.

Taylor had very mixed emotions about this man. She remembered his words to her in the library. He was abrupt and cool in his analysis of their marriage, but she believed he meant for them to have an amiable life together. He seemed to appreciate honesty. He understood why she was marrying him and didn't seem to expect more than she could give. At least there would be no illusions to be shattered. Chances were this marriage would remove her to a more congenial atmosphere at the very least. Whether he had grounds for his jealousy or not, Philip's behavior toward her was intolerable.

Soft music began playing beneath her window. Philip had hired an orchestra for the wedding and the dancing which would follow. Taylor drew herself away from the window and walked toward the door. In a little while, she would be Mrs. David Lattimer.

Chapter 2

Slowly she descended the curving marble staircase, her hand gliding over the elegantly carved oak bannister which glistened from hours of polishing by the servants under Susan's watchful eye. The tiled floor shimmered in its reflection of the crystal chandelier with its many tiny candles ablaze. She stopped at the bottom of the stairway and looked around her. She loved Spring Haven with something deep and instinctive. It was worth it to keep it in Bellman hands. This place *was* her father and mother. She couldn't bear to lose it to strangers. She might never spend another night under this roof, but it would always be home to her.

"I *am* marrying for love, Papa," she whispered softly. "For love of Spring Haven."

Philip observed her from the doorway. Never

had he seen anyone look so ravishing, so utterly beautiful. It made him angry that even he was sucked in by those deep blue pools set on both sides of her straight nose and surrounded by her milky skin. He constantly battled a desire to protect her from harm, to cherish her, to accept her advances of friendship. He could not succumb to her charms. Spring Haven was all he had, all that had not forsaken him as a child when his father brought home his sloe-eyed Creole wife.

Oh, Christina had tried to win him over, but he was too crafty to be won so easily. He wanted her to prove she really loved him. And then the baby came. From an infant, she had twisted his father around her little finger. She was gentle and kind-natured and laughed easily. Suddenly the entire plantation seemed to revolve around her. She was so very beautiful . . . and she loved Spring Haven too.

He beat down his conflicting emotions. This was simply something that had to be done. She was the usurper and must be sacrificed to save him his home.

"Are you ready, Taylor?" he asked gruffly.

She looked up with pretended calm. "Yes, I'm ready."

Taylor took his proffered arm, holding herself erect. They walked the length of the main portico in silence. The white Grecian columns glimmered in the late morning sun. She experienced a renewed panic, wanting to throw her arms around one of the strong pillars and hold on until she was safe again. She looked around her, as if to snatch one last memory of her home. The lush lawn surrounding the house, twenty acres of it, was covered with live oak, magnolias, cedars, pines, and many other forest trees. These were arranged in groves or stretched out in lines and avenues or dotted the lawn here and there. The perfume from violets, pansies, wild honeysuckle, azaleas, and roses filled the air with a sweetness suitable for a wedding.

Philip and Taylor reached the steps leading them to the east lawn. They paused for a moment. A simultaneous gasp from the guests was heard as they caught sight of the bride. Conversations ceased and every eye was upon her as she floated down the steps and across the grass. She could see David waiting for her at the other end of the long aisle, his tall body standing straight and sure.

Philip stopped. His head leaned closer to hers, his softly spoken words filtering through to her fear-fogged brain. "I *do* hope you'll be happy. There really was no other way."

Surprised by his sincerity, hope surged within her breast. Maybe he wouldn't make her go through with this. Maybe he did care what happened to her. Maybe they could be close like other brothers and sisters. Maybe. . .

Philip saw the plea in her eyes from behind her veil. He remembered how his father always melted before that look, and the chill returned to his voice as he continued. "A bride should be

21

smiling on her wedding day, Taylor," he whispered, pinching her arm. "Smile."

Oh, how she hated him at this moment! Her anger flashed across her face and her eyes snapped their fury, but she covered it quickly with a smile. Taylor turned to face her groom, determined no one would see the turmoil within her. Somehow she walked down the aisle with the look of a happy bride.

David took her arm as she reached him. They stood before the Reverend Stone, solemnly repeating their vows, promising to love and honor the other. Within moments, Katherine Taylor Bellman had become Mrs. David Maxwell Lattimer. Her emotions wrapped in a protective cocoon, Taylor listened as the Reverend instructed her new husband to kiss his bride. She was married!

David's large, aging hands lifted her veil. His beard brushed her cheek lightly as he placed a gentle kiss on her cheekbone. Then arm in arm, they walked back down the aisle together. Suddenly they were surrounded by people. They were hugged and kissed and given countless best wishes. The doors of the drawing rooms were thrown wide, and the orchestra began to play a waltz. The guests waited for the bride and groom to begin the dancing.

"Mrs. Lattimer, shall we?"

Holding her train over her arm, Taylor was swirled about the room in his arms. Soon they were joined on the floor by other couples, a sparkling mood touching all the dancers.

"Your brother has done this up proud, hasn't he, Taylor?" David whispered in her ear.

And why not? Taylor wondered. It was David's money Philip was spending so lavishly.

The celebration continued into the evening. Long tables were spread generously with food, and wine and brandy flowed freely among the guests. Watching the joyful crowd, Taylor felt suddenly worlds apart from all her friends. In minutes she had become years older than even her very best friend, Marilee Stone. A wide chasm had opened between them, one she felt incapable of crossing as the wife of this stranger.

Her head was throbbing painfully and she was weary from the dancing and noise and laughter when David said softly, "It's time to start for home, Taylor. Please make ready."

"I'll go change," she answered.

"And I'll be waiting for you in the library. I've had enough of the festivities."

Taylor went swiftly to her room. "Jenny?" she called, but there was no reply. Probably with Caesar, she thought as she began struggling with the buttons on the back of her gown. Just when she couldn't manage another one, Jenny appeared at the door.

"Miss Taylor, you should've sent fer me!" she exclaimed.

"Yes, I should have. But at least you're here now. Get me out of this. Mr. Lattimer is wanting

23

to leave."

In no time at all, Jenny had removed the wedding gown and replaced it with a lightweight traveling dress in a warm salmon color, which complemented Taylor's ivory skin and dark hair.

"Are you ready, Jenny? It's time to go."

"Yes'm. I said my goodbyes already. It's not like we was movin' outta the county. I 'magine I'll get back t'see my man now and agin."

Taylor put her arms around Jenny and hugged her. "I'm sorry you and Caesar have to be apart, Jenny," she said sincerely, "but I'm awfully glad I'll have a familiar face with me."

The journey to Dorcet Hall was spent in silence, each traveler lost in his or her own thoughts. Jenny rode next to the driver on top of the carriage. Taylor sat facing her husband and stared, unseeing, out the window as they moved farther and farther from home.

A knot was forming in her stomach as they approached their destination. A terror of the coming night was consuming her, and Taylor felt faint at the thought of sharing a bed with this stranger across from her. Her understanding of the physical side of marriage was more speculation than fact due to her sheltered upbringing. The unknown loomed in her mind, a frightening shadow on her horizon.

Dorcet Hall came into sight at last. Taylor leaned toward the window, glad for something else to occupy her thoughts. The house itself sat on a slight swell. It was much smaller than Spring Haven, being only two stories tall and the upper floor containing only four bedrooms. The red brick structure was ablaze with lights as the servants prepared for the arrival of the master with his bride.

The plantation was not a large one, consisting of about seven hundred acres, planted mostly in cotton. Taylor could see a brick kitchen off to the back of the house, but no slave quarters were in view from the drive, at least not in the darkening twilight. The lawn seemed to be neat and well kept, filled with oak trees and magnolias.

As she watched, the slaves began to assemble at the front of the house, house servants and field hands alike, about fifty in all. She realized they must be as anxious as she was, since their master himself had only arrived the day before.

"I grew up across the river from here."

The sound of David's voice set her heart to pounding again. She sat back against her seat, the icy fear returning in a rush as she was reminded why she was here.

When they had drawn to a halt in front of the house, David helped her out of the carriage, and they turned together to meet their servants.

"Most of our people have been at Dorcet Hall all their lives," he told her. "As I'm new here, too, we are still strangers to each other. However, I am sure they will serve us well."

David nodded to the watching faces as he guided Taylor up the steps with Jenny following close behind them.

"It has been a strenuous day," he said as they climbed the stairs to the second landing. "I think we had best retire without further ado."

Taylor remained awkwardly silent.

"This is your bedchamber, my dear. I hope you will approve of it. If not, you can change it any way you see fit. Your things which were sent earlier should be ready for you. I will bid you goodnight and leave you to your Jenny." He bowed slightly to her, turned on his heel, and walked down the hall to another bedroom.

Taylor felt rooted to the floor, confused by this action. Jenny opened the door to the bedroom, walked over to the bed, and turned down the covers. The huge four-poster, its white canopy nearly touching the ceiling, filled only a small portion of the large room. A thick white and blue carpet covered most of the hardwood floor, and delicately carved, very feminine, white furniture was placed in cozy groupings throughout. A vanity table with an enormous mirror sat next to a window, and there was a door leading out onto the gallery on the other side of it. A fire burned on the hearth, more as a welcome than for warmth since the windows had been thrown open to let in the sweet June air. A nightgown had been laid out over the fluffy blue quilt on the bed. Jenny held it out to her.

"Missy, you best get to bed. You look plumb wore out. There'll be plenty time later t'think 'bout it all."

After she had helped Taylor undress and get into bed, Jenny left to find her own sleeping quarters. Taylor pulled the covers up tight under her chin. She stared at the canopy above her, so still she barely breathed. Suddenly she turned and buried her face in the pillow. A muffled sob split the darkness, followed by another and another, until the night was filled with her lonely heart's cry.

Chapter 3

Taylor sat in the shade of a large magnolia, her embroidery lying idle in her lap. While it was still early in the day, the air was already heavy with the heat of August. Her eyes gazed without focusing toward the long drive. Her daydreams flitted from one subject to another like the butterflies flitting over the grass.

The two months since her wedding had come and gone quickly. She had long since given up worrying if David might come to her room in the night. This apparently was not to be a part of their arrangement. She was relieved but was left feeling somehow inadequate and unattractive at the same time. They entertained often, and each time David remarked how proud she made him.

"You are a fine asset to my home," he had told her one night after their guests had departed. "I made a wise move in marrying you. You have made it possible for me to meet and mingle with those I couldn't have otherwise."

Taylor knew he meant this as a compliment, but she was frustrated and hurt by it nonetheless. Though she still didn't know him, she had grown fond of David in her own way. Why then did she feel so lonely and hurt?

She got up and strolled through the rose garden, her embroidery falling forgotten to the ground. She paced between the bushes like a caged animal. *That's it*, she thought. *I'm in a cage, a very pretty cage.* A robin burst forth in song overhead, and she watched as he took off in flight.

"Take me with you, little bird," she cried after him. "Let me ride away on your song and be free."

Her arms were rigid, her fists clenched tightly at her sides. What was wrong with her? Why couldn't she be happy? She had so many things other women didn't have. In many little ways, David had been very kind to her. Learning of her love of horses, he had presented her with a beautiful Arabian mare. He was generous with his money, allowing her to purchase anything she needed or desired. He gave her complete control over the running of the household. True, he often seemed totally withdrawn from her, as if he wished she weren't around, as if he were unwilling to allow her to be a part of his life, but David didn't mistreat her like some men were known to treat their wives and he didn't drink heavily as

29

others did. So why wasn't she content?

"Miss Taylor, can I get you anythin'?"

Jenny stood at the entrance to the garden. A bulge around her middle indicated a baby would be added to the Lattimer household in the next three or four months.

"No, Jenny. I don't need anything . . . except maybe some exercise. Why don't you walk with me to the river?"

They strolled along in a companionable silence through the woods which separated the cotton fields from the river. Moss clung to the trees, and the forest floor was thickly cushioned with grass, old leaves and needles. The wild carpet crunched under their feet, making a pleasant melody. The aria of the river could be dimly heard wafting through the trees.

"How are you feeling, Jenny?"

"Oh, I'm fine, Missy. Ol' Mima, she keeps me hoppin', but she's no dif'rent than Susan at the old place. Sometimes I'm a bit lonesome, but I reckon that's 'cause I'm new here."

"Have you been to see Caesar?"

"Hasn't been anybody goin' that way since we come here," Jenny answered sadly.

"Does he know you're having a baby?" Taylor asked.

"Yes'm. He knowed befo' we left. We was both hopin' Masta Philip would see his way clear t'sellin' him to Masta David."

"We'll keep trying, Jenny. I promise."

Taylor felt truly sorry for Jenny. Somehow,

30

Philip had to be persuaded to sell Caesar to David. Last week he had ridden over to talk to David, and Taylor had approached him on the subject. He had refused to even consider it.

"Caesar is one of the best workers I have on the place," he told her. "Most of them don't even pay for their keep as far as I'm concerned. Shows what those damn Yankees know about slavery," he said, turning to David.

Taylor knew the subject of Caesar was closed. Philip and David were off on the subject of the growing unrest between the North and South. She quietly left the room, tired of hearing people talking about it.

They arrived at the river, and Taylor sat down on the bank. Jenny leaned against an old tree stump, resting her hands on her swollen stomach. Taylor bent down to the water and traced designs with her fingers on the rushing surface.

"Jenny, are you glad to be having a baby?" she inquired as she watched the river race toward places she had never been.

"Yes, Missy. It's part of life, what changes you from a girl to a woman. Don't know nobody who'd want t'lay with her man an' not carry his chil' inside her. Yes'm, I reckon I'm goin' t'like motherin' this chil'." She looked closely at Taylor. "You oughta get yo'self with a baby, Missy. You wouldn't be feelin' so sad then."

Taylor glanced sharply at Jenny. "Well, that might be nice, Jenny, but it's out of the question right now. Besides, I'm not all that unhappy."

"Pardon me for bein' uppity, Missy, but you sho' is. I don't think I ever seen you so lonely as you been since we come here."

"You're right, you are uppity. Master David has been very good to me. But then, I don't have to explain to you why there'll be no babies."

"You wants one, Missy, you should go after gettin' one," Jenny said firmly.

"Jenny!"

"Sorry, Missy, but it's true. You can't keep no secrets from the house darkies for long. They all knows there's not been a beddin' betwixt you and the masta."

Taylor stood abruptly, brushing the red clay from her skirt. "We're going back, Jenny," she said, and started toward the house at a brisk pace.

"Miss Taylor," Jenny panted behind her. "You could get Masta David to get you a baby if you'd a mind t'try. He really does care a heap for you."

"That's quite enough," Taylor snapped.

They arrived at the house in a stiff silence. Taylor went directly to her room. She removed her dress, soaked with perspiration caused by the humid weather and the exertion of the return walk. Dressed only in her slip, she sat at her dressing table and studied the girl in the mirror. A kaleidoscope of emotions ran amok within and she fought for control over them. Would a baby really make her any happier? Would sharing David's bed really make any difference in how she felt—about him or about herself? A knock sounded at her door. She ignored it, hoping whoever it was would go away, but the knock was repeated. Then the knob turned and the door opened a crack.

"Taylor?" It was David.

The door opened wider and he stepped inside.

"I'm riding out to oversee some harvesting. Would you care to go along?"

It was the first time he had ever asked her to join him. Her face still averted, she shook her head. She tenaciously clung to the wisp of control she still had over herself. Suddenly his hand was resting on her shoulder.

"Are you all right, my dear?"

The pent-up tears were released in a rush. Startled, David wrapped her in his arms and rocked her as he would a child. The sobs racked her body, tearing at her throat. When the storm had spent itself, he carried her to bed and pulled a sheet over her still trembling body.

"Sleep now, Taylor. We'll talk later," he whispered in her ear.

She didn't hear him for an exhausted sleep had already stolen over her. He stood beside the bed, watching tenderly her tear-blotched face. He didn't know what had happened, but he knew it was somehow his fault. He mustn't go on hurting this child-woman, his wife, any longer.

He turned swiftly to leave the room, a determined look on his face, a look closely resembling anger. He was a "take charge" person. He liked making decisions, always had liked it. What was it about her that threw his thoughts into such confusion?

Jenny saw the master leave, a black scowl warning those who didn't move quickly enough to do his bidding. She sank back against the wall of her cabin, fearing he was looking for her, but he marched on toward the stables and left quickly on his horse. She let the air hiss between her teeth as he rode away. She wondered how long she had been holding it. Her knees shook as she lowered herself carefully onto a rickety stool on her porch. She was certain Miss Taylor had told him what she had said and that she would soon be punished.

Her head went up a little higher; her back became a little straighter. A hand slipped to her belly. Then she would take her punishment. No one would ever hear her cry for mercy. Not ever.

Jenny had little reason to feel this way. From the time she could first remember, she had been well treated, a playmate for Taylor when they were children and later becoming her personal maid. She couldn't say exactly when she began to resent her lot in life, the dependency on the master of the plantation, the absence of freedom to do as she chose when she chose. Perhaps it began when she was officially given to Miss Taylor as a birthday present. Maybe that was the first time she knew she was different from the sparkling, playful child who shared her clothes and hair ribbons so generously. It wasn't that she didn't love her mistress. She did. But the advantages she had received as Taylor's maid only seemed to make slavery chafe all the more viciously at her insides.

Jenny had learned to read in Taylor's own classroom and had spent much of her free time in this pursuit, learning of faraway places and faraway peoples. She had promised herself she was going to be somebody someday. She wasn't always going to be a slave. She was going to be free like Miss Taylor. She was going to be a real lady. A free lady. Someday. Someday.

Suddenly she felt like crying. She hadn't meant to hurt Miss Taylor. She really did want to see her happy again, the way it used to be when both her parents were alive and Master Philip was away at school. Then she realized she was as unhappy and lonely as her mistress.

"Caesar," she whispered, followed by a sob. She quickly went inside her cabin. She would never let the people here at Dorcet Hall know she was unhappy. Her pride wouldn't allow it. She was more like her mistress than either of them knew.

Taylor slept—a deep, healing sleep. She didn't awaken until late in the afternoon. She poured water into the bowl on her dresser and bathed her face with a cloth. Her eyes were puffy and her cheeks bore red blotches from her crying. She splashed more water on her face, wishing it was cooler. The air was hot and muggy and no breeze stirred the curtains at the windows.

She dressed carefully in an attractive green gown before brushing her hair back from her face and securing her black curls with a matching green ribbon. She wanted to look her best. What on earth was she going to say to him?

The house was quiet as she descended the stairs. After peeking into the library and his study, she went out the back door. There she found Mima supervising the preparation of supper in the kitchen house. Her round black face broke into a wide grin when she saw Taylor.

"Oh, li'l Missy. Glad t'see you feelin' better. You set yo'self down right under that thar tree an' ol' Mima'll get you somethin' cool t'drink from the spring house."

Taylor obliged, suddenly very thirsty.

"Here be, Missy. The Marse, he went down t'check on da south fields, but he be back right soon now." She handed Taylor her lemonade, her toothless grin making it impossible for Taylor not to smile in return.

"Thank you, Mima. I think I'll finish my drink and ride out to meet him. If I should happen to miss Master David, you tell him where I've gone." She hastily finished her drink and hurried to change her dress once more.

Revived by the cool lemonade, Taylor felt ready now to face David. It was time they talked things out. The day of their wedding was the last time they had openly faced the realities of their marriage. Since then, Taylor realized, she had put a mask over her emotions, trying to be what she was not, trying to imagine her husband as someone he was not. It was time she knew who her husband was and what he wanted from her.

She was not a little girl anymore. She had to stand on her own two feet. All this pretending had led to her outburst this morning. She didn't want that kind of scene to ever happen again.

Taylor spied David on the road leading to the southern section of the plantation which bordered the river. She lifted a hand in greeting and pulled up Tasha to wait for him.

"You look lovely, Taylor," he said as he reached her. "I'm glad to see you're feeling better. Were you coming to meet me? Come, we'll ride back along the river. It may be a little cooler there."

David, not waiting for a reply, turned his chestnut stallion off the road and cut across to the river. Taylor followed him through the fallow field at an easy canter. When they reached the river, David dismounted and helped her down from her side saddle. They walked side by side along the path, leading the horses behind them. Taylor stared at her skirts, waiting for him to speak first.

"Taylor, I've been unfair to you and I'm sorry. I believe the incident this morning proves my foolishness."

She began to protest but he motioned her to silence.

"No, let me speak," he said. "We have been married over two months, yet you know little more today about me than you did the moment we met. I have resisted letting any real communication develop between us. This shouldn't be so.

"Taylor, I was born sixty-one years ago to a cracker family—dirt farmers, poor white trash—

right across the river from here. Often when I was a child, I would sit along the river and watch the owners of Dorcet Hall and their friends coming and going. I wanted more than anything to be like them. It became an obsession which has remained with me throughout my life. They had everything I ever wanted. Sometimes, I would go into Bellville with my father for supplies. It wasn't much fun being poor white. Even the negroes looked down on us. A time or two I got to see some of the great Bellman family. Your father was just a tot then. I remember his older sister too. My, she was a great beauty. Spring Haven wasn't what it is today but the Bellmans were still one of the richest families around.

"I ran away from home when I was thirteen. I worked my way to New York City. A lot happened to me which I'd rather not ever tell anyone, but I worked hard to get to the top, to be a success. I never forgot that I wanted to be like the Dorcets . . . and the Bellmans."

He smiled wryly at Taylor as he continued. "I discovered, however, that it took more than money to become one of the elite. Several times I tried to return to the South, but my poor beginnings always seemed to precede me. I was never accepted into the society where I desired to be—among the gentry. Before that time, when I was still struggling, I married a young woman from Pennsylvania. I was just twenty-five. She bore me a son after ten years of marriage. Brent is a fine young man, but I guess he is more of a

Northerner than I would wish."

David stopped by a fallen tree and indicated they should sit down. The horses grazed nearby as Taylor listened to the continuing story.

"I bought Dorcet Hall a number of years ago, but I knew from my previous attempts that just owning a fine old plantation would not accomplish what I had set out to do. I wanted to be an insider. I wanted to belong. Then Spring Haven's mortgage fell into my hands. I followed the unfortunate series of events with much interest. I must admit I gathered every bit of information I could about the entire situation—your father's drinking, your brother's jealousy, and about yourself." He patted her hand but turned his eyes toward the river. "I knew immediately that you were the key to everything I desired. And the idea of marrying a Bellman. . . Me! A Walton county Lattimer. Ah, that would be a triumph. I knew any husband of yours would be well accepted if not well liked.

"Your father's untimely death aided in my winning your hand, but I believe it would have come about in time anyway. I am a persistent and persuasive man." His voice softened. "Somehow, you were never a real person in all my scheming. You were a hostess, an introduction to the old Southern aristocracy, a calling card with the right name on it. The fact that you were still a child didn't seem to matter. It wasn't you I wanted. It was your birthright."

Taylor felt like something was piercing her

heart. Tears pricked at her eyes as she listened.

"You were never meant to be a *real* wife," he whispered painfully. "I was not planning on caring for you." He looked at her then, his gray eyes awash. "But . . . but I have grown to care for you very much, my dear Taylor. I wish I were younger or that things could be different. I wish I could be all you deserve in a husband."

David stood up suddenly and walked away from her. A groan escaped him, evidence of his internal struggle. She saw his shoulders shudder and slump; then quickly straighten again. Tears slid down her cheeks unheeded.

"You are so very young, Taylor," he went on hoarsely. "You were a prized child, loved dearly by your parents. You have little understanding of what marriage consists of except the love your parents had for each other. You only know our marriage is not a whole one. I'm sorry it can't be all you need, all you deserve. We shall never be able to have . . . what your parents had, and . . . we will . . . there will be no children in my old age." He turned again to face her, his voice slightly stronger. "But, my child-wife, I know now how much more you need than I have given or even can give. I can be little . . . No, whatever I can be, I will be. Whatever happiness it is possible for me to give to you, I'll give gladly. I hope someday you can forgive me for stealing the happiness you were born to have with the right man. And I hope you can grow to care a little for a selfish old fool."

The river sucked at its banks. A hawk swooped

toward its prey. The chatter of squirrels echoed through the trees. Life continued around them, but they seemed frozen in time, silently staring into one another's eyes. The outpouring had left them both drained. Finally Taylor rose from the old tree and walked to where her husband stood. She looked into his lined face and saw there the scorned child, the struggling youth, and the lonely man. Slowly she reached up and touched his cheek, brushing away a clinging tear. Then she leaned her face against his chest. His arms closed around her as the embers of the dying day danced across the river's surface.

Chapter 4

"You're sure you don't want to join me, David?" Taylor asked as she settled into the buggy.

"I'm afraid I have too much work on my accounts to get finished today, my dear. Besides, you don't need me slowing you down on a shopping trip. You go along and have a good time. Say hello to Miss Stone for me. I'll be looking for you sometime tomorrow." David shifted his eyes to Jenny who was seated next to Taylor. "You take good care of Miss Taylor for me, Jenny. And when you see your husband tomorrow, you tell him I'm still trying to convince Mr. Bellman to sell him to us."

"I will, Masta David," Jenny replied.

Taylor slapped the reins against the horse's back, and they trotted off toward Bellville. Indian summer had been with them for several weeks.

The leaves on the trees had turned a variety of bright reds and yellows. They rode through the fall-tinted woods and by the harvested fields in silence, enjoying the peaceful countryside.

Taylor was lost in thought. She mused on how different her life was now than just a few months before—how different *she* was. A strong bond had grown up between David and Taylor in the months since their conversation by the river. David had drawn her into his world, making her feel a part of Dorcet Hall, a part of his life. She began to understand the true workings of a successful plantation. She learned to trust his wisdom and accept his challenge to grow and change, not just pass through life. David too had changed. His drive to force the gentry into accepting him disappeared, and with its disappearance, he began to form real and lasting friendships among their neighbors.

Taylor had decided last week to make this trip into Bellville a combination social visit and shopping trip. Besides wanting material for her own depleted wardrobe, she needed to pick out several patterns of dark, washable calico or American gingham for the servants. With the coming of winter, she would also need to lay in some Cherry Pectoral for coughs and some quinine for fevers.

They had been traveling about an hour when Taylor spotted the perfect place for them to eat the picnic lunch Jenny had packed for them.

"Look, Jenny," she cried, pointing to a small

meadow bathed in sunshine and enclosed by trees in a friendly circle.

They tied the horse so he could graze while they took their luncheon. Jenny spread the blanket on the ground and then prepared Taylor's plate. Taylor cared for, she eased herself down at the edge of the blanket and began to eat her own food.

"Do you think you'll have much longer to wait for your baby's arrival, Jenny?" Taylor asked as she reclined in the sun's warmth. She knew Jenny was depressed by her separation from Caesar as the time for the birthing neared and hoped her question wouldn't upset her.

"I figured 'bout a week," Jenny answered proudly.

"Have you decided on a name yet?"

"Las' time I went t'see Caesar, he was of a mind t'call him Moses if it's a boy 'n' Mary if a girl."

"I hope we can get Caesar to Dorcet Hall soon," Taylor said. "You know Master David is trying very hard."

"Yes'm, I know . . . 'n' I shore do miss my man alot."

The meal finished, Jenny gathered up the dishes and carried them to the river to rinse them. She was awkward in her advanced pregnancy and moved slowly about her tasks. Taylor lay back on the blanket, closing her eyes and enjoying the warm sunshine on her face. She smiled, day-dreaming about her visit. Secretly she hoped to talk David into a fancy dress ball around Christmas time, and she was hoping to find something special for a ballgown. Something exciting and expensive. Maybe a velvet or a satin in an unusual shade of blue. Hopefully the little shop in Belleville would have just the right thing. She would have Pansy, her dressmaker, create a gown that would be the talk of Barrow County. Something daring, something . . .

"If I'd known angels lived in the South, I would have come long ago," said the rich, male voice.

Her eyes were temporarily blinded by the bright sunlight as she bolted upright, but at last she could make out the figure of a man standing above her, his horse waiting calmly behind him. Taylor shaded her eyes as she looked up at the tall silhouettes standing over her.

"Sir, in the South, it is *not* considered good manners to scare a lady plumb to death."

She struggled to rise and a firm hand reached down and effortlessly pulled her to her feet. Taylor found herself staring into a pair of tawny brown eyes. Involuntarily, she gasped. He was so incredibly handsome! His rugged, square jaw was clean shaven, and his dusky hair, reminding her at once of a lion's shiny coat, hung roguishly across his forehead. He was tall, well over six feet, and his broad shoulders looked as if they could carry the world upon them without effort. His shirt was open at the neck, revealing a chest lightly covered with golden hairs. He had obviously been riding for a long time, for the rich fabric of his jacket was heavily covered with a layer of red dust.

"I do most definitely apologize, Miss," he said as he executed an exaggerated bow. "I do hope you will forego the breaking of my poor heart by extending your forgiveness to me. I am simply an ignorant Yankee and unschooled in the propriety of the South." His eyes twinkled at her as he completed the flowery speech.

Taylor could not resist the banter in his voice. She batted her eyes at him and tilted her head coyly. She hadn't enjoyed herself this much in a very long time. "Why, Sir! How could any girl, least of all little, ol' me, resist such an extraordinary apology? Of course, I shall forgive you at once." She lifted her hand toward him. The oddest sensations flowed through her body as he lifted her fingers to his lips, his eyes never leaving hers.

"Missy!" Jenny's anxious call broke the spell as she lumbered toward them, alarmed by the stranger's presence. "You all right, Missy?"

Taylor stepped away from him, removing her hand from his grasp. Her fingers still tingled from his touch, and she felt her color rise in a hot blush as she turned from his admiring glance.

"Yes, Jenny," she answered. "I'm fine. Are you ready to leave?" Her voice sounded strange to her own ears.

Her maid's return had brought her sharply back to reality. She knew it was unwise for her to be here alone with this stranger—one who was admittedly a Yankee as well.

Jenny collected the blanket and food basket and carried them to the buggy, then quickly returned to her mistress's side. Turning a withering glance upon the stranger, her arm encircling Taylor's waist, she propelled Taylor toward the buggy with authority. The stranger followed close behind, his glance never leaving Taylor. He attempted to assist her into the buggy, but Jenny pushed herself in between them.

The Yankee reached out and took hold of the reins. His voice seemed to come from afar as Taylor stared, mesmerized, into his gold-flecked eyes. "I will be in the area only a brief time, but I hope I'll have the opportunity to see you again. Perhaps if I knew your name I could call at your home?"

Jenny's reply was filled with disdain. "The mistress and her *husband* don't receive Yankee callers." She clucked at the horse, and the stranger was forced back as the buggy moved forward.

They passed within inches of him, Taylor's eyes still locked with his. For one terrible moment, she felt as if she had lost something very important to her. Unable to stop herself, she twisted in her seat and watched him recede from view.

"I wonder who he was?" she whispered.

"Someone with no manners," Jenny huffed. "Approachin' women alone like that. What would Masta David think? And me promisin' to take good care 'o you, too."

At the mention of David's name, Taylor felt embarrassment run through her. She had behaved most unsuitably. She shook her head as if to clear the memory of the stranger with his piercing eyes from the grip it had on her mind. Jenny was right. If she ever met up with him again, she would snub him most pointedly. After all, she was a married woman.

The remainder of the journey passed without incident, and they arrived in Bellville shortly after noon. Her first stop was at the Reverend Stone's small white house at the edge of town to see Marilee. Taylor had been looking forward to their visit since her decision to come into Bellville. Marilee Stone, a short, slightly plump girl with honey blonde hair and laughing brown eyes, had been Taylor's closest friend since they were both schoolgirls. Taylor's father had arranged for Marilee to be tutored with his daughter at Spring Haven. She was like the sister Taylor had never had, and they loved each other. As usual, Marilee was dressed in a dark brown gown when she met Taylor on the front porch of her home. Her widower father, quite staid in many of his views, believed dark, very reserved clothing to be more suitable for the daughter of a preacher. Somehow, Marilee's gaiety and joyous outlook on life overcame her drab attire. People caught the sparkle of her personality and everyone enjoyed her company.

After catching up on each other's news over a cup of tea, the two girls set off on their shopping trip. Taylor found several bolts of fabric which pleased her and arranged to have them sent home. She was disappointed in her search for the right blue material for a ballgown, however. Giving up at last, they prepared to go on to the millinery shop. Then her eyes lit on a bolt of golden brown satin. Her heart skipped. It was just the color of *his* eyes. It made no difference whether or not the color would be flattering on her—which it would. She had to have it. This would be the special ballgown she had been dreaming about when *he* interrupted her thoughts.

Their stop at the millinery shop was short. Taylor bought one bonnet for daytime wear, but she saw nothing else she wanted. Nothing which she might want to wear with her special ballgown, which was uppermost in her mind at the moment. Next they stopped at the Bellman law office. Philip was not in, and Marilee was quite disappointed. She saw so very little of him since she no longer had the excuse of visiting Taylor at Spring Haven. Her feelings for Philip Bellman were carried on her sleeve for all to see, everyone but Philip himself. Taylor hoped she wouldn't pine over him for too long. She had her doubts that it would be a very good match should he ever notice her friend. Her experience had not shown Philip to be a very warm and loving man.

They completed their shopping list and returned home in time for dinner. The evening promised to be spent in pleasant company as Marilee's cousins, Jeffrey and Robert Stone, were joining them. Taylor enjoyed herself immensely. Laughter filled the house until late into the evening, and she was sorry the day had passed so quickly. Jeffrey volunteered to see Taylor home on the morrow since Jenny would be going to Spring Haven. Taylor happily agreed to his offer at once. Otherwise, she would have had to hire a driver. As often as she rode alone near Dorcet Hall, David would never have agreed to her coming so far alone.

Morning dawned bright and clear, but the air carried a nip in it. Perhaps winter was coming at last, Taylor thought. Jeffrey rode alongside the buggy, his bay gelding prancing smartly in the crisp weather. When they reached the crossroad which would take Jenny to Spring Haven, he tied his horse to the rear of the buggy and climbed in beside Taylor.

"Now you're sure you should be doing all this walking, Jenny?" Taylor asked.

Jenny smiled. "Yes'm, I'm sure. I need t'see my man afore this chil' comes." She turned and walked down the dusty road. Even with her swollen figure, she was pretty. Her kinky, short-cropped hair was covered in a bright red scarf, and her smooth olive skin glowed with vitality. Her walk was awkward but determined, the anticipation of seeing Caesar quickening her pace.

At the bend in the road, she turned and waved. "I'll be home afore supper tomorra, Missy," she called before vanishing around the corner.

Jeffrey clucked to the horse. They moved along at a jog, the countryside familiar and friendly.

"It was really nice to see you again, Taylor. You've been quite a stranger lately," Jeffrey said.

"Oh, I did enjoy my visit so much. I feel like I haven't seen anybody in ages. And, of course, I haven't really been away from Dorcet Hall since my wedding. But I certainly enjoyed last night, and I do thank you for accompanying me home."

"I must say you're looking mighty fine, Taylor. You see . . . Well, I'm glad you're happy." Jeffrey's ruddy complexion darkened slightly.

Taylor didn't even notice. She and Jeffrey had known each other since they were very young children. She was used to seeing her carrot-topped friend turn all shades of red. He was not very tall either and had punched his way through many childhood teasings over his hair, his height, and his penchant for blushing. He had an aquiline nose which had been broken at least twice, increasing his likeness, or so Taylor thought, to a fiery eagle. As he grew older, he had gained more control over his blazing temper, but never over his blushing. He no longer fought his way through teasings because he was so well liked. Except for his striking green eyes and red hair, Jeffrey Stone was a rather plain-looking man, but Taylor didn't seem to know this. She just liked him because he was so much fun to be with.

"Happy? Oh, yes, I'm happy," Taylor answered absently, a hint of uncertainty in her reply.

Jeffrey glanced at her nervously. "I wasn't sure you would be when I saw how old ... I mean, what a different ... I mean, when I met your husband," he finished lamely.

Taylor laughed at his embarrassment. "Why, Jeffrey Stone, I do believe that's the nicest thing anyone's said to me in just ages. To know you've been worried about my happiness is very flattering indeed." She squeezed his arm, enjoying this playful banter.

"Taylor Lattimer, all I can think about *is* your happiness!" he exclaimed, pulling the horse to a halt and grabbing her gloved hand. "If I'd known in time, Taylor, I surely would have spoken for you before ... before Mr. Lattimer did. I have loved you forever!" He kissed her hand furtively and turned back to the reins.

Taylor was stunned, her eyes wide in surprise over this proclamation of love, not knowing just what to say in reply. Jeffrey's neck and face were

51

lobster red by this time. She had never seen him so flustered as he was at this moment.

Not turning to look, he spoke again. "Taylor," he said quietly, "if you should ever need a friend or . . . or anything, I hope you'll always come to me first."

"Jeffrey, I can't tell you how much I appreciate your . . . your friendship," she answered seriously. "Believe me, if ever I have a need, I will always remember your words to me today."

When they reached Dorcet Hall, Taylor was welcomed with a warm hug from her husband. Then they invited Jeffrey to join them in their dinner before his return ride.

"Taylor," David said as they sat down to eat, "we had a visitor while you were away." She thought his voice sounded a little strange, and she looked questioningly up at him. "My son, Brent, was here."

"Your son . . . here? Where is he?" she asked.

"He had business farther south and couldn't wait for your return. But he said he would stop on his return journey. In about two or three weeks I think. He is . . . ah . . . eager to meet you."

"And I'll be glad to meet him," Taylor replied. "If he's your son, I'm sure to be very fond of him."

David smiled wryly. "I may as well warn you now, Taylor. He is dead set against slavery. He will likely try to bait you into a rousing argument over it."

Taylor lifted an eyebrow and shrugged. "It's his right to feel that way, I suppose. I'll do my best to get along with him, David."

"Thank you, my dear." David noticeably relaxed. "Brent can be quite stubborn. I did want his visit to be a pleasant one. I have seen so little of him the last few years. He was somewhat . . . surprised when I married again. And," he smiled, "I would like his blessings on my marriage to such a charming and beautiful Southern Belle."

Taylor looked tenderly at David. "Don't worry, David. I'll win him over to our side."

As the men began discussing local topics, Taylor turned her attention back to her meal. She only half listened to them as she pondered the upcoming meeting with David's son. What type of man would he be? He must be one of those awful abolitionists. At least, David had seemed to imply such to be the case. Well, if people like that kept pushing, the South would be forced to secede, just like David and Philip and all the others had been saying. How dare those stuffed shirts try to tamper with their way of life! Come to think of it, she was probably going to find Brent Lattimer very difficult to like, but for David's sake, she would do her best. Hopefully, he wouldn't stay too long.

Chapter 5

A persistent tapping on her door pulled Taylor from a deep sleep in the darkest hours of the night. Slipping a warm wrapper over her nightgown, she hurried to the door. She opened it and looked out at the slight black figure anxiously waiting there.

"Silvy? What's wrong?" she asked, rubbing her eyes and pulling her robe snugly about her.

"Missy Taylor, come quick! Oh, Missy, it's Jenny, Missy! Please come!" The girl's voice was shrill in her fright. Her shaking hands caused the candle she held to wobble, sending eerie shadows dancing across the walls and ceiling.

Taylor grabbed Silvy's hands. "Silvy, calm down. What about Jenny?" she snapped, throwing the door open wide with her free hand.

"She hurt, Missy. An' da baby, it's comin',

Missy." Tears coursed down the black face, and her words were nearly unintelligible through her sobs.

Taylor shook the girl, screaming at her, "Silvy, where is Jenny?"

Silvy's teeth rattled, her head bobbing with each jerk of Taylor's hands. "Th—the—the st—stables," she managed to stutter between sobs.

"Tell Master David. Get Mima. You hear? Silvy, do you hear?"

Taylor flew down the stairs and out of the house. As she rushed through the cool night, she could see a crowd of slaves huddled near a corner of the barn. They stumbled back in surprise as she pushed her way through. Her first view of Jenny's still body stopped her in her tracks. She felt she would either retch or faint or perhaps both.

"Dear Lord, what happened?" she gasped. Many pairs of eyes watched her kneel down to the mass of welts and bleeding sores she knew was Jenny. A moan escaped the swollen lips, the girl too weak to scream in her pain.

David's voice boomed out orders suddenly. "Quick, get her to the house. Put her in the bedroom across from the mistress. Nehemiah, you take the best horse we've got and ride for the doctor. You ride like the wind, boy, or I'll have your hide myself. Mima, you get ready for that baby."

The group around Taylor sprang into action. Jenny was carefully lifted and carried into the house. Nehemiah galloped away from the barn astride a fleet black horse. Still Taylor could not seem to find the strength to stand up. As his hands held her shoulders and pulled her to her feet, Taylor looked up into David's seething steel-gray eyes.

"Why, David? Why . . . and who?" she cried weakly, her breath coming in sharp gasps.

"I don't know, Taylor, but I will find out. I promise you I'll find out."

Taylor climbed the stairs to the bedroom across from her own. Swallowing hard, she entered. The room was stuffy and smelled distinctively of sweat and blood and pain. She sat in a chair beside the bed, pulling it up close to Jenny's battered face. Only this morning she had thought how pretty Jenny looked. Now, one eye was swollen entirely shut, a blue bruise spreading around it. Her lip was split, and the blood had dried on her chin. The beating she had endured was worse below her neck. Whip marks crisscrossed her breasts and abdomen as well as her back. Angry welts rose where the whip had struck her skin but hadn't broken through. In places the flesh hung open, blood oozing from the open sores.

Taylor gulped back the rising nausea. She took a wet cloth and sponged Jenny's face and body. Tears spilled down her cheeks. Jenny's eyelids flickered open for a moment, terror clouding her vision. When she recognized Taylor, her body relaxed slightly. She looked as if she might try to speak but a groan replaced the words as a spasm gripped her body. Taylor glanced at Mima in trepidation. The big black woman made a motion of helplessness.

"Jenny, I'm here. Fight, Jenny. You must fight," she whispered. She gripped Jenny's hand and willed her own strength to enter the failing body. "Don't give up, Jenny. Help us help you."

The night dragged on around them. The doctor finally arrived, but there was little he could do to help her. Taylor watched terrified as the small amount of strength remaining in the broken body waned. When Taylor thought she could take no more, Mima murmured, "Here comes."

Taylor leaned forward and whispered into Jenny's ear, "You're going to make it, Jenny. The baby's almost here. Help us, Jenny." She sponged the beads of perspiration from the girl's brow and then wiped them from her own. A heartrending shriek split the air, subsiding to a whimper as Jenny gave the last ounce of energy she had to rid her body of its burden. A sigh escaped through her cracked lips as she passed into oblivion.

Frightened, Taylor leaned down to her lips. She could feel shallow breathing. Lifting her eyes to Mima, she saw the old woman wrapping the tiny body in a blanket. Mima answered Taylor's unspoken question with a tear falling onto the small bundle in her arms. She turned and walked out of the oppressing silence. Taylor laid her head on her arms and wept in futility.

Ages later, or so it seemed to Taylor, she left the room herself. Hanging onto the banister, she haltingly descended the stairs. She was surprised to see the entry hall bathed in the sunlight of late morning. Hearing voices, she followed them into the library. David was deeply engrossed in conversation with his manservant, Saul, and didn't notice her.

"David."

He hurried to her side. "Taylor, you must lie down and rest. Mima told me. Don't speak of it." David guided her gently to the couch. She obediently lay down, allowing him to pull a coverlet up to her shoulders as she closed her eyes, sighing deeply.

"Go on, Saul," she heard David say softly.

"Well, sir, it appears he set t'beatin' that man. When he was done, he must've brought her here t'be found before he lit out."

Taylor pushed herself up. "What man? Why was he whipping her?"

"I thought you were asleep, Taylor. Please don't upset yourself with this."

"Don't upset myself? David, I'm upset already. Now tell me, what is Saul talking about?"

He sat down beside her. "All right, dear. I'll tell you. As near as we can piece it together, Jenny was nearly to Caesar's cabin when she was . . . accosted by Philip's new overseer. Apparently he tried to . . . tried to take liberties with her. She fought him, scratching and biting at him. He took his riding whip and began beating her. When Caesar heard her screams and found them, he attacked the fellow and then brought Jenny here.

58

He has run away, of course. There is a search going on for him now."

"Oh, it's all my fault," Taylor cried. "I never should have let her go."

"You know that's not true, dear. You couldn't have known this would happen."

"Why didn't anyone find her sooner? She must have lain out in the cold most of the night."

"Possibly. We don't know when Caesar brought her here. He must have hidden with her during the day somewhere else. They found Mr. Jackson late yesterday afternoon. He's under doctor's care at Spring Haven now. He'll be all right, but if they catch Caesar, they'll probably hang him."

"Philip is allowing that beast to stay there and be cared for after what he did?" Taylor cried.

"Now, remember, Philip hasn't seen Jenny. Besides, Mr. Jackson was attacked by a slave. That's a serious offense."

Taylor threw off the blanket and jumped to her feet. "Serious offense? What about Jenny? He's not going to get away with this," she said as she paced the floor. "He'll pay for this. I'll see that he pays for it." She walked stiffly to the doorway. "Caesar was protecting his own wife but is threatened with hanging if caught. Well, Mr. Jackson is not going to get off so easily if I can help it. I'm going to pay him a call . . . right now." She heard David's protest but ignored him, hurrying to her room to change into her riding clothes.

Threatening clouds, perfectly matching her

59

mood, filled the sky as she galloped along the road toward Spring Haven. She had angrily refused David's offer to accompany her, and surprisingly enough, he had relented.

At Spring Haven, a small black lad ran out to take her horse as she jumped down from the saddle. Susan stood waiting on the veranda.

"Miss Taylor, I do declare. We sho' does miss seein' you 'roun' here. Come on in. I'll sen' somebody a scattlin' t'get the masta."

"Thank you, Susan, but it's really your patient I've come to see," Taylor said sternly as she started for the curving stairway. "Where is he, Susan? Which room?"

"I don' think you oughta go up thar, Missy. Masta Philip, he won't be likin' it none."

"Which room, Susan?" Taylor snapped angrily.

"Masta Philip done put him in the nurs'ry," Susan reluctantly answered.

Taylor, a determined set to her jaw, climbed the stairs. She heard Susan mumble something about trash in the house as she left her behind. The wing holding the nursery had been little used for many years, and Taylor noticed how dusty everything was. Ridiculously for the moment at hand, she thought she must instruct them to correct this oversight.

The door to the nursery was open, and Taylor looked inside. The man was sitting in a chair by the window, his right arm in a sling. A large bruise darkened the side of his face, and the cheek was puffy and an angry red. His bare chest was wrapped with gauze and she supposed he had some broken ribs. He was smoking a thin cigar, the blue smoke hanging about his head like a storm cloud.

Taylor rapped sharply on the door frame and stepped quickly into the room. The small, wiry man turned to see who had entered, flinching and grabbing his side as he did so. Unwashed and unshaven, his greasy hair was matted against his head. His small dark eyes looked at her suspiciously, followed with open admiration. The bushy mustache twitched unpleasantly and he licked his lips before speaking.

"What can I do for ya? Who are you?"

"Excuse me, sir," she said politely. "I'm Taylor Lattimer, Mr. Bellman's sister. And you?"

"Jackson. Matt Jackson." He pointed to his side. "I'd get up, ma'am, but I ain't feelin' real spry these days. Had a bit of an accident."

"I know, Mr. Jackson. That's why I'm here," she said as she stepped closer to his chair.

Matt Jackson raised a bushy eyebrow in question but said nothing. It really mattered little to him why she had come. The fact was that she was standing here in his room. He was a great admirer of beautiful women and here was a beauty such as he had never seen. His eyes slithered down from her face to her lush bosom and her tiny waist. He imagined what it would be like to lay his whip across that creamy white skin instead of the usual black, hearing her cry for mercy before he took her. He smiled.

Taylor was too angry to notice his gaze or the train of his thoughts. With a calm she didn't feel, she eyed him coolly. "Mr. Jackson, the mulatto girl you brutalized yesterday is my slave. Because of your rash actions, she lost her baby. I mean for you to pay for that mistake."

Jackson dropped his cigar on the floor as if he hadn't been listening. Slowly, he placed his foot over the smouldering butt and ground it into the floor with the toe of his boot.

"Now you just hold up there, pretty lady," he said as he looked up at her. "That big nigga beat me up right good, in case you hadn't noticed. Seems to me if'n you want t'see somebody punished, you'd best see what's goin' to happen to him when he gets himself caught and just leave me be." He sneered at her. "There's a law against slaves what go hittin' their betters. He's gonna hang for what he did t'me."

Taylor felt the color leave her face as she fought to control her mounting rage. She leaned forward, her face only inches from the vile little man she was confronting.

"You, sir, are a low-bellied, slimy snake. You're worse than the filthiest and poorest sandhill tackey." She stared coldly into his eyes, gritting her teeth as she continued, "I'm going to try to explain something you aren't going to like to hear, and I hope your weak little mind can understand what it is I'm saying."

She saw Jackson's grip tighten on the arm of his chair with his good hand. The veins in his neck stood out as her insults hit home.

"It would be senseless for me to try to explain to you about kindness, about respect for another human being, so I won't waste my time. I will speak to you on your own low level. Money is something I'm sure you can understand. Well, Jenny is a valuable slave. She is worth well over two thousand dollars. Her child, a boy, which was born dead because of you, would have been worth a great deal as well. There may be nothing I can do about protecting Caesar, even if I'm glad for what he did to you, but I do intend you to repay me for my losses."

"Pay you! What d'you mean, pay you?" he erupted.

Taylor smiled wickedly as she answered. "You are to be out of the county by tomorrow or you'll pay me for the baby that was lost and for Jenny's injuries. That, or I'll take you to court for your destruction of my property. I promise you, Mr. Jackson, it will be very costly for you if you choose to stay. I'm assured of winning. If I so much as hear a whisper of your name after tomorrow, you will rue the day you crossed me."

Jackson began to rise from his chair, sputtering at her angrily. "Of all the . . . if you think just 'cause you say so, I gotta leave, you're crazy. I got me a good job here, and I ain't aimin' t'give it up 'cause you say so. I didn't do nothin' 'cept tryin' t'have a bit of sport with that dark . . ."

Taylor's open hand cracked against the side of his head, knocking him back into his chair. Her hand stung from the force of the blow she had landed, and she touched her lips to her palm as if to draw out the pain.

"Get out by tomorrow," she snarled, the last shred of control gone. She turned and started from the room.

"I won't forget this, Miz Lattimer. Matt Jackson don't never forget nothin'. Someday I'll make you eat them words of yours."

Taylor slammed the door on his shouted words. She stalked down the stairs and out onto the portico, looking angrily about for her horse. "Susan, where's that lazy boy with my horse?" she called impatiently.

"He's comin', Missy. Ain't you gonna stay t'see Masta Philip?'

"Not this time, Susan. Not this time."

She was shaking all over as she mounted her horse. Turning toward home, she saw Philip riding toward her.

"Hello, little sister," he called to her. "Have you actually come calling?"

"Well, I . . . I . . . yes," she lied. "I did come to visit, but I've waited too long. I must get back to Dorcet Hall now." She looked up at the black clouds overhead. "I may get wet before I get home as it is."

"Well, I won't keep you, Taylor. Say hello to David for me. Next time, send someone to tell me you're here. It was good to see you if only for a moment."

Taylor looked at him cynically, but his expression remained sincere. She said a quick goodbye and kicked her horse into a fast lope, one eye on the gathering storm. The storm began when she was halfway home.

At first she kept going, but the rain continued to fall harder and harder until it came down in icy sheets so heavy it nearly knocked her from the saddle. Tasha stumbled as the thick red mud sucked greedily at her feet. Finally, the palomino fell to her knees, sending Taylor tumbling to the ground.

"If that doesn't settle the hash!" she grumbled as she stood up, her clothes covered with mud. She was wet clear through to the skin. She had lost her hat some time back and her hair was heavy with rain and ice. She brushed wet tendrils from her face, looking about her. Grabbing Tasha's dangling reins, Taylor led the horse toward a clump of trees, seeking some shelter from the freezing storm. She placed her horse between herself and the wind; then stood with chattering teeth while she waited for it to stop.

"I'm sorry, girl," she spoke above the storm. "If I'd used my head, we'd have stayed at Spring Haven." She stroked her little mare's golden neck and looked up at the ugly sky, whispering again, "If I'd only used my head."

As the rain continued, Taylor lost all track of time. The freezing rain continued to batter her as she huddled against her horse, trying to share some of the animal's warmth. Violent shivers began to grip her body and she felt sleepy as the darkness of the storm turned to the darkness of nightfall.

When the rain finally began to taper off, Taylor mounted her horse, throwing her leg over the saddle to ride astride, and the pair began the exhausting trip home. Tasha fought for every step, slipping and stumbling on the muddy road. Taylor gripped the saddle horn. Her head nodded forward again and again, her chin bumping against her collarbone. She no longer watched—or cared—where her horse took her. The bitter wind which had followed the rain encrusted her wet clothing with ice. Still Taylor felt hot. Unaware of what she was doing, she removed her cloak, threw it to the ground, and loosened the collar of her riding habit.

"Swimming. I'd like to go swimming," she mumbled. Then she was convulsed by a fit of shivers. "No, too cold. Papa, where's my coat? Why don't I have a coat anymore? Where's Papa? Don't leave me, Papa . . . I'm so cold. I don't want to be alone . . . Papa, look! Mama gave me a new riding habit. Can I have a horse of my very own? Oh, I lost my coat. Papa, I'm sorry. I didn't mean to . . . So hot. So hot . . . Papa, look at me ride . . ."

Taylor's words rattled on as Tasha fought her way toward the warm stable she instinctively knew would be waiting. Taylor swayed from side to side, nearly falling off and then righting herself. Tasha's pace became quicker as Dorcet Hall came into view. She was moving past the house, unguided, heading directly toward her stall and the waiting hay and grain, when David rushed out. He had been anxiously watching for Taylor's return, hoping she was still at Spring Haven. He caught Tasha's slack reins and pulled the nearly unconscious Taylor from the horse.

"Papa?" she whispered hoarsely. "I'm home, Papa. I lost my coat."

She went limp in his arms.

David sat by her bed, holding her hand, trying to still the nightmares raging in her brain as the fever ravaged her body. She had been delirious more than a week now, and David knew if she didn't improve soon she would die. The thought frightened him terribly. Who would have thought that he, David Lattimer, shrewd, businesslike, matter-of-fact David Lattimer, would ever care enough for anyone that their illness would frighten him like this? Oh, he loved his son, he'd loved his first wife, but this was more. This was so very much more.

"Taylor," he said softly, "don't leave this old fool behind. You've brought the only real joy I've ever known into my life. I always thought it was money I needed to make me happy, but you . . . you made me laugh. You taught me to enjoy living. You brought me sunshine." He kissed the palm of her hand and then the back ot it. "Let me die instead," he prayed.

"Papa! No . . . no . . ." she cried and began thrashing wildly about.

David grabbed her arms and pulled her tightly

67

against him. The same scene had been played out so many times now that he did it automatically, speaking soothingly to her in an attempt to drive away the dark shadows, the ghosts and goblins which tormented her sickened brain.

"Dear God, don't take her from me!"

The fever broke that night. For another week, Taylor was unaware of the constant care she received, of who gave her sips of cool water and warm broth, of who smoothed her blankets and held her hand, of who sponged her tired body. Winter had arrived during her illness, and it was a cold gray afternoon when she opened her eyes and startled Mima who was dozing by her bed.

"I'm hungry," she said weakly.

"Marse David!" Mima hollered as she pushed her bulky body up. "Marse David, the Missy's awake!"

Taylor looked up into Mima's wide grin, squinting her eyes against the unaccustomed light. David was soon standing over her too, an expression of relief and joy written across his brow.

"Have I been ill?" she croaked, her throat dry and her lips cracked.

David gathered her into his arms. "My dear, you gave us a terrible fright. Thank God you're getting better now."

"Jackson?" she asked, remembering. "Is he gone?"

"Shhh, Taylor. Don't you worry about him. He's gone. You just forget him and regain your strength." He kissed her forehead. "I never would have forgiven myself for letting you go if . . . if you weren't going to be well again."

A wan smile touched Taylor's pale face. Her deep blue eyes were hidden in dark circles and her usually rich black locks hung drably about her face and shoulders.

David hugged her again. "You're the most beautiful woman in the world," he whispered into her hair as he held her against him. Laying her back down, he told Mima to bring some hot soup up to Taylor.

"How's Jenny?" Taylor asked when Mima was gone.

"She's much better. She comes to sit with you every day. After you've eaten, if you feel up to a visit, I'll send for her. Here, Mima has your broth. Eat now and we'll talk again later."

After sipping sparingly of the broth and eating a few bites of bread, Taylor slept again, but immediately upon awakening she asked to see Jenny. The weeks since Jenny's assault had softened the marks of her trial. A small scar cut across her right cheek, but Taylor was relieved to see her face had lost nearly all other traces of the abuse she had taken. She moved stiffly, as if pain racked her every motion.

"Jenny," Taylor sighed as she lifted her hand to her trusted servant.

"How are you, Missy?" she asked.

"Much better, Jenny. I guess I was pretty sick for a while."

"Yes'm, you sure was."

Taylor looked critically at Jenny. "And how are you, Jenny? Honestly. Any word from Caesar?"

Jenny shook her head, staring at her hands which were now folded in her lap. "Oh, I'm gettin' better all the time, Miss Taylor. I'm doin' a little more ever'day." She paused. "No'm. Caesar been jus' swallered up. Ain't been so sign o' him anywheres."

"I'm glad, Jenny. I hope he escaped some place they'll never be able to find him. I'm sorry he's gone for your sake, of course, but I still hope he's free." She touched Jenny's hand again. "And if we ever learn where he is, I promise you that you two will be together somehow."

A tear traced the pretty mulatto's cheek as she sat quietly at her mistress's bedside.

Chapter 6

The winter months turned to spring during Taylor's frustratingly slow recovery. The infection that had threatened her life settled stubbornly in her lungs, denying a quick return to her normally robust health. However, her convalescence was not allowed to be boring. Marilee and Jeffrey rode out often to entertain her, and even Philip stopped in several times. The Madsens from Rosewood and the Johnsons from Oak Lawn were also frequent visitors. She was always glad to receive her guests, but she became quickly tired of the constant talk of possible secession from the Union, a possibility which had grown following John Brown's raid at Harper's Ferry. It seemed all her gentleman callers could think about was war—and the ladies were nearly as bad, if not worse!

As the paint brush of spring brought color and life to the trees and flowers around Dorcet Hall, so too did it touch Taylor. With each breath she took into her weakened lungs, she grew stronger. A glow of health returned to her cheeks, a bounce appeared in her step, and her laughter filled the house once more, a very welcome sound to her husband.

David Lattimer's joy was evident to everyone. He doted on his young wife in every possible manner. At last he was even persuaded to accept some of the dinner party invitations which seemed to pour in. On return from one of these parties, a very pleasant evening at Oak Lawn, Taylor announced her decision to give a grand celebration on their anniversary. She wanted an orchestra for dancing. They would construct a dance floor on the lawn as Dorcet Hall wasn't *nearly* large enough for all the people she planned to invite. Lanterns would be hung about the gardens and around the dance floor. They would have a delicious barbecue before the dance. Everyone would be talking about it for months afterwards.

David marveled at her enthusiasm. "Are you sure you're up to this, Taylor?" he asked.

"Of course I am. Oh, David, I'm really quite well again. This is something I want to do *very* much. We both know that people expected this marriage, one of convenience, to bring us both unhappiness. I'd like them to know that I've grown up since then and that we are very happy with one another." She grasped his hand and pulled him out onto the south lawn. "See, we could have the dance floor right here and the buffet over there and the trees are perfect for the lanterns over here . . ."

David watched as she skipped and twirled from one spot to another. Suddenly he felt very old beside the bubbling girl. You are old, he thought to himself, and she'll leave you behind someday.

"David?" Taylor asked softly, seeing his thoughtful frown. "What's wrong?"

"Nothing's wrong, my dear. I think it's a wonderful idea." He smiled quickly. "Whatever you want, we'll do. Plan away!" He laughed with her as she started telling him all her desires for the party.

Preparations for the ball began immediately, setting the plantation into a constant turmoil. Taylor put her dressmaker to the task of making her a spectacular gown. Pulling the golden brown satin from its storage place, she caught a fleeting glimpse of admiring eyes looking down on her from a warm fall day. She had a feeling of loss as the vision faded, but it was soon forgotten in the busy days ahead.

David received a letter from Brent, stating he would be arriving for his previously aborted visit now that Taylor was well again. Taylor was pleased he would be arriving in time for the celebration and that he was planning an extended visit. She knew David missed his son very much and was hurt over the continuing estrangement between them. David loved Brent deeply, and Taylor hoped whatever troubled the two could be resolved during Brent's stay at Dorcet Hall.

Taylor watched in excitement as the dance floor, big enough for fifty or sixty couples, neared completion. Mima helped her decide on the menu for the barbecue. Gardeners were set to work from dawn to dusk on the grounds, and the maids scrubbed and dusted until Dorcet Hall gleamed, even in nooks and crannies.

Ten days before the ball, Marilee came for a visit. Her father had chosen this balmy June day for making pastoral calls, and Marilee had decided to stay with Taylor until his return that evening. The two girls spent the morning talking about the party. Taylor showed Marilee her dress which was nearly finished. Marilee fussed over it very satisfactorily and stated how much she wished she was married so she could wear something as sophisticated as Taylor was going to be wearing.

"I just know if I could wear something really daring, I could get Philip to notice that I'm alive," she confessed to her friend.

"Somehow, Marilee, we'll think of a way to get the two of you together. Let me show you what David has designed for the lighting of the gardens. Maybe you can get Philip to take you for a stroll under the lanterns."

Taylor left her friend in the room and went down to David's study alone. She ruffled through the papers on top of his desk. Failing to find what she wanted, she opened the top drawer. Her eyes fell on a letter addressed to David. She was unable to resist reading it when she saw the words "your wife" near the top. As her eyes scanned the pages, the color drained from her face and then returned in a blazing rage.

I was sorry to find your wife so ill on my visit to your new home. I hope she is fully recovered by the time you receive this letter. . . . Father, I cannot express how distressed I was to find you the master of a slave-owning plantation. The tragic incident with your wife's servant just before I arrived last fall should be enough to wake you up. . . . Naturally, I hope I will be as charmed by your wife as you obviously are. I'm afraid, however, that I shall not be as easily swayed by a pretty face and a soft accent as you seem to have been. . . .

Taylor put the letter back in the drawer as if it was burning her fingers. That egotistical, closed-minded, opinionated, hypocritical Yankee! How dare he say such things? What hogwash! However did David raise such an oaf? And how was she going to manage to be civil to him during his stay?

"Taylor, what's keeping you? Did you find what you were looking for?" Marilee asked as she peeked around the door.

"No," Taylor answered curtly, slamming the

desk drawer closed. "It doesn't matter anyway. Let's take a walk. It's rather stuffy in here."

Marilee, bewildered by Taylor's smouldering anger, hurried to keep up with her friend's brisk pace as she marched about the gardens as if in a military drill. The angry look never left her darkened eyes, and Marilee went home that evening still wondering what had brought on the sudden thunder clouds.

Taylor's black spirits persisted over the next several days as she thought of various ways to put this pompous Yankee in his place. She would show Brent Lattimer. She would be kind, gracious, forgiving. She would prove to him once and for all the superiority of the South. Show him what a catch his father had made. Show him how wrong he was about the way they felt about their people.

David, too, was anxiously awaiting his reunion with his son. He feared Brent's reaction to Taylor's age. He had never mentioned just how large a difference there was. A tired feeling began to seep through him. He was plagued with guilt over saddling this beautiful creature with their shadow of a marriage. He felt even guiltier because he was so happy himself. He knew anything his son might say to him he would deserve. He also knew it wouldn't make any difference. There was no way he would ever be happy without Taylor Bellman Lattimer.

Three days before the party, Taylor decided to ride over to Spring Haven, hoping to relieve her growing tensions. She had been pleased that Philip had called on her during her illness and he had sent word he would be happy to attend the barbecue. She decided it was time she thanked him in person. It did seem as if they became closer every time they met these days. Whatever had driven him for so long, whatever had caused him to be so unaware of himself and spiteful to her seemed to be disappearing. She would like to do whatever she could to continue this improvement.

She loved to ride through the countryside this time of year. The flowers on the cotton plants had already turned from their creamy white to pink, and the ocean of color as one field flowed into another was breathtaking. Some fields were green with kudzu, which would later be used for hay for the cattle and horses. The light green vines spread eagerly wherever they were allowed to go.

Once off Dorcet Hall land, she rode for several miles through unused land. Someday this too would belong to someone's plantation, but for now, the wild vegetation and trees ruled with a free hand. An old deserted cabin stood near the river in a clump of trees, but that was the only sign that anyone had ever used this land before.

The first sight of Spring Haven never ceased to thrill her. Today was no different. The house rose white and proud in the bright sunshine, its columns reaching toward the sky, a picture of strength and endurance, of a marvelous civilization. Surely Spring Haven was a symbol of all the

South held dear to her heart. Field hands could be seen everywhere, their backs bent to their labors. The smell of food cooking wafted past her nose from the kitchen. She could see black children playing a game of tag behind the house as their mothers washed clothing in big wash tubs.

Philip stepped out on the piazza as she pulled up her mare. "Hello, Taylor. This *is* a surprise."

"Thank you," she said as he helped her from her saddle. "I was feeling a bit anxious over the party, and I thought coming home for a visit might help. You don't mind my dropping in? I wanted to thank you for coming to see me when I was ill, too."

A cloud shadowed his eyes momentarily. "No, of course not. Glad to have you here."

As they walked into the house, Taylor breathed deeply of the place. In her last visit she had been too angry to savor the elegance, the stability of the house as she usually did. This time she hungrily consumed every detail.

"Oh, Philip," she sighed as they sat down across from one another in the drawing room. "How I miss being at home."

This time she saw him stiffen as he answered her. "Isn't it time you thought of Dorcet Hall as 'home'? You've been there a year now."

"But no place could possibly be like Spring Haven, even if I lived there a thousand years. Can't you understand that?"

The look on her brother's face as he replied was one she was all too familiar with. "Just remember that Spring Haven is mine. You are married. Spring Haven will go to *my* heirs when I die, not to you."

How did they get into this so quickly? she wondered. Didn't he realize that she had no desire to threaten him, to take Spring Haven from him? Taylor tried to think of some way to return them to the more companionable tones of just moments before.

"Please, Philip, let's not argue. I didn't come over here to renew bad feelings between us. I know that Spring Haven is yours." A thought popped into her head. "Speaking of heirs, Philip, when *are* you going to bring a mistress here?"

Philip studied her carefully before answering. "I suppose it is time I thought about it. Perhaps your barbecue will be just the place for me to consider the prospects." He smiled thoughtfully.

"You should look no further than Marilee," Taylor suggested boldly.

"Marilee Stone? Why, I'm like her brother!"

"You're wrong about that, Philip. She loves you very much."

"Marilee Stone," he repeated softly. "Maybe you're right. Perhaps she's just the sort of wife I'm looking for. Hmmm." He paused before turning a searching glance at her. "And you, Taylor. Are you about ready to give David Lattimer an heir for Dorcet Hall?"

She shook her head as she flushed deeply. "No. No children yet," she replied, flustered both by the question and the answer.

Philip stood up suddenly. "Come on, Taylor. You look as if you could use some air. Let's walk and do some reminiscing. There must be some times when we were both happy here that we could remember together."

She was glad to leave their embarrassing conversation behind and rose quickly from her chair. It looked as if the day might turn into a pleasant one after all.

Taylor turned her small palomino mare onto the river path. She felt relaxed and quite pleased by her visit with Philip. The weather had yet to turn really hot and the trees along the river were filled with birds singing joyous carols above her head, adding to her feeling of well-being. Sunlight sifted through the heavy branches, throwing a lattice-work of light and shadows on the path before her. The water gurgled in glee across the smooth stones lining the floor of the river. It was shallow along this point and she could see fish darting about beneath the surface.

"Let's stop for a whil, Tasha," Taylor said to her mare. "I feel like getting my feet wet."

She tethered her horse to a bush and removed her riding boots and stockings. She squealed as she stepped into the surprisingly cold water. Clenching her teeth to discourage any chattering, she waded farther into the current, holding up her skirts to keep them dry. She felt alive and healthy and wonderful as she splashed about, scaring the fish. Dismissing the threat of freckles, she removed her bonnet, letting the sun warm her scalp. Taylor felt as if she were a part of the river itself, racing toward something unknown but much desired.

Downstream, a pair of deer appeared from out of the trees. Taylor froze, watching their careful approach to the river. The buck stood alertly by while the doe drank daintily, then he too quenched his thirst. Their seemingly perfect togetherness stirred her heart. Unintentionally, Taylor sighed at their beauty. Two pairs of startled eyes turned on her. Quickly the deer bounded away, disappearing back into the forest whence they came.

"They're like two young lovers," she whispered. With the thought came a deep yearning for something she didn't even understand, something she couldn't put a name to but was just beyond her grasp. She felt a restlessness replace the joy she had experienced only moments before. She wanted to run after the deer; she wanted to escape—escape *to* something, not from it.

"I always seem to find you in the strangest places."

Taylor jerked around to face the bank. She hadn't heard the rider's approach. As familiar as if it had been only yesterday when they first met, his tawny-colored eyes were smiling at her antics in the water.

"And your legs are absolutely the loveliest I have ever had the privilege to gaze upon," he finished with laughter.

Taylor gasped and dropped her skirts. Her

81

bonnet floated away unnoticed as her dress became heavy laden with water, pulling at her legs in the current and threatening her balance. Seeing her predicament, her admirer rode into the river and effortlessly lifted her up into the saddle with him. He carried her to shore but kept her in his arms, the laughter dancing in his eyes as he looked at her.

"Please, sir. Set me down," she whispered meekly. She seemed unable to turn her eyes from his. An unfamiliar heat spread through Taylor. Her skin tingled; she felt breathless.

His hands were firm yet gentle as he lowered her from his side. His touch still burned when he released her and dismounted. He stood before her, and Taylor realized with a tremor that there was no longer any laughter in him. The mood had changed, deepened. The air was charged around them.

The stranger's hands touched her shoulders lightly and slid down her arms. Somewhere, deep within her mind, she knew she should leave; she should break away and run from this man whose very presence held her mesmerized. Ever so slowly, he gathered her to him. Her head tilted backwards, her eyes locked with his. The intensity in his handsomely carved features sent a chill of something akin to fear into her blazing heart. When his head bent forward, his mouth descending to claim hers in a kiss, she melted against him. Her arms responded of their own volition, wrapping around his neck, as much to support herself as anything; her legs seemed totally powerless, unable to hold her up.

This. This was what she had yearned for, dreamed about. This was what she needed, what had been missing. This was what could make her heart, her very soul, whole.

He released her fevered lips. He held her waist firmly, showing no intention of letting her go. His eyes traveled like a caress from her darkened eyes to the heightened color on her cheeks and then to the quick rise and fall of her rounded breasts, the soft swell visible above her dress bodice.

"You are beautiful, so very beautiful," he whispered huskily. "I've wanted to do this since the day I first saw you."

Reckless abandon swept through Taylor. Her heart told her that before long this man—his arms, his kisses, his voice—would be gone, and she would return to her real life. But for this brief encounter, she wanted to *feel,* to feel everything. She stood on tiptoe and swayed toward him. He caught her, and again his mouth claimed hers greedily. He crushed her against him, his heart thundering against her breast. She could feel the tautness of his hard, masculine body. Her own blood pounded in her ears.

Taylor felt him tremble. A low groan slipped from him as his kisses softened. He nibbled at her lips, barely touching them, then moved from her mouth and down her throat. She found his gentle touch sapping what little strength remained. She quivered violently. This tenderness was harder to bear than his forcefulness.

This time when his lips released her, he stepped away. Slowly, Taylor opened her eyes, gasping for air. She found him gazing at her intently, searching for something that seemed to puzzle him.

"Who are you?" he asked.

His question sent a shock wave through her. She turned and ran to her horse. Once mounted, she jerked Tasha's head up hard, harder than she had intended, and set off in a frantic gallop toward home. She never heard his cry of "Wait!"

Like the coldness of the river on her feet, her behavior shocked her. How could she have done it? How could she have acted like . . . like . . . like common white trash?

But he took advantage of me, she thought, grasping at anything to justify her loss of sensibilities. *Why, I was at his mercy! Thank goodness I need never see him again.*

She drove the little mare on at a mad pace. By the time she reached the barn, a thick lather covered the golden coat. Taylor felt a prick of shame when she saw the horse's heaving sides as she tossed the reins to a groom and ran to the house.

"Jenny!" she called as she flew up the stairs. "Get me a bath."

She tore off her wet clothing and dropped onto her bed while she waited. Unbeckoned, his face stared down at her from the ceiling. Her body trembled and her lips burned. She pulled a pillow over her face to shut out the stranger's image.

Go away, she pleaded. *Go away, whoever you are.*

Chapter 7

Taylor lingered in her bath, allowing the warm water to smooth away the tenseness of her body. She closed her eyes. The sweet perfume of the soap drifted up from the water. She thought she could almost touch the jasmine floating about her head. Jenny's tap at the door brought her back to earth.

"Yes?" she sighed, unwilling to be disturbed.

"Mis Taylor, Masta David sent me to tell you that his son is here. They's waitin' for you in the parlor, Missy." Jenny moved to the tub with a large towel.

"Oh, no," Taylor growled. "Not him on top of everything else! I'm not up to conversing with that mule-headed cad today." Taylor frowned darkly at Jenny, but she stayed beside the tub, holding out the towel to Taylor.

"All right. You win," she snapped and pushed herself up from the water. Tiny droplets glittered on her pale skin as she wrapped herself in the towel. She pulled the pins from her hair. Her black curls cascaded into freedom down her back and clung damply about her face.

"Get my blue linen, Jenny."

Taylor sat impatiently as Jenny carefully wove satin ribbons through her hair, pulling the hair back from her face and slipping in combs to hold it in place. Then it was allowed to tumble free in ringlets. The ribbons brought out the bluish highlights of Taylor's raven hair.

The linen gown, the same color as Taylor's eyes, had a large hooped skirt and blousy sleeves. The bodice showed only a glimpse of her white throat about the lighter blue collar, and tiny blue buttons accented the front from neckline to waist. Putting on her blue slippers, she turned in front of her mirror, well pleased with the results.

"Well," she said to her reflection, "let's go face the lion's den. He *couldn't* be any worse than we think he is."

As she descended the stairs, Taylor could hear David's laughter mixed with another's coming from the parlor. Above all, she thought when she heard it, she must not lose her temper, no matter what. She didn't want to spoil the good humor which seemed to exist at the moment. Placing a smile on her face, she entered the parlor. David was standing near the door, and she stopped at his side.

"Ah, you're here at last, my dear," he said.

She leaned foward and kissed his cheek lightly. "I'm sorry it took me so long, David, but you know how we women are." She laughed softly as he took her arm and guided her across the room. She intentionally kept her eyes on David until they stopped, doing her utmost to show their guest her utter devotion to her husband.

"This, Taylor, is my son, Brent," David said, his voice filled with pride.

Taylor turned her eyes slowly from David's face to the rising figure in front of her. She felt the color drain from her cheeks as she recognized the strong jaw, the golden eyes, and golden-brown hair. Like shattering glass, she felt her composure crumbling around her feet.

"Brent, this is my wife, Taylor," David finished, unaware of Taylor's horrified silence.

For an instant she sensed his surprise, saw that he too was unsettled by her identity. At any other time she would have admired his supreme acting ability as all recognition vanished, replaced by a polite, sincere smile.

"How very pleased I am to meet you at last, Mrs. Lattimer," he said as he took her hand and kissed it. As he looked up, she saw something flicker behind his eyes. He squeezed her hand. "Or should I call you *Mother?*"

Taylor heard and understood the irony behind his question. She knew she should respond in kind; she also knew she should pull away her burning fingers. Yet all she could do was remember the feel of his lips at her throat and wish they were back by the river once more, still loving strangers.

"Brent, would you like some sherry?" David asked, moving to the sideboard and filling two glasses.

Brent released her hand. He moved to a chair across from the couch but waited for her to be seated before sitting down himself. The distance between them seemed to help a little. She tried to emulate his superb calm and control, and she lifted her chin in a slightly defiant gesture.

"David and I are happy you were able to come for our anniversary party. We hope you'll enjoy your stay." She was irritated to hear the faint quiver in her voice.

"Thank you, Mrs. Lattimer. I'm only sorry I wasn't here for the wedding." He paused to take the glass of sherry from his father. "When I was through here last," he continued, "you were terribly ill. I never would have guessed it. You look remarkable. It's a wonder Father lets you out of his sight."

Again the irony, the sting. Taylor's eyes darkened as the thorny missile hit its mark. *Why, he really is a pompous oaf,* she thought. She had been right. Their encounter by the river had been entirely his fault. He was overbearing and cruel. Taylor failed to see that Brent's words were his own protection—protection against his violent desire to make love to his father's bride.

Her instinct toward self-preservation added an

additional lift to her chin as she answered with brilliantly feigned courtesy, "How very nice of you to think so. I assure you, however, my recovery is entirely due to my *husband's* attentions. We are *utterly* devoted to one another."

"I'm sure."

Lout, her eyes screamed.

Coquette, his accused.

"Ah," David said, uncomfortably aware that things were not going well but uncertain as to why, "here's Jenny with a tea tray for us."

Taylor's words were sugary sweet as she asked Brent, "You are still planning to stay a few weeks, aren't you, Mr. Lattimer?"

"I wouldn't want to miss it for anything, *Mrs.* Lattimer."

She turned aside. "Jenny, please see that our guest's room is ready. Oh, and see to the dinner arrangements as well."

"Yes'm."

Brent's eyes followed Jenny's departure and remained on the empty doorway after she was gone.

"Tea, Mr. Lattimer?"

"What . . . Oh, no. No, thank you," he answered, his gaze returning to her. "Tell me. Was that your maid who was beaten last fall?"

"Yes, that was Jenny."

"Very pretty," Brent said thoughtfully. "It's too bad . . ." Seeing Taylor's puzzlement over his remark, he continued, "I mean it's too bad about what happened to her. Of course, if she was thought of as a human being instead of a piece of property, this might not have happened. Or, at least, the attacker would have been punished."

"Brent . . ." his father warned, but it was too late. Brent had waved the red flag in challenge, and Taylor, whose emotions were already raw from this day's rubbings, could not control her anger.

"Mr. Lattimer," she said, her voice as icy as the river water he had pulled her from, "do you employ any servants in your home in New York?" He nodded. "Tell me, you pay them a wage, I trust. Is it enough to provide them a home as well as clothing and other food supplies? Is it enough for them to have a doctor come if they are ill? Do you even know where they live if it's other than your attic or basement?"

"Well, I . . ."

She leaned forward, her blue eyes stormy in her growing wrath. "And when you've fired them because you were dissatisfied with their services, did you find them another position with someone you felt would be a kind employer? Or what about when they were too old to serve you any more? Did you provide them with a place to live out their old age? Did you know or care if they still had a roof over their head?" She stood up, her voice trembling as she continued. "Mr. Lattimer, might I submit to you that you know nothing about our institution of slavery. We care about our people. Your father has gained the respect and loyalty of his slaves, and they, in turn, have no fear for their tomorrows. We are not so stupid that we do not recognize the problems which slavery can cause or the injustices which sometimes accompany it, but we do reserve the right to live our lives without Yankee interference.''

She stalked to the door, stopped and looked back at him. "Get down from your judgment seat, Mr. Lattimer, and find out who we really are. Now, if you'll both excuse me, I have things to see to. I'll see you at dinner.''

She swept from the room, leaving a stunned silence in her wake. She didn't stop her march until she reached the porch. Taylor sagged into one of the waiting wicker chairs, her entire body drained of strength. The magnitude of her feelings flashed in her eyes as one emotion after another rushed through her.

She felt shame burning in her stomach when she remembered her response to his embrace, his kisses, his throaty words of desire. Confusion followed on its heels. How could this have happened with David's son? Anybody; he could have been anybody, but not Brent Lattimer. Then she remembered his barbed words, his speaking glances, the aspersions he had cast on her morals and her character, and rage began to boil in the very depths of her soul. How dare he? How dare he do this in her own home? His attitude would be unbearable to cope with while he stayed with them.

Stayed with them! Her anger vanished, swallowed up by desperation over her current circumstances. However was she to manage with him around all the time, his eyes accusing her of impropriety, his nearness reminding her of that part of life she had yet to taste, reminding her of the spark of passion he had brought to life inside her.

Taylor hid her face in her hands, succumbing to the sheer weight of her troubles, and wept.

Brent's eyes were glued to the girl as she flounced angrily from the room. *Gads, what an exit! She was as gorgeous in wrath as she was in passion.* The desire to hold her, to love her, to possess her, still burned in his loins.

David cleared his throat. "Sorry, son. It wasn't quite the welcome I had planned. I should have warned you how sensitive my wife is about the slavery issue. Like many Southerners, she feels a bit guilty, yet doesn't know how to get along without them."

His father's wife. He forced himself to drag his thoughts back to the conversation. "And you, Father. Don't you feel guilty?"

David's gray eyes studied him for a long time before he answered. Could they really discuss this without anger between them? Could he make Brent understand what drove him back to this land, to these people?

"Brent, none of us can live without guilt." He shook his head. "That's no answer, is it? Yes, I do feel guilty sometimes, but these people are a part of the South. They're how we survive, how we live as we do. I'm a kinder master than many bosses in the factories of the North. I'm good to my people and they know it."

"Do they, Father? Isn't a yoke, no matter how light, still a yoke? Do they stay willingly?"

"Perhaps we'll soon find out, Brent, if the Republicans have a say in it."

They fell silent, David lost somewhere in the future and Brent lost in a dream from the past.

He had never forgotten her. As if it were happening now, he could see her black hair spread freely about the blanket, one arm about her head, the other tracing patterns on the quilt. A pleased, almost mischievous smile played across her full lips, their color lusciously pink in comparison with her fair complexion. It was so real he could almost feel the sun warming the back of his coat.

She had spirit too. He remembered how coyly she had played with him when he complimented her, but her eyes had given her away. Another picture framed her in the river, her laughter joining the gurgling water in a sound of joy. He had held her, wanted her, loved her.

But she was his father's bride.

A chill held Dorcet Hall in its grip for the next two days. Taylor and Brent were icily polite but tried to avoid each other whenever possible. At dinner the first night, Brent seemed about to apologize, but Taylor pretended not to hear him and asked David a question about the cotton crop. Her rebuff was well understood. Brent did not try again.

It was with great relief that the sun rose on the day of their anniversary. The sky was dotted with fluffy white clouds floating lazily above when Marilee arrived early that morning. The two young women set to work in a flurry of preparations. The house crawled with servants, and David suggested to his son that they ride out to the fields to avoid being in the way.

Marilee watched them walk toward the stables, then turned to Taylor with a smile. "My goodness! If I weren't so stuck on your brother, I could lose my heart to that Yankee stepson of yours," she giggled.

"Marilee!" Taylor exclaimed, her cheeks flaming. "He is definitely not your type."

In early afternoon, the two girls lay down to rest but both were too excited to sleep. Guests would begin arriving within just a few hours. Taylor vacillated between imagining failure to assurance it would be *the* ball of the year.

When it was time, Jenny and Silvy came to Taylor's room to help them dress. Marilee had convinced her father at last that she needed something gay for the occasion. Her gown was a sunny yellow color with an enormous belled skirt which, unfortunately, added some unneeded weight to her already plump figure. Silvy fixed her hair in tight ringlets pulled over to one side of her head. When Marilee turned to see how Taylor was coming, she was struck dumb.

The decolletage of the gown's bodice revealed

Taylor's snowy neck and shoulders and exposed a hint of cleavage. Below her tiny waist, the skirt, clinging to her feminine hips, flowed freely to the floor. Taylor's hair was intricately piled on her head with tiny topaz gems peeking out from each curl. Wisps escaped about the nape of her neck and about her face, carefully creating a casual appearance.

"Oh my!" Marilee finally managed. "Taylor, it's so . . . so French! You're positively beautiful."

"Marilee, do you really like it? Is it too much?" Taylor asked, suddenly very unsure of herself. She had so wanted to appear adult and sophisticated tonight.

Marilee caught the hesitant note in her friend's question and rushed to her side. "Oh, Taylor, it's perfect. You'll be the belle of the ball. There'll only be eyes for you."

A knock interrupted them. David's voice called out, "Taylor, our guests are arriving. Are you ready to greet them?"

Taylor swallowed her fear, returned Marilee's hug and walked to the door. David's eyes lit with understanding and appreciation when he saw her. He knew better than she did herself just how important this party was to her. He knew she had much to prove to others, but mostly to herself, about who she was. He placed her hand in the crook of his arm and they moved together toward the stairs.

"My dear," he said sincerely, "I am truly the luckiest man alive. I'm married to the most thoughtful and beautiful of women. Thank you, Taylor, for the happiness you've given me this last year."

David and Taylor moved easily among their guests, welcoming them to their home. The women fussed over her gown, some commenting later that it was absolutely scandalous. The men silently admired her glowing beauty and wished it was their own arm she was leaning on. The barbecue was an enormous success with more than enough for everyone to eat. People stood in cozy groups, visiting and laughing, as they waited for the dancing to begin. Just as the music began to play, Taylor saw Brent for the first time since that morning. He was talking with Eugenia Johnson, his head bent close to hers. Taylor was strangely upset at the sight and snapped her eyes away from the couple. Why should she care who he talked to as long as he wasn't bothering her?

"Shall we begin the dancing, my dear?" David asked. He escorted her to the center of the specially fabricated dance floor. She was soon lost in the crowd of twirling dancers. She had a new partner with each new song and had just finished a particularly taxing reel with Jeffrey Stone when she looked up to see who would claim her next dance and there stood Brent Lattimer.

"May I have the honor?" His deep voice reverberated around her. She nodded. His strong hand was firm in the small of her back as he guided her expertly about the dance floor. His eyes held hers firmly in their spell. She tried to summon up her disdain but it eluded her. *It would be heaven to always be held like this,* she thought dreamily. She didn't hear the music stop and was surprised when his arm released her. He bowed slightly to her before leading her to David who was sitting under a tree. She smiled weakly at her husband as she sat down beside him.

"You seem to be enjoying your party, Taylor," he said.

"Our party," she said automatically, her eyes following Brent's back as he walked toward Eugenia. As he claimed her for another dance, Taylor was once again gripped by a strange feeling. She turned back to David. "Would you like to dance again?"

"I'm afraid I'm feeling too old to keep up with you young folks," he answered.

His reference to their age difference depressed her suddenly. She excused herself and walked alone into the gardens, the soft light of the lanterns adding a dreamlike quality to the night. Occasionally she came upon couples strolling about, mostly young lovers, and her depression increased. The night was filled with lanterns of its own, the stars twinkling brightly and a three-quarter moon suspended overhead. She left the gardens behind her, automatically following the familiar path.

She stood at last beside the river, its surface multiplying the lights of the night sky many times over. She stared at the flowing water. Somehow she always seemed to find solace here.

By the river her father had talked to her of lasting love, the kind he felt for her mother. Here it was that David had bared his soul to her and brought some contentment to their marriage. *And here it was that* he *held you in his arms,* she thought.

"Do you plan to go wading in that beautiful gown?"

She gasped as Brent moved to stand at her side. She looked up, but his eyes were on the far shore. "Must you always sneak up on me, Mr. Lattimer? It's most disconcerting." She spoke softly. The night air carried her words swiftly away from them.

They remained where they were for several minutes, neither of them moving or speaking, both gazing at the river, lost in their own thoughts. At last Brent turned to her.

"Why did you marry my father?" he asked, his eyes seeming to bore into her skull to seek out her answer.

She looked into his handsome face, his eyes so very serious, his hair moving lightly in the soft breeze. "Because I was told to," she answered.

"For his money?" Brent asked, his voice nearly expressionless.

Taylor shook her head. "No. Not for his money. Not for me, at least. For Spring Haven." She paused. Hesitantly, she reached out and touched his arm. "But I have grown to care a great deal for David. We really are quite happy with one another." She pulled her hand back and turned away. "Really," she sighed, "we are quite happy."

"But it isn't a real marriage, is it? I'm not blind, you know. And you're so young and he's so old."

Taylor didn't reply. The silence grew thick between them. Suddenly he gripped her shoulders and turned her abruptly to him. His hands bruised her bare skin, but she remained silent as she returned his searching look. Just as suddenly, he loosened his hold and stepped away.

His voice was low and angry. "Why, of all people, did it have to be you?"

He was gone. She stood still, his words repeating themselves in her mind. *He must hate me very much,* she thought.

David's worried eyes settled on her as she emerged from the garden some time later. He hurried over and took her hand. "Where have you been, Taylor? I've been searching everywhere for you."

"I'm sorry, David. I walked down to the river for a moment. It was so pretty, I guess I lost track of time."

"Well, no matter. Here, come with me." He led her to the raised platform where the orchestra was playing. He lifted a hand and the music stopped. Soon he had everyone's attention. Then he pulled her closer to him and smiled merrily.

"My friends. I came here a stranger and have found the warm hospitality of the South to be very generous to me, indeed. I cannot express what your friendships have meant." He looked seriously at Taylor, lowering his voice slightly. "Most of all, this woman, my wife, has brought me a great deal of happiness." Turning back to the listening crowd, he smiled again. "I have thought long and hard about the perfect gift to give Mrs. Lattimer on this first anniversary. I've finally come up with it. We're going on the honeymoon we never had. I am taking her on a tour of the states. We will leave within the week."

Taylor's mouth dropped open as the guests applauded, the sound thundering in her ears. David hugged her and then held her at arms length. "Are you surprised? Are you pleased?" he asked, his voice anxious over her silence.

"David, I had no idea," she said softly. "Of course I'm pleased!" She threw her arms around his neck and squeezed him as hard as she could. *It was wonderful. A chance to get away. To get away from . . . everything.*

Chapter 8

The hotel suite was the most luxurious one they had stayed in yet. Taylor gazed about her in awe. Even she, who had been raised in wealth among imported French and English furnishings, under crystal chandeliers and looking into gold-framed mirrors, was overcome by the elaborate decor of the room. The chairs were covered in royal blue velvet, and their delicately carved legs were inlaid with gold leaf. A thick persian rug covered the floor. Rococo carvings edged the high ceiling. Ornate chandeliers hung overhead. The velvet draperies, in a matching shade of blue with the chairs, were covered with arabesque designs and bordered windows which overlooked a private park.

David paid the bellman and closed the door. His eyes ran over their room, then met hers. "A bit ostentatious, isn't it?" he commented.

Taylor laughed. "You are so right."

She opened the door to what was to be her room. She found it to be just as elaborately furnished as the sitting room but the color theme was a bright red. "Oh, my!" she breathed.

David had looked into his room and found the same thing in a princely purple. "We won't want to stay here long, my dear, or we will surely go mad in our surroundings."

Taylor agreed wholeheartedly. The place was garish in its attempt to appear patrician. She much preferred the timeless elegance of her plantation.

True to his word, David and Taylor had left Dorcet Hall only four days after the party. They had progressed leisurely, visiting Charleston, Savannah, Montgomery, and New Orleans in the South. Then they had traveled to Concord and Boston in the North before arriving here in New York City. From what she had seen of the city so far, she was prepared to leave already. She found it dirty, shabby, and overcrowded. The people she met seemed boisterous, talking too much and too fast.

"I've sent word to Brent that we've arrived," David was saying. "I'm going over to the bank this afternoon and told him to plan to dine with us this evening in the hotel dining room. Would you care to go with me to the office?"

She shook her head. "I'd just as soon not. As you will recall, your son and I have some problems getting along together. We'd best limit our meeting today to dinner.''

"I wish the two of you could mend your differences. Are you certain you won't come with me?''

Taylor touched his shoulder affectionately. "I'm sure. Perhaps I'll go shopping. Jenny and Saul can chaperone me. I'll be fine. You go talk business. You're dying to see how they're managing without you, you know.''

David chuckled. "You *are* perceptive, Taylor,'' he replied.

The afternoon had been pleasant. Taylor found several gowns imported from Paris which she liked, and she had them sent back to the hotel. David returned looking exhilarated from his excursion as well. Apparently he approved of Brent's handling of business in the past year and more. She surmised that the gap which David's return to the South had caused was narrowing at last.

As Taylor dressed for dinner, she determined that nothing would spoil this evening for David. She liked to see him as happy and relaxed as he was now, and his son's disapproval of her would just have to be ignored the best she could.

The emerald green gown she had found that afternoon seemed the perfect choice for the evening. The bodice was cut just low enough to expose the soft rise of her bosom. Her hair was left spilling freely down her bared back. When she walked into the sitting room of their suite, David nodded approvingly, then lifted a hand to stop her and went to his room. When he returned, he was carrying a small black case. He stopped in front of her and held it out. Hesitantly, she took it from him, opening it carefully. She gasped.

"I bought them in New Orleans and was saving them for just the right moment. This seemed to be it."

Taylor looked up as he spoke, then returned her gaze back to the contents of the case. Lying on the white satin lining were a pair of perfect emerald earrings and an emerald studded choker.

"Put them on," he encouraged her.

She carried the precious items back to her room, still quite speechless. Never had she seen anything so lovely. When she came back out, she stood quietly in front of her husband.

"Ah, I was right. You were meant to wear emeralds. They bring out the sea in your eyes."

Suddenly she threw her arms around his neck, her feet lifting off the floor as she squeezed him with all her might. "You're *too* good to me, David!" she exclaimed.

He laughed, throwing his head back as his mirth filled and shook his body. He unfastened her hands from around his neck and lowered her to the floor. "Taylor. Taylor. You are such a lovely mixture of woman and child. You make me young again. Come," he said, taking her arm. "Let's dazzle all New York with a true beauty of the South."

David felt like a new man since they had begun

their trip. In showing Taylor the sights, he had seen them again himself through fresh eyes. He felt younger than he had in years and was proud to escort this lovely sprite through the hotel lobby. Let the other men look on in desire. He knew she was utterly devoted to him.

Brent was waiting for them in the dining room. He had obtained a secluded table in a corner of the large, ornate restaurant. He rose when he saw them enter. He hadn't changed since she had seen him last, over four months ago. His strong, handsome features and golden brown eyes and hair still gave her the impression of a mighty lion overseeing his kingdom. She was definitely the envy of the other women in the room as she sat down with these two men.

Brent and David were also the recipients of much envy. Taylor's beauty was something quite rare. She was unaware of the effect her appearance was having, however, as she accepted Brent's greeting and was seated.

"You look as lovely as I remembered, Mrs. Lattimer," he told her.

"Thank you, sir," she replied softly.

Brent had already ordered for them, and the waiters brought them each a bowl of steaming clam chowder as an appetizer. The main course which followed was stuffed partridge, baked to perfection. Taylor concentrated on her food, only half conscious of the men's conversation. She took an interest in what they were saying, however, when the talk turned to politics and their voices grew louder and more intense.

"But surely you can see that Lincoln is the man we need at this time?"

"The last man we need in the White House is that black republican," David growled. "There'll be war if he's elected. You can be sure of it. No matter what good intentions he might have, no matter if you believe in slavery or not, his election will bring disaster."

"Maybe it will take a war to make the South realize she can't go on owning people, no matter what their skin color."

Taylor was immediately miffed. "And just what do you know about the South anyway, Mr. Lattimer?"

"Please don't get your feathers ruffled. I still believe a man like Lincoln just might be able to bring about the necessary changes without the trouble Father and everyone else is predicting if he were just given a chance. The South is a beautiful place, Taylor, full of beautiful people, including the darkies. I'd like to live there myself as my father has chosen—my roots do go back there—but I can't under the present circumstances."

Her thin thread of control over her temper snapped. "Mr. Lattimer, the South doesn't want you!" She rose stiffly. "Forgive me. I find this place intolerable. Too many Yankees. Most undesirable for the digestion."

Her dramatic sweep from the room was most impressive, but she was severely depressed upon

106

reaching her room. Why had she done this to David again? If only Brent wasn't so opinionated! Taylor threw herself across her bed and waited for David's return. She was sure it wouldn't be long. She had spoiled the evening for everyone with her hot temper and wild tongue. David made no mention of her angry display, however, when he came in. He only commented that he was tired and planned to retire early.

"If only I'd stayed out of it," she mumbled to the accusing ceiling.

They remained in New York for another week before going to Washington City. Taylor did not see Brent again. David went each morning to the bank but spent the afternoons with her, showing her about the city and surrounding countryside. The subject of their first evening was never brought up, but Taylor felt its presence nonetheless. She wished she could mend some bridges with Brent but felt sure she had totally burned them all. Finally she put it out of her mind, so confused did it leave her.

The Lattimers arrived in the capital city on a dreary November afternoon. Taylor was surprised to find it a city under construction, crisscrossed by many muddy streets. An overpowering odor drifted in the air off the fetid waters of the Old City Canal. She was disappointed that the capital of her nation was without the quiet nobility she had imagined it would have.

David dined that evening with Senators Chesnut and Toombs, but Taylor declined the invitation to join them. She knew politics would be the only subject open to discussion. Even though they would most likely be in agreement with her, being Southerners like herself, she felt she had caused enough trouble already. Two days later, the election results were in. Lincoln had won. David announced they would leave at once for home.

"There is no way to stop it now, Taylor," he told her sadly. "There will be war. An ugly, destructive, drawn-out war. God help us all."

They had been on the train only a short time when David collapsed. Although he rallied immediately, Taylor could see that he was desperately ill. She wanted to stop until he was totally recovered, but David insisted they continue. "I must reach Dorcet Hall," was all he would say.

With the help of Saul and Jenny, they proceeded slowly toward home, resting for a day or two whenever the travel became more than he could handle. When they reached Athens, Taylor was convinced he was dying. She sent word to Brent that he should come quickly if he wanted to see his father before he died. Then the weary foursome continued their journey home to Dorcet Hall.

Chapter 9

Taylor tucked the blankets around David's legs and then plumped the pillows behind his head and back. She stepped away from him, smiling encouragingly. "There now. Isn't that better?"

David tried to return her smile as he nodded. His illness had left him weak, the battle he had fought for his life showing distinctly on his face. The skin sank back from his cheekbones, no longer enough flesh to fill out his face, and he was jaundiced. The yellowish tint even touched his eyes which were sunken in their sockets. The hair on his head and his beard was white instead of gray. His weak attempt to smile tugged painfully at her heart.

In the weeks since he first fell ill, Taylor had watched him age quickly. Those who saw them traveling home together had thought her a very devoted grandchild. Her concern for him was real as she faced the strong possibility of his dying. She cared a great deal for David Lattimer, she realized—nearly too late. For all the wrong reasons, they had married, but he had been good to her. He had removed her from an environment where she was unwanted and placed her in one where she was very special indeed. She had been a child when they married, but he had helped her to learn about the world and about herself. It wasn't until his illness that she realized just how empty her life would be without him. She depended on him just as she had on the only other important man in her life. She had lost her father. She wasn't prepared to lose David, too.

Taylor sat on the floor beside his couch. She had been trying to read *The Marble Faun* but was unable to keep her mind from wandering to other things. The fire burned brightly, chasing the cold air back into the corners away from the invalid. Rain splashed against the windows. Taylor was grateful they had made it home before this awful weather. Christmas had come and gone unobserved as she fretted over her husband and wondered when his son would come. She also wondered why he wasn't here already. David had asked for him often in recent weeks.

"Miss Taylor," Jenny called from the doorway. Taylor glanced at David before rising. He was sleeping peacefully again. She slipped away quietly.

"What is it, Jenny?"

"Somebody jus' rode in, Missy. I saw him take his horse 'round t'the barn."

"In this weather?" Taylor pulled the draperies back from the window beside the door and peered into the inky darkness. She finally made out the figure of a man bending into the rain as he walked swiftly toward the house. She opened the door as he climbed the steps. He lifted the hat from his head and shook it as he looked up at her.

"Brent?" she cried. "You've come at last! Come in." She reached out, caught his sleeve and pulled him inside. He stood dripping on the parquet flooring, looking nearly drowned.

"How's Father?" he asked as he removed his sopping rain gear.

"Better. Why didn't you come when I sent for you?"

"I wasn't in New York. Your message just reached me last week. May I see him?"

"Wait just a little. He's sleeping right now. Come into the library and have a cup of coffee while you dry off."

Taylor led the way, instructing Jenny, who was taking his wet things, to bring a coffee tray to them. Brent followed her, halting in front of the fire to warm himself. She watched him silently, thinking how like his father he was and yet so different too. He turned and caught her staring at him.

"How are you, Mrs. Lattimer? You avoided me in New York."

New York. It was a lifetime ago.

"As I recall, we were both better off not seeing each other. Besides, you and your father didn't need me around while you talked business day in and day out," she said. "And please let's stop this silly formality. Call me Taylor." She handed him his coffee cup while she spoke. They fell silent as they drank the warming brew. Taylor wished she wasn't always so uncomfortable around him. She knew he disliked her thoroughly. Suddenly another thought popped into her head. What if David did die? The place would surely go to Brent. If he didn't want her here, she would be turned out. She wasn't sure Philip would want her at Spring Haven, no matter how much better they were getting along.

"I'd like to see him now," Brent said, oblivious to her new worry. "What has the doctor had to say about him?"

Walking beside him, she answered, "When we first got home. Dr. Reed didn't think he had a prayer. Now, he's rather noncommittal, but I think he's at least more hopeful. I'm certain he's better, and I know your being here will help, too. He's asked for you often, you know." She stepped closer to the couch and gently touched David's shoulder. "David? Look who's here. It's Brent."

David blinked, the light too bright after sleeping. Brent knelt next to his father and took his shriveled hand. Taylor could see him bite back his shock over his father's appearance.

"Father," he said simply, yet it said so much.

"Ah . . . Brent. You've come. How nice, my

112

boy." He closed his eyes, too tired to say more.

Brent lifted his eyes to Taylor. "This is improved?" he whispered incredulously. She nodded. He looked again at his father and Taylor slipped out of the room, leaving the two alone together.

A bitter northeaster blew against the house the next morning but the clouds were gone for the time being. Taylor awoke early but stayed snuggled down in her warm bedding until Jenny came to stir up the fire. She stared at the canopy above her, wondering how long Brent would stay with them. Jenny entered with a tray, breaking her train of thought.

"Mornin', Missy. You ready t'get up?" she asked as she set the tray down and turned to the fireplace.

"Is our guest about yet?" Taylor asked, pushing herself up against the headboard and drinking the hot chocolate. By the time she was finished, the chill was leaving her room. She dressed in a hurry, not paying much attention to what Jenny pulled from the closet for her to wear. "I'll see to my hair," she told Jenny. "You see if Master David is awake yet and if he wants Saul to carry him down to the parlor right after breakfast."

Taylor ran a quick brush through her hair and fastened the unruly curls back with some combs. She leaned closer to her image in the glass with a slight frown. "My, you're pale," she said as she pinched some color into her cheeks.

Taylor found Brent already in the dining room

eating his breakfast. The sideboard was covered with several delectable choices, but Taylor paid little attention to what she was putting on her plate. She sat across from Brent and spread preserves on the roll she had taken.

"How lovely you look this morning, Taylor."

"Why . . . thank you, Brent. You . . . you look well yourself." *What a silly thing to say,* she thought as she looked back at her plate.

"Is Father up yet?"

"No. He's still sleeping. After he breakfasts, Saul will bring him downstairs. Dr. Reed is supposed to drive out again today. I'm sure you'll want to speak to him. He can tell you much more than I can."

Brent left the table and walked to the window. He stood, his hands clasped behind his back, looking out at the bleak winter scene. The leafless trees struggled to stand straight against the prevailing winds. The lawn seemed colorless, the flowers all gone now, the grass sleeping through the winter. Taylor tried to concentrate on her meal rather than his broad back. She tried to think of something interesting to say to break the silence but was unsuccessful. At long last, or so it seemed to Taylor, she finished her breakfast. Still he stood staring out the window. Occasionally he rocked back on his heels; otherwise he was perfectly still. Deciding not to interrupt his thoughts, Taylor pushed back her chair and quietly started from the room.

"Taylor," he said just as she reached the door.

She stopped and looked in his direction. His back remained turned toward her as he continued. "Do you suppose we could start over again with each other? I've treated you unfairly and I'm sorry. I had my mind made up not to like Father's new wife from the moment I heard he was marrying again, and then, when I saw it was you, I ... I was ... Well, never mind," he said, turning at last. "I would like us to be friends. I've seen how devoted you are to him."

She looked thoughtfully at him, then nodded. "Yes, Brent, I would like us to be friends." Suddenly, she was afraid she would cry and left hastily. Why was she never quite in control of herself when he was around?

Brent turned back to the window as she disappeared through the doorway. The weather looked just like he felt—cold and wind-battered. Like his father, he was a man who liked to be in charge of every situation. He decided what he wanted and made whatever decisions were necessary to obtain it. But this was different. He was definitely not in charge here, especially of himself. And he couldn't go after what he wanted. She wasn't available for the taking.

He hadn't wanted to see her again. His father was enamored with her but he was no fool. He was bound to read Brent's feelings if he was here for very long. How long could he stay himself from crushing her in his arms and kissing those sweet lips if he must see her day in and day out?

A fire raged within him. He leaned his forehead against the glass to cool himself and prayed he would never betray himself to anyone.

Dr. Reed arrived before noon. Taylor led him into the parlor where David and Brent were sitting together. The doctor was surprised at the increased vitality of his patient since he had seen him last. He shook hands with Brent as Taylor introduced them.

"Yes, I remember Mr. Lattimer," he commented. "We met last summer at your barbecue."

Taylor stayed with David when the examination was over while Brent and Dr. Reed went into the library to discuss his findings.

"A brandy, Dr. Reed?" Brent offered as he closed the door behind him.

"Yes, I believe I will, thank you." The doctor settled himself into a comfortable chair near the fireplace and accepted the proffered glass. "Mr. Lattimer," he began, "I must say your father has indeed made a significant recovery since his return home. I honestly didn't hold out much hope for him to survive when I first began caring for him. I must admit that his progress is due primarily to Mrs. Lattimer's felicitious care. And now your presence seems to have helped him too." He pushed his glasses back on his nose as he spoke. "I hope you will extend your stay as long as possible."

"You can be sure, doctor, that I will remain as long as he needs me," Brent answered, his emotions at a tug-of-war within him. "Dr. Reed, what caused his illness?"

The doctor sighed and shook his graying head. "I don't know what brought it on, Brent. But his primary problem now is his heart. He's getting old, as are a lot of us. He must slow down. He'll

116

never be able to do all he was used to doing before this illness." The doctor finished his drink and stood up. "Whatever his ailment, my boy, you and Mrs. Lattimer seem to be just the right medicine for him. Just keep it up. Now, I must be off. I have one more patient to see before I can return to my warm hearth in Bellville."

Brent saw him to the door and shook his hand again. Dr. Reed placed his hat on his head, buttoning his overcoat up tightly before opening the door. "You send for me if you need me. I'll stop by again next week. Good-bye for now."

Brent watched as the doctor climbed into his buggy and drove off. Then he joined Taylor and David in the parlor. His father was sleeping once again, and Taylor motioned for him to be quiet. They moved to a corner of the room.

"What did Dr. Reed tell you?" Taylor asked anxiously.

"He said Father is improving and that it's because of you that he is. Father is going to be fine."

"Oh, that's wonderful. I'm so glad you're here, Brent," she whispered, smiling brightly.

Brent looked at her solemnly, his face so close to hers he could smell her soft perfume. "So am I, Taylor," he replied. "So am I."

Chapter 10

"Well, tell me your news, Marilee. I can see you're just bursting with it," Taylor said as her friend sat down across from her.

"Oh, Taylor, you'll just never believe it!" Marilee exclaimed. "Philip has asked me to marry him."

Taylor's eyes widened at the news. She jumped up and hugged Marilee. "I'm so happy for you, Marilee. I know you've been hoping and praying for this. When did he ask you? When is the wedding?"

"After you left last summer, Philip started to pay court to me. Papa was beside himself that a *Bellman* was actually calling on his daughter, I assure you. Philip was with me last week when the news came that Georgia had joined with the other states in seceding. He said there'll be trouble for sure now and that he'd better not wait any longer. I couldn't imagine what he meant." Marilee giggled. "Then he asked me to marry him. You can imagine just how long I had to think about it before saying yes. Papa consented to us getting married next Friday."

"So soon?"

"Both Philip and Papa think there'll be war, and we want to marry before then." She reddened. "Besides, Philip says a son is needed for Spring Haven."

"I know."

"Anyway, Taylor, I want you to stand up with me. We're going to have just a small ceremony at Papa's church. He's going to officiate, of course, and Philip has asked Jeffrey to be his best man. You will, won't you, Taylor? Will you be there with me?"

Taylor hugged her again. "Of course I will. Where else would I be? I'm so very happy for you, Marilee. I hope Philip knows just how lucky he is."

"I'm the lucky one, Taylor," Marilee said earnestly.

The two young women went upstairs hand in hand. Together they went through Taylor's closet trying to decide just what she should wear. There certainly wasn't time to have anything special made. They visited and laughed as Taylor tried on and discarded gown after gown. Finally a decision was made, and Taylor took Marilee to tell David the news before she left.

"Miss Stone, I'm very pleased for you and Mr. Bellman. As Euripides said, 'Man's best possession is a sympathetic wife.' Philip Bellman is a lucky man." He took Taylor's hand and pressed it against his cheek. "As am I," he continued. "I wish I felt strong enough to attend the wedding with Taylor. Perhaps you would allow my son to escort her in my place."

Marilee agreed heartily. "Of course. I would be honored to have Mr. Lattimer in attendance if he would be interested in coming."

"I would be glad to come, Miss Stone, if you wouldn't mind a Yankee among your guests," Brent said, smiling wryly.

"Oh, pooh," Marilee declared. "What nonsense! You're part of Taylor's family. Your father's a Southern gentleman if ever there was one."

Brent sighed. "I'm afraid most people won't be quite so gracious as you, my dear Miss Stone. Nonetheless, I'll be at your wedding with my best wishes in hand."

The Friday of the wedding brought with it a promise of spring. David said good-bye to Taylor and Brent from his chair on the porch early that morning. "You two have a nice time. Give my regards to the bride and groom."

Taylor kissed him and tucked his blanket around his feet, a habit now after so many weeks. "I wish you were coming with us, David," she said. Then she shook her finger at him. "Don't you overexert yourself. I've told Jenny to take care of you, and I'll be checking with her to see if you've behaved yourself. If you haven't, you'll have me to face for it."

David chuckled. "Thank you for fussing so. See what I put up with?" he asked Brent.

"Yes," Brent answered gently. "I see."

The horse stepped at a lively trot under its harness during the ride to Bellville. The air was crisp, but the sun burned brightly overhead. Touches of green were everywhere. Taylor felt the surge of renewed hope which spring always brought her.

"You love this land a great deal, don't you?" Brent asked as he observed the excitement on her face.

"Oh, yes! There's no place like here."

"Tell me about your Georgia, Taylor . . . and about yourself. I find I really don't know you at all."

Taylor glanced at him, then returned her eyes to the fallow fields they were trotting past. "Like what?" she asked.

"Your childhood," he suggested.

She settled back against the seat, losing herelf to the story she was telling. "My father was born on Spring Haven," she began, "although it wasn't called that then. It was just a big farm really, but the Bellmans were already the most influential and wealthiest in the area. Bellville was named in honor of my grandfather. Papa married the daughter of a neighboring farmer, Philip's mother, and the two lands merged. It wasn't a very happy marriage, I've been told. By the time she died of yellow fever, Papa was a successful lawyer and had built the manor house that's there now. He met my mother in New Orleans. They were very much in love." Taylor sighed wistfully. "I'm just beginning to understand how hard it was for Philip. He was still just a boy. Suddenly he had lost his mother. Then his father became all wrapped up in a new wife and very quickly a new daughter. He was off to schools while I was growing up. When he was home, he made it very plain that he didn't like me very much. Maybe he had reasons for it. But he's always loved Spring Haven. He would die for it. That's why he forced me to . . . that's why he . . . Well, that's all best forgotten." She paused in reflection.

"Mama died in a buggy accident when I was fourteen. Papa couldn't handle it. He changed, almost overnight, from the strong, loving man I'd always known to someone lost, floundering for a grip on life. He drank and gambled . . . and it finally killed him." Tears clung to her thick lashes. She blinked furtively. "I was a pretty spoiled child, I guess. My parents gave me everything I ever wanted. David's helped me to grow up; at least, I hope that's so. And it's because of your father that Philip and I are growing closer to one another at last." She looked down at her hands as she finished, a thoughtful expression across her beautiful face.

Suddenly, Taylor looked up, a smile returning to her mouth. "You've never seen Spring Haven! Oh, just wait till you do. It's a little piece of heaven right here on earth. The land is so fertile you can see its richness. The trees and the flowers, the river, the horses, the house ... Oh, I just can't describe it. Spring Haven is more than mere words could ever describe."

Brent returned her eager smile before asking, "And Dorcet Hall?"

She gestured in apology. "I'm ... comfortable there. And I'm still in Georgia. But no place could ever be the same as Spring Haven."

"You would return if you could?"

She shook her head sadly. "I'll never be able to return home. The plantation is Philip's and will pass on to his children. There's no chance I'll ever live there again."

The wedding was performed just before noon with about twenty guests in attendance. Marilee wore a gown of illusion over silk. Her veil flowed full and free over her face and person like a shower of pure white mist. A wreath of white and yellow blossoms crowned her head, and she carried a matching bouquet. Taylor stood by Marilee's side, misty-eyed, while Marilee and Philip said their vows. She knew how much in love with him Marilee was and hoped Philip returned her love in kind. She still found it hard to believe he did—or could.

The wedding party and guests rode out to Spring Haven after the ceremony. Tomorrow the newlyweds would leave on their honeymoon to

Charleston. A bountiful dinner was set before them, and toast followed toast as everyone drank their best wishes to the bride and groom. Taylor sat between Jeffrey Stone and Dr. Reed. Lively conversations surrounded her and she enjoyed herself as she hadn't in months. When people began to depart, Taylor gave Brent a tour of the house and grounds before they, too, started for home.

"I can see why you feel the way you do, Taylor," he said as he helped her into the buggy. "There's a mystique about this place." He paused. "Just as there is about you."

Taylor looked at Brent from beneath heavy lashes, trying to understand what he meant by her "mystique," but he was already turning the horse toward home and not looking at her. She felt strangely reluctant to return to Dorcet Hall. The day had been so lovely. She had enjoyed Brent's company and loved showing him Spring Haven.

"If we can keep up this pace, we'll make it back before nightfall," Brent said.

She looked up at the sky in surprise. She had no idea it had gotten so late. Even the air was turning cool, a reminder that winter still ruled the nights. Instinctively she snuggled up against him. A warm shock spread from that touch into her stomach and down through her thighs. She slid away quickly, her eyes locked on the horse's ears, a blush heating her cheeks. What on earth had come over her?

A loud crack split the air. Taylor felt herself

flung into space as the buggy twisted and rolled. She hit the ground with a thud, the wind knocked from her lungs. An excruciating weight fell against her leg as she fainted.

"Taylor? Taylor!"

She could hear a voice calling to her from far away. Someone was shaking her shoulders. She opened her eyes, looking directly into Brent's concerned face.

"Are you all right?" he asked.

"I . . . I think so. What . . . what happened?" Taylor asked as she pushed herself up and looked about her, disoriented.

"The wheel. It's broken. No way to fix it. We're going to have to walk home. The horse has a broken leg."

"Oh, no! Are you sure?"

Brent held his hand out to help her stand. "I'm sure. Come on. Up you go." He pulled her to her feet, but as she tried to stand, she crumpled into his arms.

"My ankle!" she cried, the pain searing up her leg like a hot iron.

Brent carefuly lowered her back to the ground. He pushed away her skirt and gently probed her ankle. A worried frown furrowed his brow. "Well, it could be broken; it's definitely a bad sprain." He sat back on his haunches and looked up at the sky. "We've got to get to some kind of shelter. It's going to be completely dark soon and the nights are still pretty cold." He stood up and looked around as if seeking an answer. "I'll just have to carry you," he said finally.

"You can't pack me all the way home," she protested.

He shrugged. "No other choice that I can see."

Brent walked over to where the sorrel gelding lay, caught in a tangle of harness. Pulling out a pistol, he aimed it carefully at the animal's head and fired. Taylor jerked as if it was she who had been struck by the bullet. The horse flinched and then fell still as Brent returned to her. Effortlessly, he lifted her from the ground. He began walking at a determined pace toward Dorcet Hall. Taylor felt each jarring step he took, her ankle throbbing painfully. Tears threatened to cascade down her cheeks as she gritted her teeth against the torment. She hid her face against his chest, gripping his shoulder as she tried to support herself better. His shirt was torn and her hand felt warm and sticky. She looked at it and found her hand covered with blood.

"Brent, you're hurt!" she exclaimed. "You shouldn't be carrying me."

"I'm afraid you're right, Taylor. I don't think I can get us home. Do you know of any place we could take cover? Think hard."

She shook her head in reply. "Wait," she cried as she remembered something. "There's an old shack along the river near here. It should be just a little farther."

Brent pressed on, finally shouting, "There it is." He cut across through the trees toward the river.

The door of the dilapidated cabin, built from scraps of lumber, was swinging free in the evening breeze. The interior was thick with cobwebs and dust, the single room occupied by an old cot sitting on the dirt floor and a rickety table in the center of the room. Brent set Taylor on the cot and closed the door. He pulled the table over to hold it shut, the latch on the door long since broken. He found the stub of a candle in a rusty holder on a shelf near the fireplace along with some matches. Striking one, he carried the light over to Taylor.

"I'll try to get a fire going. Are you all right?"

Taylor nodded as she accepted the candle. She put it on the floor and watched as Brent knelt before the fireplace. She shifted on the cot, trying to find a position which would relieve the painful spasms in her right leg.

A fire blazed at last before them and Brent returned to the cot. "We may get a little heat out of that. At least the chimney isn't plugged up. Let's have a look at that foot again."

Tenderly, he held the calf of her leg and examined her ankle. It was swollen and turning black and blue. When he turned it, she groaned.

"We need to secure it," he told her. His eyes ran over the room, searching for something he could use. "Nothing. Well, we'll have to use your petticoat. Give it here."

"Now just wait one minute!" It was bad enough to have him looking at her bare legs, but to have him ripping up her undergarments—it just wasn't done!

Brent laughed at the expression on her face. "Don't go getting all prim and prissy on me, Taylor. This is a real fix we're in and your ankle needs attention. Your petticoat is all we have to use. Either give it to me or I'll take it from you. Come on."

Taylor glared at him for a moment, but the intensity of her pain convinced her he was right. "Turn around then," she ordered him in a clipped tone. Brent, still smiling, turned his back to her. She lifted the skirt of her dress and started tearing the fabric of her slip. "Is that enough?" she asked as she dropped her dress back over her legs.

Brent held out his hand to accept the strips of material, nodding as he did so. Again he held her calf with one hand while with the other he set the foot in the position he wanted. Taylor grasped the sides of the cot, bracing herself against the new stabs of pain. Beads of sweat dotted her forehead as he wrapped the foot and ankle tightly. She tried to concentrate on anything else which might keep her tears from falling. Waves of blackness threatened to overtake her.

Brent looked up from his completed work. Taylor's face was as white as a sheet. Her long dark lashes were pressed against her pale skin. She looked so helpless, so . . .

"Taylor?" he asked. "Are you still with me?"

She opened her eyes, her voice weak and strained as she spoke. "Are you finished?"

"Yes. I'm sorry it hurt so much, but I think it's as it should be now." Brent pushed himself up from the floor and walked over to the single window in the room.

Outside, the night had covered everything in inky darkness. The wind had risen and blew in around the small, dirty panes of glass and under the door as well. He wondered if he should try to make it to Dorcet Hall tonight, leaving Taylor here alone. The room was growing colder, their fire providing little heat in the drafty shack.

When he turned back toward the cot, he found Taylor leaning against the wall, her eyes closed again. Traces of the tears she had been unable to hold back any longer streaked her cheeks. A dirty smudge under one eye showed where she had tried to wipe away the evidence. Her arms were held rigidly across her breasts, and she shivered occasionally. Again he searched the room, this time for something to cover her with, but there was nothing to be found.

"Taylor?"

She shook her head, her mouth set in a grim line, her eyes still closed. Brent sat beside her on the cot. He pulled her to him and wrapped his arms tightly around her shivering body. She stiffened, then relaxed and finally, she slept. Brent's arms and back grew tired. A gnawing ache persisted in his shoulder as the hours dragged by. Still he held her snugly against him.

She awoke sometime after midnight. The embers from the fire cast a red glow around the room. "Brent," she whispered as she tried to pull away from him. She looked up, a strange sensation piercing through her as her eyes met his in the flickering light.

"Taylor."

It was only her name he spoke, but somehow it was so much more. She felt paralyzed as he lifted her chin with his finger and brought his lips against hers. Her head spun. Surely she floated somewhere above the earth, for this couldn't be an earthly sensation. His hands held her head firmly between them as his lips moved hungrily across her cheek and down to her throat. Her breath came in short gasps. Again his mouth claimed hers, and she was lost in his power. She groaned as she leaned toward him, her hands pressed against his chest. She could feel his heart pounding as did her own. She returned his kisses, amazed at herself, at the hunger which filled her.

Suddenly she pulled away from him, the spell broken, a look of horror in her eyes, clear even in the dimness of the room. "Your father," she whispered, her voice breaking. "Stop this! We mustn't. What about David?" Her eyes were wide and she braced herself as she had against the pain in her leg, gripping the sides of the cot.

Their eyes locked for an eternity. She could hear his breathing, rapid and shallow. At last, his hands released her. He rose from the cot, crossed to the fire, and crouched down, his head drooping forward, cradled in his hands. The blackness of night filled her aching heart. She felt empty, alone, afraid. Then his whisper cut through her with an agony she had never known. Again, it was only one word, but its futility filled the room and echoed through her spirit.

"Taylor."

Chapter 11

She was alone when she awoke. Sunshine tried to peek through the dirty window and the fire had been rekindled. She sat up from the slumped position she had slept in, aching all over. She tried to stand but was quickly reminded of her injury by the hot pain flashing up her leg. She fell back onto the cot. For a moment, she thought she might cry. She was alone, hungry, and thirsty. Her foot throbbed without respite. Her elegant gown which she had worn for the wedding yesterday was rumpled and stained. She felt dirty and wanted a bath. It had been a long time since she had felt this sorry for herself.

Taylor wondered where Brent was and when he would return. Memories of his embrace flooded over her. Even when he was gone, Taylor was caught by his magnetism.

She tried to shake away her thoughts. "Well, I must have something to drink," she said aloud. "I can't just sit and wait for him." Holding her skirts out of the way the best she could and leaning against the wall for support, she hobbled around to the door.

Taylor blinked at the sudden brightness when she pulled open the door. Birds sang merrily in the nearby trees, rejoicing in the freshness of the morning. A tree limb lay on the ground next to the shack. She picked it up and using it for a crutch, slowly made her way to the rushing water. Ignoring the muddy river bank, Taylor dropped down and lowered her cupped hands into the water. She splashed her face, then dried it with her skirt. Next, she took a long drink. The water tasted gritty, but she was too thirsty to care.

Her thirst quenched, she straightened with a sigh. Looking around her, she wondered how long she would have to wait before Brent came back. *Maybe he's not coming back,* she thought. What if he was angry after she pushed him away and had left her here? The possibility loomed before her. She was frightened at the thought—and was suddenly convinced it was true. She couldn't just wait here indefinitely. She would just have to try to make it home on her own.

Standing at the river's edge, she knew her ankle wouldn't support much weight. She would just have to rely on her makeshift crutch. As she limped back toward the cabin, she began to grow angry. How dare he just leave her here without a word! She leaned against a tree before proceeding through the heavily wooded area. The ground was uneven and covered with brush. It wasn't going to be easy walking through there with her bad ankle, but she had to try.

"Taylor!"

She turned to see Brent riding up to the cabin, leading Tasha behind him.

"What do you think you're trying to do?" he scolded her. "Make your ankle worse?"

Brent tied the horses and hurried over to her. He placed both hands on her shoulders, smiling. "My, you truly are beautiful, Taylor," he said, laughing softly.

"Why, you worm you!" she snapped. "I know all too well just how I look. Why did you leave me without a word? If I weren't so glad to see Tasha, I would surely have been happy never to have set eyes on you again!"

The smile disappeared. "I didn't want to disturb you. You needed the sleep badly. You didn't think I'd left you, did you?" He stared at her incredulously. "You did!" He cupped her chin in one of his hands. "Taylor, after last night, don't you know how much I care for you?"

He bent to kiss her. Taylor allowed herself to be drawn into his embrace and succumbed to the indescribable feelings his kiss sent through her. Before she was ready, he gently released her. Silently picking her up, he carried her to her horse. "It will not happen again, Taylor." The finality of his words, the emptiness of his voice, stung her. She knew he was right. It must not happen again. She nodded as he lifted her to her saddle. Taking the reins from him, she turned Tasha toward home, not waiting for Brent.

David was waiting on the porch. He watched anxiously as Brent helped Taylor from her horse. He thought she seemed more hurt somehow than just her ankle. Her smudged face looked defeated, without hope.

She accepted his hug meekly. "How are you, Taylor? Brent told me what happened," he said as he released her.

"I'm fine, really, David. A few days' rest and my ankle will be as good as new, I'm sure." She smiled wearily. "What I need right now is a bath."

"I'll have Jenny get one for you. Brent, carry her to her room. I've sent for Dr. Reed and he should be here soon."

She was caught up in his arms once again. How good the bath was going to feel, she thought. Perhaps it could warm her aching heart as well.

Later that morning, Dr. Reed confirmed that it was only a nasty sprain. "You were very lucky, Taylor," he said as he finished wrapping the ankle. "It could have been much worse." He turned to David. "I saw the buggy and horse on the way out. It's a wonder they weren't both killed by the looks of it." He shook his head. "Now I'd best see to Brent's shoulder. You stay off that foot for at least two weeks, Taylor Lattimer. Hear me?"

"Yes. I will, Dr. Reed," she answered. "Thank you."

134

David sat down on the edge of the bed, his face drawn and tired. She was sorry to have caused him this worry and felt guilty as well. She must forget Brent's kisses. And she must forget the way she responded to those same kisses. She owed too much to David to ever treat him so shabbily.

Taylor reached out and took David's hand. "Why don't you go lie down. I don't want you having a relapse now that you're getting well again."

"Maybe you're right, my dear. I am a little tired. I'll have Jenny come sit with you in case you need anything."

Taylor closed her eyes and lay back on her pillows. She heard Jenny come in but feigned sleep. Soon she was not pretending. When she opened her eyes again, it was afternoon.

Sitting up, she said, "Jenny, I'm starved. Get my dressing gown and help me with my hair. I want to go downstairs."

"Don't you be steppin' on that foot now, Missy, else Masta David be after both our hides," Jenny said as she helped her dress.

Taylor laughed. "You're so right, Jenny." She watched impatiently as Jenny combed the snarls from her hair. "Nothing fancy. I'm getting hungrier by the minute." She felt as if she hadn't eaten in weeks.

Jenny sent for Saul to carry their mistress down the stairs. David looked up in surprise as they entered the room, promptly putting aside

135

the ledgers he was studying.

"My dear, you look much improved after your rest," he said as Saul put her on the couch.

"And I feel better, David, but I'm starving to death!"

"Jenny, have Mima see to a meal for this famished young woman," David ordered as he sat beside her on the couch. "From what Brent told me, you two had quite an adventure."

"I'd just as soon not have that kind of adventure ever again, thank you," she replied.

"Here's something you'll like," David laughed as Mima came in with the dinner tray.

"Lord-a-mercy, Miss Taylor!" Mima exclaimed as Taylor quickly started eating. "Folks'd think nobody 'roun' here ever fed you nuthin' befo'. Slow down 'fore you makes yo'self sick."

Taylor glanced up from her plate as she took another big bite. Mima's stern look almost choked her. "All right, Mima. All right. Don't get all flustered at me." She carefully cut a very small bit of meat and chewed slowly. Satisfied, Mima left the room, muttering about "some folks' manners."

David chuckled, and Taylor looked at him, returning his smile. We are happy together, she thought suddenly, then wondered where Brent was. Her lighthearted mood dissipated.

"Where's Brent?"

"He rode off some time ago. Said he wanted to look over the buggy to see what caused the accident."

136

"How was his shoulder?"

"Dr. Reed bandaged a fairly deep gash but said it was nothing to worry about. It will be mighty sore for a while, certainly," David replied.

Taylor turned her eyes to the window and stared idly through the glass. The afternoon wore on with only the rustle of ledger pages interrupting the silence. Taylor's thoughts drifted on the silence, always returning to Brent. She was so confused about him. She didn't understand what had happened between them. It all seemed so sudden, so all jumbled up in her mind. She was still looking out the window when she saw him riding toward the house. She watched him dismount and enter through the front door.

His mouth set grimly, he acknowledged Taylor with a brisk nod before turning to his father. "I need to speak with you. Privately."

David lifted a questioning eyebrow but followed him immediately across the hall into the library and closed the door. Taylor held her breath. Something must be wrong. What if he was telling David about last night? No, he mustn't. He wouldn't.

When the library door opened an hour later, Brent's long strides carried him quickly out to his horse. He kicked the stallion into a gallop and was out of sight almost at once. Taylor turned from the window. David had come back into the parlor. His manner told her he didn't wish to discuss whatever had been said between them, and she sat in apprehensive silence, listening to the

137

grandfather clock tick away the minutes.

In the days following Brent's sudden departure, neither David nor Taylor talked about him, even though he was obviously on both their minds. David treated her with increased tenderness and care, convincing her that Brent had not told him of their embrace. The warm weather persisted, and preparations began for the spring planting. Although he was unable to participate as he once had, David had Saul drive him out to the fields to watch the field hands at their labors. Taylor wandered aimlessly about the quiet house with the use of a cane, her heart anxious and strangely troubled.

It was one such afternoon when Jeffrey Stone arrived. Taylor was sitting on the porch waiting for David to return. She welcomed the diversion and waved a greeting to him as he rode up.

"How nice to see you, Jeffrey. It's been just forever since you've come out this way."

"I had to. With Cousin Marilee off to Charleston with that new husband of hers, and you laid up with that nasty ankle, I was getting terribly lonely in town. I found the urge irresistible to spend the remainder of this day in the company of the most beautiful woman in Georgia. So here I am."

Taylor laughed, a merry tinkling melody, crystal clear and crisp, allowing his flattery to chase away her troublesome thoughts and concerns. She fluttered her eyes at him, desiring to prolong this freedom from worry as long as was possible. "Why, Mr. Stone. Surely there must be many charming and more eligible ladies just pining for your company in Bellville."

"Not any I care to spend any time with," he said seriously, but she chose to ignore it.

"Tell me, Jeffrey. What news is there? I feel like I haven't heard *anything* about *anybody* for just *ages.*"

Jeffrey settled back in his chair. "Let me see. What on earth could I find to tell you? Did you know they've elected Jeff Davis president? It should have been Robert Toombs or Alec Stephens if you ask me, but... Well, it's a start, anyway."

"Will it come to war, Jeffrey?"

"Not if the Yankees know what's good for them."

"Oh, dear. This is much too serious," she said, batting her eyes coyly once more, a mischievous smile tweaking the corners of her mouth. "I thought you'd come to cheer me up. Come now, Jeffrey. Tell me the latest gossip."

He joined her laughter. "All right, Taylor. I'll tell you everything I know and a lot about what I don't." He talked on and on, making her laugh until the tears rushed down her pink cheeks; then making her gasp in feigned shock.

Jeffrey loved to hear her laugh. When they were children, her giggle had been most infectious. She loved to play innocent jokes on her father, but she often gave them away by laughing too soon. He couldn't remember a time when he hadn't loved her. He was even unsure when exactly he stopped loving her as his childhood friend and began loving her for the woman she had become. It made no difference anyway. He had always known he was invisible in her eyes as a suitor. He knew he was not the type of man to set a woman's heart to racing within her breast. He was too plain, homely really.

He remembered his fumbling attempt at expressing his love to her and felt the familiar heat rising up his neck. If only he had been able to speak sooner, perhaps she would be his bride. But words of love always seemed to stick in his throat. He could write them, though. He could spend hours, pen on paper, telling her of his love, his undying devotion to her. Then he slowly, ceremoniously, tore the sheets into tiny pieces. The time was not right for her—or anyone—to read his innermost thoughts. For now, he would have to be content with her friendship. At least he could receive that with the same honesty with which she freely gave it to him.

By the time David returned, Taylor felt exhausted, yet exhilarated, by Jeffrey's visit.

"I see you have cheered my wife," David said as he shook Jeffrey's hand in greeting. "I must thank you for that. Please stay for supper. You can return to town tomorrow."

"Thank you, David. I believe I'll do just that."

Later that evening, the threesome sat down to a table laden with ham, roast turkey, hot biscuits, vegetables, apple pie, cheese, fruits, and wine. Jeffrey assisted Taylor with her chair, then sat down beside her.

Turning to David, he said, "You know, Mr. Lattimer, your wife gets more lovely every time I see her. You are truly a fortunate man."

"Yes, my father is the luckiest of men."

Taylor's eyes darted to the doorway where Brent stood looking travel-weary and hungry. He nodded to each member at the table before taking his seat next to his father. David's eyes questioned him, and Brent answered with a slight shake of his head.

"You remember Jeffrey Stone, don't you, Brent?" David said, ending the eloquent silence.

Brent nodded to Jeffrey. "Of course."

"Good to see you again, Brent," Jeffrey said. "Looks as though you've been doing some hard riding."

"I've just returned from Atlanta, but it's good to get back." Brent turned his attention to his food, eating with relish. The others followed his example, and for a time, silence settled over them.

His hunger assuaged, Brent looked around at the others. "Quite a bit of activity in Atlanta these days. Many folks are traveling to Montgomery for Jeff Davis's swearing in."

"My father wanted to go," Jeffrey said, pushing back his chair from the table, "but he felt he couldn't get away right at this time. Too bad. He would have enjoyed it. How about you, Brent? What do you think of the latest turn of events?"

141

"Brent, what was your business in Atlanta?" Taylor interrupted sharply, trying to avoid any disagreeable arguments from starting. She saw that he understood her tactics as he looked at her.

"Nothing important. I did try to look up an acquaintance of Father's and mine but couldn't find a trace of him. He seems to have vanished into thin air."

Again, Taylor felt as if the unsaid was saying more than his words and felt the doubts of the last few days returning. "Anyone I know?" she asked.

David cleared his throat, shaking his head. "No, my dear. No one you should know." Turning to the men, he asked. "Shall we go to my study for a glass of brandy and a smoke?"

Taylor was led to the parlor and left there with David's brief peck on the cheek. Picking up her embroidery, she frowned as her hand hovered over the fabric, wondering just what was going on.

Taylor and Brent stood on the porch watching Jeffrey ride away. David had already excused himself, stating he had work to get done in his study. It was the first time Taylor had been alone with him since his return, and she found she was very uncomfortable. How was she to act with him? She wasn't even sure if she liked him at all. Besides, David loved her. He was good and kind, and he needed her. Brent didn't need her. He had left her without a word. Their kisses had meant nothing. Nothing at all.

"Your ankle is much better, I see," Brent said, his eyes still following Jeffrey.

She sat down in a rocker. "Much better. I think I'll be able to give up this silly cane in another few days."

"I'm leaving again later today," Brent said, leaning against the railing. "Back to Atlanta."

"Oh?" She tried to answer nonchalantly but found her voice sounded strained in her own ears. "Will you return soon?"

"I don't know," he said softly. "Taylor?"

She looked into his eyes. The span of the porch separated them, yet she felt the closeness of his body intensely.

"Promise me you'll take care of yourself while I'm gone."

"Take care of myself? What do. . ."

"Promise, Taylor."

"Yes. Of course. I promise. But, Brent. . ."

He stood abruptly. "I have to speak to Father before I go," he said and was gone.

She sat in a bemused silence. What on earth was he talking about? You would think she always went about falling from buggies and spraining her ankle or something. She shrugged her shoulders. Everything seemed so out of kilter lately, she really shouldn't be surprised by Brent's request.

It wasn't really so odd, and at least it showed he did care for her, if only just a little.

She sighed. Perhaps a ride would do her some good. The weather was so nice and her foot *was* much better.

"I'll get Jenny to go along," she said to herself. "I'll take a nice, long ride."

She hurried inside, finally finding Jenny in the kitchen with Mima. Sending Jenny for the horses, Taylor headed for her room to change her clothes. Brent's voice broke into her thoughts as it darted around the nearly closed library door.

"You must have someone watch her at all times. I don't think we can presume her safe until he's found."

Taylor stopped still, unable to pull herself away. They were talking about her!

"Brent, you don't think he's come back here, do you?"

"No, I don't. If I did, I wouldn't leave. I'm sure he's still around Atlanta. I've just got to keep looking."

"I wish I were stronger. I feel so useless. You know how much she means to me, Brent."

"Yes, Father, I know. And she loves you too."

A long silence followed. Taylor held her breath, afraid to move for fear of discovery. She didn't want them to find her eavesdropping.

"I'll get my things and leave now. I'll send word if I learn anything."

"Son," David said urgently. "Be careful. And . . . thank you."

The scraping chair sent Taylor scurrying to her room. She pulled off her dress and reached for her riding clothes. From her window, she could see Brent's horse being led toward the house. Holding her dress against her chemise-clad breast, she moved to the window and looked down. Brent was just swinging into the saddle. As if he felt her eyes upon him, he looked up at her. Hesitantly, she lifted a hand in farewell. He stared at her briefly but didn't acknowledge that he had seen her salute. Then he turned and rode off.

Taylor leaned against the glass. She was afraid. Brent was gone again. She was deserted, alone, an unknown enemy lurking in the shadows, and Brent had left her behind again.

"Stop it, you silly goose!" she scolded suddenly.

"You need some help, Miss Taylor?" Jenny asked as she entered, not knowing the confused state of her mistress. "Josh, he's gettin' the horses ready."

Taylor threw down the dress she was clutching and plopped down in front of her dressing table. "I've changed my mind, Jenny. We're not going after all. Go tell Josh."

"Yes'm." With a lifetime of experience behind her, Jenny's face didn't betray her wonder at Taylor's sudden change of plans or strange humor. She simply turned and left, closing the door quietly behind her.

Taylor was staring at her reflection. She had to find out what was going on. Why would anyone want to harm her? She must be letting her imagination run wild. After all, she never heard her name mentioned. She had just assumed it was her they were talking about. The best thing she could do was ask David. Confess that she had overheard them talking and ask what it was all about. Yes, that was what she would do.

She dressed again quickly and limped down the

145

stairs. "David," she called, looking into the library.

"In my study," came his reply.

David was sitting in his high-backed chair staring off into space. The room had a very masculine odor, like that of cigars, brandy, and wood. A massive desk occupied a large portion of the room. David had turned his chair toward the morning sun coming through the east window. Taylor knelt down on the highly polished wood floor and leaned against the dark leather-covered arm of his chair. David reached out absentmindedly and rested his hand on her head. They remained so for several moments before Taylor spoke.

"David, what's going on? I really must know."

He sighed, removing his hand from her head and drawing it across his eyes as if to erase what troubled him. Taylor waited, watching him struggle with his decision. His gray eyes were weary, red-rimmed, evidence of a sleepless night.

She gently traced a deep line on his forehead with her fingertip. "Please tell me, David. I know it's about me," she said, hoping he would deny it. "You're worried and it's tiring you terribly. Please tell me." She leaned closer to him. "I have a right to know."

"Yes. You do have a right to know." His eyes had returned to the sun-bathed lawn beyond the window. "There was evidence that someone was trying to hurt you. The buggy *accident* was no accident."

"Not an accident?"

"It had been tampered with."

"But who? Why?" Taylor puzzled.

David pushed himself out of the chair, moving closer to the window and away from her. Again he rubbed his eyes and then massaged his temples before turning to face her. With the light behind him, Taylor couldn't see his face very well but sensed his searching gaze.

"Matt Jackson," he said at last.

The name assaulted her with his image—the bushy eyebrows over squinty eyes, the pinched, thin mouth under his mustache, the dirty hair. She remembered his red face and bulging veins as he told her he would never forget what she had done.

"Jackson," she repeated the name in a whisper. "He wouldn't. Surely he wouldn't attempt such a thing." She stood up, reaching out to David in a gesture of unbelief. "He left the area, didn't he? He wouldn't come back for this."

"He was seen by some of the slaves at Spring Haven the day of the wedding," David answered.

Taylor was incredulous. "And you . . . you and Brent think he'll try something again?"

He nodded.

She sat in his vacated chair, trying to put her thoughts in order. No reasonable person would try to hurt her because she slapped him or even because she sent him from his job. But Matt Jackson, was he a reasonable man? She recalled Jenny's battered face and body. No, this was not a

147

reasonable man they were discussing. He was a madman, an attempted murderer.

She lifted her face as David approached her. He placed a hand on her shoulder, trying to reassure her by his touch. "It's best," he said, "if you stay close to the house until Brent returns."

Yes, she thought. *Until Brent returns. It will be all right when Brent returns.*

Chapter 12

The weeks of waiting put a strain on both Taylor and David. No word came, and each envisioned terrible reasons why not. Jeffrey came out often, and finally, Taylor realized he was there as her guard, her protector. She was unsure whether this made her feel better or worse. Jeffrey tried hard to amuse her, to take her mind off Matt Jackson and his threat, but to no avail.

It was an early April afternoon when her hopes were answered. She and Jeffrey were sitting together on the lawn. David had gone down to the barn to watch the grooming of a young stallion he had recently acquired. Taylor was only half listening to Jeffrey's idle chatter as she gazed pensively down the drive. At first her mind didn't register on the lone rider cantering toward them. As he came into focus, she straightened in her

149

chair. Jeffrey quit talking as she stood up, aware of her sudden anticipation, and his eyes swung around to find the cause.

Yes, it was him. He was home! Taylor began to run toward the rider, waving her arms above her head. "Brent! Brent!" she cried.

Jeffrey followed her. He watched as Brent vaulted from his horse and gathered Taylor in his arms. For a moment, Brent held her tightly against his chest, his face smothered in her hair, his eyes closed as he savored her closeness.

Jeffrey stopped short. Like a blind man given his sight, he saw clearly the love between them, perhaps before they knew it themselves. A dull pain spread through his chest. Now she was truly lost to him. It was no longer an old man who stood between them but her knight in armor. How could he, the red-headed county clown, compete against him? Even worse was knowing he couldn't even dislike Brent or David.

Brent pressed her tightly to him, breathing in the freshness of her hair, inhaling the very essence of her. How he had missed her! Yet even while missing her, he had learned he took her with him everywhere. Not for one moment in these past weeks had he not caught a glimpse of blue-black hair or sparkling blue eyes, not heard her lilting laughter or her angry retorts.

He opened his eyes and saw Jeffrey watching them, understanding written on his face. He slowly released his hold. Taylor looked up, her eyes revealing all the depths of her feelings,

feelings she had only just begun to realize she had for him. It was no longer a secret to her—or to him.

"Hello, Jeffrey," Brent said calmly.

Taylor twirled around. She had forgotten he was even there.

"Hello, Brent," Jeffrey answered in the same tone as he came forward to shake Brent's hand. Their eyes met in a level, speaking gaze.

"Any news?" Jeffrey asked.

Taylor spun back around, waiting anxiously for Brent's reply. Brent saw that she knew why he had been away and nodded. "He's in jail."

Taylor gasped, a combination of surprise and relief. "What happened?" she asked.

"He got in a brawl. Had nothing to do with me, but he'll be in custody for quite a while. I don't think you'll have to worry about Mr. Jackson again, Taylor."

"Come, both of you," Taylor said, collecting her wits about her. "Brent, you must be tired and thirsty, and David needs to be told of your return." She took both men by an arm and hurried them toward the house. David met them in the entrance hall. He had been told already of Brent's arrival and had come immediately from the barn.

There was much congratulating and backslapping as Brent presented the details of his trip. Jackson had been aware of Brent's relentless pursuit once he had found his trail and had led Brent a merry chase. He caught up with him in

151

Savannah. He was too late though. It seemed Jackson had tied on a good drunk and got in a fight. The other party was pretty well beaten up by the small but quick Mr. Jackson. Unfortunately for him, the man he fought with was a good friend of the mayor, and the judge had thrown the book at him.

"They won't let him out till after a new mayor is elected from the looks of it. Any and every possible charge was brought against him."

"I hope he never gets out," Taylor said with a shudder. "That wicked little weasel should be kept shut away from decent folks until he dies."

The men toasted Brent's success, even though he stated he had had little to do with the outcome.

"Well," Jeffrey said, putting his empty glass on a nearby table. "I'd best go home. I'm sure your family would like to be alone for a while."

Moving swiftly, Taylor slipped her hand through his arm and walked with him outside. "I wanted to thank you, Jeffrey, for all the time you've spent with me. It was very generous for you to keep me company during this ordeal."

"There won't be any reason for me to come out so often now, Taylor. I'm going to miss you."

"Oh, Jeffrey. You're such a good friend. I'll miss seeing you too."

He smiled wryly and swung up into the saddle. His green eyes seemed sad as he looked down, speaking softly so only she could hear. "Be careful, Taylor. You may be in more danger from yourself than you ever were from Matt Jackson."

"Jeffrey. . ."

"So long, Taylor."

She watched his ramrod straight back until he disappeared from view. It was true. She was going to miss him. What had he said about her being in more danger from herself? Yes, he was probably right, she thought as she returned to David and Brent. They stood side by side on the porch where they had been observing the farewell. She felt torn in two as she looked at them. How was she to handle it—loving father and son and wanting them both in different ways?

It felt good not to be afraid to leave the house alone. She had slipped away from David and Brent about an hour before. She needed time to think about her feelings, to think about herself and David and Brent. She breathed in the fresh air, savoring it as if she had been locked indoors for years. The scent of the jasmine filled the air like a faint smile of spring. Nature was yielding to the magic breath of the season, bursting forth with new life everywhere.

Taylor strolled idly through the pasture where the mares and young colts were grazing. Several new colts had been dropped in the last few days, and Taylor chattered soothingly to the nervous new mothers, patting some on the shoulders or stroking their soft muzzles as she stopped to admire each new addition. She felt comforted by the serenity of the pastoral scene. The gentle motion of tails swishing at flies, the noisy sucking of a hungry foal, and the tender prodding of a mother as her wobbly colt tried to make its too long legs behave gave her a feeling of security, as if there really was a plan to life, a reason for being.

She knelt down and stroked the downy coat of a sleeping foal. It started at her touch but relaxed as she murmured in a soft monotone. Her problems no longer seemed so overwhelming, surrounded as she was by such peace and contentment.

As she resumed her walk, a large black crow berated her from atop a tall pine tree. She shaded her eyes as she looked up at him. "You're right, of course, Mr. Crow. It's a wonderful, beautiful day," she called to him and laughed as he ruffled his feathers indignantly in reply.

She slipped easily under the rail fence. The road running alongside the pasture was deeply rutted by the winter rains, and she had to pick her way carefully as she followed it.

"Afta'noon, Missy, a voice called out to her.

She waved to the field hands as they plowed up the small corn field which would help to feed the families at Dorcet Hall later in the year. Soon, she turned off the road and cut through the dense trees to the river. Once there, she sat beneath a tree, leaning against the bark, enjoying the feeling on her back. She hugged her legs tightly to her breast, resting her chin on her knees. Now, she really must think about. . .

She stirred. Surprised to find she had been sleeping, Taylor straightened her back and stretched. She began to get up and then felt someone watching her. She turned to see Brent sitting on the ground against another tree. He smiled as she looked at him.

"Good afternoon," he said.

"What are you doing here?"

Shadows moved across his face, a breeze waving the tree branches above his head. "I figured you had gone off to sort things out. Thought, perhaps, we should do some sorting together."

A squirrel, his bushy tail darting nervously from side to side, moved cautiously between them. As Brent started to rise, he scampered off in fright.

"We have a problem, you know," Brent said, looking up at the puffy white clouds meandering overhead.

"Yes, we do," Taylor answered with surprising claim.

Brent offered her a hand and pulled her to her feet. "For a moment, standing here with you, I could almost believe we could be together always." His hand cupped her chin as he spoke. "Ah, Taylor. For once in my life, I don't know what I should do. . . No, that's a lie. I do know what I should do. I should get as far away from here as I can before we . . . before I do something I'll regret as long as I live."

Leave? He might leave. She felt her heart breaking.

He ran his fingers over her hair, stroking it lovingly. "Makes one wonder, doesn't it, Taylor," he said philosophically. "I came here a year and a half ago, hating the South for changing my father, or so I thought. I was determined to dislike my stepmother. Then I lost my heart to a Southern belle I discovered daydreaming in a meadow. It was already too late for me when I learned she was married to my father."

In a like manner, she replied, "And I, who didn't know how love could really feel, was determined to scorn my Yankee stepson. But I was as lost as if I'd stepped into quicksand."

"You do love me, Taylor?"

"Oh, yes," she sighed, leaning her hands against his muscular chest as she bit back her tears, already knowing what was next. "You must go away. You must go away soon," she whispered.

"Yes, I'll leave within the month. We can't take any more chances. We both care for him too much." He pulled her to him. "We won't be alone again," he whispered into her hair.

She nodded. Her throat felt swollen, and it was difficult to speak. "You know I . . . I wouldn't hurt your father for . . . for anything. He's been so good to me. So . . . so gentle and so kind. I was such a child. . ."

Brent tipped her head up with his finger. His face swam through her tears as he bent to kiss her. It was different from the other time. It was gentle, almost fearful. She choked on a sob as his lips left hers.

"No matter where I go or what I do, Taylor, I will always love you."

She kept her eyes closed tightly as he released her. She felt him moving away. Dying would be easier, she thought, than this pain tearing at her insides.

"Goodbye, my love," she whispered after him. "Goodbye."

Chapter 13

"Yeeeeeehaaaaa!"

Taylor's breath caught in her throat as the terrifying screech filled the parlor. She dropped her needlework and ran to the window just as David emerged from his study. They exchanged surprised glances and looked outside. Six riders were galloping up the avenue toward the house. They were shouting, waving their hats, and stirring up an orange dust cloud so that it was difficult at first to tell who they were. David pulled her with him out onto the porch. Jeffrey, followed by the other five, pulled to a halt in front of them.

"It's war!" Robert Stone whooped.

"Lincoln's called for a hundred and fifty thousand troops from the Northern states," someone else shouted.

Jeffrey jumped down from his saddle. Tossing the reins to his older brother, he took the steps two at a time and grabbed Taylor's hands. "It's begun, Taylor. Mr. Lattimer. They're calling up volunteers. Beauregard's taken Fort Sumter without a single loss to the Confederacy."

"We'll whup them Yankees and be back before they know what hit 'em," someone hollered. "After a week or two, we'll have peace on our terms."

The yard erupted in cheers.

David shook Jeffrey's proffered hand. "I hope it goes that easily. I do hope it does, Jeffrey."

Taylor thought he sounded despairing, as if the South could be beaten. But surely he knew that the South was in the right. They *couldn't* lose.

"Oh, it's true," Taylor said, turning a brilliant smile toward Jeffrey and the others. "We'll be done with it all by fall. You can all come here for a party in celebration. The weather's lovely in September. I'll start planning now."

Several more shouts resounded from the riders.

"Mr. Lattimer, David, I mean. I was wondering if you and Taylor might not like to join us. Philip and Marilee got in . . ."

"Marilee's back?" Taylor interrupted.

"Yes. Last night. Anyway, the Barrow County Guard is going to Atlanta in case they need to call us up. Of course, Philip is going with us—he's our lieutenant, after all—and so Marilee's joining us for a few days, and she was hoping Taylor, and you too, of course, could come along. There's bound to be a lot of people and parties and goings-on in Atlanta. It'll be great fun."

"Oh, David, could we? I'd love to see Marilee. It's been so long since she left. Please?"

David smiled tenderly at her. "I'm afraid I don't feel up to all this trip would hold in store." He looked thoughtful. "Listen, if Marilee is going, there's no reason you can't go without me."

"Are you sure?" she asked, torn between wanting to go to Atlanta—to go any place away from here—and not wanting to hurt David by going without him.

"Yes," he answered firmly. "I want you to go. It will do you good."

Jeffrey waved his hat toward the others. "You fellows ride on to Bellman's. Mrs. Lattimer and I will be along as quick as she can get her things together."

Taylor clutched Jeffrey's arm. "I'll only be a minute."

She turned and ran quickly into the house. Holding up her skirts, she flew up the stairs to her room, calling, "Jenny! Jenny, come quick. We're going to Atlanta."

She rifled through her closet. There would be dances and parties. She would need something really nice, even if she only stayed a day or two. Jenny helped her select several gowns, then packed them in the portmanteau along with nightgowns and undergarments.

"Go get whatever you think you'll need, Jenny. I'm going to ride over to Spring Haven on Tasha with Mr. Stone. You can follow with my things in the carriage. Oh, Jenny, isn't it exciting?"

Taylor was too caught up in her own excitment to notice Jenny's sullen, "Yes'm."

Jenny watched her mistress from behind shrouded eyes, anger boiling up inside her. Sometimes she would like to grab those lily white shoulders and shake her till her teeth rattled. She really was fond of Taylor, but she hated being owned and ordered about unthinkingly. Couldn't Taylor understand that she didn't feel this war was a party? The North had to win. They just had to!

Taylor chattered on, but Jenny had learned to close her ears when she chose to. It wasn't that Taylor was mean or cruel. She just went through life not thinking about it, accepting things as they were or excusing them away. Really, Taylor was no worse than even the slaves themselves. They too accepted the yoke as theirs without question. Not her. Not Jenny. She wanted only two things— Caesar and freedom, preferably at the same time.

Dressed in a teal-blue riding habit and wearing a matching bonnet set at a saucy angle, Taylor almost skipped down the stairs. The men, no doubt, would have ordered only the carriage. She would have to let them know she wanted to ride over on Tasha so she could get there faster. She turned down the hall toward the back door and plowed directly into Brent.

"Whoa," he cried out, grasping her shoulders to

steady her.

"Oh!" she gasped, shrinking back from him. They had avoided each other so carefully this past week, she was suddenly unsure how even to talk to him. "Have you heard?"

"Yes, I heard." Brent's eyes held the same dread she had seen in his father's.

"I'm going to Atlanta with Philip and Marilee."

"I'm leaving too."

"Today?" she whispered.

"I was leaving soon anyway, Taylor. This just hurried the departure a little."

"Don't go," she suddenly pleaded. "Not North. You love the South. You told me so. Stay. Fight with us."

He shook his head miserably. "I can't, Taylor. I can't fight for the South when I feel she's wrong. Not even for you."

She felt angry, which was better than the empty, hollowness that had been her primary emotion lately. She stamped her foot in vexation. "Oh, you . . . you stubborn . . . Always the same thing with you!"

Brent's answering smile was a sad one. "Taylor, will you never see?" he asked softly.

Her blue eyes darkened, and she tossed her head. "All right, go on, Yankee. You'll be begging for our mercy soon enough. Get out. Get out of here and get out of Georgia. I hope I never see you again. I was certainly mistaken about you!"

She turned in a huff, but he caught her shoulders. She glared straight ahead as he spoke

161

to her back. "I pray you'll never see what war can do, Taylor. Please be careful." He seemed to choke for a moment. "Take . . . take care of Father for me." His hands released her, but she didn't move. "If ever you need me, I'll come if I can . . . I love you, Taylor Bellman Lattimer."

The whispered words seared through her. She ran out the door, not looking back. She was better off without him, the blasted Yankee! How could she think she loved him? Good riddance to him. She flicked away a fallen tear, swearing it would be the last she would ever shed because of him, and ignoring the dull ache and returned emptiness which gnawed at her heart.

She found Tasha saddled and waiting for her. Jenny was already seated beside Josh atop the carriage. Jenny must have told them she wanted Tasha. She could always count on Jenny. A groom helped her into the saddle, and she rode out to where Jeffrey and David were waiting. Jeffrey mounted up when he saw her approaching.

She stopped beside David, and he placed a hand on her leg as he looked up at her. "If you'll be staying more than four or five days, send word. And be careful. People will be pouring into Atlanta like bees to honey and some will act pretty crazy."

"Are you sure you won't come?"

"No, this isn't for someone my age and in my state of health. It's for you young folk. You go on now and have a good time."

He watched them ride off, catching the sounds

of their mingled laughter. "This may be the last good time many of you ever have again," he said sadly as they disappeared from view.

It was about eleven o'clock when Taylor and Jeffrey cantered up to the front lawn of Spring Haven. At least fifteen men, all in their twenties, were milling about on the veranda. Marilee came rushing out of the house to meet her before she could dismount. They fell laughing into each other's arms. Taylor stepped back to look at Marilee. She had lost the roundness that Taylor had always known her to have. Her brown eyes twinkled happily, and her cheeks were lightly brushed with color.

"You look absolutely marvelous!" Taylor exclaimed.

Marilee blushed. "I feel marvelous."

"Taylor?"

She turned toward Philip's voice. She was immediately impressed with a change in him but was unsure exactly what it was. The scowl which had lived on his forehead for many years was erased. He seemed more relaxed, even pleasant. He had grown a mustache while they were gone, and Taylor decided she liked it on him. She had been wrong. This *was* a good match. They were both happy.

"You look well, Taylor," Philip said, hugging her.

"And so do you!"

"Taylor, I . . . Thank you," he said seriously.

"I'm sorry . . ."

She covered his lips with her hand. "Hush. Don't say any more, Philip." She hooked his arm. "Come on, you two," she said, taking Marilee with her other hand, "tell me about Charleston."

They climbed the steps together. Several of the young men joined them as they entered the house.

"We thought we'd serve a light luncheon to everyone before leaving for Atlanta," Marilee told her. "If we don't run into any problems along the way, we should get there by supper time. While it's still daylight, we hope."

"Tell me about your honeymoon," Taylor requested again as they sat down at the long dining room table. "It's obvious the two of you had a wonderful time."

Philip reached over and lovingly squeezed Marilee's neck. "Yes, we did. We saw some old family friends and made some new ones. Mostly, we kept to ourselves."

The blush returned to Marilee's cheeks. "Taylor, you should see all the activity in Charleston," she said, changing the subject. "They started preparing for war months ago. They have their own militia. We went out to see them drilling in their dress uniforms. My, how handsome they were." She addressed the men at the table. "Of course, we all know that Georgia is destined to be the true heart of the Confederacy. Our men cannot be outdone by anyone, even other Southerners."

They laughed and cheered in response.

"And what about you, Taylor?" Marilee asked.

"Oh, it was rather dull around here," she replied innocently. "Someone did try to kill me, and Brent Lattimer, you remember David's son, chased him all over Georgia before he was put in jail in Savannah, but other than that, nothing's happened." She took a bite of an apple and then laughed at Philip's and Marilee's gaping looks.

Jeffrey joined in her laughter, helping her answer their questions which began pelting them as soon as the Bellmans had recovered from their initial shock.

"Jeffrey was my dearest friend through it all," Taylor concluded. "I couldn't have stood it without him."

Jeffrey experienced the unwelcome warming of his neck and face and became deeply engrossed in his meal.

The entourage of young men on high-strung, blooded horses, fashionable young women in comfortable carriages, and colored servants to care for their every need grew in size as they neared Atlanta. Taylor wondered if there would be any place left to stay by the time they got there. Everyone in Georgia must have been heading for Atlanta, Taylor thought. They were lucky, however. They obtained rooms on the fourth floor of the Trout House on the corner of Pryor and Decatur streets. An atmosphere of carnival filled the air of the city. Taylor had never seen anything like it before. Atlanta, a combination of proper society and tough frontier town, was bursting at the seams.

Gas lamps cast their eerie lights on the streets full of people as Taylor peered out the window of her room. She was tired and felt gritty from the journey. She was suddenly homesick for the peace and quiet of Dorcet Hall and wondered if Brent was already gone. "Silly goose," she whispered to her reflection in the window glass.

She was waiting for Philip and Marilee along with Jeffrey. They had all been invited to have dinner with George Mason and his family. Mr. Mason had been a colleague of Martin Bellman. They had met him unexpectedly as they entered the bustling city.

"Well, I'd best get changed," Taylor said aloud.

She washed the dust off the best she could with water from a porcelain pitcher on the dresser. She dressed in a burgundy cotton gown with a large hooped skirt.

Jenny had just finished brushing her hair when Marilee knocked and entered. "Ready, sister?" she asked, then giggled. "Oh, it's wonderful to have you for a *real* sister."

"My thoughts exactly."

They joined their escorts and went down to the waiting carriage. The horse picked his way carefully through the dusty streets. Revelers, many of them drunk, were singing songs, whooping and hollering, as they celebrated the defeat of the Yankees, somewhat prematurely.

"Atlanta will never be the same after this," Philip stated, looking out the carriage window as they moved through the streets.

Lights blazed in every window of the Mason home, a simple yet handsome structure located on Peachtree Street. Dogwood, peach blossom, wisteria, and Cherokee roses surrounded the house, and the lawn had a white fence separating it from the street. The house, like the town, was overflowing with people. They obviously had not been invited to just a simple dinner party.

Taylor was surrounded by handsome men, some already in uniform, flirting with her and paying her outrageous compliments. All were bragging about how many Yankees they would single-handedly slay before returning home. They knew she was a married woman, but she was beautiful and they flocked to her side regardless.

Jeffrey never left her, however, and finally it appeared he had had enough of the crowd around them. He took her arm and firmly led her away from the others and outside. They walked slowly through the elegant gardens behind the house.

"Thank you, Jeffrey. I was beginning to think I would suffocate under so much attention."

"It's only natural. You are the prettiest woman in Atlanta."

"Really, Jeffrey. Don't you go being as silly as all the others now. I've had enough empty compliments to last me till I'm an old, old woman," Taylor cried in exasperation. "Look at how clear the sky is. You could almost touch the stars tonight," she said, changing the subject.

They moved leisurely amid the rose bushes and

under the weeping willows. It was hard to imagine that their country was now at war, that men could already be dying somewhere while they were enveloped by the peacefulness of these gardens.

"I didn't see Brent this morning. Has he left Dorcet Hall again?"

"He has by now," Taylor sniffed, her good mood dispersing.

Jeffrey stopped walking. "You sound angry. Anything wrong?"

"I am angry. He's gone to fight for the North," she spat out in disgust. "Hopefully, we'll never see that Yankee again."

Jeffrey leaned closer, examining her face. "Are you trying to convince me or yourself?"

"What do you mean? I don't have to convince anyone," she protested. "It's the truth."

"All right. All right. I believe you. It's just, you . . ."

"I what?"

"Nothing, Taylor. Let's go back inside."

They were nearly to the house when Jeffrey spoke again. "Taylor, I love you very much. Will you remember that? Remember it always," he said seriously.

"Oh, Jeffrey. You and Marilee are my dearest friends. I love you, too."

She missed the unhappiness in his eyes as he smiled and nodded. "All right, Taylor. All right."

She was glad to leave the party and return to the hotel. Taylor lay on her bed, staring at the ceiling. She hadn't had nearly as much fun as she had thought she would. Something kept nagging at the back of her mind. She should have been blossoming under all that flattery, even if it were all nonsense. What was wrong with her tonight?

As she closed her eyes, it seemed David and Brent both stood before her. She could see their sad eyes clearly. Their words echoed again and again in her ears.

I hope it goes that easily... I pray you never see what war can do... hope it goes that easily... never see what war can do... what war can do... what war can do...

She bolted upright, holding her hands over her ears as she stifled a scream. Her vision disappeared, a red sea washing over her tormenters as they faded away.

What war can do, Taylor, what war can do...

"No," she moaned. "No!"

I love you, Taylor.

Chapter 14

Taylor dabbed at her forehead and throat with the already damp handkerchief. This awful heat. Would it never stop? Her linen dress clung uncomfortably to her skin, and tiny drops of perspiration trickled between her breasts. She felt angry. Angry at the world and everyone in it. Stupid war!

". . . and when Dr. Reed told me about it, I thought I would faint right there on the spot. I did. I swear I did."

Taylor thought her nerves would explode any second. Did that woman never shut up? She looked up from her task and met Marilee's twinkling eyes from across the porch. How did she keep her good humor listening to that woman carry on? Every Tuesday and Thursday, she and Marilee met with the other women from the

170

Bellville Ladies Aide Society to do their part for the war effort. Today, they were wrapping bandages to be sent to the front. Sometimes they were involved in the preparation of cartridges for both muskets and cannon. At other times, they cut out and sewed flannel shirts or knitted warm items such as hats and socks. The other women had arrived at Dorcet Hall early this morning, and Taylor was wondering if they would ever go home.

"Excuse me. I think I'll see to some more lemonade."

She jumped up from her chair and almost bolted into the house. She stopped and leaned against the banister, closing her eyes. She took slow, deep breaths, trying to calm her ragged nerves. How she hated these sessions!

"Taylor?" Marilee's soft voice said beside her.

She opened her eyes. "Oh, Marilee, I don't think I can stand much more. This heat. This war. David working himself to death. Mrs. Reed telling us every gory detail that Dr. Reed passes on to her. If I hear of one more amputation, I'll scream. I swear I will."

"I know. I feel the same way. You just have to learn to ignore her. Think about something more pleasant."

"But, Marilee, there isn't anything pleasant anymore. It just drags on and on. They thought they'd have them whipped in six months. It's been over a year, and we're no nearer winning now than before. What's all the killing for?"

171

Marilee put her arm around Taylor's shoulders. "Come on. We'll get that lemonade you were talking about." They moved slowly toward the kitchen. "Taylor, the South has had some brilliant victories. Sure, we've had some losses, too, but we'll have more victories soon. I know we will."

Calming down a little now, Taylor replied, "I'm sorry, Marilee. I don't usually lose control like this."

"I know you don't, dear."

They had reached the kitchen. Mima was sitting in the shade of the brick building, dozing, her head dropping forward onto her ample bosom.

"Mima," Taylor whispered in her ear.

The large black woman jerked awake. She blinked her sleepy eyes at the two women beside her. "Oh! Missy Taylor. I's sho' nuf sorry."

"It's all right, Mima. Would you see to some more lemonade for our guests?" Taylor couldn't suppress a grin at the flustered servant.

"Right now, Missy." Mima scurried inside.

"There," Marilee said with satisfaction. "You feel better already. We'd best get back to the others."

Taylor nodded, resigned. It wasn't that she minded doing her part, she told herself. She just wondered if it really did anyone any good. More and more men died everyday. At least, she thought, no one close to her had been seriously wounded or killed. She had that to be thankful for.

Probably her biggest worry at the moment was David. He was working far too hard. He was overseeing both Dorcet Hall and Spring Haven. He had planted no cotton this year, only corn and wheat. He fretted over the crops continuously and spent a great deal of time in the fields. His face had turned gray from the stress, and Taylor feared he was putting an awful strain on his already weakened heart. He refused to slow down, though, and he also refused to see a doctor. He said doctors were too busy these days with men who really needed them. Besides, Dr. Reed was in the army and so was not available. He didn't want to see the new doctor, Dr. Marsh, even if he was as good as everyone claimed.

It wasn't just the work causing him all the worry, either. He had received no word from Brent since he left Dorcet Hall. Mail between the Union and the Confederacy had been severed more than a year before. Taylor knew he wondered often if Brent was even alive, especially after the Confederate rout of the Union army at Manassas. She refused to think about it herself.

Taylor took up her work again. Lizabeth Reed, Dr. Reed's spinster daughter, had taken up her mother's chatter, and Taylor tried, unsuccessfully, to shut out the high-pitched voice.

"I, for one," she was saying, "think it must get better this fall. We've given those Yankee scoundrels too much ground already. Just think. We've lost New Orleans to them, and now they hold Fort Pulaski on our *own* coast. I shudder to think of it. And that awful Captain Andrews. To think of him being as close to us as Marietta. Dirty spy."

"George Richards lost a leg. He's in Atlanta now. Poor boy. He and Rosetta were to be married this summer."

"Poor Rosetta, you mean."

"I heard George Allen died from dysentery. Dr. Reed says the disease runs rampant once anyone gets it."

"Have you seen the prices they're asking for foodstuffs? It's positively outrageous, I tell you."

"There won't be a man left alive anywhere if it doesn't stop soon. They killed and wounded over 15,000 of our men at Shiloh, and the Yankees lost about the same."

"Who's going to be left to marry?"

"Henry says we need a decent commander of the armies before we'll bring this way to its rightful conclusion."

"It would be different if we had a different president. Mr. Davis just doesn't know what he's doing. Of course, I'm only a woman and we're not supposed to understand these things but . . ."

"At least we have a good governor in Joseph Brown. He, at least, knows how to protect Georgia."

"Dr. Reed says . . ."

On and on they went. Taylor mopped again at her beaded brow. Wisps of hair had escaped her severe bun and stuck to the back of her neck. She sipped at the drink Mima had served, which was already warm, and began to daydream. Wouldn't it be nice to be discussing someone's recent party instead of someone losing his leg, discussing a new dress instead of the price of food, discussing someone's wedding instead of someone's dying.

"Taylor. Taylor, are you listening to me?"

Reluctantly, she pulled her thoughts back to the present, looking up at Mrs. Reed.

"Lizabeth asked you what time you will be coming next Tuesday? We'll be meeting at our house."

"Oh, I'll ride in with Marilee. The usual time."

As if on cue, the remainder of the women stood up and, with hurried goodbyes, entered their buggies and carriages and started for their homes.

"You are staying the night with us, Marilee, aren't you?" Taylor asked as the last buggy disappeared down the road.

"Yes, I'd rather planned to. I do hope tomorrow will be a little cooler."

They sat down in the parlor. Two young black girls waved fans nearby, stirring the sweltering air without cooling it. Both women were silent, each feeling exhausted by the heat and the day's labors. When David entered sometime later, they were still sitting quietly, nearly dozing as Mima had done.

"Hello, dear," he said as he brushed the top of Taylor's head with his lips. "Hello, Marilee."

"Hello, David," they replied simultaneously.

"Are you staying, Marilee?"

"Yes."

"I'll take you home in the morning then. I need to look over a few things at Spring Haven tomorrow." He poured himself a glass of the lemonade. The cool beads of moisture had long since disappeared from the sides of the pitcher and the drink was as warm as the room. "Will you join us in the morning, Taylor?"

"I don't think so, David, but thank you for asking."

"If you two ladies will excuse me, I'm going up and wash off this dust. I'll join you in a little while."

"He looks awfully tired," Marilee said when he was gone.

"Mmmm," Taylor agreed. "I'm so very concerned about him, Marilee. He is doing too much . . . and his worries depress him."

Marilee tried to encourage her with a smile. "He's a strong-willed man, Taylor. He'll come through this. Look how much his health has improved since he became ill on your trip."

"But he nearly *died* then, and he didn't have all this extra pressure on him either." Taylor twisted her handkerchief nervously.

"You do love him, don't you?" Marilee said softly. "I . . . sometimes I've wondered about you . . . about your marriage."

Taylor tilted her head slightly, her eyes and voice conveying her weariness. "I thought we had put those rumors to rest long ago, Marilee."

"Oh, my. I didn't mean to . . . I am sorry. I guess I just sometimes compare the two of you with Philip and me and . . . Well, you know what I mean," she ended weakly.

Taylor sighed. "Yes, I do know. It's a different kind of marriage, but I do love him . . . and I *am* happy."

"Of course you are. I knew that. Oh, let's change the subject."

"Yes, let's."

Silence filled the room once more, Marilee's embarrassment tangible. Suddenly she giggled. "Oh, Taylor, I can certainly mess things up, can't I? I always could. I'm glad you always forgive me."

Taylor laughed with her. "How can I help it, you silly goose. Come on. Let's see about dinner. David will be hungry after his hard day."

They ate late in the evening, trying to outwait the hot afternoon air. The fare set before them was simpler than it would have been a year before, but there was still plenty of good food to choose from. They raised nearly everything they needed in their home gardens. They also had their own cattle, goats, and sheep as well as hogs to supply their meat and milk.

A few tallow candles provided the only light during their meal. The large windows stood open to receive even the slightest stirring of air, but the candles burned unmolested by any breeze. Taylor and Marilee sat on either side of David, but conversation was limited as they each picked at their food.

David pushed his plate away, his face looking pinched as he lit his pipe. "You'll forgive me for smoking, ladies?"

"Don't give it a thought," Marilee said quickly. "I rather miss the scent at Spring Haven."

"Any word from Philip?" David asked.

Marilee nibbled on her lower lip. "Not recently. He wrote me just before the fighting at Pittsburg Landing, but I haven't heard anything since."

"If he was hurt, you'd have heard, Marilee." Taylor reached across the table and touched Marilee's clenched hand. "Try not to worry. I'm sure he's just fine."

Marilee smiled stoically. "I know. I'm sure he's just very busy. I'm sure I would feel it inside if he were hurt or . . . or anything." She slid her chair back from the table. "I think I'll go on up to bed. Goodnight, David, Taylor." She kissed them both on the cheek and went upstairs.

"I didn't know it had been so long since she'd heard from him," David said. "I wouldn't have brought it up if I'd known. I know what she's going through, not knowing, not hearing anything." There was no mistaking the raw edges of his nerves.

"You should go to bed too, David. You're so very tired."

"I believe I will. We'll want an early start tomorrow. Are you coming up?" he asked.

Taylor shook her head. "I think I'll sit on the porch for a while. It's too hot to try to sleep yet anyway."

She walked with him to the stairs, kissed him goodnight, and followed him with her eyes as he climbed each step toward his room. When his

178

door was closed, she went outside. The night air was quiet. Even the crickets were too hot to chirp, it seemed. She sat down on the steps and gazed up at the stars. It was hard to believe that somewhere to the north or to the west people had been fighting all day, killing each other with guns and cannon. What were they doing it for anyway? It was a very unpatriotic thought. Everything had been so clear at first, a year ago, two years ago. Now she wasn't so sure. Could war be right when father and son were on opposite sides, when brother killed brother, when a nation was torn in two?

"Miss Taylor, you need anything?" Jenny had walked up behind her unnoticed.

Taylor patted the step beside her. "No, I want nothing. Sit down, Jenny."

Jenny obeyed, waiting silently for her mistress to speak again.

"What would you do if the Yankees won, Jenny? Would you leave here?"

Jenny hesitated only briefly before answering in a firm voice, "Yes'm, I'd leave."

"Where would you go?" Taylor asked in surprise.

"I'd go north. I'd go to find Caesar."

"You think he made it then?"

"Yes'm. I'm sure of it. And if he can't get t'me and if I got the freedom t'find him, I'll be lookin' ever'where I can."

Taylor was thoughtful before asking her next question. "If it weren't for Caesar," she asked,

179

"would you still go?"

Jenny stared at the hands folded in her lap as if they were the most interesting things around.

"Jenny, would you?"

"Yes'm," came the whispered response.

"But why?"

"So I'd know I was free."

Taylor felt her mind struggling to understand. "But haven't we always treated you well? Probably better than you would ever be treated as a free darky in the North."

"Yes'm, you've always treated me right good. Always."

"Then why?" Taylor repeated.

"Miss Taylor, you and the masta, and Masta Martin before you, you've all treated me real fine. I've had things most my people never even dreamed about. You never laid a hard hand on me, and 'cept for one time, I ain't never seen anyone get treated unfairly by you or yours. But even when you give me so much others don't have, even freedom t'do things what I want t'do, I'm still a slave, somethin' that can be bought 'n' sold anytime you like. Somethin' that can be taken from her family and even sent down the river to some other plantation. If the Yankees win, and I never left here, I'd never know'd I'd been freed. So if they win, I'll go. Yes'm, if they win, I'll be findin' my way north."

Taylor was amazed as the words poured forth from Jenny. She couldn't help asking, "And if the South wins?"

Jenny's mouth was set in a wry line. "Then, I guess I'd stay right here with you ... and be as happy as I'm able. I wouldn't have no other choice nohow, now would I?"

Taylor turned Jenny's words around and around in her mind. She knew she should reject outright all that Jenny had said, but something nagged at her troubled spirit, something told her that there was a ring of truth to what Jenny was saying about freedom and her right to know it.

"Thank you, Jenny. Thank you for answering me so truthfully," she said at last. "You can go on to bed. I'll take care of myself."

"Yes'm." Jenny stood up and turned to go. "Missy," she said as she reached the end of the porch. "You always tried t'be kind of a friend t'me as well as bein' my mistress. I know that. Never been nobody as lucky in who was their mistress than I been. Don't you go ever thinkin' no different."

"Thank you, Jenny. Goodnight."

"Goodnight, Missy."

Chapter 15

A slight breeze was stirring the curtains at Taylor's windows when she awoke. The air was slightly cooler, but it still promised to be a hot day. Taylor had slept in a cotton shift with only a light sheet over her. It had been the wee hours of the morning before she had drifted off to sleep, both her body and mind exhausted. Now she slid her feet over the edge of the bed. Moving to the window to catch more of the breeze, she noticed a few clouds dotting the sky. Perhaps they would bring some relief.

Taylor suddenly decided to dress and ride to Spring Haven with Marilee and David. A change of scenery might settle her thoughts. She splashed her face with the tepid water in her pitcher. A swim was what she would really enjoy, she thought. She heard a door close out in the hallway. That was probably Marilee. She walked swiftly to her door and looked out in time to see David starting down the stairs.

"David," she called to him.

He stopped and looked back. "Good morning, dear." He still looked very tired, she thought, even after a night's sleep. Of course, this hot weather didn't help either.

"I'd like to go along with you today if that's agreeable with you. Will you wait for me?"

"Of course. We'd love to have your company," he replied. "I'll have your horse saddled."

"Thank you," Taylor called as she rushed to get dressed. She tried to control her abundant tresses by pinning them up in a bun, but she knew they would be breaking loose before the day was over.

Marilee and David were already eating a light breakfast when she entered the dining room. She took a piece of toast and poured herself a cup of coffee at the sideboard before joining them. Coffee had become a dear possession, and they rarely served it anymore. She savored the hot liquid as she sipped at it.

"Are we about ready?" David asked a few minutes later.

Both Marilee and Taylor replied in the affirmative, and the horses were brought around for them. Taylor's mount, a saucy gray gelding, was tied to the back of Marilee's buggy. He pawed impatiently at the ground while Taylor patted his neck and spoke gently to him. She liked Apollo but could hardly wait for Tasha's foal to be weaned so she could have the use of her favorite mare again. David helped Taylor into the buggy beside Marilee before mounting his own horse. Taylor took the reins and the three started off in the early morning warmth.

By the time they reached Spring Haven, the relentless sun was again baking the earth and everything on it. David rode immediately to the fields, leaving the two women on the piazza. Marilee brought out some knitting. It seemed Southern women were always knitting socks or sewing shirts or something similar these days. Whether they had a man in the war or not, someone would need what they set their hands to. Taylor and Marilee worked in a companionable silence for several hours, breaking only for a light repast at noon.

The sun was still high when Taylor laid the needles and a partially finished sock in her lap. She gazed across the front lawn, resting her eyes after so many hours of close work. She noticed the grass had suffered over the past year. Somehow, the meticulous manicuring of the lawn and flowers and shrubbery lost its importance when a country was at war. The large oaks bordering the avenue had not lost any of their strong beauty, however. As this thought crossed her mind, she caught sight of a man leading a weary horse up the drive. He wore a dust-covered Confederate uniform.

"Someone's coming," she told Marilee. "A soldier. Do you suppose it's anyone we know?"

Marilee looked up from her knitting and watched as the tired duo came closer to them. Suddenly she stood up. "Taylor, it's him. It's Philip!" she cried. "He's alive!"

She flew down the steps, halting abruptly when she reached the ground, struck by uncertainty, her arms held out toward him. His steps quickened. He dropped the reins, leaving the fatigued beast behind as he hurried forward. As Taylor watched from the porch, not wanting to intrude on their reunion, Philip stopped in front of Marilee, grasping her outstretched hands. The two stood quietly staring into each other's eyes. Suddenly, he pulled her to him, crushing her against his chest.

"Marilee."

Marilee was both crying and laughing now and couldn't speak.

Philip saw Taylor watching them. "Hello, Taylor."

"Welcome home, Philip."

Marilee gasped. "You're home. How long, Philip. How long will you be home?"

"I have a week," he answered, his eyes traveling over the house, caressing the building with his glance. "It's good to be home. It's so good to know there's something this damned war hasn't touched, that there's something besides dirt and death in the world." His words left a taste as bitter as bile in Taylor's mouth.

Marilee took his arm and led him past Taylor and into the house. Taylor hung back, giving them time to be alone with each other. She felt a surge of relief wash over her. She hadn't realized just how frightened she had been. Frightened for his survival. But it wasn't just her brother. It meant, if he was able to survive, so might . . . others.

"Taylor, come in here," Marilee called. "Philip has gone up to change, and I've sent word to David that he's here."

They sat down in the drawing room, waiting for their husbands to join them. David arrived first.

"Philip is here?" he asked as he stepped through the archway, his hat still in his hands.

"Yes," Marilee answered. "He wanted to wash up before he eats. Susan's fixing him something right now. David, he looks wonderful."

"Then he wasn't hurt at Shiloh?"

"No," Philip answered himself as he entered the room. "I've managed to avoid those Yankee bullets so far." The two men shook hands heartily, grabbing the other's shoulder with their free hands as they did so.

"You look good, Philip. Very good."

"A brandy, David? I could use one." Philip poured them both a generous glass from a decanter, then sat on the arm of Marilee's chair, sighing deeply. "You have no idea what it means to be home again."

"How goes the war, Philip?" David asked soberly.

A shadow crossed the lieutenant's face. "All things considered, it goes well. We didn't give the Yankees enough credit to begin with, and they do have greater numbers than we do, but we have

186

greater leaders ... or will have as soon as somebody gives them the authority. It's going to take longer to end the war than we thought, but we'll end it as the victors, rest assured."

"How much longer?" Taylor wondered aloud.

Philip shrugged. "A year, maybe two or three."

"Three years?" Marilee asked faintly.

Her husband's gentle look caressed Marilee's face. "We'll hope not, won't we?" He sighed again before smiling broadly at everyone. "Now, let's change the subject for a while. David, how are the crops? Can we feed our troops well this winter?"

"Why don't we ride out, unless you're too tired, and I'll show you. We've had a good spring wheat crop. The corn is doing well although this drought may hurt us yet ..." He continued talking as they left the room.

"He really does look all right, doesn't he?" Marilee asked, still unable to fully believe he was home. "I'm a very lucky woman, Taylor."

Taylor left before David and Philip returned. She had sensed Marilee's desire to be alone, probably to freshen up for her husband. Taylor wondered what it would be like to eagerly anticipate your husband's loving embrace, his kisses, his whispered words of devotion. Against her will, she remembered Brent's arms about her, his lips claiming hers.

She shook her head to rid her mind of the intruding memories. She had managed to erase him from her thoughts for the most part since their parting words. She refused to recognize that the *others* she cared about in this war included

Brent. David would have to do the worrying about his Yankee son. She wasn't going to do it herself.

Taylor rode slowly along the river path. She hadn't fogotten her desire this morning for a swim. The clouds that had welcomed her upon arising had since drifted away without shedding any rain, and Taylor looked forward to slipping into the cooling waters. She had discovered the small backwash, heavily shrouded by pine trees and cedars, shortly after she came to Dorcet Hall. Now she nudged Apollo to hurry him toward their destination, feeling hotter just thinking about it.

When they arrived, the gelding plunged his nose into the shallow pool and drank thirstily before she tied him to a tree limb. After a quick glance about, Taylor peeled off her moist, sticky clothing and dove in. She came to the surface with a gasp, wiping the water from her eyes. Treading the water with her feet, she pulled out her hair pins and submerged once more. She swan across to the opposite shore under water. Her hair tugged heavily at her scalp as it swirled about her. She rested on a ledge beneath the surface and looked above her. The sun no longer seemed so fierce, its rays filtering through the thick branches as the afternoon waned. She relaxed and allowed the water to draw the heat from her body.

Closing her eyes, Taylor listened to the gentle sounds of the forest and river. She could hear the soft lapping of the pool at its shores, the stronger rushing of the river not far away. She could hear a crow calling harshly and a squirrel's chattered reply. She could hear the contented chewing sounds as Apollo nibbled at the forest grasses. She felt at one with nature, safe and secure from any troubles.

She pushed away from her ledge and swam back and forth from one shore to the other. She knew it was time to leave but felt reluctant to quit this peaceful place quite yet. At last, grudgingly, she stood up, allowing the water to trickle in tiny rivelets down her smooth skin. She picked up her shift and dress and wished she had a towel to dry off with.

Suddenly, Taylor tensed. Icy fingers of fear moved up her back. She wasn't alone! She whirled around, her eyes scanning the trees and bushes. She saw nothing, but she couldn't rid herself of the feeling that someone or something was watching her. Her hands shaking, Taylor dressed with haste. She tried to still the loud pounding of her heart, telling herself how silly she was being. Again, she searched the dense foliage, listening intently for a clue to her fright. Still nothing. Taylor swung her leg over her horse's back. She kicked him into motion. A hasty glance backward revealed only lengthening shadows. Still the terrifying feeling persisted. Only when she sighted the chimneys of Dorcet Hall above the trees did she feel safe from whatever apparition stalked her. She knew she wouldn't soon forget the feeling of evil eyes surveying her naked body.

David had arrived before her and was just handing his mount over to a stable boy when Taylor rode up. His startled look reminded her in just what kind of state she must appear, sopping wet and riding astride. Her hand flew to her tangled mop of hair. She felt herself flush as David strode quickly to her.

"Taylor, what happened?" he asked as he grabbed Apollo's reins.

"Nothing. I'm fine, David." She felt thoroughly foolish now. "I just went for a swim. When I realized how long I'd been there, I came home in a bit of a rush is all." She leaned into his waiting arms and dropped from the saddle. "I'm sorry I frightened you."

"Are you certain nothing is wrong?" David persisted, still alarmed by her appearance.

"David, I'm just fine. Really. I know I look a mess." She grinned weakly. "And if you don't mind, I'm going to go up to my room and straighten up a bit before someone else sees me looking like this."

He nodded, and she ran away from him, disappearing into the house. David watched her go, a questioning frown wrinkling his brow. "Take care of the horses, Josh," he ordered absent-mindedly before following her inside.

In her room, Taylor had already pulled off the damp dress and shift. The coolness of the pond was forgotten in the heat of her room. She sprawled across her bed, pulling the sheet over her nakedness and squeezing her eyes against her thoughts. Sleep overtook her unawares, a dreamless, deep slumber, closing out all memories; good or bad.

Chapter 16

"I tell you, David, this is more than I can stand. We have to find out just who is behind it and put a stop to it."

Taylor paced angrily back and forth across the library floor, her arms folded across her chest, her mouth pinched together, and her anger boiling behind her eyes.

"Taylor, I've done everything but flog them one by one until we get a confession. Is that what you want me to do?" David asked, expressing his own futility.

Taylor sagged down into a chair, her rage ebbing. "No," she answered softly. She knew as well as David that there was little else to be done. Unable to stop herself, she began to sob, her face hidden in her hands. She felt his touch on her shoulder but didn't look up.

In the last two months, Taylor had been plagued by unexplainable occurrences—torn or stained dresses, missing items such as mirrors or combs, a feeling of being constantly watched by someone. When they had realized these were no ordinary coincidences but intentional efforts to annoy her, they had sought to find out who was responsible but had come up empty handed. Everyone professed their innocence. No one knew anything about it. Taylor could think of no reason why any of the servants would seek to hurt her, not like this.

"'Scuse me, Marse David. Mis Mar'lee jus' drove up," Mima interrupted from the hallway.

Taylor quickly dried her eyes. "I don't want Marilee to know anything about any of this, David. Not that I've been crying and especially not about Princess."

Princess was the latest unexplainable occurrence. Taylor had found the kitten several weeks ago, scrawny and hungry and obviously an orphan. Too young to be on her own yet, Taylor had made a pet of her and the two had quickly become inseparable. The kitten slept on her bed and followed her around wherever she went. But this afternoon, Taylor had been unable to find her. When she returned to her room after a thorough search of the ground, she had found Princess lying on her pillow, her little neck broken. Someone had maliciously killed her and left her to be found by Taylor.

"Hello, David. Taylor," Marilee said as Mima

brought her into the library.

Taylor returned her greeting, noting that Marilee was positively twinkling from ear to ear.

David had noticed too. "My, you do look like the cat that swallowed the canary. You must have brought us some good news. Word from Philip?"

"Not really," Marilee answered him, slowly untying her bonnet as she sat down near Taylor. She teased her audience with a smile.

Taylor couldn't stand it. "Tell us, Marilee. Quickly. I'm dying to know what you're keeping from us."

Marilee giggled merrily, sounding more like a little girl than the young woman who appeared before them. "I *do* have good news for you." She paused again.

"Marilee!"

"All right. I'll tell you . . . Philip and I are going to be parents." A stunned silence met her announcement. "Well, have you nothing to say?" she asked.

Taylor leaned forward and took her hand. "Oh, we are very happy for you. For you both. We're just so very surprised. It was certainly not what we expected."

"Indeed, we are pleased for you," David added. "Does Philip know?"

"I sent him a letter this morning. I know he's going to be thrilled." She blushed. "We certainly didn't expect his leave to be so fruitful."

"Do you think he'll be coming home again soon?" Taylor wanted to know.

Marilee shook her head. "Not likely. Remember, he only returned to the war seven weeks ago. Maybe at Christmas he'll be able to come. I don't think it will be sooner unless we see some remarkable changes in the war effort."

For a moment, Taylor felt a wave of jealousy wash over her. Why was it Marilee who was so much in love and having a baby? It should have been herself instead. It wasn't fair. It just wasn't fair. Taylor was the one who had been born to the gentry. She should have been guaranteed happiness by her right of birth. Ashamed of herself for these secret thoughts, Taylor turned an extra special smile upon her friend.

"Marilee, you must stay with us while Philip is away," she said. "We must pamper you. After all, you're to be the mother of the next generation Bellman."

"Oh, thank you, Taylor. I was so hoping you would ask me just that. Spring Haven has seemed so awfully empty lately. It just doesn't feel like home with Philip gone."

Taylor stood up, glad for something different, something happy, to think about. "We'll send someone for your things right now. You'll begin your stay with us this very moment."

Taylor felt herself being sucked down into an enormous black hole. The air was thick, and it was hard to breathe. She thrashed about wildly, trying to grasp something that would save her. It was hot, so very hot. Deeper and deeper, she felt

194

herself being plunged into the waiting abyss. Fear welled up inside. She tried to scream but no sound was heard.

A cough racked at her chest. She couldn't seem to get any air into her lungs. She was dying. She knew that when she reached the bottom of this black pit, she would die. There would be no more tomorrows, no chance of ever seeing anyone ever again, of telling them she loved them. Why didn't someone help her? Why didn't anyone care that she was dying?

Suddenly, Taylor bolted upright in her bed, the nightmare still vivid in her mind. It still seemed real as she opened her eyes. The air *was* thick in here. Then she heard the crackling noise. The thick air—it was smoke! The house was on fire. As she was watching, flames reached out of her burning closet and spread along the wall to her door. She sat frozen by fear, watching the eager fire lick at the walls and furniture. She must still be dreaming. This couldn't be real.

A scream pierced through the fire from the hallway. Marilee! Spurred into action, Taylor ran toward her door, but the growing inferno beat her back. She turned toward the window. Although certain it had been open when she fell asleep, it was shut tight. She tried to open it but found it jammed. The door leading out onto the gallery was, likewise, stuck shut. For a moment, panic threatened to overwhelm her. Over the noise of the fire she could hear voices, but they seemed very far away. Her eyes watered and her throat burned from the dense smoke filling the room, stealing her oxygen.

Reason returned to her. She couldn't just stand there and wait for the fire to reach her. She had to do something. Taylor picked up the nearest object, the chair beside her dressing table, and flung it out the window. Tiny particles of glass flew in every direction. She was still unable to escape through the hole. Jagged pieces of glass remained stubbornly clinging to the frame. Taylor glanced quickly over her shoulder. The hungry orange fingers were consuming everything they touched, and the heat from the fast approaching blaze seared her skin. There was no time to lose. Grabbing her hand mirror from the dresser, she smashed at the remaining glass. A sharp pain stung her hand as it hit a ragged edge. Hurriedly, she climbed through the window, her foot catching in the folds of her nightgown, causing her to fall awkwardly onto the gallery floor. For a moment, she stayed where she had fallen, feeling too tired to bother going any farther.

"Miss Taylor, where are you?"

Taylor lifted her head. Through the dense smoke billowing out of her window, she could see Saul standing only a few feet away, fighting to open the gallery door to her room.

"Saul! Here. Here I am!" she cried, pushing herself up from the planks of wood.

He grabbed her arm and, without a word, began dragging her along the gallery toward the stairway leading down to the lawn. Blistering tentacles of fire reached out at them, angered by the humans' attempt to escape their fury. Taylor covered her face with her free arm as Saul pushed her before him down the steps. As her feet touched the grass, Taylor paused to gain her breath. Suddenly, Saul knocked her to the ground and began to beat her with heavy blows. For a moment, she thought he was going to kill her. Then she realized her nightgown was ablaze. She screamed and began tearing at the gown to free herself from it.

"Missy! Missy, it's all right," Saul yelled at her above her own screams. "I got it out, Missy. It's out."

When she couldn't stop, he picked her up in his arms and began running toward the grove of trees where the others had gathered to watch the fire. By the time he laid her at Marilee's feet, her screams had turned to whimpers.

"Taylor, you're safe, dear," Marilee whispered as she knelt down beside her. She cradled Taylor's head in her arms and rocked her gently.

"Where's David?" Taylor asked, her panic subsiding. "I haven't seen David."

Marilee pointed mutely to a large oak. Propped up against the mighty trunk was David, his face smudged with soot, looking strange in the eerie flickering light cast by the burning house. He stared blankly as sheet after sheet of sparks fell from the brick walls. It seemed to Taylor she could see David's own spark dying out, as if the raging fire drew its strength out of him.

Taylor followed his gaze. There seemed to be little left for the fire to feed upon, yet it still persisted. The brick walls stubbornly refused to crumble, but the interior ... Several pieces of furniture dotted the lawn, all that remained of their possessions. Servants stood around the house, buckets hanging idle in their hands, the hope of saving the house entirely gone. Several of the women were sobbing.

"Miss Taylor?" It was Jenny. "Miss Taylor, you'd best let me see to that hand. Missy?"

Taylor slowly lifted her hands in front of her. She was surprised to see blood dripping from her right hand and tiny squirts of the red liquid pulsing from her wrist. Unobjectingly, she watched as Jenny wrapped the hand and wrist securely.

As the first rays of dawn began to streak the eastern horizon, the flames began to die out for want of fuel. Empty black eyes stared hauntingly back at the silent people gathered in front of the devastated shell of Dorcet Hall. One by one, the servants began to drift away to their cabins until only Jenny and Saul remained to watch over the three white folks sitting on the grass. Taylor now leaned against the same oak tree as David, her left hand firmly holding his in a reassuring grasp. Marilee sat on his other side. All three were dressed only in their sleeping attire. Taylor's had been burned and torn, hiding little of her smoke-blackened skin. Jenny had brought her a rough blanket to wrap up in. David hadn't said a word to anyone for hours. His silence and the look on his face—as devastated as the house—pulled painfully at her heart. She was afraid for him.

Marilee was the first to rise. "We can't just sit here forever. You'll just have to move into Spring Haven until you can rebuild."

Taylor's heart jumped in her breast. Spring Haven! Of course, they could go to Spring Haven to live. It wasn't so bad really. They still had a home. Yes, they could go home.

"It's gone," David said, his voice so low they almost couldn't hear him. "It's all gone."

"Oh, no, David," Taylor said to him, trying to share her renewed optimism. "We'll be happy at Spring Haven. Honest we will. You'll love my home. You can rebuild while we stay there. You'll build something even better than before."

David's eyes met and held hers. She held her breath. He had given up, his beloved gray eyes shrouded in despair. "My dear, I'm an old man. I have seen my dream disappear before my eyes. I'll not live to see this house rise again."

"David, please! Please don't talk that way. Of course you'll rebuild. You love this place."

"Taylor, it's time for me to return you to your home," he said softly. "I should never have taken you from it. Your heart has never left."

She began to cry. How could she have been so cruel, only thinking of herself, always thinking only of herself.

"Both of you stop it," Marilee said sternly. "We must get ourselves organized. We're all overwrought and saying meaningless things we shall all be sorry for later. Jenny, see to something for us to wear; Saul, get the carriage ready for us. We'll leave for Spring Haven at once."

The bedraggled troop started up the avenue, turning their backs to the smouldering black rubble in the midst of the rich summer green, the morning sun bright regardless of the sorrow the night had wrought.

Chapter 17

A rainbow of color had been showered upon the garden and each hue had its own fragrance. A sweet song was chirped from a tree branch over her head. Taylor snipped another flower with her sheers and laid it in the basket on her arm. She hummed softly as she searched for another blossom for her arrangement. Her contentment increased here in the gardens of Spring Haven. She couldn't help it. She was so glad to be home. She looked over the hedge. David could be seen sitting on the portico, staring into space. It was how he spent most of his time. If only he were better, Taylor's contentment would be complete.

Guiltily, she lowered her eyes. Although she wanted David to get over this despondency, she knew that it would mean renewed interest in Dorcet Hall. She wasn't ready for it to be rebuilt, at least not yet. They had only been here little more than a week. Taylor wanted to stay for as long as she could. Until the war was over and Philip returned. They would have to leave then. Philip would be returning to his wife and child and to rebuilding his life. There would be no room for them here then.

She cut another flower and turned toward the house. A boy was handing the mail to Marilee as she climbed the steps onto the porch. Marilee looked quickly through the envelopes, hoping for a letter from her husband. She found a letter for David and one for Taylor. Passing them out, she sat down to read one from her father. The Reverend Stone was serving as a chaplain with the Georgia 8th regiment near Richmond, Virginia.

Taylor opened her letter, sitting down on the top step to read it. It was from Jeffrey Stone, who was also near Richmond.

My dearest Taylor,

I hope I am not becoming too bold in my address, but you are truly dearest to me. I pray that a kind Providence is keeping everyone well at home. Give my regards to David.

I am right now camped about fifteen miles from our young nation's capital. We can thank God for a thorough rout of the Federal forces and the saving of Richmond. McClellan, the young Napoleon, has been beaten back. The battle lasted about a week. We fought against heavy odds and won. The Lincoln forces must have numbered nearly two hundred thousand men. In my own division alone, nearly a thousand men were killed and over four thousand were wounded. The carnage was terrible for both sides. I saw many friends, both new and old, die all around me. They are a great loss to our country, and we shall mourn them for a long time to come.

The physical difficulties, met at every step by our advancing troops, were great indeed— deep swamps and rivers, miry roads and dense woods. For now, we wait ... and wait. Only a skirmish with the enemy here and there. They are now rebuilding their forces, no doubt planning to try once again to reach Richmond. We took many prisoners during the heavy fighting, and the capital took in well over three thousand of them during the week.

The tide has turned, Taylor. The Confederacy will retreat no more. The hearts of the men have needed a victory and we were granted a great one. I shouldn't share with your tender spirit the nightmare of battle. I will only say that I am well in spite of the shells and bullets and bayonets. Sickness, an even greater danger than the Yankess I believe, has also been avoided.

As I sit writing beside the campfire light, the mosquitos are so thick they appear a solid wall. The flies are drawn to the smell of battle which hangs heavily around us, an odor of death and destruction. Fleas scramble to find a spot upon my legs which another has not already claimed as his. Unpretty things to be telling one such as you, but these are the things of war.

Enough of this, Taylor. How much more would I rather be sitting near you under one of the grand old oak trees of Dorcet Hall as we did not so very long ago—the cleanly swept lawn, the lovely gardens, the freshly sanded walks, the gentle voices of the people at work all around us. The past year seems both a minute and an eternity to my weary mind. I would remember you and Marilee, and David, too, as you were in my most pleasant memories of you.

I hope to be able to come home soon. If the righteous prevail, then we shall have finished with this unjust war before the year is gone. I would be most pleased if you would write me direct rather than through Marilee. I remain

Your ever faithful,
Jeffrey Stone

Finished, Taylor looked up from the letter. She always enjoyed receiving one from Jeffrey. He was surprisingly more eloquent on paper than in person, even if his news was of the grimness of war. Marilee was still reading her own mail, but David had finished. A subtle change had come over his countenance. Taylor saw it immediately.

"Who was your letter from, David?" she asked.

"A very dear friend, Taylor. A very dear friend." He pushed himself out of his chair. "I think I'll go up to my room and change. I could use a walk in the gardens afterwards. Will you join me then, my dear?"

Taylor nodded as he left the porch. She and Marilee looked at each other, bewildered.

"What brought that on?" Marilee wondered. "He hasn't looked like that since before the fire."

"I know. Whoever wrote him that letter, I owe them my thanks."

David held her hand tightly against him as they walked slowly along. It was good, he thought, to have the last years of a man's life spent in such pleasant company. He glanced at Taylor out of the corner of his eye. She was so good to him. She had always had a sweet nature but now this was complemented by her blossoming maturity. She was a woman, not a child. A woman ripe for love.

And so she is loved, he thought. I love her. Marilee loves her. Jeffrey . . . and Brent, they loved her too. Yes, Taylor was loved. If he died today, she would be cared for. It put his worries to rest to know that.

"This has been most pleasant, Taylor. Thank you for accompanying me."

His smile crinkled around his eyes. David would never again be as strong and vital as he had been when Taylor first met him. Too many things had happened since then. However, she was relieved to see that his health and spirits were so much improved. She still wondered who the mysterious friend was who had raised him from his doldrums but resisted the temptation to ask again. If he wanted to tell her, he would.

"We had best get ready for dinner. I smell something delicious coming from the dining room," Taylor said as they stepped inside the house.

They climbed the stairs together, and David left her at her bedroom door. The old room had been kept just as she had left it. Luckily for her, many of her old dresses had been left in the closet after she was married. Otherwise, the fire would have left her truly destitute. She freshened up quickly, choosing a pretty pink and white frock from the wardrobe. The style was quite outdated as well as a bit childish on her, but it still fit her as it had four years ago. Feeling sixteen again, she picked up the skirts and practically skipped down the stairs. She stopped outside the drawing room, smoothed her dress, and walked demurely into the room. David was waiting for her, and as soon as Marilee joined them, they walked into the dining room.

The good news from the front, David's revived spirits, and the expertly prepared food spread before them improved everyone's appetites. For the moment, the recent difficulties which had befallen them seemed far removed. They laughed and visited as Taylor had not enjoyed doing for many months. By the time David pushed back his chair and lit his pipe, Taylor was feeling overwhelmingly pleased with her life and family.

"I'm sorry to break up our evening," Marilee said, "but I'm going to retire. I'm afraid I'm much sleepier these days. Goodnight, Taylor dear. Goodnight, David."

After returning Marilee's kisses and watching her leave, David offered his arm to Taylor and they walked leisurely into the drawing room.

"Would you like me to read to you, David?" Taylor asked as they sat on the couch together.

The rhythmic tick-tock of the grandfather clock in the foyer and the soft sound of Taylor's voice as she read aloud lulled David to sleep. When she realized he was no longer listening but dozing, Taylor quietly closed the book. She slipped a pillow under his head on the arm of the sofa and tiptoed outside. The weather had been unusually mild for July. It was nice not to be so worn out from the heat. It felt as if it might even rain soon. Only a few clouds hugged the edges of the sky tonight, however, and they glowed strangely in the moonlight.

Taylor leaned against a large white column near the steps. All things considered, she was a very lucky woman, she thought. While things had not always been as she would have chosen—or as she had dreamed they would be when she was a child —happiness had not entirely deserted her. Only when she lost Brent . . .

Brent. How very long ago since she had said her angry goodbye to him. She allowed herself for the first time to examine her feelings about him, to feel and to wonder, to hurt and to love. She wondered if he was still alive. So many men had died already. No, she would be like Marilee. If he were hurt or dying, she would feel it. Taylor closed her eyes and remembered his arms around her, his lips pressed against hers. Her body quivered. She folded her arms across her chest, hugging the memory close against her. A wisp of a smile touched her full lips and she felt flushed.

"My, my. Ain't we feelin' pleased 'bout somethin'."

The whispered words sent a chilling terror through her body. She knew that voice. She twirled around, poised for flight.

"Who's there?" she hissed, trying to cover her fear.

Her eyes searched the darkness to find her visitor. At last, she could make out the shadow of a short, slight man and the glow of his burning cigar at the far end of the portico. Slowly he began to walk toward her. The dark night, though filled with stars and the waning moon, made it difficult to tell who he was, but something about him was familiar. When he was only a few feet from her, she realized he carried a gun at his side. His final step brought his face into view. Taylor sucked in her breath.

"You!"

He chuckled, his thin lips breaking into an ugly grin. "Yes'm, Miz Lattimer, it's your ol' friend, Matt Jackson. Bet ya been missin' me around the old place."

Taylor straightened her shoulders and tried to sound confident. "Mr. Jackson, I suggest you get off Spring Haven land. You were dismissed from here for gross misconduct, and you're very unwelcome here."

Matt puffed on the stub of his cigar, chewing slowly on the end. Then he took a quick step closer. Taylor could smell his unwashed body, and her lip curled involuntarily as she leaned away from him.

"Miz Lattimer, I don't 'tend t'go nowheres right now."

"Then I shall call for someone to remove you," she said bravely.

He lifted the gun, stopping it just inches from her nose. "You make one peep, and it'll be your last," he whispered.

The color drained from her face. Her legs seemed to turn to putty beneath her and she feared she would collapse in front of him. He chuckled at her fright as he reached out with his free hand and stroked her arm. She flinched, but her eyes never left his face.

"Mr. Jackson, take your hand off me ... please."

"Why, Miz Taylor, did I understand you t'say please t'the likes o' me?" Again he laughed. "Before tonight's over, I think you'll have said it many times."

Her eyes widened, a new horror spreading through her veins. "No!" she cried. "You wouldn't. You can't get away with this. There are

209

others here to stop you."

He lowered the gun, jabbing it against her midriff. He leaned against it with his body, bringing his eyes only a hairs breadth from her own. "If you care what happens t'those folks in there at all, Miz Taylor, I'd suggest you shut up. I could twist that sister-in-law of yours head 'round just as easy as a tiny kitten."

"You . . . you killed Princess?"

"And I could fix it so's the old man you married slept right through the next fire, too."

A new wave of terror followed in the wake of understanding. "No," she gasped. "You burned it? You hate me so much?"

His rough hand gripped her chin, pinching it painfully. "Oh, no. I don't hate you, Miz Taylor. Ain't no man could look upon this lovely face 'n' hate you. And there ain't no man who could watch you swimmin' naked in the river 'n' not want t'have you." He felt her tremble. "Oh, yes. That was me you could feel watchin' ya. I ain't never seen nothin' so lovely in all my life, 'n' I've made it my business t'see as many as I could, white 'n' black." His voice rasped with emotion. "I aim t'show ya what a real man can do for you. I ain't jus' some nobody you can turn up that purty li'l nose at." He released her chin and caressed her cheek.

Jackson smiled, his teeth so yellow she could see it in the dark. His hand slid down her side and stopped in the small of her back. "I think it's time we found us someplace more comfy, don't you?"

Taylor felt nauseous.

"I think your room might be just the place. Let's go."

"No. Please, no," she whimpered.

"Move it!" he snapped.

But she couldn't. She felt frozen to the spot. Think quick, she thought. Somehow she had to get free of this madman before he . . . before he . . .

"I said move," he snarled again, digging the gun into her side.

This time her legs obeyed. Shakily, she entered the house. Her eyes darted nervously about, looking for something, anything, which might help her escape.

Jackson whispered in her ear as she reached the stairs, "You try anything', I'll kill Miz Bellman and your husband while you watch. And it won't be a purty sight, neither. You 'member that, ya hear?"

The cold nose of the gun resting against her back pushed her steadily toward her room. Don't let this happen, she prayed. Please don't let this happen.

"Taylor, is that you? Could you come here a moment?" Marilee called from her room.

Taylor stopped short, holding her breath. What was she to do?

"Taylor?" Marilee came to the top of the stairs. For a moment, her eyes locked with Jackson's; then she began to scream.

Taylor saw his arm jerk out beside her, the terrible blast thundering in her ear. A flash of blue flared from the gun, and Marilee fell backwards, as if someone had struck her before she crumpled to the floor in a heap.

"Quick, git up those stairs. Your husband will be up now." He shoved her roughly, his eyes locked on the top of the stairway, watching for David.

Taylor stumbled and fell to her knees. She felt herself being pulled up by the collar of her dress. She was choking, trying to pull the fabric away from her throat, when suddenly the grip was gone. She fell forward again, gasping for air. She turned her head in time to see Jackson and David tumbling down the stairs, locked in each other's grasp. Taylor braced herself against the railing, watching the struggle between the two men. As they wrestled on the floor, she could see the strength begin to ebb from the bigger and older of the two. Her eyes fell on the gun at the foot of the stairs. She had to reach it.

Taylor inched toward the gun, her eyes on the combatants. She read the look of victory in Jackson's features. He, too, knew that the older man was failing. As Taylor's fingers wrapped around the weapon, Jackson dealt a wicked blow to David's chin, following it with another to his stomach. David sagged to the floor on his hands and knees, his face a ghostly white. He coughed and blood spattered the floor. With each breath, a gurgling sound filled the quiet room. Then David fell forward onto his face.

Matt Jackson laughed. His chest rose and fell

with his heavy breathing as he turned toward her. His eyes burned, the depths of his evil heart lighting them with an unnatural fire.

"Put the gun down, little lady. Can't ya see I've won?"

"Don't you take another step," she warned him. "I'll shoot."

Again, he laughed, his courage inflated by the fallen man behind him. He began to move in her direction. As the bullet slammed into his chest, his face held a grotesque look of disbelief before he hit the floor.

"Miss Taylor!"

Saul stood in the doorway, his eyes taking in the scene before him.

"Quick, Saul," Taylor cried, springing back into action. "See about David." Taylor raced up the stairs to Marilee. Blood was flowing from a wound in her shoulder. She was unconscious but alive.

Hearing other voices below her, she leaned over the banister, calling, "Josh, ride for the doctor. Tell him to hurry. Then get the sheriff. Susan, help me with Miss Marilee. How's Master David?"

"Not good, Missy," came Saul's response.

"Can you get him to his room? I'll join you in a moment."

Standing there, watching them hurry to obey, she thought this nightmare must surely end soon. She would wake and find that everything was all right.

They carried Marilee to her room and bound the

wound. Taylor left her in Susan's care and rushed to David's room. Saul and Mima were standing on either side of his bed and watched mutely as she knelt beside her husband, taking his hand.

His eyes were circled in a ghastly blue tinge. The opaqueness of his skin was frightening. Never had she seen anyone look like this.

"David?" she whispered. "David, please try. Don't leave me, David."

His eyes fluttered and opened. They looked at her from far away. Already he was removed from her. He spoke softly, causing her to lean her ear down to his lips in order to hear.

"Taylor, my dear. Thank you."

She waited for him to say more, but all she could hear was the terrible gurgling in his lungs. She lifted her head away from him. His eyes were closed again.

"David! David!" she cried. "Please. I need you. Don't leave me. Not now. Please," she sobbed.

His lips moved again.

"Brent," he said. "Take . . . care . . . of Brent. You and . . . he . . . take care . . ."

His spirit slipped from his body, and she was left with only his empty shell. Taylor laid her head on his chest.

"Goodbye, David. Th . . . thank you, too."

Chapter 18

Sometime in the night, the rains began, the black clouds dropping their heavy burden upon Spring Haven. Taylor stood up at last, stiff after so many hours without moving. She bent and kissed the cold cheek one last time, and then turned, walking slowly from the room. Only emptiness was left. She wished she would cry. She would know then that she could feel something, anything.

At the other end of the hall, several servants were waiting outside Marilee's bedroom. Taylor wished she could just go to her own room, curl up in her bed and forget, just forget. But she couldn't. She must take charge of things. She was the only one left to keep things running. David was gone. He was really gone. Wearily, she proceeded toward the closed door.

"Rachel," she asked the nearest woman, "how's

Miss Marilee?"

"Ah don' know, Missy. Docta Ma'sh, he come 'n' been hyar a long time now, but he ain't said nothin' t'any us folk 'bout her. Ol' Susan, she's he'pin' him. 'Lor 'I's awful fearful fo' da Missy, ma'am."

Taylor knocked softly and opened the door. Dr. Marsh was bending over Marilee, his face harsh in the light of the burning pine knots. He stopped her with a finger to his lips and came to meet her near the door.

"Doctor?"

"It's not good, Mrs. Lattimer. I'm afraid she's going to miscarry. There is nothing more I can do. Her shoulder should heal nicely, barring any infection, but . . . I'm sorry about the baby." He shook his head sadly. "I'm sorry about your husband, too," he added. "I . . . I wish I'd had the chance to know him better since I came here."

"Thank you, Dr. Marsh. May I speak to Marilee?"

"You'd best let her rest. It's been a difficult time for her. She needs whatever sleep she can get."

Taylor left the room, her shoulders sagging under the weight of her sorrows. She passed through the group outside the door, not answering the questioning looks written on each black face. Her eyes averted, staring at the floor, she nearly collided with Saul.

"Miss Taylor, I need to talk with you," he said urgently.

216

"Not now, Saul. I can't right now. Can't it wait? I'll talk with you later." She started around him.

"Miss Taylor, that Matt Jackson. He got away."

Cold fingers clamped down on her grieving heart as she turned to look up at him. "But . . . but he's dead," she whispered hoarsely.

"No, ma'am. He must have jus' been wounded. We thought he was dead, and whilst we was takin' care of Marse David and Miz Bellman, he got away. But he left a trail of blood," he said encouragingly. "He'll be easy for the sheriff to find, Miss Taylor. Don't you worry yourself none."

"Worry?" she said strangely as she walked away from him. "Why should I worry? What more could he do to me?" she finished as she opened the door to her bedroom.

She lay on her bed, waiting. She waited to feel. She waited to cry or scream or just plain hurt. She waited and nothing happened. She lay there, staring at the ceiling, wondering at the apathy which gripped her mind and body, wondering if she would ever care what happened about anything ever again. Wondering until she fell asleep. When she opened her eyes again, Jenny was sitting by her side.

"Afta'noon, Missy," she said.

"Afternoon?" Taylor turned her head toward the window. The sky was still dark with rainclouds and seemed not to have changed since she closed her eyes. Sitting up, she asked, "Where were you last night, Jenny?"

In explanation, Jenny held her arms out for Taylor's inspection. Raw sores circled each wrist. "Mr. Jackson," she answered simply.

"Jackson?"

"He tied me up in the barn las' night. Told me he'd be back to finish what he'd started, but he never came back. I tried to get loose but couldn't. Josh, he found me this mornin'."

"He should be dead. I thought I'd killed him. I should have killed him."

"Sheriff's been here. He says, way he's bleedin', he can't live long. They'll find him, Missy. You don't go worryin'."

Taylor laughed harshly. "That's just what Saul told me." She moved her legs to the side of the bed. "Is the sheriff still here?"

"He'll be back soon."

"And Marilee?" Taylor asked hesitantly. "Is Dr. Marsh still with her?"

Jenny dropped her eyes. "No, ma'am," she answered softly. "He went back t'town. Says he's be back agin tomorrow."

And she began to feel. Knowing Marilee's baby was lost was like a knife plunging into her heart. She wept. She wept for David, for Marilee, for the lost baby, and for herself. She wept for the lost chances to show David how much he meant to her. She wept for a love never known and for a love known and lost, for a mother's empty arms and for a father's lost hope. Taylor wept. She wept for everything and for nothing.

The rains continued. The red mud clung to everything, slowing all travel to a near standstill. Even so, a large number of people had arrived for the funeral, fighting their way slowly along through the thick clay mud. Taylor stood at the graveside, a lonely figure in black. Jenny was beside her with an umbrella, doing her best to keep her mistress dry. The Reverend Stone, arriving on furlough in time to perform this sorrowful task, was reading from his Bible, his voice barely audible over the pounding rain.

". . . so saith the Lord, 'For ye are dust, and to dust ye shall return.' But let us not lose hope, for as he believed upon the Lord Jesus Christ, so might we be assured that today he is with the Lord in paradise. Amen."

Taylor picked up some mud, dropping it on top of the coffin. Slowly, she turned and walked away from the grave site. One by one, she could hear others dropping earth, the thick, red earth that David had loved so much, upon the box. She tried to shut the sound from her mind. It was so very final. The darkies began to sing softly, a haunting, stirring melody. She wished he could have been buried at Dorcet Hall. At least he should have lain where his heart was. Perhaps, when the rains stopped, perhaps then they could move his body.

Lifting her eyes, she found Marilee standing at the window in the master bedroom. The doctor had forbidden her to attend the service. In fact, he had confined her to her bed, but there she stood.

Taylor was glad that the Reverend Stone was here. Never had she known Marilee to be so depressed. As she met Taylor's glance, Taylor noticed again how very pale and drawn she was.

Taylor herself looked pale. The black mourning gown and bonnet accentuated her naturally white skin. Her dark eyes dominated her face now, making one think instantly of a poor waif or a forlorn puppy.

The slaves laid planks down over the muddy ground as a walkway to the house, and Taylor could hear her guests following her. She steeled herself for what lay ahead—the words of sympathy, the offers of help, the tears and remembrances. She felt so inadequate, so unable to cope with it all. But she did cope, and somehow, the hours moved on.

Taylor sat wearily in a chair near the fireplace. The last guest had finally departed. The library felt cold, she was unsure whether it was the weather or just her soul. A fire had been started in the fireplace, and she waited eagerly for its warmth to remove the chill from her body.

She closed her eyes, feeling the lonesomeness and deathly quiet of the mansion. She told herself that this would pass, the pain and the tears. She remembered when her father had died, how very lost, alone, even betrayed she had felt. But little by little, the pain had lessened until all that was left were the happy memories. She knew it would happen again, but for now, only the pain was real.

Susan cleared her throat, announcing her presence. "Sorry t'disturb you, Missy. Rev'rend Stone asked if you might join him 'n Miss Mar'lee in her room."

Taylor sighed. "Yes, I'll go up right now, Susan."

Marilee was sitting on her bed, propped up by large fluffy pillows. Her father sat nearby in a straightbacked chair. They both turned expectantly as she entered the room.

"How are you feeling, dear?" Taylor asked as she bent to kiss Marilee.

"Better, I think. And you? Are you holding up?"

Taylor sat down on the edge of the bed. "I suppose so. I'm a little tired is all."

"Taylor," the reverend said gently, "Marilee has decided to come home to stay during her convalescence. Perhaps she will even stay until the war is over. If it isn't too much to ask, she'd like you to remain here to oversee Spring Haven."

"Leave Spring Haven? But Marilee . . ."

"Taylor, I'm sorry," Marilee said softly, tears brimming in her brown eyes. "I can't bear to stay here. Try to understand, please. The house is so large and empty without Philip, and now . . . now I've lost our baby. I can't help it, Taylor. I just . . . I just want to go . . . home. I want . . . want to be with Papa . . . at . . . home," she finished, choking on sobs.

The Reverend Stone gathered his daughter in his arms, comforting her as she cried in earnest.

The sorrow of a parent grieving for his child was etched on his face, and he stroked her hair lovingly until her sobs died down.

"T . . . Taylor," Marilee continued, wiping her tears from her cheeks and eyes. "I . . . I know how you love Spring Haven. You think it's the only place on earth. I think it's lovely, too. I always have. And I'll be glad to . . . to return here when Philip comes back, but not before, Taylor. I don't think I'll come back before then. I . . . I'm sorry."

Taylor tried to think of something to say. Marilee was right. She couldn't understand anyone wanting to be anyplace else than right here. Why, this place restored her, gave her courage to go on.

The Reverend Stone spoke again. "We'll make sure you have a responsible overseer, of course. And you have many reliable servants here. I know Philip would be glad to know you're watching over things in his absence."

"Of course, I'll stay," Taylor answered firmly. "Where else would I go?"

"Why, you could come home with me if you'd rather," Marilee interjected. "It is a lot to ask of you, that you stay here alone."

"No. No, Marilee, that isn't what I meant. I want to stay here, and I *do* understand why you're going. You need some time to get well, some time to forget. You needn't worry. I'll watch over things here. I really do know how to run a plantation. David is . . . David *was* a good teacher. He made certain I knew the workings of the land

222

as well as the home. I'll be fine."

Marilee took Taylor's hand. "Thank you for understanding. I know you're suffering too. I'm sorry to be so selfish. I wish I could help somehow, but . . ." Her voice trailed off.

"We'll plan on leaving as soon as the roads have cleared for travel," the Reverend Stone said, filling the awkward silence. "We want an easy journey for Marilee."

"Of course. Now, I think I'll leave the two of you alone again. I'll look in on you later, Marilee."

Taylor closed the door quietly behind her. So, she thought, I'm to be really alone now. She descended the stairs, her hand caressing the banister. Mistress of Spring Haven. It brought the first real smile to her lips in several days. Yes, she would be fine. Spring Haven would give her the strength to go on. She would be fine as long as she was here.

Chapter 19

Taylor rode back to the barn in the late afternoon heat, hot and sticky after supervising the harvest of the corn. She was happy with the good crop and had heard from Dorcet Hall that the yield there was large too. It helped to ease her anger over this morning's news. Ten field slaves had disappeared during the night, and she was livid over it. It had never occurred to her that *her* slaves would want to run away. She jumped down from the saddle, handing her horse to Josh before starting toward the house. Her dress was chafing under her arms, and she was eager to get bathed and changed.

It hadn't taken her very long after Marilee and her father left to settle into a comfortable routine. She had refused to hire an overseer as she felt quite confident in her ability to manage the plantations on her own. Saul had become her right hand. Although trained as a valet, Saul knew a great deal about planting as well. He was an educated negro, a rare quantity in the South or North. He helped her with the accounts and made sound suggestions and decisions. He was not averse to hard physical labor either. Taylor and Saul became familiar figures to the slaves as they worked in the fields of corn, wheat, and beans.

Jenny, too, had become indispensable. Taylor was too busy with the crops to undertake the household operations as well, and Jenny had the uncanny ability to keep each of the servants working happily at their tasks without realizing Jenny was even in charge. This talent was particularly a blessing when it came to Susan and Mima. Both of these women had been house-keepers of their own plantations too long to get along well together. Until Dorcet Hall could be rebuilt, though, there was nothing else to do but bring Mima here. Jenny seemed to know just how to make each of them feel that hers was the most important duty being performed and that she was the only one who could do it.

Taylor still missed David, but her days and nights were kept very busy, too busy to feel sorry for herself. When she did think of him, it was with a spirit of gratitude. She was thankful for the enrichment he had added to her life in their three years together. He had carefully nurtured her from childhood to young womanhood. He had been a second father to her, and so much more besides. Because of him, she felt better prepared to face these difficult times. Sometimes, she would awake in the night crying, but for the most part, her tears had been conquered.

She followed the war less closely these days. Her main concern was in growing food to feed the troops, not in who was winning any particular battle. Fewer people rode out to visit with her, and she rarely sent for the news. Josh had brought news today of heavy fighting in Virginia at a place called Cedar Mountain. Some called it Slaughter Mountain, Josh said. She hadn't heard about casualties yet and hoped no one she knew would be among them when she did.

Taylor allowed herself to relax in her bath. When she was done, she would still have work to do in the estate books, but for now she intended to just enjoy the refreshing water. Washing her arms with the perfumed soap, she felt a twinge of annoyance at the darkening of her skin. She did her best to protect it, but it had still become tanned from all her time in the sun. She knew the ladies of the Bellville Aide Society would feel it a scandal to have skin like this. Thank goodness, she was no longer expected to join them. Well, she thought, at least her skin was still soft and her complexion was still flawless. What did it matter anyway? The only people she saw anymore had much darker skin than she did. Her stomach growled angrily, and she realized she had skipped supper again. Immediately, she felt as if she was starving.

"Jenny," she called. "Have Susan prepare a

supper tray for me, please. I'll eat in the study tonight. Oh, and have Saul meet me there in about fifteen minutes."

The servants had long since retired by the time Taylor closed the leather cover of the accounts book. Her eyes burned and she rubbed them with her finger tips.

"That's enough for tonight, Saul. You go on to bed. I'll see you in the morning."

"Yes'm, Miss Taylor. I'll be stayin' with ol' Henry tonight, if you needs me. He's feelin' poorly, and I said I'd sit with him a spell."

When he was gone, Taylor put out the lights, and carrying her candle with her, proceeded to her room. She was surprised to see Jenny sitting up in her own tiny room near Taylor's.

"Jenny? Still awake?"

"Jus' thought I'd see if you needed anythin' before I turned in."

"Nothing, thank you. Goodnight."

"Night, Missy."

The windows in Taylor's room stood open to the night air, and a slight breeze stirred the curtains. Her room was awfully warm despite this. Moonlight spilled in across her floor, turning her carpet to silver. Removing her dress, she lay down on the bed in her slip, but before she could drift into sleep, her door opened again.

"Miss Taylor," Jenny whispered urgently. "Miss Taylor, somebody's comin'. And they're not actin' right about it, neither."

"What do you mean?" Taylor whispered back, fully awake once again.

Jenny motioned her to the window. "Come see."

Taylor crossed quickly to where Jenny had parted the curtains. The moon cast her white light over the earth, nearly as bright as day, but the shadows were deeper, darker. It took her a moment to locate the spot Jenny was pointing at. Yes, she could see them. Two men leading their horses and clinging to the shadows, moving cautiously toward the house and avoiding open spaces.

Taylor grabbed her dressing gown. "Jenny, get me David's gun," she hissed as she pulled the gown snugly about her. "There's no time to get Saul. They're nearly to the door now. Quick, Jenny! Get it now!"

Taylor glanced furtively out the window again while she waited for Jenny's return. She couldn't see them anywhere. How close were they?

Together, Taylor and Jenny crept quietly to the top of the stairs. They stood horrified as they heard the latch being wiggled. Thankfully, it was locked.

"Come on," Taylor whispered, girded by a growing anger.

They glided swiftly down the stairs and into the drawing room just as the latch gave way. Taylor cocked the gun and readied herself to shoot. She had no doubts who her intruder was, and she was fuly prepared to kill Matt Jackson and his friend

228

too.

The well-oiled door made no sound as it swung open, soft light flooding the entry hall. The two men's silhouettes were thrown across the floor before them. As they stepped inside, Taylor raised the gun in front of her. She checked herself just in time. Both men were extremely tall. It wasn't Matt Jackson after all.

"Stop right there and don't move," she said as the men reached the stairs, trying to sound braver than she was. "Who are you and what do you want?" She wished she had sent Jenny for Saul, but it was too late now.

In unison, the men turned toward her hiding place in the drawing room. The closest man, she could see now, was a Negro. The other was partially hidden behind him and could not be seen clearly. Before she could demand that they leave, she heard Jenny gasp. Suddenly, she pushed past Taylor and ran toward the two men. Taylor lowered her weapon, shocked as she watched Jenny throw her arms around the black man's neck and heard her weeping.

The other man stepped around the pair, the light from the moon falling upon his face as he said softly, "Taylor?"

"Brent?" she gasped, feeling as if someone had knocked the wind out of her.

It seemed forever before his feet brought him across the entry hall and his arms were closing around her. She sagged into them, allowing his strength to support her. As Jenny lit several candles, Taylor pulled back from him, looking into his face. Several days' stubble covered his chin, and he was thickly covered with dust. But he looked good. Oh, how very good he looked. Her eyes swung around to Brent's companion.

"Caesar!" she exclaimed.

The big black nodded stiffly; a smile flickered on his lips and then disappeared.

"What happened at Dorcet Hall?" Brent asked her.

She looked back at him, her eyes wide. Of course, he didn't know. There was no way he could have.

"Let's sit down," she said, pulling him toward the sofa.

"We found Dorcet Hall in ruins. What happened to it?" he prodded her.

"Matt Jackson burned it down."

"Jackson. I should have know it." Brent pulled a worn piece of paper from inside his coat pocket and gave it to her. "Read it."

My son,
I hope this note can find its way to you. I fear that Jackson is back in the county. Strange things have been happening to Taylor. She doesn't suspect yet, but we need you. I am not strong enough to protect her from him. If there is any way you can come to us, I beg you to do so.

Your father

The letter was dated only a few days before the fire.

"Oh, Brent," Taylor said, blinking back the unexpected tears. "After he sent this note, Jackson set fire to the house. No one was seriously harmed, but your father was deeply wounded in his spirit. We came here until we could rebuild."

"But nothing's been done yet from what I could see," he said.

"No. David was so very depressed at first. He lost all heart. Then, when he was beginning to pick up, when it looked as though . . . Jackson came back. He was going to . . . he threatened me. He had a gun and he shot Marilee and your father struggled with him. He was too strong for David. Your father's heart . . ." Her voice caught in her throat. "I shot Jackson with his own gun, but he got away. David . . . your father died that night. Marilee lost her baby, but she's healing from her wound. She went to stay with her father."

Speaking at last, Brent asked, "You're alone here now?"

She nodded.

"Is he . . . is Father buried here or at Dorcet Hall?"

"He's here. It rained, and the ground turned to mud, and I had no other choice . . ."

"Where?" he asked hoarsely.

"I . . . I'll show you." She looked toward the corner of the room where Jenny and Caesar were quietly standing, arms around each other. "We won't be long."

They walked side by side through the long grass. The family cemetery was located a short walk from the house in a lovely grove of magnolia and peach trees. Neither of them spoke as they walked. The moment seemed too private to disturb with words. When they reached the wrought-iron fence surrounding the grave sites, Taylor silently pointed to David's resting place, and Brent continued on alone.

He knelt beside his father's grave, staring at the stone monument in disbelief. How could this have happened in so short a time? Did he even know Brent was coming in reply to his letter? Had he received Brent's reply?

"Father," he whispered. "Father, I came like you wanted. I came to protect her. You knew I loved her too, didn't you? Did you know how very much?"

He was crying quietly now. "Father, you and I . . . we didn't see eye to eye on much, but . . . but we loved each other. I'll try to take care of everything just like you'd have wanted." His hands grabbed the stone, anger choking out the tears. "And I swear to you, I swear Matt Jackson will pay for what he's done—to you and to Taylor. He'll pay. I swear, he'll pay."

She watched him talking and weeping, and she cried with him. Yet, even in his sorrow and her own, she was glad he was here—here with her.

Here? But he was a Yankee! How had he made it through the lines? Taylor's fright chased away her sadness. She knew little about war and military matters, but she was certain that a Yankee dressed in civilian clothes in the middle of Georgia would quickly be hung or shot as a spy. She waited anxiously while Brent paid his respects and said his goodbyes to his father.

Brent stood up and drew his sleeve unceremoniously across his eyes, wiping away his tears. Then he turned abruptly, walking swiftly away. Reaching Taylor, he took her arm and propelled her alongside him back to the house. She hadn't any chance to ask him about his being there. His face forbade her from asking. Caesar and Jenny were still waiting for them, and Taylor sent them away as she and Brent sat down together on the couch.

Brent stared into the cold fireplace for several minutes. Taylor waited for him to begin the conversation, and finally, he did.

"I suppose you're wondering about Caesar and me, about us being here?" he asked quietly.

She nodded.

"I still don't know how Father managed to get that letter through the lines. When it reached me, I asked my commanding officer for an emergency furlough. I showed him the letter and told him the story. I eliminated the fact of it being in Georgia. I hadn't taken any leave before this and our regiment hadn't seen much fighting for a while, so he could spare me. Anyway, I was able to arrange for about six weeks.

"I'd met Caesar some time before, and I needed a good cover once I was in the South. He agreed to help me if I could assure him he wouldn't be taken as an escaped slave when we got here. I took the liberty of giving him that promise. We traveled as master and slave, slipping through the lines quite undetected. Once we arrived in this county, however, we moved more carefully. We're both known by too many people hereabouts. When we got to Dorcet Hall and saw what had happened, I feared I had lost you for good. My only hope was that you and Father had taken refuge here."

Brent took her hands. "I know this isn't the time or place, but I've learned in this war that there is no spare time. You must act quickly on everything. If there is something you want, you must get it before someone else does." He paused thoughtfully. "Taylor, I love you. Since the day you rode off with Jeff Stone for Atlanta, I've thought of nothing else. Do you . . . can you love this Yankee once again?"

Taylor's eyes dropped to their clasped hands. She was blinded by unshed tears, but a smile brightened her lips as she looked up once again. "I never stopped loving you, Brent, in spite of what I said that day."

Brent stood, drawing her up with him. "I think you had best show me where I'm to sleep tonight," he whispered.

They mounted the stairs, their hands still clasped together. Taylor stopped at Philip's old room. She started to leave him there, but his hands held her shoulders tightly, halting her departure. Slowly, he pulled her back to him. His mouth came down to meet hers. At first the kiss was tender, gentle, but soon the hunger of their love was fully expressed in their embrace. Her body was melded with his, and she yearned for something she didn't even know. Taylor tried to make herself pull away from him but was powerless to make her limbs obey.

His lips parted from hers. Only inches away, he said, "Marry me, Taylor. Say you'll marry me."

"Oh, yes. I'll marry you, Brent. I'd do anything you told me to do. I couldn't live again without you."

He kissed her again, more gently this time, the sweetness of it flowing like honey through her veins. When he set her aside this time, she had no desire to leave his arms, to even try to leave them. He understood her and shook his head.

"No, Taylor, my love," he whispered huskily. "We'll do it right. We'll marry first."

Unwillingly, they separated, each to their own rooms.

"Goodnight, my sweet," he whispered to her departing shadow. "Goodnight, my love."

Chapter 20

The following days passed as if in a dream for Taylor and Brent. They walked hand in hand along the river. They sat dreaming under the shade trees. They visited late into the night as they learned everything they could about each other.

It was early in the day, this hot August Friday. The young lovers were sitting on a large rock beside the river, Brent tossing stones into the water and watching the ripples float away on the current, and Taylor lying with her head in his lap, her eyes closed. Suddenly Brent drew her up and kissed her urgently, leaving her breathless once she was released. Her eyes, wide with wonder, stared at him as she tried to regain her equilibrium.

"I can't wait until the end of the war, Taylor.

Marry me now."

"But Brent, how? We can't allow anyone to know you're here. It's too dangerous."

He pushed himself up from the rock and walked a few steps away from her. His hands were clasped behind him, and his head was thrust downward in concentration. "We must find some way," he said, his voice husky and strained. "I cannot bear it any longer. Don't you understand?"

Taylor moved to his side. Laying a hand on his shoulder, she answered, "I think I do. Yes, I understand. I'll see what can be done. We'll manage somehow, Brent. I love you."

Taylor sat nervously in the parlor of the parsonage. The skinny, pinched-looking wife of the minister sat across from her, a frown hardening her mouth.

"Let me see if I understand you, Miss Andrews," the pastor was saying as he walked behind her. "You have a *cousin* who desires to marry a Yankee if he can somehow get through the lines of fighting? And you are trying to find someone to perform the ceremony? Where did you say you're from, Miss?"

She wiggled in her chair. "Near Macon, Reverend," she lied smoothly. It was becoming easier with each new minister.

He stopped his pacing beside her. Leaning his knuckles on the table top next to her chair, he bent closer to her. "Miss Andrews, I have a strong

237

suspicion that you're lying to me. I doubt that Andrews is even your name. But I will tell you this. If your *cousin* wanted to marry a Northerner, she had best find some way to go to him because no honest Southern minister would marry one of our women to a heathen Yankee."

"But I . . . but she loves her home. She doesn't want . . . she can't leave the South. She's the only one left to watch over the plantation and her people until the war is over."

"Hurrumph," he snorted as he began to pace again. "Seems to me she has no care for this land if she thinks she can love one of them. She'd be better off dead. If she were here right now, I would pray for . . ."

Taylor stood up dejectedly. She was exhausted and didn't want to listen to any more of this discourse. She knew only too well what else he was going to say to her.

"Thank you, sir. I appreciate your advice for my cousin. I'll do all I can to discourage her from making this disastrous alliance," she said as she hurried toward the door and escape.

Josh was waiting outside by the carriage. Seeing her approach, he opened the door and helped her inside.

"Let's go home, Josh."

"Yes, ma'am!"

For five days they had been driving from one town to another. Always it was the same thing. No one would help them. No one considered love of a Yankee as any reason to marry one. All she wanted to do now was go home, but another long day of travel would have to be endured before she got there. If they were lucky, and if Josh pushed the horses hard enough, they would reach Spring Haven before midnight. How was she going to tell Brent that she had failed once she did get home? How was she to look into those beloved golden eyes and tell him they couldn't get married? How was she to deny them both the warmth of each other's arms?

Wearily, she lay down on the seat. She would cry but she was too tired even for that. The sway of the carriage quickly lulled her to sleep.

The carriage pulled to a halt outside the front door. Before Josh could jump down from his seat atop the carriage, Brent was out the door and down the steps. He almost yanked the door from its hinges in his rush to lift Taylor out of the conveyance.

In the light of the entry hall, he could see dark circles under her eyes. She hadn't slept again after a light supper and short rest in Athens, and the toll of her journey was clear on her delicate features. Brent already knew the trip was a failure just by looking at her.

His arm firmly around her waist, he guided her gently up to her room. They didn't speak of it. There would be time enough for that tomorrow. He kissed her a soft goodnight at her door and quickly left her in Jenny's care. Every muscle in his body was tense, strained to its limit. How he wanted her! Never had he felt so frustrated. To be so close to her every day. To proclaim his love and hear it returned, yet stopped from claiming her for his own. By sheer willpower, he had left her behind and gone to his own room. He stood by the window, staring into the night without seeing. Soon he would have to return to his division. He had been gone far too long already. He couldn't bear to leave her behind without his protection. What if the army—either of them—came near here. She would be defenseless.

He would make her come with him. Somehow, she must be made to leave Spring Haven and go north with him.

Jenny, understanding her mistress's heartache, quietly helped her out of her traveling clothes. She washed the dust from Taylor's body and then slipped a nightgown over her head. She helped her into bed, and putting out the light, she left the room.

Taylor listened to the door close softly behind her maid. She knew Jenny would be hurrying even now down the back stairs and out to the cabin. Out to *their* cabin. As if she were there, she could clearly see in her mind Jenny rushing into Caesar's waiting arms and the cabin door closing out the rest of the world to their love.

She was wide awake now. Her room was very dark. No moon tonight. For hours, or so it seemed, she stared into the darkness, feeling her heart aching in a most painful manner. Sometime in those lonely minutes or hours, she knew what she would do . . . what she *must* do.

She moved silently down the hall, hardly even breathing, the swish of her satin nightgown the only sound to be heard throughout the house. She opened the door and crossed to the bed. Even in the darkness, she could see his face, the gentle rising and falling of his chest. He looked unhappy and lonely in his sleep. She stood there, staring down at him and willing her love to touch his heart.

His eyes opened. "Taylor?"

Never had she known that her name, spoken softly in the night, could be a statement of love. Deliberately, she slipped her nightgown from her shoulders. It crumpled to the floor, encircling her feet.

"I am yours, Brent. By all the love inside me, I am yours forever. Surely that makes me your wife. Surely our love makes us one," she whispered. "Love me, Brent. Make me a woman."

He sat up, reached out and took her hands. He held them tightly as he stared up at her. Then, he gently pulled her down to him. His body was strong and warm against her. His lips on hers held more love, more tenderness than she had ever known. A storm of emotions washed over her as she drowned in his lovemaking.

Chapter 21

Harvest continued. The hot August sun relented some as September claimed its rightful place in the scope of things. For Taylor, there was no war, no season, no passing of time. There was only the happiness of her life with Brent at Spring Haven. It mattered little what else was happening in the world. The sun still shone. The crops still grew. The slaves still sang while they worked. And the nights still came. The nights in his arms.

Her euphoric happiness blocked out all other thoughts. She was, therefore, unprepared for Brent's serious expression as they sat down to breakfast one morning.

"What is it, Brent?" she asked. "What's wrong?"

"Taylor, I've got to get back to my company. There's been another battle at Bull Run."

She blanched. Words eluded her.

"You must come with me now, Taylor." Brent's words were full of his love, his yearning for her. "It would only be until the war is over. When we come back, no matter which side wins, we can rebuild Dorcet Hall. We could make it another Spring Haven. Whatever you want, you would have. I know you don't want to leave here, but we could be together whenever I could get a furlough."

"How soon?" she asked, still confused. "How soon are you leaving?"

"A few days at the most."

What was she to do? She loved him. She didn't want to be without him. But live up North? And she would be without him there, too. He would be away with the army, fighting, maybe even dying.

"Can I think about it for a while, Brent?"

His face fell. "Of course."

"Oh, my love, don't look like that! You must know I want to be with you, but there is more to consider. There's Spring Haven and . . . Please. I *do* love you so."

Brent nodded as he got up from the table. "I've got to discuss our leaving with Caesar." His lips brushed her forehead and then he was gone.

Taylor followed him with her eyes, then swept them around the room. Leave Spring Haven? Go north? Live among the Yankees on the hope of seeing him now and then? Could she do it? There would be no letters if she stayed here; no news would be able to reach her. She wouldn't know if he was alive or injured or dead. Could she bear that? She laid her head on the table. What was she to do?

"Missy. Somebody comin'," Susan called from the hall.

A visitor? They hadn't had a visitor since the funeral. Taylor went out of the dining room to the large window at the front of the house. It was Marilee's buggy she saw coming up the drive, and she hurried out to meet her sister-in-law.

Expecting to see Marilee, she was taken back as Jeffrey Stone climbed out of the buggy, his right arm in a sling. He saw her and smiled, the usual twinkle in his eyes. She noticed how white his face looked under his red shock of hair. He was thin, and pain creased the area around his eyes.

"Hello, Taylor."

"Jeffrey Stone!" She hugged him, carefully avoiding his arm. "Come in. When did you get back? What happened to your arm? Is there word from Robert or Philip?" She guided him into the library as she chattered on.

"I'm fine. I'm fine," he insisted as they sat down across from each other. "And how are you, Taylor? You look wonderful."

"Thank you. I'm very well."

"I was sorry to hear about David."

"Thank you, Jeffrey," she said softly, a flush of discomfort flooding over her face. How thoughtless she must appear to him. "Now, do tell me about your injury," she said to change the subject.

"I took a bullet in my wrist and one in my

shoulder at Cedar Mountain. Had a bit of a problem with it. Doesn't seem to want to heal right, so they sent me home for a while." He paused a moment, the smile gone from his lips. "I watched better men than me meet their death this last year. I'm lucky to have survived this long. Believe me, Taylor, it's better to fall dead on the field of battle than to get ill or be wounded and have to stay in one of those hospitals."

A shadow crossed his green eyes, his skin turning gray all of a sudden. "It's hell, Taylor," he whispered hoarsely. "Right here on our own Confederate soil. They've brought hell with them into our land."

For the first time, Taylor understood the reality, the nightmare of war.

"Sometimes," he continued, "the waiting is the worst part. When you can hear the battle some place else but you're not involved. Not yet. The noise, the smell, the yelling and screaming. And after I was hit, I fell among others, some dead, some dying, all around me. I prayed I'd die just before I passed out. I woke up in a field hospital. Taylor, they had a pile just for the sawed-off limbs. Legs and arms everywhere. Piled up where everybody would see them . . . But I wasn't about to let them have mine." Jeffrey shuddered, reliving the nightmarish memory. "They shipped me off to a hospital in Richmond, then to Atlanta. Finally, I persuaded them to let me come home. And I couldn't very well come home without seeing you, now could I?" he finished, a smile returning to his face.

Tears sprang to her eyes. "Oh, Jeffrey, it's so good to know you're all right. I hope you don't have to ever go back."

"I will," he said, shaking his head. "The war is going to last a long, long time. They'll be using old men and boys before it's over. We were wrong, Taylor, so very wrong. We thought it was all a lark."

She thought of Brent. He was one of them. He was one of the Yankees who were tearing apart her country, who were killing and maiming her friends and loved ones. How could she bear to go live among them, even for Brent?

Jeffrey noticed the thoughtful, somewhat strange look on her face. "Is something wrong?"

"No. Nothing," she answered, mentally shaking herself. "Would you like something to eat or drink?"

"No, but I would like to walk with you about the grounds. Would you mind?"

"I'd love to, Jeffrey," she replied softly.

"Remember the Mason home in Atlanta?" Jeffrey asked as they strolled arm in arm through the gardens. "Remember the walk in their gardens we took back in April of sixty-one?"

"Yes, I remember."

"We were all very brave back then, weren't we? You were even planning a party in honor of our victory. In September. It didn't happen that September and it won't happen this one either."

Taylor pressed his hand. "Jeffrey, you're home

246

to rest, to regain your strength. Let's talk of more pleasant things, shall we?''

They continued their walk in silence, making a solemn picture—Taylor dressed in black and Jeffrey in a faded gray uniform, his arm bandaged and in a sling. It was a sight all too common in the South.

Taylor thought again about going North with Brent. After listening to Jeffrey, how could she go and live among the enemy? She would have to say no. She would have to wait for him here. When the war was over . . .

She steered Jeffrey back to the house. He looked tired, and he was so thin and pale, she was sure he must need some good food to eat. Sitting Jeffrey down at the table, she called for their lunch. While they waited, she poured him a cup of "Confederate coffee," a concoction of parched particles of corn with sorghum added to provide sweetening.

"I'm sorry this isn't the real thing," she apologized.

Jeffrey chuckled. "No one gets much of a chance to drink coffee anymore. Actually, Taylor, I doubt I could stand real coffee. You get used to the taste of this stuff after a while.''

They ate heartily on corn, sweet potatoes, peas, and chicken. Jeffrey was just touching his napkin to his mouth when Brent came charging into the room.

"Taylor . . .'' He stopped abruptly.

The room was deathly still as Brent and Jeffrey

247

looked directly into each other's eyes, both men trying to take stock of the situation before speaking. Jeffrey was the first to move. He rose from his chair, putting his napkin on his plate, and then held out his hand to Brent.

"Excuse the left hand, Mr. Lattimer," he said.

Brent accepted the offer, and they shook hands silently.

Taylor poured coffee into another cup. Her hand was shaking so badly that she spilled much of it into the saucer. "Join us, Brent?" she asked nervously, wishing she had had the good sense to have sent word to him that Jeffrey was here.

Jeffrey turned to look at her. She loved him more than ever, he realized. There really was no hope for him now. David was gone, but Brent would always stand between them. He dropped his eyes from her face. He would be happy with only a fraction of her love if he could only call her his own. Damn him! Damn Brent Lattimer. Why did he have to be so tall and handsome and charming!

Picking up his slouch hat and placing it on his head, he turned his face toward Taylor again. One look at her face, silently pleading for Brent's life, and he was lost. He couldn't hurt her, even if it meant not having her. He also knew he must protect her from others doing what he had wanted to do. He must get Brent away before he was caught.

Jeffrey took her hand and spoke softly. "Thank you for the delightful time, Taylor. It was wonder-

248

ful to spend the day in your company." He looked meaningfully into her eyes, squeezing her hand as he did so. "Strange things happen in war, you know. For example, I heard not long ago of a Yankee sneaking through to a Southern plantation. Don't remember why he was there, but I do remember that a Confederate officer recognized him, and even though he was a friend, he was obliged to report him to his superiors. Don't remember now what happened to the man. Hung him I suppose."

He released her fingers. "Well, I'd best get started back to town. I may have troubles with my buggy or my horse or something else that would slow me down in getting home." He saluted her casually, a gentle smile in his eyes. "Good afternoon, Taylor."

She watched him walk from the house in search of his horse and buggy.

"That was good of him to give us that warning," Brent said at her side. "We'll have to leave within the hour if we're to get a good head start on them. I'll tell Caesar. You get your things together."

Taylor's head was spinning. She had decided she wasn't going with him only a short time ago. Now that the time was here, she knew he was right. She had to go.

She hurried up to her room. They would have to travel light, and she was unsure what to take. As she stood helplessly in the midst of her room, Jenny came rushing in to help. Seeing her mistress's confusion, she took command.

"You go on, Missy," she said, giving Taylor a little shove toward the door. "I'll get you packed."

Taylor nodded obediently and left the room. She was frightened by how fast everything was happening. Thoughts tumbled out of control in her mind. Never had she felt so confused, finding it impossible to think clearly. Her head felt as if it would burst any moment. She was leaving Spring Haven. She was going north to live among strangers, the enemies of her home. She might never see Spring Haven or Bellville again. Her heart aching as did her head, she was still trying to put her thoughts in order when she reached the barn. Brent's voice carried clearly through the doorway to meet her.

". . . I'll get rid of her anyway once we get there. The danger will be over then."

Taylor stepped back quickly as if she had been struck. In her confused emotional state, his words could only mean one thing. He was talking about her. He had tricked her into believing he loved her. He had used her and only wanted her along as a hostage, to save his own skin. Why? Why wasn't it true that he loved her? He had to love her. He had to. She turned to run back to the house.

"Taylor."

She froze as he called her name.

"Taylor, are you ready?"

I won't cry, she thought as she turned to face him. He was walking toward her, an air of urgency about him.

"Taylor, we must leave. Are you ready?" he repeated.

"I . . . I'm not going," she said in a whisper.

The smile vanished. "Not going? But don't be ridiculous. Of course you're going. You have to come with me."

She shook her head stubbornly.

"Taylor, what's wrong? I love you."

Her chest hurt. Her head pounded. He spoke to her of love. Oh, how she had loved him. But he had lied. He lied! She knew it now, but she wouldn't let him know she knew.

"Brent, I can't go with you. I . . . I've thought it over carefully. I'm not going. I'm not leaving my home. These people need me here. Spring Haven is too important. I love . . . I love Spring Haven too much to go with you."

"Taylor." He said her name as he had said it to her so many times as they lay in each others arms, their love surrounding them in the intimacy of their bedroom. His hand reached out to caress her cheek.

"Don't!" she cried, stepping back quickly. "Don't touch me, please. I can't go. I just can't go with you." The tears began, falling unchecked as she looked at him.

Brent stared back at her helplessly. He didn't know what to do, what to say. He didn't know what had gone wrong. "Taylor," he pleaded, "we . . . I . . . there's no time to waste. We must leave now. Say you'll come. Come with me now."

Oh, I want to believe you, she thought as she

shook her head in reply.

Brent's shoulders sagged. He turned his back to her and began his slow walk to the barn. Taylor resisted the urge to tell him to wait, to run to him with outstretched arms and a heart full of love, to risk whatever might happen later just to have him now.

"Miss Taylor?"

Taylor turned to face Jenny. "I'm not going," she told her.

Jenny gasped, her body tensing.

Taylor touched Jenny's shoulder, understanding her fear. "You're still going, Jenny. I promised you would be with him if we ever found him. Go with Caesar now. Love him always, Jenny. I wish you happiness."

Jenny studied Taylor carefully, a wide range of emotions playing across her face. Then she turned and ran to the waiting men and horses before Taylor could change her mind.

Taylor, a cold chill beginning to take hold of her heart, watched Brent ride toward her. His eyes searched her rigid face for a clue to her change of heart.

"Taylor," he said, pulling his charge up short. "It's not too late."

"It's too late, Brent. It *is* too late."

The finality of her words were like a slap in his face. He didn't understand what had gone wrong. They had been so happy these past weeks. He searched his mind for something he had said or done that would have brought about her decision.

252

He could see the emotional upheaval she was going through. He thought of bodily picking her up, forcing her to go with him, but he discarded the idea. She must want to go with him or it would be no good. No, she had decided against him. She had decided Spring Haven was more important. Or perhaps it was Jeffrey's appearance that had changed her mind. Perhaps she had realized she could love the Confederate soldier more than him. She hadn't even told him to come back after the war. She had only said it was too late for them. Too late.

"Goodbye, Brent," she cried suddenly and ran into the house.

From the window, Taylor watched their departure. It was his death she saw in her spirit. The death of all she held dear. The death of her one love. The death of her heart.

Chapter 22

Taylor waited for the soldiers, wondering what she would say to them, knowing she couldn't betray him even now. But they never came, and at last she knew they weren't going to come. Jeffrey hadn't reported Brent after all.

The first night he was gone, Taylor sat up in a chair, staring at the bed they had shared. A coldness filled her veins, leaving no room for feelings nor even room for tears. As day followed night, again and again, she found it impossible to sleep but a few hours now and then. With sleep came dreams, visions of Brent, and with them, threats of emotions, a danger of feeling the pain. So she locked herself up in a cocoon of nothingness and moved lifelessly through each day.

Jeffrey's arm was healing admirably now,

though the doctor insisted it remain in the sling for a while longer so he wouldn't be tempted to overuse it. Out of his mother's sight, however, he had rid himself of the restraint and was thoroughly enjoying the feeling of control over the spirited animal beneath him as they thundered along the road toward Spring Haven.

It had been a month since he had been there, twenty-nine agonizing days since he had turned his back and walked away, not knowing if he would ever see her again. This morning he had heard from one of the kitchen servants, by way of who knew how many other servants and field hands, that Taylor was still there—and alone—at Spring Haven.

Jeffrey brought his steed, snorting and blowing, to a halt at the porch. He mounted the steps two at a time, nearly barreling through Mima as she opened the front door.

"Sorry, Mima," he said, laughing. "Is Miss Taylor receiving?"

Mima's round face moved slowly from side to side. "Oh, Marse Jeffrey, I shore am glad t'see you. Miss Taylor, she's in an awful state, she is."

His jubilation disappeared. "What is it? Is she sick?"

"Yessir, she's sick all right. But not like you're thinkin'. She's sick someplace harder t'cure." Again she shook her head sadly.

Beginning to understand her meaning, he asked, "Where is she, Mima?"

"In the cem'tery, Marse Jeffrey. She goes there

'n' sits by Marse David's restin' place fo' hours 'n' hours, not movin' or talkin' or nothin'. Jus' sits there." Her eyes grew big as saucers. "Sits der jus' like a zombie, she does," Mima whispered.

Deliberately, Jeffrey turned and walked toward the tiny cemetery. Dear Lord, don't let her suffer, he prayed.

She didn't look up as he approached, even though he didn't stop until he was only a few yards away. His own heart cried out for her. Taylor's eyes stared blankly at the ground, dark circles smudging her pale skin beneath them. Her face was neither sad nor happy. It was simply expressionless, empty.

"Taylor."

She lifted her gaze slowly. It seemed to him that he could see her returning herself from someplace far away. For a brief moment, he thought she wouldn't make it back, that she wouldn't know him. It was a frightening sensation.

Taylor felt mildly irritated. She resented being dragged back from her place of retreat, a hiding place her mind had found where she wasn't required to think or feel.

"Jeffrey?" she said as she recognized him. "I didn't expect you. How are you?"

He studied her carefully. "Much better, Taylor. My arm is nearly as good as new. And you?" he asked as he sat beside her.

"Mmmmm," was her only reply as her eyes drifted away again, looking at nothing in particular. It was as if she was unable to concentrate on any one thing for very long.

Jeffrey put his arm around her. He wanted somehow to wipe away the hurt he knew was hiding inside her. He wished he could somehow will his own strength into her. All he could do for now was offer whatever support and comfort she would accept from him, and he made that offer with his eyes. She leaned her head against his shoulders in silent acceptance.

"I love you, Taylor. Marry me," he whispered, surprising even himself.

Taylor pulled away from him, staring at him, eyes wide, as if he were a stranger. Just who was it that had asked her to marry him? Suddenly, she came crashing into the present, into understanding and pain. He was gone. He had left her. They weren't to marry. She choked on a sob, and Jeffrey was quickly holding her tightly against him, a sentinel against the pain in her heart, a guard to hide behind.

"I'm sorry, Taylor. I . . . I shouldn't have asked. I'm sorry. I'm so sorry."

The tears didn't come. Only the one, dry sob. She lay against his chest, eyes open. As quickly as it had come, the pain receded behind the wall of emptiness she had so carefully constructed.

"Yes. I'll marry you, Jeffrey."

"You'll . . . Are you sure?" he stuttered, holding her away from him.

"I'm sure. When would you like the wedding?"

Stunned, he ventured, "This month? Before I have to go back?"

"Fine. Whenever you'd like."

They said no more—Taylor because there was nothing left to say, and Jeffrey because he was afraid to say anything for fear she would change her mind. Jeffrey wasn't fooling himself. He knew she loved Brent, but he was certain she would grow to love him, love him even more than she had loved Brent. He knew he would always love her as he did now. And if Brent had really loved her as he did, he thought, he would have taken her with him. Jeffrey knew he wouldn't have left her behind.

A quiet wedding was planned for early November. Marilee, of course, would stand up with Taylor. Jeffrey's best man would be an army surgeon he had met during his recuperation. Taylor paid little attention to what preparations were made. It made little difference to her. There was some whispering in Bellville about the impropriety of marrying so soon after the death of her husband, but most people accepted it well enough. Jeffrey and Taylor were both well-liked, and the war seemed to be affecting all the old and accepted traditions anyway.

What Taylor had been unable to do for herself, time began to accomplish for her. Little by little, her mind was pulled back to reality. She began to feel again—first the pain, then the loss, the rejection, the anger. Finally, even these were paled by the passing of time until she came to accept Brent's absence, his betrayal, as she accepted

David's death. She had loved him, loved him still, but nothing would ever bring him back. Not ever. The time she spent with Jeffrey was salve on her wounds, and she learned to treasure their moments together.

Taylor sat quietly before her dressing table, staring at her reflection. Could she see it in her face? Wasn't there a special glow about her now that had never been there before? Could anyone look at her and know? Last night, when she herself had realized it, she was filled with horror, but now, in the light of day, she felt a peace and joy filling her heart like she had never known. Brent's child. Brent's and hers. He hadn't left her. Not totally. He had given her a part of himself to keep forever. He must have loved her at least a little to have given her this child.

And Jeffrey—dear, sweet Jeffrey with his plain face, red hair, and large heart, with his gentle words and blushing passion. How would this news affect Jeffrey? Would he still want her for his bride? How would she ever find the right words to tell him?

Even these thoughts couldn't still the happiness swelling within. Somehow she would tell Jeffrey, and somehow she would weather whatever came. She wasn't alone anymore.

Jeffrey returned from a medical examination in Atlanta four days later. As they sipped their coffee, Taylor observed him from behind lowered lashes. He was in an exceptionally good mood. And why not? In just three days he was marrying the girl of his dreams. His arm had been pronounced sound. He was alive and life was beautiful. What more could he want? Even returning to the war couldn't diminish his exuberance.

Taylor set down her cup and walked over to the window. She knew she couldn't look at him, couldn't watch the hurt replace his smile when she told him. Instinctively, she placed a protective hand over her abdomen.

"Jeffrey, there's something important I must tell you."

He knew it! He had felt something in the air ever since he arrived, but he had refused to believe anything could go wrong now. Not when everything was going so well.

"What is it?" he said, ready to go to her.

She lifted a hand. "No, stay there." Somehow, even with her back to him, she had known he was about to rise. "This . . . this is very difficult for me to tell you, Jeffrey. I . . . I've tried for days to think of some way to . . . to tell you so that it wouldn't hurt you."

Was she going to refuse to marry him? He jumped from his chair.

"Jeffrey, stay there!"

He stopped.

She cleared her throat, ready to speak again. He thought how lovely she looked, framed by the bright fall day outside the window, the sun reflecting tiny prisms of light off her shiny hair. He thought how lonely he would be without her, now that he had gotten used to thinking of her as his.

"Jeffrey, I'm going to have a child."

A child? She was going to have a baby? Who would have thought? Well, that wasn't so bad. David Lattimer was a decent sort. He deserved an heir by Taylor. Jeffrey would love the child as if he were his own. He . . .

"It's *Brent* Lattimer's baby," she said, reading his mind.

The silence. The loud silence. At last she turned to face him. Jeffrey had sat back down. He stared at her in disbelief, his mouth working as if he wanted to speak but couldn't.

"Tell me about it," he said at last.

Her eyes dropped to where her hand still rested on her trim stomach. "You knew I loved him. Even before the war, I loved him. He came back because of Jackson. David had sent for him to come. He came even though it was so dangerous for him to do so. But when he got here, it was already too late. David was already . . . dead. We . . . he wanted us to marry, but there was no one who could . . . or would." Tears traced her cheeks and dropped to the floor, but her voice remained clear. "In my heart, in *our* hearts, I thought, we were married. He was my husband. I was to go with him when he left, but . . ."

A sob escaped her. She twisted her hands together, trying to calm herself. Jeffrey waited, feeling as if a mighty fist had been driven into his gut, knocking the very life from him. Brent's baby. Not my baby. His. Jeffrey felt sick to his

261

stomach. If Brent Lattimer walked in the door right now, he would kill him. His hate was bitter bile in his throat.

"I learned . . . he didn't really love me," she continued softly, "so I stayed behind."

"You still love him." It was a statement, not a question.

"Yes," she sighed. "I still love him. But it's over. I was his wife in my heart. Now I'm his widow. I love you, too, Jeffrey. I . . . I'm sorry about . . . about the baby. I understand that you can't marry me now."

"Not marry you!" Jeffrey exclaimed, jumping to his feet again. "Of course, we'll still marry."

It was her turn to be stunned. "But . . . but the scandal. Jeffrey, you . . . they'll know . . . everyone . . ."

"Everyone will think as I did, that it's David's child. Even if they don't I don't care. I love you, Taylor. I'll love the baby. I promise to love you both forever and always. We'll get married just as planned."

And so Taylor found herself standing before the Reverend Stone once again. Again she repeated her vows, and again she knew this was not the right man. She had learned to love David. She already loved Jeffrey. But neither of these men was the one she loved totally, passionately and forever.

They returned to Spring Haven alone. There was no celebration, no honeymoon. There was only Jeffrey and Taylor and a large house full of empty rooms and haunting memories.

One thing would be different this time from her first marriage—Jeffrey would not be leaving her at her bedroom door before going to his own room. She was not the frightened, naive child she had been then. She knew what the night would hold. What troubled her were her memories of Brent, knowing his child rested within her while she lay with another man, husband or not.

Chapter 23

They stood quietly together amid the noise.
Private farewells were being said all along the
station platform as the engine puffed and panted,
impatient for departure. Somewhere in the crowd,
Marilee was saying her goodbyes to her father.

Jeffrey Stone, handsome in his new uniform,
his epaulets proclaiming his recent promotion to
captain, gazed silently at his wife. He was trying
to absorb into his mind, into his very soul, how
she looked at this moment. He wanted to keep it
with him forever.

Taylor was not dressed in black today in
deference to Jeffrey's request. She had donned a
rose-colored gown with a full hooped skirt and
was wearing a matching bonnet over her tight
ringlets. The warm color brought out the pink in
her cheeks and accentuated the delicate white-

ness of her complexion. She looked so helpless and defenseless standing there, her eyes staring out at the train from beneath her bonnet. Yet, he knew that she was really quite strong and capable. She was a mixture of obedient, pliable Southern womanhood and the grit and backbone it took to manage a home and oversee a plantation, even without the help of a man if necessary.

"Taylor," he said, barely audible above the hubbub.

She turned her dark eyes to meet his. He wished he could read what was really hidden in the depths of those blue pools. He wished he could remove the protective veil he had seen lowered over them in the last few days.

"Write me often, Taylor," he said.

She nodded. "I will. Be careful, Jeffrey. Don't get hurt again."

They had said it all before, yet they seemed unable to say anything else.

"You'll let me know about . . . about the baby?"

"Yes," she replied, her eyes dropping from his.

His fingers gripped her shoulders. "I love you," he cried, almost desperately.

For a moment, she didn't reply. When she lifted her head again, she was gazing through a sea of unshed tears. "I know you do, Jeffrey."

He waited for her to say she loved him too. His eyes begged her to speak those words. His heart ached to hear them.

"Yes," she said, finally speaking them. "I love you too."

Perhaps it would have been better not to hear them. The words were empty of the passion, the intensity he longed for.

"All 'board!"

The cry caused an immediate flurry of kisses and hugs all along the platform. With hasty, last minute farewells, people began to board the train. Jeffrey pulled Taylor against him, kissing her forehead tenderly. As he stepped away, she leaned quickly forward and returned his kiss, her lips lightly brushing his.

"Jeffrey, please be careful. Come home . . . come home safely."

The Reverend Stone appeared beside them. "We must go, Jeffrey."

Once more, he held her shoulders, searching her face, searching it for something to take with him during the long nights and nightmarish days ahead. She was crying now, and he knew he was pressing her too hard and too fast. She needed time. He must give it to her. God willing, he would return home and be able to give her the time to learn to love him completely.

He kissed her forehead again, not trusting himself to kiss her lips. He thought, briefly, that if he did kiss her as he wanted, he would turn his back and walk away from the train. He wouldn't care about the court martial or hanging for desertion or anything if he could only be with her a short time longer.

"Goodbye, love," he whispered in her ear, and then turned away.

Through her tears, she watched him go, becoming a blur of gray before disappearing into the black car. She tried to clear her eyes as the train began to chug away from the station. She lifted a gloved hand, hoping he was sitting where he could see her.

Marilee's fingers touched her elbow. "Let's go home. We'll have some tea."

Taylor nodded, her body chilled by the long wait in the crisp November air. She felt suddenly drained of any energy. A cup of tea would be nice.

The ride to the Reverend Stone's home from the railroad station didn't take very long, and Taylor was glad of that. She was growing colder by the minute. The small parlor was warm, a fire burning cheerfully on the grate. Taylor untied her bonnet, laid it with her gloves on the table near the door, and then sat down in front of the fire. Marilee brought in the tea, and they sipped it in silence, both of them remembering their separate farewells. Taylor regretted her inability to send Jeffrey off in a brighter spirit. Her life seemed so tangled, so mixed up.

She had known the marriage was a mistake almost at once. Jeffrey adored her, almost worshipped her. While this had been just what she needed at first, it soon became an irritant. He worked so hard to make her happy; he wanted so much to make her love him as he loved her. She understood this, but she was unable to give him more than she already had.

Their wedding night had been a disaster. When

Jeffrey put out the light and slipped into the bed beside her, all she could think about was Brent. And Jeffrey *knew* it. He knew her mind was on another man—the father of the child she would bear. He feared the comparison and was awkward in his lovemaking. They both lay awake long into the night, filled with frustration, not touching, each pretending to be asleep but knowing that the other was awake and pretending too.

They never spoke of it, and Jeffrey hadn't made love to her again. Instead, he showered her with affection, waiting on her hand and foot, as if to make up for his failure. She tried to assure him that it was all right, but even she knew it wasn't. She hoped time would make the difference for them just as Jeffrey did. Poor Jeffrey. He was one of her dearest friends. He had always been like a brother to her. He was never meant to have been her husband.

"Don't be too depressed, Taylor," Marilee said, misunderstanding her silence. "Jeffrey will return in fine form. As much as he loves you, he'll be careful. He'll be eager to raise a family with you."

Taylor looked at her blankly, putting down her cup. "This seems as opportune a time as any to tell you, Marilee. I'm going to have a baby."

"But, Taylor, you can't possibly know that after only four days. You'll have to wait . . ." She stopped. Something in Taylor's face told her she was wrong.

"This child is a Lattimer."

"A Lattimer?" Marilee mimicked. "But I thought . . ."

A fragile smile illuminated Taylor's face. "Yes,

Marilee, a Lattimer. A wonderful son to inherit Dorcet Hall and to make his father . . . to make David proud."

Marilee found her voice. "Why, I must say I'm nearly speechless. You took me so by surprise. David's child. I didn't have any idea. I mean, you and I talked about it. I thought you and he weren't . . ." She stopped, blushing. "I mean . . . Well, no matter. A baby! It's wonderful. I'm truly happy for you. When?"

"Late spring," Taylor answered evasively. She could almost see Marilee's mind counting the months since David's death.

"Mmmm, about mid-April at the latest, I'd say."

Taylor didn't reply. She certainly couldn't tell Marilee the baby wouldn't arrive until the end of May. She would just have to hope for some good explanation by the time the baby came.

"Taylor, I just thought of something. You can't stay out there alone. Why don't you move in here with me? Papa and Jeffrey won't be home again from Virginia very soon."

"No!" Taylor nearly shouted. More calmly, she continued, "I want this child born at Spring Haven like I was and like my father was before me. Besides, someone has to keep an eye on the place for Philip."

Marilee looked crestfallen.

"Oh, Marilee, I didn't mean that the way it sounded. Of course, I understand why you're not there. I . . . I . . ."

"It's all right, dear. I know you didn't mean to suggest that I have deserted Spring Haven, my husband's home, but I have. It's time I went back. I'll come stay with you at Spring Haven myself."

"You mustn't feel you have to, Marilee, if you're not ready. I know you must still feel very badly, about . . . about all that happened."

"Well, I'm coming," she said firmly. "You don't even have a reliable lady's maid to care for you since you sold Jenny." She turned to pour more tea. "And I still don't understand whatever possessed you to sell that girl. And to a stranger no less. She was with you since you were both children. You'll never again have as good a servant as Jenny was."

Taylor made no reply, thinking it better to ignore it than to lie further about it.

"I think you'd best stay the night here, and we'll both go to Spring Haven tomorrow," Marilee continued her original train of thought.

Taylor sighed softly. "Very well, Marilee."

She knew that Marilee had made up her mind. Nothing Taylor could say now would change it. Marilee was determined to come take care of her, and she might as well get used to the idea.

Chapter 24

Taking care of Taylor was precisely what Marilee attempted to do, usually without success.

Taylor totally engrossed herself in the management of the large plantation. She spent long hours in her father's study going over the plantation accounts, and her days were spent planning the planting or the harvesting or the selling of one crop or another. Thanksgiving and Christmas were spent quietly at home, and the New Year arrived without fanfare. Some stored bales of cotton were lost to a fire early in the year. More slaves ran away before January was over, and nearly all the livestock still at Dorcet Hall was stolen in February. The army purchased many of their horses in early March, greatly reducing their breeding stock.

Yet throughout these troubled months, Taylor

grew more beautiful than ever before—serene and even radiant. Nothing seemed able to disturb the mantle of contentment which she was covered with as the baby grew inside her. To Taylor, the child was a link with his father, a sign that he had loved her after all. At times, she awoke during the night and reached out to touch him. Discovering the empty bed beside her, her hand would return to rest upon her enlarged belly. The young Lattimer within would once more assure her that everything was all right, and she would drift back to sleep.

It was only when she received letters from Jeffrey that her serenity seemed disturbed. She would find herself again burdened with guilt— guilt over her continued love for Brent, guilt over her child, guilt for marrying Jeffrey when she knew she loved another. She tried to respond lovingly to him in her letters, but she knew she failed. It would take her nearly a week after one of his letters arrived before she could shake off her gloom and resume her normal routine.

These difficult times did not go unobserved. Marilee saw and fretted over them. She loved Jeffrey as the brother she had never had. Taylor was like a sister to her. It seemed to her the best thing that could ever happen for Taylor and Jeffrey to marry. The two dearest people in the world just had to belong together. She tried to ascertain what it was that troubled Taylor and did her best to cheer Taylor up when one of those black clouds dropped around her.

The fruit trees were all in blossom and the flowers were in a glorious blaze. The very air was thickly sweetened by their perfume. The pretty expectant mother sat in the shade of the veranda, a letter in her hands. She felt the usual feelings of guilt rising in her chest as her eyes followed the familiar scrawl across the pages.

My dearest wife,

How I long to be with you! Our regiment is being sent to reinforce the armies of the West. It is my belief that a great battle will soon be fought somewhere in Tennessee, probably near Murfreesboro. The recent troubles near Charleston are attempts by the enemy to stop this reinforcement.

It is with great disappointment that I must forego the pleasure of seeing you before going to Tennessee, but we will not be traveling in that direction, and I must remain with my company. Give my love to Marilee and my howdies to all the servants. Of course, you know my heart is filled to overflowing with love for you and the coming child. I await your confinement with great anxiety. If only I could be with you through you ordeal.

Sometimes, my darling wife, I can almost make myself believe that this camp and this war are all a nightmare, and I will soon wake up and find you with me. If only that were so.

There are many duties yet to be seen to before

I can rest tonight, so I must close. I hope your letter will find me before we leave for the West. You cannot know just what they mean to me, your words upon the paper, knowing they were written with your beautiful hand. I'm grateful that you write more often than I am able to write to you. It's most difficult to go so long without hearing from you. Remember that I am always

Your devoted husband,
Jeffrey

A frown darkened Taylor's eyes as she finished reading. She wondered if they would always go on pretending with each other or if they would learn to face their problems with honesty. For now, she must try to compose a reply that would give encouragement to her soldier husband. She pushed her cumbersome body up from the wicker rocking chair. She would go at once to her desk and write him a letter. Something to brighten his days.

As she turned toward the house, a group of riders came thundering up the avenue. She recognized who they were at once and stiffened as she waited for them to reach the house. The lieutenant, a handsome young man, jumped down from his horse, and with long, confident strides, climbed the steps to meet her.

"Afta'noon, Miz Stone. I hope we find you in good health."

Her answering nod was rather void of the

customary courtesy. "How can we be of service, Lieutenant?" she asked, eyeing the motley group of men waiting below.

"The Confederate Army is in need of more of your fine horses, ma'am. We've come to buy some of your stock."

"Sir, you must be aware that you're already in possession of most of our horses. If you should take any more, there will be no future horses for the Confederacy from our stables." Her voice was tinged with sarcasm. They never *bought* their horses. They gave rock bottom prices for valuable animals, paying with the already nearly worthless Confederate paper.

"I'm sorry, Miz Stone," he said casually, "but my commanding officer was most explicit. If you choose to deny us, we have the authority to impress what animals we need."

Taylor gave him a stony glare. How could the army do this to their own people? Weren't they supposed to be causing hardship to the enemy? She tried to think, tried to find some way to outsmart this man.

"Very well, Lieutenant. If you and your men would like to take some rest in the shade over there, I'll see what we can do for you."

The soldier touched the brim of his hat, which he had never removed, as a sign of agreement. She watched them move over to the grove of trees and dismount before she hurried toward the barn. The army certainly retained the most distasteful men for this job, she thought. From the looks of them, most were poor whites. At best, they were farmers or tradesmen. The lieutenant appeared to have had some education, but his manners lacked any true breeding. With as much dignity as she could muster, she hastened toward the barn.

"Saul?" she called, stopping to let her eyes adjust to the darkness of the barn.

He stepped out of a stall at the end of the long aisle. "Yes'm, Miss Taylor?"

She waited for him to come to her before speaking again. He quickly surmised that something was amiss by how agitated she appeared.

"Saul, the soldiers are here for more horses."

Calmly, as if he didn't understand the seriousness of the situation, he turned and said to Josh, "Quick now, you get Miss Taylor's mare and yearlin' and get 'em to that meadow we talked about. Be careful. There's men out front." Turning back to Taylor, he said, "You distract 'em for a bit, ma'am, and I'll try t'get the best of 'em hid."

Taylor couldn't even nod in agreement she was so surprised. It had never occurred to her to provide hiding places, especially from their own soldiers, but apparently Saul was prepared. Josh had already disappeared out the back of the barn with Tasha and her copper stud colt, Amen-Ra, and Saul wasn't about to waste any more time either. He immediately moved toward the stall holding Sheikh Hazad, their most prized stallion. He grabbed the halter hanging on the wall and approached the wary animal.

"Yes, ma'am. You were certainly wise to start

with the best for us. My general will be most pleased with his new stallion."

Taylor spun around to face the grinning lieutenant. "You are mistaken!" she sputtered. "Sheikh is not for sale."

"Is that right?" he smirked, a lazy smile turning up the corners of his mouth.

"Saul, put Sheikh in the pen and then bring the lieutenant the horses we have available."

She started to walk out of the barn. "Come with me, Lieutenant, and I'll get your men something to quench their thirst."

She saw him join his men before thankfully entering the house. He had apparently decided to let her pick which horses he would take, and she was grateful for at least that concession. She was stopped by Marilee on her way to the kitchen. Her eyes were still sleepy from an afternoon nap.

"Why are those soldiers here?" she asked.

"More horses."

"But we've sold them all the expendable horses. You told them that, didn't you? Surely you aren't going to let them have more?"

"I don't have any choice," Taylor snapped. "I either let them have them or they take them."

Suddenly, Taylor was overwhelmed by a feeling of vulnerability. She was helpless, unable to control any of the events in her life. What was the use of fighting it? She couldn't change anything anyway.

Marilee saw these emotions flicker across Taylor's face and was immediately full of remorse.

She had come here to help Taylor and all she did was cause more worry. Taylor needed her support now, not questions about what she was going to do.

"No," she said, "I suppose we don't have any choice. But we can put forth our best efforts. Come along, I'll help you talk to these men. Surely, they'll listen to reason."

Marilee took Taylor's arm and marched her back to the front door. Taylor made no objections. She hoped there was something they could do. Perhaps Saul had still been able to hide some of the horses.

These hopes were quickly shattered. As they looked out the open door, their eyes fell upon a yard full of milling horses. It looked as if every one of their stallions, including Sheikh, was on a lead line, and many of their best mares and two-year-olds as well. Taylor gasped at the disorganized commotion. They couldn't take all those horses! She picked up her skirts and rushed toward the lieutenant.

"Sir!" she cried. "You have no right to take all these animals."

Ignoring her, he swung into his saddle. She grasped at the reins of his mount to stop him. Scornfully, he looked down at her.

"Madam, let go."

"Lieutenant," she pleaded, "you mustn't take Shiekh Hazad. We must have him here."

"Miz Stone, he's needed more by the army. You'll be sent payment for all of them."

He kicked his horse forward. She stared, unbelieving, as the soldiers began to move the horses out of the yard. A coarse-looking sergeant pulled roughly at Sheikh's halter. Unused to this type of treatment, he reared back, his legs flailing the air, his nostrils flared and eyes wide. The sergeant was nearly unseated. He cursed angrily. Suddenly, a whip was in his hand, appearing out of nowhere. The tip of the lash struck the regal animal across the shoulders, increasing his terror. Again he reared, and again the whip cracked across the chasm. A shrill whinny pierced the air as the whip cut into his chest.

"Stop!" Taylor cried.

Without thinking, she threw herself into the melee. Her hands clawed at his pant leg. Caught unawares, he turned his attention to her assault. Instinctively, his hand came down to break her grip. The butt of the whip hit her across the forehead, stunning her, and she stepped back and into the path of the crazed stallion.

"Taylor!" Marilee screamed.

The sergeant, realizing too late what was happening, tried to reach out and pull her back. A red pain burst across her eyes and she crumpled to the ground. The lead rope was suddenly lax, and Shiekh thundered away to freedom. A triumphant neigh echoed across the courtyard but no one noticed. No one even tried to stop his escape. They were all running toward Taylor who was lying unconscious in the dust.

Marilee gathered her head in her lap. There was

279

no blood, but a large lump was quickly rising on the back of her skull. "Taylor?" she whispered.

She looked up at the lieutenant, now standing over them, a worried expression on his face. "Sir, I hold you directly responsible for whatever happens to my sister-in-law."

A groan interrrupted whatever else she might have said. Her eyes broke away from their angry glare at the lieutenant and returned to Taylor whose hand was now carefully feeling her head. She winced as she found the goose egg. Hesitantly she opened her eyes, looking at the world through glazed vision. She closed them, moaning again.

"Taylor, the . . . the baby. Are you hurt?" Marilee asked anxiously.

"I . . . I think we . . . we're both all . . . right. Jus' . . . just a headache," came the weak reply.

She opened her eyes again. As the lieutenant's face swam into focus above her, the color returned to her cheeks. "Get off my land," she snarled with as much force as she could muster. "If . . . if I ever see you on my property again, I . . . I'll shoot you myself."

He straightened, looking as if he'd been struck.

"Get out," Taylor cried, holding her throbbing head as she lifted it up from Marilee's lap. "Get out *now!*" With that, her eyes fell shut again as her head dropped back into Marilee's lap.

"Let's go, men."

Taylor listened to the hooves pounding the road until it was only a faint thumping in her chest.

Then she forced herself to sit up and look around. Marilee sat on the ground beside her. Saul towered over them both, blocking out the sun's bright rays while Susan and Mima watched from the porch.

"Did they take them all?" she asked Saul as he helped her to her feet.

"No, Missy. Sheikh got away from 'em. I sent Josh t'fetch him."

"Which ones *are* left?"

"Well, your Tasha 'n' Ra are hid out. They only took two of the plow horses, and Apollo is down at the blacksmith's so they missed him. Probably about five mares left plus the yearlin's. That's 'bout it 'cept for that worthless li'l red mare. Nobody ever wants her."

They were slowly walking toward the house now.

"Which one is that, Saul?"

"Oh, you know, Missy. The one Mr. Brent was going t'take north so's t'be less noticed than one of them fancy horses would have been."

Taylor glanced nervously at Marilee, but, of course, there was no need to be nervous. Marilee had no way of knowing it was since the outbreak of war he was talking about so carelessly.

"Mr. Brent planned on gettin' rid of her as soon as he got t'the North, but then you . . ." Suddenly he remembered himself. "Then he changed his mind," he ended abruptly.

But Taylor had ceased listening. Her thoughts had returned to the day she had overheard Brent speaking those words. ". . . get rid of her once we get North."

She stopped still. Good Lord, he had been talking about a *horse!* He had loved her and she had thought the worst of him. She had thrown him away, the most important person in her life.

She turned sharply toward Marilee, but her words froze in her throat as a jagged pain tore around from her back into her stomach. She sucked in her breath and grabbed at Marilee's arm as she doubled over. She felt something warm trickling down her legs.

"The baby!" she gasped.

Saul's strong arms had scooped her up before the words were hardly spoken. His long, strong legs carried her quickly into the house and up the stairs with Mima and Susan both following in his wake. Taylor looked up at Mima as Saul laid her on her bed.

"It's too soon, Mima. The baby. It's coming too soon."

Mima's black face leaned down close to her own. "Don't you worry none, Missy. I been seein' t'birthin's roun' these parts for nigh on forty years. This hyar baby's goin' t'be jus' fine."

"Too soon," Taylor repeated in a whisper as another pain gripped her.

Marilee took her hand. "Shhhh, Taylor. Don't fret. The baby's not too early. He was due to arrive any day now."

Taylor shook her head slowly but said no more. Now Susan was bending over her. "Docta's been sent for, Missy." To Marilee, she said, "You best clear out now, Miss Mar'lee. Miss Taylor don't look like she tends t'wait for no docta. That babe's in a hurry."

It was true. The pains were coming faster and faster.

Taylor grasped Marilee's hand tightly. "Let her stay, Susan," she pleaded. Beads of perspiration popped out on her forehead. She tried to pray that the child would be all right. That he wouldn't be too little to survive. So many babies died. This child must live. She tensed with the next spasm.

"Easy, Missy," Mima scolded gently. "Don't go fightin' dis. You gotta let your body do its work."

As the pains increased in intensity and frequency, Taylor began to slip into a semi-conscious state. She imagined that David and Jeffrey stood on each side of her. Both were frowning angrily at her. They seemed to be speaking but she couldn't hear anything they said.

"I'm sorry, David," she mumbled. "You really don't mind that they'll think he's yours, do you? You would love him if you could stay. You'd be a wonderful grandfather."

David shook his head sternly and turned away from her. Next she looked at Jeffrey.

"Oh, Jeffrey. You said you'd love him anyway. He can't help our mistakes. Perhaps we can learn to be happy, to be a family. Please don't hurt him."

Jeffrey turned away too.

"Brent!" she cried as a fresh pain tore through her. "Come for us. We need you. Your son needs you. Help us. Brent. Oh, Brent. I'm so sorry. Oh, Brent."

David and Jeffrey turned to look down at her again. She still couldn't hear what they said, but she suddenly knew what they meant to do. They were going to take away her baby. They were going to steal him and then she would have nothing.

"No! No, you can't have him. He's mine. He's Brent's. You'll not take him. Jeffrey, David. Don't. Go away. Leave us be. He's mine. I love him. I love him. Please, don't do this. Don't make me lose him too. I love him. Oh, Brent. Brent . . ."

She whimpered as a searing hot pain clutched at her body. She rose part way off her bed. Through her fogged brain, she could hear someone talking to her, calling out her name.

"Harder, Miss Taylor. Push harder."

She *did* push. She held her breath and bore down with all her might. A groan slipped out through her dry lips, building, along with the pain, to a crescendo that filled the room with its sound.

Taylor gulped at the air, her eyes tightly shut, waiting for the next pain to overtake her. Suddenly, she heard a baby's cry. It was over. She opened her eyes and tried to find where Mima stood with the baby.

"Is . . . he . . . all . . . right? Is he . . . big enough?" she croaked, her throat parched as she panted for more air.

Marilee squeezed her hand. Her voice was

284

warm and filled with the wonder of new life. "The baby's a little small. I'm afraid there is one definite problem with *him*, Taylor."

"No. Oh, please, no."

Marilee smiled, her familiar giggle reassuring Taylor. "*He* is a girl. You have a daughter."

"A . . . a girl?"

Mima placed the bundle in Taylor's arms. Cautiously, she pushed away the soft blanket in which the child was swaddled. She was so very tiny. Her head was covered with raven black hair, as soft as down. Taylor continued to remove the blanket until she could see all of her baby. The tiny hands and feet were perfectly formed. How could anything so small, so helpless, and so beautiful belong to her?

"She's beautiful, Taylor," Marilee whispered, mirroring her own thoughts.

The new mother unbuttoned her nightgown and held her child against her breast. The little one continued to cry for a moment. Then, age-old instinct prevailed. Her little mouth clamped down over the nipple and loud sucking sounds filled the room. Taylor's eyes were wide in awe as she gazed at the tiny bit of humanity in her arms.

"She is lovely, isn't she?"

Marilee nodded. "What will you name her?"

"I haven't any idea what to call her. I was so sure she would be a boy."

"Perhaps you should try to contact her father. Maybe he would have a suggestion."

"Her father?" Taylor asked, turning so sharply toward Marilee that the baby lost her hold on the breast. She objected strongly, and Taylor helped her resume nursing before speaking to Marilee.

"Oh, you mean Jeffrey. Well, I . . ."

"No, I mean her father. I mean Brent."

Taylor dropped her eyes to the baby's soft head, silence her only answer.

"Taylor, what about Jeffrey? Does he . . ."

"He knows. He knew about it all. I thought Brent didn't love me after all. But he did. Maybe he still does. Jeffrey still wanted to marry me, even after I knew I was carrying Brent's child. I should have said no to him. It was unfair to both of us."

They watched the baby give up her sucking as she fell asleep, exhausted after her traumatic extrance into the world. Faint mewing sounds could occasionally be heard in the otherwise still room.

"What now?"

"I'm married to Jeffrey, Marilee. I have no choices to make. I have my daughter now. I . . . we'll be happy."

They left her alone at last. She slept undisturbed, without dreaming, for several hours. The room was filled with lengthening shadows when she awoke. The baby was still sleeping peacefully in the crib beside her bed. Taylor looked at her in wonder as she carefully picked her up, drawing her into bed beside her.

"You really are mine," she whispered in awe. "Only happiness will be allowed to touch your life, my daughter. You will grow up knowing only love and beauty and you will marry the man of your dreams as you ought. You will be wiser, so much wiser than I. You will never make the mistakes your mother made."

She kissed her soft forehead and rocked the child gently. Awakened, the baby opened her eyes and gazed up at her mother for the first time. Those eyes! *His* eyes. Taylor felt a tear slip down her cheek. How she loved his golden eyes. And now they looked at her again. To others they would seem the same, nondescript color of most babies' eyes, but she knew better. The promise was there. They *were* his eyes.

"Brent. Oh, Brent, she's beautiful. I wish you could see her. I wish you could even know she exists. I'll try to love her enough for both of us. I promise. Oh, my darling, how I miss you."

Kissing the baby again, she whispered, "You are my memory of Brent, of your father. Brent . . . Yes, that's it. I'll call you Brenetta after your father."

As if pleased by this decision, Brenetta closed her eyes and slept again. Mother and child were cloaked in the night's darkness, yet Taylor's heart was filled with the light of a mother's joy. Her tomorrows would be happier because of Brenetta.

Chapter 25

Taylor looked over her shoulder at her reflection in the mirror. She turned slowly before the glass, sucking in her breath and tightening her stomach muscles. Seeing her, Mima chuckled. Taylor shot her a scathing glance and then continued her scrutiny. Although she was really quite slender, in her own eyes she was still too fat. She was impatient for the return of her tiny waist, which Mima had unpleasantly informed her would never be the same.

Mima was humming softly to the baby again, and Taylor walked over to Brenetta's cradle for another look at her sleeping child. Mima grinned merrily at her. Being appointed the baby's nurse had restored the displaced housekeeper's good nature as well as her importance among the other household staff. Now, she thought, she was even more important than Susan.

Taylor patted the diapered bottom lightly and kissed the soft head. A feeling of well-being flowed through her veins every time she looked at her.

" 'Scuse me, Miss Taylor," Susan said as she tapped on the open door. "Miss Lizabeth Reed has come callin'."

Taylor lifted her eyebrow. "Really? She and her mother were just here two days ago. Well, tell her I'll be right down. Prepare a tea tray please."

Taylor ran a quick hand over her hair before starting for the stairs. She was more than a little surprised that Lizabeth had come again so soon. It wasn't as if they were close friends. Lizabeth was four years her senior and had always been quite aloof whenever they were among the same group of people.

As she entered the drawing room, she placed a friendly smile on her lips. "Why, Lizabeth. How nice of you to call again so soon. Did your mother come with you?"

"No, not this time. Is Marilee going to join us?"

Taylor sat down in a flossy chintz chair. "She's out visiting today herself. Would you like some tea?"

"Yes, thank you."

The amenities over with, the conversation ceased as they sipped their refreshments. The silence was not companionable as between two intimates, but instead was strained. Taylor grew apprehensive and told herself to cease being such

289

a silly goose.

"Is the baby awake?" Lizabeth inquired finally.

"Brenetta's sleeping right now, but as soon as she wakes, I'll have her brought down if you'd like."

Lizabeth put her tea cup on her lap. Her eyes seemed cool as she turned them upon Taylor. "I meant to ask you the other day. Where on earth did you get the name Brenetta? It's so unusual. Did *Jeffrey* help you pick out the name?"

"My daughter is named for a member of David's family," Taylor answered calmly—and truthfully.

"And Jeffrey had no say in the matter? How strange," Lizabeth persisted.

Taylor eyed her visitor warily, wondering just what was behind all these questions. "Jeffrey left it up to me to name the baby."

"Well, I suppose he really doesn't care," Lizabeth said with a thin smile. "It's not his child after all."

Taylor felt a rising anger warming her breast as she replied, "Of course, he cares about the baby."

Lizabeth snorted.

Taylor felt a sudden loathing for this plain, skinny woman who had seemingly come just to antagonize her. "Just what was it you came to say, Lizabeth?"

"I would have thought you were bright enough to figure it out, Taylor," she said as she stood up. "If it weren't for you, Jeffrey would have married me."

Rising as had her guest, Taylor stared at her in amazement.

"Oh, don't give me that innocent look, Taylor Bellman. Everyone knew our parents meant for us to marry. It was simply an accepted fact. Jeffrey . . . he was a little confused after he went off to the university, but he would have proposed to me soon enough. But the war came."

Taylor found her voice. "But, Lizabeth. Jeffrey didn't want . . . he had no intentions of. . ."

An unflattering color rose in Lizabeth's pinched face. "Yes!" she screamed, cutting off Taylor's sentence. "He and I *would* have been married. But somehow you tricked him. I don't know what you did, but I know it was all your doing. And you, all the time carrying another man's child. It's not decent, I tell you. I would have given him sons. *His* sons."

"Lizabeth!"

"You'll be sorry you stole him from me, Taylor. Someday, you'll pay for my sorrow."

This was all really too unfair, Taylor thought as her anger flared. "I think you should leave now, *Miss* Reed."

Lizabeth, however, didn't budge. "I would have raised his children in *his* home, children with *his* name. I would have been mistress of Southside. You . . . you don't even *live* there!"

The anger had disappeared as quickly as it had come. It was all so senseless, so pointless. Taylor sighed and replied, "I don't have to explain my actions to you, Lizabeth, but I'll tell you anyway.

Jeffrey plans to rebuild Dorcet Hall for my daughter to inherit. His parents aren't old. He isn't needed there, and he's not their oldest son. His mother is the mistress of Southside, so I'm not needed there either." She moved as if to touch Lizabeth's arm in sympathy, but the other woman stepped sharply back, and Taylor withdrew her hand.

"You're right about one thing, Lizabeth," Taylor continued softly. "I don't deserve him. He's a good man. Too good. He loves Brenetta without even seeing her, even though she isn't his own."

"If he loves her so much," Lizabeth said acidly, "why didn't he give her his name?"

"That was my own decision. Her father would have rejoiced had he known of her and would have loved her as he loved me. She deserves his name and he deserves her to wear it."

The truth in her voice and in her words somehow broke through Lizabeth's jealous tirade, stopping her retort in her throat. Confused now, she walked quickly from the room, Taylor following quietly. Lizabeth entered her carriage hastily, but before the door was closed, she looked back at Taylor standing on the veranda. She looked as if she would speak again, but pulled the door shut and ordered the driver to move on.

Thoughtfully, Taylor watched the carriage disappear down the avenue of oaks. It had never occurred to her that Lizabeth Reed had ever even *thought* of getting married, let alone that she would think Taylor had stolen Jeffrey from her. Wryly, she acknowledged that she had told the truth in everything she said about Brenetta and her father. Perhaps that was some sort of consolation for the day's unpleasant turn.

She tried to shake off the gloom that Lizabeth's visit had left as she returned to the house, but her mind would not let go. To think that Lizabeth loved Jeffrey. And Jeffrey? Had he really grown up thinking they were to marry? Had Dr. Reed and Charles Stone really thought it such a good match, or was it all just Lizabeth's imagination?

She sat down on the sofa in the drawing room and tried to piece her thoughts together. Jeffrey was raised at Southside, a magnificent plantation southwest of Bellville. His father, the Reverend Stone's older brother, and his mother had raised their sons to be planters. The education they received was a necessary break in the more important business of planting, but both boys were naturally expected to return to Georgia—first helping their father and then establishing their own plantations.

Taylor had seen Jeffrey frequently when they were growing up. She had always considered the older boy her friend. After all, he was Marilee's cousin. She remembered how surprised she had been by his proclamation of love. It had never occurred to her that he might fall in love with her, but even more impossible seemed the thought of him marrying Lizabeth Reed.

Taylor shook her head slowly. How very little a person knew about their friends or even their own family. She wondered now how Jeffrey's parents really felt about his marriage to her. Had they been disappointed with his choice? She had never even considered it before. Jeffrey and she had visited Southside for two days after they were married, and Taylor had felt most welcome. Now she was unsure.

"Miss Taylor," Mima called from the head of the stairs. "That babe o' yours says it sho' is feedin' time, and you're t'get yo'self up d'rectly."

"I wonder," Taylor whispered to herself as she went up the stairs to the nursery. "Will anything in my life ever be as it should be? Whatever happened to my dreams of marrying my Prince Charming and living happily ever after? Does it ever happen for anyone?" And then she wondered how many other lives were as mixed up and twisted as hers. How many of the people she knew spent their lives wondering what could have been if only they had made a different choice at some point in their lives? Would hers be any better if she had made different decisions? Would she be happier? She opened the nursery door and looked in upon an angry, red-faced, and hungry Brenetta.

No. Any decision which would have kept her from holding this child in her arms as she did now would not have been worth it. No matter what else might be awry in her life, Brenetta made it all worthwhile.

Chapter 26

The South reeled under the weight of disaster following disaster. Stonewall Jackson, known as the "first man of the Confederacy," died at Chancellorsville, Virginia in May, shot accidently by a Confederate soldier. In June, Rosecran's campaign in Tennessee sent a steady stream of wounded into Atlanta. The news from Gettysburg reached the South, the name becoming synonomous with horror and loss in the hearts of thousands. Thirty-five hundred Confederate soldiers had died in three days of fighting. Nearly fifteen thousand of their men were wounded, many to die later or be crippled for the rest of their lives, and over thirteen thousand soldiers were missing when the fighting was over. The latest blow was the surrender of Vicksburg to General Grant. Brave Vicksburg. She had fought long and hard.

Amid this gloomy pall, people were only too glad for an excuse for celebration. The church, therefore, was packed on July 19, 1863 for the baptism of Taylor Stone's daughter, Brenetta Bellman Lattimer. The air was hot and still inside the tiny Presbyterian church, and there was barely room to wave a fan before one's face to keep from passing out. Still, it was a happy, though solemn, occasion.

After the service, guests were invited to the Reverend Stone's home outside Bellville. The house was too small to hold such a large gathering, so tables and chairs had been set up on the lawn. Marilee, acting as hostess in her father's absence, insisted that Taylor merely enjoy the day and let her take care of the details.

Three-month-old Brenetta charmed everyone, smiling prettily at whoever held her and chortling when spoken to. Everyone commented on how like her mother she looked except for her odd-colored eyes. Taylor had one bad moment when someone recalled how different they were from David's gray ones.

"Oh, remember, Tom," Eugenia said. "Mr. Lattimer's son . . . now what was his name? . . He had the same colored eyes as his little half-sister. Well, nearly the same color, I think."

Taylor's sigh of relief was hidden behind her fan.

The day proceeded without another hitch, and Taylor bade farewell to the last guest in the afternoon. She sank wearily into a rocker on the porch. Marilee followed suit in another chair nearby.

"Whew," Marilee gasped. "What a day! Brenetta must have been welcomed by everyone in the country."

"Everyone that's still around, anyway," Taylor said . . . *and Lizabeth Reed,* she thought to herself.

Marilee nodded. "Speaking of who's left, Taylor, there's something I need to tell you. I've decided to go to Atlanta. There are so many injured there now and I want to do something to help. You don't need me here anymore . . . if you ever did."

Taylor started to protest.

"No. No, I didn't mean it that way, Taylor. Besides, with Philip in Tennessee now I might be able to see him more often if I were in Atlanta. I could take the train up to Dalton like so many of the ladies do and meet him there. Mrs. Mason has said I could come to stay with her as long as I wish."

"Of course," Taylor responded thoughtfully, "you must go if it's what you think best. Are you sure, though? After all, this is your home. We don't know how long this war will go on, and Atlanta may not even be safe for long."

Marilee nodded firmly. "Oh, yes. I'm sure. All I've done to help the cause is wrap a few bandages and sew a few shirts. I'm certain that's important, but I want to do more. Every day the

297

Yankees take more land from us. Taylor, and kill more of our brave men. There must be more that I can do for those who are giving so much to protect us from those infidels. And I'm going to do whatever I can to help."

Surprising even herself, Taylor suddenly answered, "Then I'm going with you. I want to help too."

"But, Taylor," Marilee protested, taken off-guard, "the plantation. The baby."

"Oh, pish posh. You know as well as I do that Saul can run Spring Haven with no help from me, and Mima can care for Brenetta as easily in Atlanta as here. It's settled, Marilee. I'm going along."

The small caravan left for Atlanta on a hot morning in July. Taylor and Marilee rode in the buggy, pulled by Apollo, who was thoroughly insulted by this assignment. Two of their large plow horses pulled the wagon carrying Mima and Brenetta as well as all the luggage. Taylor wished she could bring Tasha but the threat of her being impressed, or even stolen, had forced her to leave her behind. A close eye would have to be kept on the horses they had as it was.

The road was dusty. There had been no rain for several weeks now. The crops they passed were already suffering from the drought. Taylor wondered what the army would be eating if the rains didn't come soon.

They met a large number of travelers moving

away from Atlanta and visited for a short while with a family of refugees from Tennessee while the horses rested. His wife standing close at his side, as if afraid he would suddenly disappear, and his children sitting quiet and wide-eyed in the wagon, the head of the family told them how he had been ordered to take "the oath" with rifle butts staring him in the face. He had escaped while the Yankees were plundering his home, destroying whatever they found that was useless for their own needs or pleasures. After the soldiers were gone, he had crept back to get his family. They had moved carefully to avoid capture until they were inside Confederate lines, reaching Marietta after several terrified, wearisome weeks. Then they had moved on to Atlanta. People had been most kind to them, but there were so many soldiers and refugees, it was hard to find food or lodgings. When they did find food, it was mostly unaffordable. Milk at forty cents a quart. Chickens near six or seven dollars a piece. Beefsteak almost five dollars a pound.

"I was a wealthy man before the war," he finished. "Now I'm ruined. I have nothing."

"Where are you going now?" Marilee asked gently.

A futile shrug. "We're on our way to Athens. My wife has an aunt there who will take the family in. Then I'm going to join up. If only I'd . . ." Again he shrugged.

As they parted company, Taylor looked behind her and watched the tired family moving slowly down the road. Suddenly she felt like crying, like weeping until she could cry no more.

Taylor scarcely recognized Atlanta. The population had nearly doubled since her last visit. The streets were filled with people and carriages everywhere. Josh hurried the horse through the congested streets to the Mason home. Taylor looked at the white house with affection. It was still as lovely as she remembered, the yard a little less well-kept and the siding needing to be whitewashed, but it was still a most elegant home. It was hard to believe all that had happened since that night just over two years ago when she was here last.

Sophia Mason stepped out onto the porch, shading her eyes with an open hand. Her hair was graying and deep lines etched themselves around her eyes from perpetual worry. Recognizing her guests, she called out a greeting and hurried forward to meet them.

"Marilee! Taylor! You're here at last. How glad I am to have you." She hugged each of them. "Come in. Come in. Jack will show your servants where to put your things. Mr. Mason is so busy with the Home Guard. Those not in the army must be prepared to defend their city, you know. He won't be home for several more hours I'm afraid. He'll be so glad to see that you're here."

Rattling on about one thing and then another, she led them into the parlor, a small, friendly room on the east end of the house. Shaded by large trees, the room was much cooler than the rest of the home.

"You'll forgive the disorder," Sophia continued. "They have impressed many of our servants to work on the fortifications outside the city—dreadful looking things—and Mr. Mason donates our house servants several days a week to work in the hospitals. Such inconveniences we have to put up with these days, but it's all quite necessary, of course."

Taylor and Marilee exchanged concerned glances. This nervous chatter was so unlike the Sophia Mason they had known since childhood.

"Mrs. Mason," Marilee said softly, "we aren't going to be causing you any hardship, are we?"

"Oh, my, no! It will do me a world of good having you here." She emitted a sharp laugh. "George hopes it may distract me a little. I get quite distraught with the Yankees breathing down on us like they are, everything so different, you know, than before the war."

"Mrs. Mason, don't you worry," Taylor said quickly. "The Yankees won't even reach Georgia soil. Our army will see to that."

"But they've done it already. Just last April that awful Colonel Streight nearly reached Rome."

Marilee moved to sit beside the agitated woman. "But, Mrs. Mason, General Forrest stopped him and captured all sixteen hundred of his men. Surely that must show you that General Bragg won't let them have even a bit of Georgia soil."

"But he's always in retreat!"

There was no arguing with her. Many Southerners wondered about the policy of falling back to gain a stronger position, something that never seemed to happen. Neither Marilee or Taylor could think of a reply, and silence filled the room.

Suddenly the older woman shrugged off her dark cloak of depression. "Taylor, I must see your daughter. From all reports, I hear she is the prettiest child ever born."

"Now, how can I disagree with that?" Taylor laughed as she rose from her chair. "I can't help but concur. Come. We'll go see her."

Taylor lay awake long after the rest of the house had fallen into silent slumber. She knew instinctively that her life had entered a new phase and that things would be very different for her for a long time to come. She wondered what her tomorrows would bring.

As she closed her eyes, she could see clearly in her mind the family of Tennessee refugees walking down the road to Athens, moving away from her. They were joined by another family, and then another, until there were thousands of people moving, beaten and weary, down a road of despair.

Chapter 27

Taylor waved at the flies over the young man's face. It was a useless gesture. There was no ridding themselves of the swarms of flies in this wretched room. You brushed one away and ten more took its place. If there was even a little breeze, it might not seem quite so oppressive, but the day held no promise of any such relief. The hospital room, once part of a government office building, was so stuffy it seemed a great effort to even draw a breath.

But it was the smell that bothered her the most. Taylor knew she would never get used to the particular odor of flesh laid bare. Every day when she arrived, she was forced to brace herself once more to face the reek of blood, disinfectant, and other miscellaneous smells.

The soldier beside her had received a wound to

the head. His eyes were bandaged, and she knew the doctors did not expect him to regain his sight. He was just a mere boy, eighteen at the most.

"What else can I do for you, Henry?" she asked him.

"Miz Stone, would you be so kind as t'write my ma for me? I shore would like t'let her know I'm all right. She's shore t'be powerful worried 'bout me."

"Of course. I have some paper right here with me. You just tell me what to put down and I'll write it for you."

"You tell her that it ain't nothin' too serious but I cain't be writin' myself, and I got the he'p of one of 'lanta's nice ladies . . . and then put down your name, Miz Stone. You tell her for me that I'm gettin' real good care and that I think I'll be mustered out soon so's she can be 'spectin' me home to he'p with the farm."

Taylor wrote furiously to keep up with him.

"Miz Stone, you ever been over t'the Carolinas? Our place, it's in the hill country up from the Savannah, not too far from Augusta. Ma'am, it's real purty country. It's hard land t'farm but it's ours and it's purty. I . . . I shore do hope I gets t'see it agin."

The break in his voice brought tears to her eyes. She swallowed hard to repress the corresponding quiver in her voice. "Of course you'll see it again. And soon too. Didn't you just tell your mother you'd be out of here soon?"

"Ah, Miz Stone. You know better. Them doctors cain't save the sight of a man what took powder like I did. I can feel it. I ain't never seein' nothin' agin. I may be goin' home, but I ain't goin' t'be seein' it."

She couldn't say anything more. As she sat there, he seemed to fall asleep. She whispered his name, but he didn't reply. She picked up her basket and moved on among the cots and pallets, speaking an encouraging word here, taking someone's hand there, trying to relieve whatever misery she could. Marilee was likewise employed on the other side of the room.

"Mrs. Stone, would you come here please?"

Taylor turned to see the blood-speckled coat of Major Jones, the army surgeon who cared for this room full of patients. He was standing beside a new arrival. His face was grim and foreboding, and she went over to him filled with trepidation.

"Mrs. Stone, I need your help. All my aides are busy downstairs at the moment. I just removed this man's right arm. There was a great deal of infection, but with a little luck, we'll save his life. If you would just stay here with him until he comes to. Call me when he does." He turned quickly, muttering to himself, "If I just had the right supplies. Do they think I can help these men with so little?"

Taylor pulled up a stool beside the cot, her eyes averted. She knew her face must be quite pale as she summoned up her strength to look at him. A moan drew her eyes to his unconscious, pain-ravaged face. Beads of perspiration dotted his forehead and spasms of pain caused him to move restlessly on his bed. Taking a cool rag, she leaned closer to wipe his brow. Good Lord! It was Robert Stone!

She glanced quickly across the room, afraid she had cried her dismay aloud, but Marilee was reading to another patient, unaware of the newest sufferer in their midst or his relation to her.

Taylor turned back to her brother-in-law. Leaning close to his ear, she whispered, "It's all right, Robert. You're safe now. It's me. Taylor. We'll take good care of you. Be strong. Be strong, Robert."

She wiped the sweat from his face as she spoke. As if his unconscious brain understood what she was saying, he ceased his moaning and appeared to sink into a deep sleep.

More than the stump of an arm she knew was hidden under the sheet, it was his face that told the story of the last two years. The lines etched deeply around his eyes should belong only to old men who have lived long and seen much. They didn't belong on a man only twenty-nine this summer. His hair, once a deep auburn color, was streaked with gray, and he was extremely thin. She remembered how he had looked the day he and Jeffrey and the others had come whooping up to Dorcet Hall to tell them of the start of the war. Oh, they were all so handsome, so gallant. Were these the same men with their pain-worn faces, mutilated bodies, and ragged souls who had filled those first exciting weeks and months with romantic and heroic visions?

She looked away from him. Marilee had to be

told.

"Marilee, could you come here for a moment?"

Marilee lifted her eyes from the book she was reading, said something to the soldier, and then got up, weaving her way between the beds to Taylor.

"Marilee," Taylor said hesitantly. "Robert's here. He's hurt."

"Robert Stone?"

Taylor pointed to him. "It's Robert. He's lost an arm."

Marilee sat down on his other side, her heart feeling like lead. Never did she see one of these injured men without imagining Philip in their place. Now it really was a loved one before her, yet he seemed a stranger. Could this be her cousin?

When Marilee had decided to come to Atlanta, she had had no idea it would be like this. At first, the doctors had forbidden the women to help in the hospitals. The belief that only women of "shady character" became nurses was stubbornly held to. Finally, for want of enough help and out of sheer desperation, the ladies were allowed to visit with the injured men, bringing at least miniscule comfort to them. Eventually, they were each doing some sort of nursing duties and the original prejudice was hidden behind closed doors in the doctors' minds for the time being. But there was so little they could do to really help, so helpless to stop the suffering.

Now her own cousin lay on a cot before her very eyes, minus an arm, and she felt her mind go blank. She couldn't help him. She couldn't help any of them. They would go on fighting, blowing away parts of a man, parts of their country, and she couldn't help any of them.

His eyelids fluttered, and he moaned again. Slowly, he opened his eyes and looked about. Still somewhat drugged by the morphine, he didn't recognize either of his female attendants at first.

"Water," he whispered.

Taylor went quickly for a cup of cool water, sending word to Dr. Jones that the patient was now awake. Upon returning, she placed the tin cup against his lips while Marilee braced his head. He drank sparingly. With a sigh, he lay back down.

More lucid now, he looked at the two women again. "Marilee?" he said slowly, as if certain it couldn't be true.

She nodded, tears beginning to roll down her cheeks as she smiled tremulously.

He turned. "Taylor?"

"Yes, Robert. It's really me."

"Where am I? Are we at home?"

Marilee kissed his grizzled jaw. "No, dear. We're in Atlanta. You're in a hospital here."

His face blanched. "They ... they took my arm?" His left hand grasped the light sheet and threw it off, revealing the bloody bandage where his arm had been. All three stared at it in horror.

Suddenly, the room was filled with a sound such as Taylor had never heard before. The cry, coming from Robert's innermost being, was filled with the haunting knowledge of pain and despair, of all the lost future and wasted past. The lament seemed to make its way into Taylor's very soul, leaving her cold, stripped bare of any protection

308

against such anguish.

When it stopped, the room was deathly still. Most of those in this room understood all too well the meaning of such an eerie wail. Many would live with the sound in their hearts for the rest of their lives.

Never again did they hear Robert complain. He mourned the loss of his arm privately and emerged from his intense but brief time of grief determined to meet life's challenges under the new terms fate had thrust upon him. In a remarkably short time, he was out of his bed visiting with other occupants of the hospital. He laughed and cried with them and bade farewell to new friends daily as they went home or back to the front . . . or died.

He left the hospital on a warm afternoon in mid-September. Soldiers had been pouring into the city all day and dust from the heavy traffic filled the air. No rain had fallen in two months, and now even the shrubbery was covered with finely pulverized red clay. They saw many men on their way to join Bragg's forces. They also saw a large group of blue belly prisoners near the car shed as they drove toward the Mason home.

Mr. and Mrs. Mason were both there to greet Robert, and Sophia hurried him up to his room immediately. She wouldn't hear of anything but that he get into bed at once and allow them to take care of him properly.

"Honestly, Mrs. Mason, that's all Marilee and Taylor have done for weeks now."

It was a total waste of words. He had to get into bed. Once there, he was served biscuits and red eye gravy which he ate under three pairs of very watchful eyes. When he was finished, he asked Taylor to let him see Brenetta.

"She's all Jeffrey has talked about for months, you know."

Mima proudly brought in her charge and placed her on Robert's lap. Brenetta stared at him seriously for a moment, and then, deciding he was definitely a friend, broke into a captivating grin.

"Hello, there," he said to her, returning her smile. "You should have seen your husband, Taylor, after he got your letter telling him of Brenetta's arrival. We were on the way to Tennessee when it reached us. Yes, sir, he was one proud papa."

"Do you suppose there's a chance of him getting a furlough soon?" Taylor asked as she watched Robert and her daughter together. Strangely enough, she suddenly felt it very important for Jeffrey to get to meet Brenetta.

"Not unless the fighting dies down. Now that Rosecrans holds Chattanooga, they may hold up for the winter. Then, I imagine they'll let the men have a furlough, a few at a time."

Marilee had been sitting quietly beside Taylor. Now she spoke up thoughtfully. "Robert, if we aren't strong enough to keep them from taking our strongholds, however shall we drive them out once they have taken them?"

The question lay heavily in the air. It needed no reply. Each one present already knew the answer.

"Miz Stone, thar's a soldier at the door askin' fer you."

"Who is it, Ellie?"

"I don' know, ma'am, but he's powerful dirty."

Taylor got up. "I'll be back soon. Don't let Brenetta tire you out, Robert. It's your first day out of the hospital, remember." She turned to the young maid. "Where is he, Ellie?"

"I tol' him t'wait on da porch, ma'am. Massa George is out 'n' I didn't wanta lets him in. He's powerful dirty 'n' I don't trus' him, none."

"Perhaps he needs some help, or maybe I'm needed at the hospital," Taylor said.

Ellie had closed and bolted the door before she had gone to get her, and Taylor was amused by Ellie's aversion to a dirty soldier, thinking she should be used to them by now, the city was so full of them. She thought at first that he had left without seeing her. Then she caught sight of a butternut uniform at the end of the veranda. He was sitting on the top step facing the gardens. His back was rounded with fatigue and a bedraggled slouch hat covered his head. He didn't hear her approaching, and she wondered if he had fallen asleep while sitting there.

As she came closer, she could see the epaulets on his uniform. "Major? What can I do for you?" she asked, gently touching his shoulder.

He jumped up quickly, his body immediately tense and alert as he spun around.

"Jeffrey!"

Chapter 28

"Is it really you?" she cried, throwing her arms impulsively around his neck.

His hands, red and calloused, took hold of her forearms, disengaging himself from her spontaneous embrace and holding her back from him.

"It's me, all right," he answered.

Yes, it was him. The red hair, the green eyes, the slight build. Yet something was different about him. His hair was longer. His eyes were without their sparkle. His body, though slim, had been finely honed into a wiry endurance machine. Yet the real difference was something else, something still indefinable.

"How are you, Taylor?"

"I'm fine, Jeffrey," she answered. "I haven't had a letter from you in two months. I was worried. Did you get my mail?"

"No. I haven't been receiving mail."

He looked around him slowly, his eyes squinting against the afternoon glare. She waited for his lead, wondering that he didn't hug or kiss her.

"This place hasn't changed too much," he said finally. "I'm glad."

She nodded silently, still waiting. Suddenly he smiled and pulled her to him, kissing her cheek softly.

"I'm a bit travel-stained and would like a chance to clean up. Then we can talk."

Again she nodded. "Jeffrey, did you know that Robert is here?"

"Robert?"

"Yes. He was injured, Jeffrey. Badly."

His jaw tightened, the muscles in his shoulders stiffening as he asked, "Is he going to live?"

"Yes. It's his arm. He lost his right arm."

He grimaced, then sighed. "I'll see him after my bath."

An inexplicable fear nestled in her heart as the day progressed. Though she searched for the cause of her anxiety brought on by the subtle changes she felt had occurred, she searched in vain.

After Jeffrey had his bath and dressed in a clean uniform, they went together to Robert's room. Taylor sat silently beside Jeffrey as the brothers visited. He held her hand tightly the entire time but seldom turned his gaze upon her. Adeptly, he steered the conversation away from the war. They talked about Robert going home to

313

Southside and how he would cope as a one-armed planter. They discussed crops and the weather, their parents and their friends. Finally, exhausted from his first day out of the hospital, Robert drifted off to sleep.

Quietly, they slipped out of the room. "The baby now," Jeffrey said as he carefully shut the door behind them.

Taylor nervously led the way to the nursery, suddenly filled with uncertainties. Mima flashed her toothless grin as they entered her domain.

"Good t'see you, Massa Jeffrey. Miss Brenetta, she jus' woke up from a good nap and is waitin' t'see ya."

Jeffrey approached the crib cautiously. The baby, clutching her feet with her fingers and babbling merrily to herself, looked surprised by the appearance of this new face and shocking red hair. They seemed to size each other up, green eyes staring into round golden-flecked brown ones. Brenetta was the first to voice her opinion. She released her toes and lifted her arms toward him, a squeal followed by a giggle bubbling forth from her lips. Like a lantern just lit in a dark room, Jeffrey's face came alive as he lifted the infant from her crib.

"So I'm something to laugh at, am I?" he laughed with her, holding her high above his head.

Taylor observed them from her station by the door, her husband and her daughter now sitting on the rug on the nursery floor, Jeffrey making faces and Brenetta obliging him with more

314

squeals of delight. It was good to see the sparkle return, to see him as he had been before the war, before all the hurt began. She felt warmed and comforted by the familial scene.

When they left the nursery, Jeffrey looked at Taylor wistfully, becoming once again touched with that same quality of change she was unable to define, and said, "She's so beautiful. Just like you, Taylor. I wish I could be around to watch every minute of her growing up. I wish . . ." His voice trailed off.

Again, uneasiness tugged at her heart.

After a pleasant supper with Marilee and the Masons, they took the buggy, riding silently in the cool September evening, stopping atop a rolling hillside overlooking Atlanta. As if for their benefit, a full moon dressed the earth with white. Jeffrey was again holding her hand tightly in his own.

"It looks very ordinary and quiet from here, doesn't it?" he said softly.

"Mmmmm."

The rooftops of Atlanta were all lined with silver, a gift from the moon. Lights from the buildings and from the town's gas lamps seemed spun about with golden filigree. Overcrowded hospitals and soldier-filled streets could not be seen from this vantage point. In fact, it was easy to imagine they didn't exist at all.

"Taylor, there's something I must tell you before . . . before I go back." He turned toward her but his face was lost in the shadows of the

315

buggy.

"What is it, Jeffrey? What's been troubling you?" She wished she could see his face.

"I leave early in the morning. This night will probably be the last time I'm with you for a long time."

"Jeffrey . . ." she began. He sounded so ominous.

"No, Taylor. Let me talk." His hand tightened on hers. "Dearest, since I went to Tennessee, I've been transfered to another division. We . . . ah . . . work behind the lines."

"A spy?"

"Yes, I'm a spy. It's important work and someone must do it."

"But it's so danger—"

"Taylor, don't interrupt me," he warned. "That's one of the reasons I haven't written or received any letters. It just wasn't possible."

Unexpectedly, he leaned closer, his face free of the shadows as he kissed her eagerly. "I love you, Taylor Stone. Nothing could have made me as happy as your marrying me. I don't . . . I know we didn't start off too well, and it hasn't made it better with us being apart because of this blasted war. I think Brenetta is wonderful, too, and I'm proud to be her stepfather."

He sat back, enveloped in the darkness again, the passion leaving his voice as he continued. "You never lied to me. I knew Brent Lattimer was still tied up in your heart when we married. But I knew you cared for me too, and I hoped it would grow into something deeper, something lasting. I had a chance for that as long as we both believed he didn't love you, didn't want you anymore . . . But he does still love you."

"Why do you say that?" Taylor whispered.

"Because . . . he told me so himself."

She felt herself tremble and her head seemed very light. She stared at the shadows shrouding Jeffrey, eyes wide and waiting.

"I was on an important mission in August. I was discovered. They would have shot me on the spot, but they wanted to learn what information I had gleaned, so they took me to be interrogated . . . and *then* shot. My captors took me to their colonel. Colonel Lattimer."

He paused, and she knew he was scrutinizing her for her reactions.

"Neither of us indicated we recognized each other. He spoke sharply to me inside his tent for a few moments, treating me as he would any spy, then told the others I had admitted there were other rebels still to be caught. He sent them out to find my *partners*, saying he would personally see me to the stockade.

"We barely had any time to talk after he led me outside their camp. However, the first thing he did was ask about you. He wanted to know if you were happy and well. He asked what you were doing, if you were safe. He wanted to know how you looked. Of course, I couldn't tell him since I hadn't heard from you or seen you in so long myself."

His voice was strained as he continued. "He told me he hoped Spring Haven wouldn't be harmed by the war since he knew you loved it more than anything in the world. He . . . he was

317

sincere, you know. He really cares about it, and he cares about you. He said . . . he said he loves you, but he knows you couldn't ever be expected to marry a Yankee. He asked *me* to take care of you . . . as I've always done before. Ironic, isn't it?" he asked, seeming to choke on his question.

"I told him we were married. I meant to tell him about Brenetta but . . . but I didn't. I . . . I'm just a coward, I guess. He sent his best wishes to you. Then he had me strike him over the head with his own gun. Taylor, he helped me escape. I'd be dead now if it weren't for him. And he did it for you, because he loves you."

The swish of the horse's tail was the only sound in the silence that ensued.

"It wasn't fair to leave him thinking you loved me," he continued at last, "but I did. I cracked him over the head just hard enough, I hope, to convince the others of a real escape. Afterwards, I was able to complete my mission and then return to report my findings."

Once again he leaned into the moonlight, saying, "Taylor, I love you too much to keep this from you. I . . . I'm so very sorry. Sorry about so much."

Poor Jeffrey, she thought and kissed him. Even so, her heart felt like singing. It was true! Brent still loved her.

"The truth, Taylor. Do you still love him? If he were here now, would you choose him or me?"

She drew sadly away from him. "Jeffrey. . ." she pleaded. "Don't . . ."

He gripped her wrists, pinching her skin in the tight squeeze. "The truth, Taylor," he demanded.

318

Her eyes fell to where his hands held her prisoner. Why was he doing this to her, to them? It seemed so pointless to bring up the past. The truth. He said he wanted the truth.

"I still love him, Jeffrey, but . . ."

His mouth covered hers, stopping the rest in her throat. When he released her, he finished her sentence for her. "I know. You love me too. It just isn't the same though, is it?"

Jeffrey took the reins, and clucking to the sleepy animal, he turned the buggy back toward town.

"Why, Jeffrey? Why did you want to know? Why did you even tell me about it?"

There was no pause this time. "Because I love you, Taylor Stone. I love you and want you to be happy. Only by knowing the truth can I help make you happy."

Stopping the buggy by the front gate, he embraced her tightly for a long time; then he kissed her, a lingering sweet kiss that caught her by surprise. He took her face between his hands, and by the dim light shed from a distant street lamp, drank in her face, the sparkle in his eyes now caused by tears.

"Go on in, Taylor. I need to put up the horse. I love you."

Bewildered and confused, she obeyed. From the porch, she watched him drive the horse around to the stables, and then went up to her room to wait.

Chapter 29

She was surprised to find she had fallen asleep in her chair. The crimp in her neck brought on by her awkward position woke her. The light was still burning on the night table, and she wondered what was keeping Jeffrey. As if in answer to her question, the grandfather clock in the parlor chimed out the hour. Five o'clock!

Taylor jumped up from her chair. Quickly, she looked about the hallway and then went to Robert's room, but there was no sign of Jeffrey there. One by one, she searched each room of the house until the only place left that she could think of was the stables. Josh, sleeping on a cot in a closet-size room near the barn door, was instantly awake as the old hinges creaked, announcing her arrival. He was quickly up and at her side, a low burning lantern in his hand.

"Josh, have you seen Master Jeffrey?"

He looked a little sheepish as he answered, "Yes'm. He brought back da buggy las' night 'n'then left. He tol' me not t'say nothin' t'nobody 'n' t'give you this in da mornin'."

Apprehensively, Taylor accepted the proffered paper and began reading it.

Taylor dearest,

I couldn't bear another goodbye, so I have left only this note to say it for me. I'm a coward, indeed. By the time you read this, I should be northbound on the train.

My love, when I came to town, it was to say goodbye to you in truth, to free you to love the right man. I have thought of nothing else for many months. But when the moment came, I couldn't bring myself to tell you. I can't free you because I am unable to free myself. If you are to be free from me, it is something you must do. I am helpless to help you.

My only desire is to make you truly happy. I pray I'll have the chance to do just that. Whatever our marriage is to be is up to you, my darling. If I should be lucky enough to survive this war, we will face the decision together, even if it means living apart.

Give my love to Robert and Marilee, and give my thanks to the Masons for their kindness.

Yours,
Jeffrey

Taylor rubbed her forehead, trying to erase the foreboding sensation that his letter had left her. Josh shuffled his feet nearby, his sleepy eyes fighting to stay open, reminding her of his presence.

"Go back to bed while you can, Josh," she said as she folded Jeffrey's letter and carefully placed it in her dress bodice. Dejectedly, she hurried back to the house, hugging her shoulders from the cold. She went directly to the parlor and stirred up the fire, after which she snuggled into an overstuffed chair nearby, staring at the renewed flames.

Why was it she had hurt him so? She was a fool to have said she still loved Brent. Had she no feelings, no compassion for Jeffrey that she could hurt him in that manner? What was it about Brent—no, about herself—that caused her to be untrue in her heart to both her husbands, both of them good men who loved her and treated her wonderfully? What perverse hope kept her thinking there was still a chance she and Brent would someday be together?

Tortured by what seemed unanswerable questions, Taylor chewed at her lower lip. She knew what she must do, but she was reluctant to be forced to make the decision herself. The night was ticked away by the clock. But there was no decision really, she thought. She was married to Jeffrey. She must stay married to Jeffrey. There would never be a time for her and Brent again. He believed her married to Jeffrey out of love, and no matter what the reasons for that marriage, married she was. But Jeffrey had left without knowing she would choose to stay with him, to somehow repay his goodness to her.

She sat up straight. Wait! Perhaps he hadn't left yet. Maybe she had read this in time. Maybe he was still at the station. She rushed upstairs for her shawl. Catching sight of her hair in the glass, she grabbed a bonnet and tied it carelessly over her wild curls. Her dress was wrinkled from sleeping in it, but that couldn't be helped at the moment. She was in too much of a hurry.

Once again, she brought Josh out of his sleep. This time, however, he was sent scurrying to ready the buggy for her. Taylor ignored Apollo's less than happy snorting as he was backed up to the buggy and strapped into the harness. Before Josh could even get the door clear open, she was clucking at him to hurry.

The streets were quiet but not deserted in this pre-dawn hour. She passed near a bakery, the warm, friendly scent making her stomach growl in anticipation. Occasionally, she would pass men loitering against buildings, making her thankful for the light from the gas lamps and her swift steed. She reached the depot without any delays but was soon faced with another dilemma. How was she going to go about finding him even if he was still here? She allowed herself only a brief moment of hopelessness before looping the reins and beginning her search.

The depot was busier than she would have

thought for this hour of the day. Civilians and soldiers alike, coming and going, filled the board sidewalks and other waiting areas. In desperation, she stopped a soldier and asked him if he knew who Major Jeffrey Stone was or where he might be found.

"Which division is he in, ma'am?"

"Division? I . . . oh, dear. I seem to have forgotten. I'm not sure. Oh, I can't remember," she repeated awkwardly. "But . . . but he's been in Tennessee."

The sergeant grunted. "So's everybody, ma'am. Sorry."

He walked away from her, shaking his head. Undaunted, she proceeded on her way, stopping anyone in uniform, always asking the same question, always getting the same answer. No one could help her. Suddenly knowing she was going to cry, she dropped onto a bench and fought, unsuccessfully, the tears of frustration.

"Excuse me, ma'am. Are you all right?"

Taylor swallowed, not looking up immediately at the owner of the shiny boots in front of her. When she answered, her voice broke, choked by her tears.

"I . . . I doubt . . . it, sir. No one . . . seems to be able to . . ."

A white handkerchief was thrust forward, and she accepted it gratefully, dabbing at her eyes.

"Thank you," she said, lifting her eyes as she handed back the newly dampened linen square. They settled on a friendly, aging face and the

324

insignia of a general. "Oh, my," she said breathlessly.

The general smiled warmly, his eyes wrinkling up at the corners. "Now then," he said. "Will you tell me what's wrong? Perhaps I really can help."

"Oh, sir, if only you could. I came to see my husband off, but I can't find him. I don't remember his division or company or brigade or whatever. He may have already left. He wasn't expecting me. It was to be a surprise . . ." Her voice trailed off.

"Perhaps if I knew his name?"

"Jeffrey Stone. Major Jeffrey Stone."

"Jeff Stone! Why, bless me. You're young Jeff's wife? Ma'am, it's a pleasure to meet you. And how's that new baby of yours? Girl, isn't it?"

"Yes, ah, General . . . You know Jeffrey?"

"Know him? We've served together almost the entire war. He's a good boy, our Jeff."

"Yes, he is . . . but General . . . ah . . ."

"I'm sorry, Mrs. Stone. The name's Baker. General Baker." He inclined his head in introduction.

"General Baker. About Jeffrey. Has he left yet?"

The friendly face lost its smile. "I *am* sorry, Mrs. Stone. You've missed him. The train pulled out about twenty minutes ago."

Missed him. She had missed him. It was too late to send him away knowing she cared enough to stay with him always, regardless of anything else, including Brent.

"Can I see to someone to take you home, Mrs. Stone?" the general asked, his voice filled with concern.

"No, thank you, General Baker. I have my own buggy here. But thank you for your help."

He took her arm as she started to walk away and fell into step beside her. "Got to make sure you get home all right. For Jeff, you know," he said as he escorted her through the crowds. He helped her into her buggy and handed her the reins, again expressing his sorrow at failing to have been of help.

"It's not your fault, General Baker. Thank you for taking the time to try. Will you be seeing Jeffrey again soon?"

"I hope to reach Dalton before he leaves there. May I give him a message for you?"

"No. Wait. Yes, you can. Tell him I tried to see him and that I'm hoping he'll come home to Brenetta and me very soon. Home for ever."

General Baker touched the brim of his hat. "I'll do just that, ma'am. Goodbye."

Taylor turned Apollo toward home, allowing him his head once they reached Peachtree Street. He would have no problems finding his warm stall from there. She didn't hurry him. She was too busy mulling over all that had taken place since yesterday afternoon.

A twinge of self-pity raised its ugly face, causing her to wonder why these things always happened to her. Why couldn't she have met and married Brent and lived at Spring Haven forever?

Why did these disappointments only happen to her? Couldn't she find real happiness? Why? Why? Why? By the time she reached the stables behind the Masons' home, she was in a pronounced blue funk, thoroughly depressed with her lot in life.

"Taylor, where on earth have you been?" Marilee quizzed her as she came into the house. "Josh said you'd gone to see Jeffrey off. Is it true?"

"Yes. He's on his way to Dalton right now. But he left his love for everyone here. Excuse me, Marilee," she said as she walked by her. "I'm tired. I'm going up to my room to sleep. We'll talk about it later."

The fresh white sheets welcomed the emotionally exhausted woman into their fold, and she quickly succumbed to their offer of temporary escape.

Chapter 30

"Taylor?"

Marilee's call slipped through to her sleep-fogged brain.

"Taylor," she repeated, "wake up."

One eye still held tightly shut, Taylor looked over at the door, cracked open just far enough for Marilee to peek in at her. The room was bright with late morning sunshine. Even the flowers on the wallpaper seemed to grow and bloom under its golden spell.

"Come on in, Marilee," Taylor mumbled, closing her eye again quickly.

The door opened and was closed swiftly. She listened to Marilee's shoes clip across the wood floor, silenced suddenly when she reached the thick rug around the bed. Taylor pushed herself up against the headboard, resolutely commanding her eyes to open.

"How are you feeling, Taylor? Rested?"

"Mmmmm. I suppose so," she answered, stretching languidly. "Is it time to go in to the hospital already?"

"Almost. Taylor, you'll never guess who's downstairs. Dr. Reed! He's going to be working in the hospitals in Atlanta from now on. But there's the most dreadful news. Mrs. Reed is dead. Typhus, he said."

"Not Mrs. Reed!" Taylor exclaimed, suddenly wide awake, disbelief written in her eyes.

"That's not all. Lizabeth is going to come here to stay with her father. Mrs. Mason has offered them both rooms *here.*"

"Ohhh, nooo," Taylor groaned, slipping down under the sheets.

Marilee giggled as she yanked the covers from Taylor's face. She knew of Lizabeth's infatuation with Jeffrey and of Taylor's dislike for the woman.

"Coward! Don't worry. Dr. Reed said they would only stay until they find a house for themselves."

Dropping her legs over the side of the bed, Taylor pouted prettily. "But that could be until after the war. I could be driven crazy before then."

Marilee laughed again. "Come on. Get dressed. You must come down and welcome Dr. Reed, no matter what your sentiments."

Taylor agreed, forcing herself out of bed. She noticed Marilee was still smiling merrily and turned a cocked eyebrow in her direction.

"What's up?"

"Dr. Reed did bring some good news. Philip will be getting a furlough soon. I'll be able to meet him in Dalton."

"Marilee, how wonderful!"

Two pairs of arms flew into the air as the friends hugged each other. They twirled about the room in dizzy joy, Taylor's white nightgown and black hair mixing with Marilee's brown dress and blonde locks. Released, Marilee fell onto the bed and watched as Taylor splashed her face with water and then dressed. Marilee helped comb Taylor's hair, twisting it into a neat chignon at the nape of her neck.

"Well, let's go," Taylor said, checking her reflection one last time in the mirror over the chiffonier.

"Dr. Reed, how are you?" Taylor asked, her voice betraying her shock at the difference in her merry old friend. His face was wizened, hardship and worry having etched deep furrows around his mouth. His eyesight was failing, and he peered at her from behind thick glasses. The webbing of smile lines at the corners of his eyes had become ugly grooves.

"I'm fine, Taylor. Just fine. And you?"

"Well, too, thank you."

Taylor planted a feather-kiss on his cheek as they hugged lightly. Then everyone sat down, Mrs. Mason sitting on the couch beside the doctor, and Marilee and Taylor sitting across from them in matching chairs. Robert had announced he was coming down soon. He would not be kept abed any longer. In the meantime, Sophia Mason served them all tea and ginger cakes. Taylor noticed Dr. Reed's hands were unsteady as he lifted his cup and wondered how much longer he could go on working when he was like this. It would be terrible, no matter how much she disliked her, if Lizabeth were to lose her father too.

Sophia's nervous chatter was again filling any silence which might have occurred among the little group. Dr. Reed replied politely to all her questions, sometimes allowing the little smile to return.

"Taylor," Sophia was saying now, "did Marilee tell you that Dr. Reed will be staying with us for a time? And Lizabeth too."

A shadow drifted across the doctor's eyes. "I'll be glad when Lizabeth arrives. I've been worried about her since her mother died. Her letters . . ." He left it there with a shrug.

Sophia poured more tea. "Oh, my. Yes. It will be wonderful to have her here with us, won't it, ladies? My, what a fine bunch of friends we will make. If only it weren't because of this dreadful war. We used to have such fun. All the boys were at home then. We had such great parties, too. My, this house used to be filled with laughter and music, the doors thrown open to the spring perfumes."

She fell silent, her face growing sad, her own

memories accentuating the dismal circumstances of her present life, her husband working long hours for Atlanta's protection and her sons fighting in the war.

Compassionately, Dr. Reed patted her hand. "Ah, Sophia. We all remember those happy times. I fear we won't see days like them again very soon. But the war can't last forever, and better times, if not as good as of old, will still find us. Once we've whipped the Yankees . . ." he ended weakly.

What an empty, overused phrase that has become, thought Taylor.

Robert came down just then, and soon after, Taylor and Marilee left for the hospital, hoping he would be able to rekindle some cheer in the parlor for the two older friends.

The hours at the hospital had thoroughly drained her today. In each man's face, Taylor had seen Jeffrey, hurt and not knowing she cared enough to stay with him. Several of the patients asked her what was wrong, alerted by her preoccupation, her missing gaiety, but she merely shrugged and tried to turn her attention—and her smile—upon them.

She wearily mounted the steps to the porch, Marilee silently following behind her. All Taylor could think about was a relaxing bath and going to bed. Tomorrow she would write to Jeffrey and hope it reached him before he left on another mission that would keep him from his mail. So deep in thought was she that she almost ran into Sophia in the entry hall.

"Oh! Sophia, I'm sorry. I wasn't paying attention to where I was going."

"No harm, Taylor. Guess what, dears? Lizabeth Reed has already arrived. She's in the parlor with her father now. Do go in and greet her."

Taylor exchanged a speaking glance with Marilee and proceeded to the parlor as directed. As she stepped through the doorway, her eyes met with Lizabeth's, sending a warning shiver down her spine. The woman, dressed in black, her harsh features underscored by the mourning clothing, was perched on the arm of her father's chair, hiding him from Taylor's view. Marilee was still behind Taylor in the hall. For a moment, there was only the two of them, and the hate in Lizabeth's eyes were palpable and paralyzing. She stopped abruptly, her eyes caught in the almost hypnotizing gaze. As she returned the look, Lizabeth's face seemed to go totally blank, unregistering. Lizabeth turned away, and when she turned back, she was smiling.

"Taylor. Marilee. Oh, how good it is to see some familiar faces." Lizabeth left the chair and came toward them. Her arm went briefly around each woman's neck as she kissed them. Taylor forced herself not to cringe at her touch. She searched the other woman for some sign of insincerity but could find none. She tried to shake off the icy feeling left over from their initial eye contact. Perhaps she was mistaken about what she had thought she had seen there.

"Marilee and I were very sorry to learn of your mother's death, Lizabeth."

"Thank you, Taylor. It was very unexpected and tragic. But at least my father is in Atlanta now so I can be with him. I didn't want to stay at home. It was just too empty without Mother."

"Of course. It would be that way for anyone," Marilee said as they all took their seats.

Lizabeth, returning to her father's chair, placed a hand on his shoulder and asked, "How's your baby, Taylor? Half grown, I suppose."

"Yes, she's growing all too fast. She's a wonderful baby."

"It's too bad Jeffrey hasn't been able to ever see her or spend any time with you, his wife. But, of course, the war must come first."

"Oh, but he has seen Brenetta," Marilee broke in. "He was here just yesterday. Played with Brenetta for the longest time and was thoroughly taken with her, as is everyone. I've never seen a father more in love with his child than Jeffrey is with Brenetta. And with his wife too."

"Jeffrey was here? And I missed him?" Lizabeth asked in a whisper. "When will he be back?"

"He . . . he didn't know, Lizabeth," Taylor answered, suddenly filled with pity for this love-starved spinster who thought herself in love with Taylor's husband.

A hard glint returned to Lizabeth's gaze. "If he'd known I was coming, he would have waited to say hello."

"I'm sure he would have wanted to," Taylor answered stiffly, her pity vanishing in a flash, "but he was unable even to stay with his *family* for a full day. We'll all hope he comes home again soon to his family and friends. Then you'll have a chance to see him."

A sneer was Lizabeth's only answer.

Her stomach churning, Taylor jumped up. "You must excuse me. I really must go up and look in on Brenetta. It's nice to have you here, Lizabeth."

As if pursued, she fled the room for the nursery and sanctuary with her child.

Chapter 31

The heavy numbers of wounded from the fighting at Chickamauga in September and later at Chattanooga, Lookout Mountain, Orchard Knob, and Missionary Ridge kept Taylor at the hospital for long hours every day. She was glad for the bone-tired exhaustion that accompanied her to her bed every night. It kept her from lying awake and worrying. She had heard nothing from Jeffrey since his departure, not any response to her letters at all.

The long hours themselves were even a blessing. They saved her from much contact with Lizabeth Reed. The Reeds, father and daughter, continued to reside at the Mason home on Peachtree Street. Taylor's belief that Lizabeth was filled with an irrational hate for her continued. At times, the woman's odd behavior caused

Taylor to think Lizabeth was becoming unhinged. She mentioned this to no one, however. Not even to Marilee.

It was just four days before Christmas. Taylor was alone in her room, furiously working on a muffler she was making for Marilee. She had taken the afternoon off from her hospital duties to work on her Christmas gifts. Her room was bitterly cold, even with a fire on the grate, and she was finding it difficult to make her fingers perform properly. People were saying this was the coldest winter since '34. Taylor was convinced it was true.

Mrs. Mason had just closed the door, having brought Taylor the news of the fire which had raged through the fairgrounds hospital the previous night. Twenty of the forty buildings were destroyed, but apparently no lives had been lost. However, valuable bales of blankets were burned, and it was estimated the fire would cost the government nearly one hundred thousand dollars. Sophia was so distressed she had gone to her room to lie down.

It seemed to Taylor that only a few minutes had passed before another tapping was heard. Ellie's turbanned head poked around the door. "Miz Stone, thar's a so'dier at the door askin' fo' you."

With a sigh, Taylor put down her work. If these interruptions kept up, she would never be ready for Christmas. She rubbed her cold fingers as she walked down the stairs, trying to stir up their circulation and ease the ache in the joints.

The tall, middle-aged officer was standing just inside the front door. He was nearly blue with the cold himself and was shifting his weight from one foot to the other.

"Lieutenant, I'm Mrs. Stone," she said to him, holding out her hand. "What can I do for you?"

"Mrs. Stone, my name is Richard Adair. I've been sent here from . . ." He sneezed, then sneezed again. "Excuse me, ma'am. As I was saying . . ." Another sneeze cut off his words.

"Lieutenant Adair, please, allow me to get you something hot to drink. Come stand by the fire and warm yourself."

She saw he was about to decline, so she took his arm firmly, stopping any further protest, and almost thrust him before her into the parlor. She was rewarded with a grateful smile as he stood beside the blazing hearth.

After handing him a cup of coffee, such as it was, she asked, "Now, what did you come to see me about?"

He stiffened as he placed his cup on the mantle, his eyes looking anywhere but at her. "Mrs. Stone, ma'am, I was sent to you by General Baker."

His suddenly impersonal tone gave Taylor a moment's warning.

"It is with sorrow that the general must inform you of the death of your husband, Major Jeffrey Stone. The general sends his deepest regrets and sympathy to you and your daughter."

Taylor stared into the fire as she sank into the

nearest chair.

"Ma'am?"

"Yes, Lieutenant. I heard you. Do . . . do you know how he . . . how he died?"

"It's my understanding he was rescuing some wounded men, ma'am. Soldiers from both armies."

Taylor nodded sadly. "Yes, that sounds like Jeffrey."

The soldier stepped closer to her, holding out a packet of letters. "The general wanted you to have these now. His other possessions will arrive later."

Vision blurred by tears, she accepted them, saying, "And his . . . his body? Will they be sending him back to us?"

"Yes, ma'am."

He continued to hover nearby, wanting to help the beautiful young widow if he could. He waited for her to begin to cry hysterically as he had known others to do. Instead, she sat very still as silent tears poured from the deep dark pools above her high cheekbones.

A swish of skirts caught his attention. Two women stood in the doorway to the hall. The pretty blonde, a petite young woman, was nearest to him; the other, older, sharp of feature and extremely thin, glared at him suspiciously.

"Taylor, what on earth has happened?"

Marilee's quickened steps brought her to Taylor's chair. She knelt down, taking Taylor's hands in her own, but there was no reply. Marilee turned

339

her gaze upon the lieutenant.

"What's happened here, sir?" she demanded of him.

"I have had the unpleasant task of informing Mrs. Stone that ... that her husband is dead, ma'am."

"Jeffrey? Dead? Oh, Taylor..."

Marilee sat beside her and pulled Taylor's face against her breast, rocking her as she would a child, stroking her hair and crooning comforting sounds.

Taylor looked up at her friend with red-rimmed eyes and said faintly, "I always failed him so, Marilee. It was I who should have died. He had so much more to give this world. It really... it really isn't fair." She choked on a sob. "I ... I hurt everything I touch."

"Shush, now, shush," Marilee said in a soothing tone. "That's just not true, dearest Taylor. You've given everyone your love. Jeffrey was terribly happy because of you. Shush, now."

Taylor said nothing more, allowing Marilee to continue her tender administrations as the grandfather clock ticked loudly from its corner of the room, counting off each second of grief. Finally, Taylor pushed herself away and dried her tears. She rose gracefully from the couch, her face perfectly composed. Again she held her hand out to Lieutenant Adair, a faint smile touching the corners of her mouth briefly.

"I know this hasn't been an easy job, Lieutenant Adair. I thank you for your concern. Will you be returning to General Baker shortly?"

"Yes, ma'am, I will."

"Then please send him my regards and thank him for all his concern on my behalf. I'll be forever grateful." She walked with him to the door. "I'm sorry you must travel in such cold weather, Lieutenant. May God grant you good health and a safe trip back to your station."

The soldier, protocol forgotten, his eyes filled with admiration, took both of her hands in his own. "Mrs. Stone, I'll remember you for a long time. You *are* the Confederacy—strength in the face of adversity and grief, the ability to continue when all seems lost, quiet beauty. If . . . if there is anything I could do . . ."

"Thank you, Lieutenant Adair," she said as she shook her head. "There is nothing anyone can do now."

"He must have been a good man for you to have loved him."

The gentle smile illuminated her face. "Yes," she whispered, "he was a good man. A very good man."

Sensing he should leave, he bowed slightly and stepped out into the chilling wind. He bent his head into the cold as he heard the door shut behind him.

"Marilee?" Taylor said quietly. "Stay with me. I don't think I could bear being alone right now."

"Of course, I'll stay with you."

"I . . . I think I'd like to go up to the nursery for a while."

Marilee held onto her elbow as if she were a feeble old woman. Together, they climbed the stairs to the third floor, sorrow sounding in each step. The door to the nursery stood open to them, and a voice other than Mima's drifted out to them. They stopped short, sighting Lizabeth bent over the baby's crib.

"Your mother is a fool," she said shrilly. "She thinks he's dead, but I know he's not. I saw him just this morning. But he told me he hates you both. He intends to pay you back for all the harm she has brought to him. He won't ever play with you again. He'd as soon you were dead, you know."

Taylor darted to the crib and grabbed up the surprised child. "Lizabeth, what are you babbling about?" she asked in horror.

The answering smile was cold. "You *really* are a fool, Taylor. But Jeff knew that. He never loved you. He only wanted to possess your beauty. But he truly loves me. He wouldn't lie to me. He is sick of you and would only like to hurt you. Jeff loves me."

Gently, Marilee touched Lizabeth's arm. "Jeffrey's dead."

"No, he's not! I know where he is, and he's not dead."

"Where is he?" Taylor asked carefully. "Tell us, Lizabeth."

An ugly cackle slipped from her thin lips. "So you can try to take him again? Never! He hates you as I do. Don't try, Taylor Bellman. Don't you ever try to find him." Skirts rustling, she swept out of the room, a laugh punctuating her final words.

"She's mad," Marilee whispered. "She's really insane."

Taylor was still holding her child tightly against her, and Brenetta had had enough. She wiggled and cried out, breaking the spell that held her mother and aunt. Taylor lowered her back into the crib where she stood holding onto the side rails, smiling up at them.

"Do you think she might harm Brenetta?" Marilee asked.

"I don't know, but I'm not taking any chances. She's moving into my room tonight. And she'll never be alone for a moment while that woman lives here. Mima will just have to let others fix Brenetta's meals and wash her clothes. She'll have to be with her every moment that I'm not."

"Taylor," Marilee said hesitantly, "what about you? Perhaps you're in danger, too."

"I'll be fine, Marilee. What could she do to me, anyway? She thinks she has Jeffrey, and as long as I don't try to take *him* from her, she'll forget about me. What can it hurt to let her go on believing in this imaginary Jeffrey? We know he's gone. And besides, I couldn't bear to tell Dr. Reed."

The matter was settled, and Brenetta's things were quietly moved into Taylor's room. Mima was given her instructions, especially being cautioned about when Miss Reed was in the house.

"You don't have t'tell me, Missy," she replied. "I seen how her eyes go dead sometimes. That woman's got an evil spirit livin' in her, Missy, that she does."

The fire cast dancing figures across the ceiling. At other times, under happier circumstances, the dancers would have seemed cheerful and friendly. Tonight, they were sinister. They seemed to be laughing at her loss and jeering at her fears, taunting her for her failure as a wife.

Jeffrey dead. It seemed she had known this would happen for the last three months. If only she could have talked to him again; if only he had written. He had saved her letters. Why hadn't he taken the time to answer them?

Remembering the packet of letters, she sat up and lit the lamp. Perhaps reading them, seeing what she had written again, would ease her turmoil. Carefully, she untied the bow that held them. She found a number of them unopned. These were the most recent ones she had sent, obviously reaching his headquarters when he was unavailable. He never returned to read them.

She found the letter she had written the day after his departure back in September. The envelope was well-worn and stained. As she unfolded the letter, another slip of paper fell out. It was a letter from Jeffrey, dated December 1, 1863.

Dearest Wife,
    Your letter informing me of your decision filled my heart with unbelievable joy. I swear

to you, Taylor, that I will make you and Brenetta happy all of your lives.

Now, when my life seems to have begun again, may seem a strange time to say what I'm about to say, but feeling so aware of love and life also makes a man more aware of death. If I should not return from this war, I would not have you feeling you had failed me in anyway. You see, I know you, Taylor my love, and I know you would blame yourself for everything. You loved me honestly, without falsehood. What more could any man ask? In our single year of marriage, we have had less than a week together. Yet that week was worth it all to me.

I love you, Taylor. Forget it not. Kiss Brenetta for me.

Your Jeffrey

Dear, dear Jeffrey. To the end thinking only of her. Even in death, he had managed to reach out and save her from her own condemnation. Having freed her from guilt for not loving him more, he had allowed her to grieve honestly for the loss of what they had truly had.

Taylor turned down the light and lay back again. The evil dancers had fled from her ceiling, unable to remain in this new atmosphere, mixed with love and pain.

Holding his letter close to her breast, she whispered, "Jeffrey, your place in my heart can never be filled by another. You'll always be with me as you always were when I needed you. I wish . . . I wish it could have been different."

Chapter 32

Taylor leaned closer to Robert, trying to find some relief from the bitter wind cutting around the carriage doors. She knew Josh must be near frozen to death up on his perch. Mima sat across from them, Brenetta asleep while tucked inside the woman's coat for extra warmth.

"We're almost there, Taylor. How're you doing?" Robert asked.

She forced a weak smile around her chattering teeth in reply.

The hours since they had left Atlanta had been torture. The three adult occupants and the child had bundled up as best they could against the arctic weather, but it was not enough.

"Thank Providence I was ready to travel," Robert added. "I wouldn't have wanted you making this trip alone."

Taylor didn't hear him. She was listening again to the noisy clatter of the wagon behind them—the wagon carrying the coffin. She took Robert's hand, suddenly aware of his pain too. Aware that he also could hear and understand.

"My poor parents," he said softly. "Their oldest maimed; their youngest gone. What this will do to them . . ."

She tried to squeeze his fingers reassuringly but her own were too cold to move. There was nothing she could do anyway. In silence, they shared their mutual pain.

Southside stood in the cold dying day like a fortress, opening her arms to the weary travelers. Likewise, the master and mistress of the great plantation welcomed them inside. No thought was given to anything but the immediate comfort of the new arrivals. Taylor found herself whisked away and tucked tightly into a warm bed, a heated stone at her feet and a blazing fire in the grate. Sleep overwhelmed her. There was no resistance to it.

"Good morning, Taylor dear."

Joanna Stone sat beside her bed. The morning sun, belying the winter weather outside, highlighted the silver strands which now streaked her lovely auburn hair. She was holding a steaming cup in her dainty hands which Taylor accepted gladly.

"Did you rest well?"

"Yes, I did, Mother Stone. I had no idea it would

347

be morning when I awoke."

"You had a very trying journey, daughter. You needed your sleep."

"Well, I must get up now and look in on Brenetta," Taylor said, pushing back the covers.

Joanna laughed airily. "Don't you worry about her. She's been entertaining Mr. Stone and Robert for the past hour. Such a wonderful child. I . . . I hope you'll allow us to . . . to remain her grandparents."

A crack had appeared in Joanna's carefully constructed composure, and Taylor held out her hands to her mother-in-law. "Oh, Mother Stone, who else would have the right but those who love her as you do. Of course, you will always be her grandparents."

"Without Jeffrey, I was unsure if . . ."

They wept, holding the other's hands, drawing some strength from their shared grief. Taylor kissed Joanna on the cheek and hugged her warmly.

"I suppose we had better go downstairs," Joanna said, drying her tears. "Shall I wait for you to dress?"

"No, you go on. I'll be along shortly."

Taylor stood alone in the well-heated room, her bare feet sinking into the thick carpeting. The room was elegantly and tastefully furnished. The delicate French furnishings stated unequivocally that this was a thoroughly feminine domain. It was so very beautiful, more so even than Spring Haven, but suddenly, Taylor knew that was where she truly wanted to be.

"Yes, I'll go home for a while. I'll go home to Spring Haven, to where I've always been the happiest. I'll go home as soon as I can."

She dressed in her worn black gown, noting she would really have to have another one or two made. She would be needing nothing else for a long time to come. If she were vain, she would have acknowledged how flattering to her complexion the black clothing was anyway.

Taylor found the Stones in the library. Brenetta was inching her way along the side of the couch on very wobbly legs, her grandparents and uncle providing a very satisfying audience. Spying her mother, she squealed joyfully and let go of her anchor. She plopped unceremoniously to the floor, a look of utter dismay in her eyes. Everyone laughed, stopping the threatening tears, and she crawled quickly toward Taylor.

Taylor knelt down to meet her daughter's charge, and the two hugged each other, Taylor kissing Brenetta several times about the face. The child was so lovely and growing so fast, it made her head spin.

Charles Stone came toward them as she stood up, Brenetta braced on her hip. "Daughter, it's good to have you here," he said affectionately, giving her a warm embrace. "Would that it was not for such sad reasons."

"Thank you, Papa Stone. I'm glad to have the family to come to."

Taking her free arm, he said, "You will stay with

349

us until the war is over, of course."

"No," she answered gently. "I won't be staying for long. I'm needed in Atlanta, and before I return, I'm going up to Spring Haven for a while." She kissed the older man's whiskered cheek. "But thank you for wanting me. It helps. It really does."

"You won't leave us too soon, will you, Taylor?" Robert asked, already dreading her absence.

"No, I'll stay here a week or two."

They buried Jeffrey on a blustery day at the close of 1863. His grave was on a small rise overlooking Southside and her many acres of land. It was the sort of place Jeffrey would have liked, Taylor thought. She leaned on Robert's arm throughout the service. Her tears, at last, were spent. Now she stood dry-eyed, listening to the minister's voice and her mother-in-law's gentle sobbing.

The service over, she picked up some earth and sprinkled it over the coffin. Twice widowed in less than two years. How very strange her life had turned out to be.

The week or two Taylor had intended to stay turned into six and then seven and finally eight. It was difficult to leave. Her in-laws resisted any mention of her departure from Southside, declaring how deeply they needed Brenetta and herself in their lives. Robert was no help. He desired her to stay as well. He had come to depend on her lovely presence, on her gentle attendance of him for the past six months, and he was reluctant to lose her—and the feelings he had for her now.

Only through almost heartless determination did Taylor find herself looking out the rear window of the carriage at the shrinking vision of Southside and a family she loved deeply.

"Bye-bye, bye-bye, bye-bye," Brenetta chattered merrily, waving at her mother in the seat opposite her.

"Yes, Netta. We're going bye-bye. We're going home."

Even Mima smiled at that. "Won't they all be su'prised t'see us, Missy?" she said. "Shore will be good t'be home, all right."

This journey was very different from the trip to Southside in December. Wildflowers had sprung up in a mosaic of colors—bright yellows, merry pinks, vivid reds, cool blues. The eternal promise of spring. As they passed one familiar landmark after another, Taylor's excitement increased. She sat on the edge of her seat, hands gripping the window edge, looking anxiously ahead.

"There it is! There's the drive," she cried. She pulled Brenetta into her lap. "Now watch, honey. We'll see it any minute now."

Taylor held her breath. She hadn't realized just how much she had missed this place. Then it was before her, the same as she remembered—strong and proud. Home.

Hardly before the wheels had stopped rolling, Taylor was jumping out to the ground. Saul and

Susan were out to meet her in a flash. Hungrily, she looked over the lawn, the gardens, the pillars, the portico.

"Never again. When this war is over, I'll not leave here again," she promised herself. This was where she belonged and this was where she would stay.

Taylor took long walks nearly every day, sometimes alone, sometimes balancing Brenetta on her hip. Sometimes she would ride out on Tasha, the spirited mare stretching her limbs under her as they galloped across the fields and over fences. It was a time of renewal for Taylor. A time to remember the past but also a time to look to the future. April crept upon her unawares. Already she had been away from Atlanta for three months, yet she hardly thought about it, so contented was she.

She was lying in the soft grass at the edge of the spring pasture. In other years, it had been filled with mares and new foals. Now it was empty, save for herself and Tasha. She could hear the mare's contented chewing as she moved leisurely through the lush forage. Taylor stared dreamily up at the powder blue sky dotted with puffy white clouds. This morning she had awakened knowing it was time to go back. She couldn't keep hiding here like this. The war wasn't over yet. She had to return where she could be of some help. Yes, she would plan her trip back tonight. But first, she would enjoy the peace of this place.

The aimless wanderings of her mind stopped

finally on a question—where would she be now if she had refused to marry David? Would things have turned out very differently, better perhaps? She decided she would probably have married Jeffrey anyway. Would they have found more happiness if she had been married only to him? Would she have been content as his wife?

And Brent. What about him? Would she be better off never to have met him? She was surprised at the wealth of feelings his name still caused her. She had thought she had successfully closed the door on the past. Now, she allowed herself to consider him and found that, if anything, her love, her longing for him had increased while it lay hidden inside her heart.

"I would trade everything, even Spring Haven, to be with him," she whispered.

As she jumped to her feet, Tasha shied away, then eyed her warily. Taylor couldn't believe her own thoughts. Always she had wanted Spring Haven. Always. Hadn't she promised herself upon arrival that she would never leave here again when the war was over? Hadn't even Brent thought her love for Spring Haven was greater than her love for him?

"But I would," she said, louder this time. "I would leave it without even a look back if I could have him at my side."

Chapter 33

"Saul, I need to talk to you. Please see me in the study as soon as you can."

Taylor walked quickly away from the barn and up to the house, deep in thought. She felt as if a veil of spider webs had been swept from her brain and away from her eyes. Everything seemed much clearer to her now. There were decisions to be made, and she had to make them.

"Mama! Mama!"

Brenetta's clear cry of welcome greeted her from the veranda where she had been playing with some wooden blocks. Mima sat in a rocker close by, her face wrinkled up in a grin.

"Mima, it's time we returned to Atlanta. I want us ready to travel in two days," Taylor said as she swept Brenetta up from the floor. "And how about my little Netta. Are you ready to see Aunt

Marilee again?"

Brenetta's black curls bounced wildly as she nodded enthusiastically. Although too young to remember Marilee or Atlanta, she loved to go with her mama anywhere. Taylor kissed her cheek and set her against her hip.

"Mima, we must prepare things here in case we don't get back before the Yankees come."

"Yankees! Here, Miss Taylor?"

Taylor nodded grimly. "I'm afraid so, Mima. We can't go on pretending to ourselves. It's going to end differently than we all thought."

Mima shook her graying head, her troubled eyes looking at the floor. "Yankees at Spring Haven," she mumbled. "The Hall burned t'the groun' an' Yankees at Spring Haven. Never thought t'see it."

"I hope I'm wrong, Mima. I do hope I'm wrong . . ." Taylor let the words drift off as she looked around her. The enemy here. It *was* unthinkable. Her free hand caressed a pillar lovingly.

"Well," she said, mentally shaking herself, "we must be ready for anything. Ah, here comes Saul. Mima, get Susan and meet me in the study."

Taylor led the way to her father's old study, still holding her daughter in her arms, and Saul following close behind. As she entered the room, she caught a fleeting image of her father behind the large oak desk. It was only the light playing tricks on her, but her breath caught in her throat. *Papa.* How things had changed since he had sat behind that desk.

Absentmindedly, she put Brenetta on the braided rug and sat in the old leather chair she had imagined him in. She remembered clearly the happy hours she had spent with her father in this room. She also remembered that last time, just before his death, when he wept in her arms. Poor Papa. It was better to remember him in those happier days when her mother was still alive. How very wonderful they both were.

Christina, a Creole from New Orleans, small and dark with snapping black eyes and vibrant moods. Martin, a tall and handsome native son. They had loved intensely, and from this love, a child was born. How good it would be if, for even a short time, she could return to those days when she was protected and spoiled by her parents, unconcerned with the worries of war and death.

She heard the door close and looked up as Mima and Susan approached her. She studied their apprehensive faces before beginning. "Saul. Mima. Susan," she said carefully, looking at each one directly as she spoke their names. "You have been trusted servants to me. No one could have been as favored as I have been by your faithfulness. I want to thank you, each of you."

Taylor paused as Brenetta tugged at her skirt, demanding up. "I realized on my ride today," she continued as Brenetta settled in her lap, "that there is much to be done in order to be ready for the future, much that I must do and that you must do too. I've managed to ignore the war for

356

several months now, using my widowhood as an excuse. Well, my black dresses won't protect me from the Yankee invaders."

"Miss Taylor, if'n any Yankees dares t'try t'harm you . . ." Mima sputtered.

"It's all right, Mima. I know you'd help me. What I want to say is this: When the Yankees get closer, most of the slaves are going to run off. I must be very careful who I take into my confidence. You three, and Josh as well, are the only ones I feel ready to do that with."

"Ain't no Yankee livin' could get me t'tell him nothin'," Susan said in a huff.

"I know that, Susan. Now, what we must do is hide, without the others seeing us, all the valuables that are left at Spring Haven. The house won't be safe from their pillaging. Besides, it might be burned down. So we must hide them elsewhere. I'll need your help. We must be very careful."

Taylor stopped talking and looked around the room for a moment, her eyes gathering memories for the future.

Observing the look, Susan spoke up. "Miss Taylor, you fo'get what you're thinkin'. No Yankees gonna burn down this here house while I's still livin' an' breathin'."

Taylor smiled. "You're right, of course. Now, we must work swiftly and carefully. Each of you must help with the silver and jewelry and anything else of value. Understood?"

The three nodded solemnly.

"One last thing," she said as she stood up. "No matter how this war turns out, I'm giving each of you your freedom. I'll draw up your manumission papers before I leave for Atlanta. I should have done it long ago. If you want to leave, I'll understand. If you choose to stay on, I'll be very grateful, and I'll pay you what I can ... *if* the Yankees leave me anything."

Taylor walked from behind the desk and would have left the room had not Mima's hand fallen on her arm, arresting her exit.

"Miss Taylor, I been a slave fo' nigh on fifty years 'n' I ain't never cared much who I served, long as they didn't beat me much. But I don't wants t'work fo' nobody else, fo' money nor nothin'. I'll stick by you 'n' da li'l missy."

"Me too," Susan chimed in.

Saul's serious nod made it unanimous.

Feeling a little choked, Taylor said, "Thank you all again. Now, let's get busy, shall we?"

Taylor sat at her mother's dressing table, a candle providing the only light in the room. Fondly, she ran her fingers over the delicate bottles which covered the top of the dresser. Her father had left everything as it was when her mother died, and neither she nor Philip had done differently after his death. Opening a vial, her head was engulfed in a cloud of Christina's favorite verbena cologne. It seemed as if she could feel her mother close by. Taylor remembered watching Christina comb out her rich black hair in the evenings at this very dressing table. She remembered her mother's pretty, lilting accent and her sparkling laugh.

She sighed, caught up in her yesterdays, and pulled open a drawer to begin the task of sorting out the priceless objects, both of monetary and sentimental worth.

It was after midnight when her hands fell upon an envelope in the back of the bottom drawer. With surprise, she saw it was addressed to her in her mother's flowing hand. Her fingers shook nervously as she broke the seal and read the letter, nearly eight years after Christina Bellman's death.

June 16, 1843

My darling Katherine Taylor,

Today you celebrated your first birthday. Next to your darling papa, you are the most important person in the world. I'm so proud of you.

As I watched you with your cake, I thought how quickly you have grown in your first year, and before I know it, you'll be grown up and away from me. This is why I write now. I write this as a prayer for you, Katy T. I pray that you will grow in wisdom as well as beauty. I pray you will love those around you. I pray you will be compassionate to others. And most of all, I pray that you will love and marry a man like your papa, someone who will love you above his own life. Watch carefully for him, my daughter, and when you have found him, never let him go.

Happy Birthday, Katy T.

Your loving Mama

A tear splattered on the page. *Katy T.* How very long since anyone had called her that. Her mother had written this almost twenty-one years before, and now Taylor had a one-year-old daughter of her own.

"I did find a man worth loving, Mama," she whispered, "but I lost him. I didn't know to watch carefully. But we have a beautiful daughter. I wish she could have known her grandmother. Oh, Mama. Papa. How I miss you both."

She laid her head in her arms on the dressing table and wept, seeming to drown in the flood of memories and heartaches.

"Come on, Missy," Mima's voice whispered in her ear. "Time you was t'bed, I'm thinkin'."

Taylor found herself gently propelled from the room and into her own. Mima's tender urgings got her into her night clothes and into bed where a troubled sleep washed over her, holding onto her until morning light flooded her room once again.

Taylor stood beside the carriage, looking around her for a last time before beginning the trip to Atlanta. Mima and Brenetta were already ensconced inside the carriage, and Josh stood nearby, waiting to help her in too. Susan and Saul watched from the steps, Susan quietly sniffling. Each had been handed their manumission papers only moments before, and again each had sworn not to desert her, no matter what.

"Goodbye, Saul, Susan," she said one last time, and then stepped into the carriage, suddenly wishing to leave quickly. She had a foreboding premonition that Spring Haven would not go too many months without witnessing tragedy again. She shivered.

As the horses trotted down the drive, she huddled back in her seat, closed her eyes against the passing ground, and prayed that when next she saw Spring Haven, it would be the same.

As the small party of travelers neared Atlanta, they found themselves going upstream against a river of refugees, mostly women and children and old men. Some led broken down beasts of burden pulling carts stacked with whatever possessions they had managed to save. Others pulled the carts themselves. Still others had nothing left to bring. Their faces filled Taylor's stomach with gnawing trepidation. They were faces of anguish and exhaustion.

"Hardly a soul left in Marietta or north of there, ma'am."

"General Johnston won't ever let the Yankees take Atlanta."

"Johnston is expected to fall back again, to Kingston this time."

"It's lost. It's all lost."

Words of despair sprinkled with shreds of hope answered her questions.

"Ma'am, if you don't mind my askin'," the

wizened old man said, "where you been hidin' these last months so you don't know 'bout the war?"

Where indeed! Taylor sat back in the safety of her carriage and wondered what she would find in Atlanta. Why had she requested no letters? And why had Marilee acquiesced? Was everyone safe? Why had she stayed away so long?

Atlanta itself was filled with soldiers and homeless people making their way farther south. Many fought to obtain space on the next train for themselves and their belongings. Taylor wondered if perhaps the Masons and Marilee might have fled the city. Would she find the house empty?

After so much activity in the streets, the Mason home seemed desolate in its silence. Taylor rapped sharply on the door and waited. Just as she was about to try the latch herself, the door was opened a crack. Ellie's familiar wide eyes peered carefully out at her.

"Ellie? Open the door. It's me. Mrs. Stone. Ellie, what's wrong?"

Slowly the door swung open.

"Lor', Miz Stone. You done come at a sad time," the girl whined.

"Where's Marilee?" Taylor asked hoarsely.

"She's upstairs with Marse Bellman."

"Bell . . . Philip's here?"

She didn't wait for a reply. Skirts flying, she raced up the stairs to Marilee's room. Without a rap of announcement, she flung the door open before her. Startled, Marilee looked up. Philip, his face flushed with fever, lay sleeping restlessly in the bed beside her. Even Marilee's appearance was a surprise to Taylor, her abundant gown unable to hide her pregnancy.

"Taylor, you're back!" Marilee cried, her arms thrown wide in greeting.

"Marilee," Taylor asked as they hugged each other. "What's wrong with Philip? Where are the Masons?"

"Sit down, Taylor," Marilee said, relaxing her embrace. Her eyes returned to her husband. "The doctors don't know for certain what's wrong with him. Sometimes he's perfectly well and then he'll be struck with the fever again. He's so delirious during these bouts. We just have to wait them out."

"And you, Marilee. When's your confinement? Why didn't you tell me?"

Marilee smiled. "I was just beginning to suspect when we learned of Jeffrey's death. I couldn't tell you then. You were so very upset." She touched her abdomen. "The baby's due in July."

"I'm so happy for you. I know how very much you and Philip wanted a child."

Marilee sponged the perspiration from Philip's brow. "Yes, I want this child. And I want him to grow up knowing his father, too." She choked back a sob.

Taylor knelt beside Marilee's chair. "Oh, honey," she cried, holding Marilee's hand. "Philip

363

will be all right. You'll see. He has so much to live for. You, the baby, Spring Haven. He'll get well. He just has to."

"I couldn't live without him, Taylor. Dr. Reed says there's no cure for something they don't understand. He'll either get over it . . . or have to live with it . . . or die."

Taylor cradled Marilee's head in her arms and let her cry. And she cried with her. When the tears had dried up at last, Taylor continued her questioning.

"Where is everyone, Marilee? Ellie seemed so afraid."

Marilee shook her head. "It's tragic. All three of the Mason boys are gone. One right after the other. When news of Tom's death came, it was the last straw. Mr. Mason just lay down and died too. Dr. Reed said his heart just stopped for want of any desire to live. Sophia left Atlanta last week to live with her sister in Savannah."

Taylor was speechless. Poor Sophia. How could so much tragedy strike one family so quickly? Tom Mason and John and Charlie. All gone. All of them. And now their father too.

And Jeffrey.

And David.

And almost Robert.

And maybe even Brent. She would never even know about Brent. Perhaps not knowing was worse.

Philip mumbled incoherently, and Taylor looked at him. Only thirty-three years old, he looked older and hardened. She had helped in the hospitals long enough to know that war could change a man. She had seen it in Robert and Dr. Reed, but this was Philip. This was her own brother.

"I think the fever is starting to break," Marilee whispered. "He always needs lots of water as soon as he awakens. I must call Ellie."

"You sit still. I'll get her," Taylor said. She paused at the door. "Dr. Reed, does he still live here?"

"Yes, he's stayed on . . . but Lizabeth moved out several months ago."

"Really? She moved out alone?"

"No," Marilee answered slowly. "She said she got married."

Now Taylor was truly surprised. "Married? Now *that* is something. Who to?"

Marilee dropped her eyes nervously.

"Marilee, who did she marry?"

"I've never met him but . . . she calls him . . . Jeff Stone."

A shocked quiet filled the room.

"She's crazy," Marilee said emphatically. "Even her father thinks so. He hardly ever sees her, and when he does, he's depressed by her condition for days afterwards."

"Has . . . has Dr. Reed . . . has he ever seen this man? Does he really look like Jeffrey?"

"No. He's never seen him. I've even wondered if he really exists, but Ellie saw Lizabeth walking with a man, hanging on his arm and kissing him

365

right there in the streets, calling him Jeffrey."

A cold hand closed around Taylor's heart. "Well," she said, shaking off the encroaching fear, "we buried Jeffrey so we know it's not him. Why would any man allow himself to be called by another name? He must be as crazy as she is."

"Maybe he really loves her. Maybe he just humors her," Marilee offered hopefully.

"Maybe," Taylor said, doubting it. She remembered Lizabeth as she stood over Brenetta's crib, saying that she had seen Jeffrey and that he hated her and her mother. She remembered the coldness in Lizabeth's voice and eyes. "Maybe," she whispered again.

"Taylor, look!" Marilee cried. "Philip. He's sleeping peacefully again. He'll be well again soon."

"I'm so glad, Marilee. I'll get Ellie." Taylor slipped from the room, Lizabeth's phantom dogging her heels as she hurried toward the kitchen.

Somehow his tormented brain knew when he must begin the struggle back to consciousness. Each time it became more difficult to leave the peaceful darkness that followed the fever. It would be so easy to just let it take him, keep him from the harsh world he must return to. He could hear voices murmuring close by. Marilee. It was always Marilee who stayed beside him. Marilee. Yes, that's why he pulled himself back. For Marilee. And for the child.

"Philip? Darling, can you hear me?"

A cool cloth brushed his forehead and his bristly cheeks. Slowly he opened his eyes, knowing even the dimly lit room would hurt his eyes after so long in darkness. He smiled weakly at Marilee, her face blurred, yet so clear in his mind.

"I made it again," he croaked.

She kissed his brow, her lips cool and dry against his skin. "Yes, darling," she replied. "You're going to be fine. Philip, look who's here."

He turned his head on the pillows, his eyes falling on the familiar, unrelieved black gown worn by women throughout the South.

"Hello, Philip," she whispered as she kissed him lightly.

"Taylor?"

"Yes, it's really me. I'm so sorry to find you ill, Philip."

He could see her better now, the unruly blue-black curls forced into a semblance of order, the white complexion, the deep, dark eyes. It was there, in those blue eyes, that he saw most readily the difference in this young woman from the girl he had known as his little sister and David Lattimer's bride. She had grown up. She had been widowed twice. She had known loss and fear and love.

Taylor took his limp hand in her own and kissed the rough, work-worn palm, her eyes still meeting his in an understanding gaze. They had both suffered. They had both changed. And they would both go on suffering and changing as the South died around them. Few Southerners knew this or would admit it, but brother and sister saw it clearly and each were glad for a confidant for their knowledge.

Included in their glances was something else, a final recognition of and forgiveness for the jealousy, the bitterness, and the unhappiness they had known five years before. Five years and a civilization ago.

Philip tightened his fingers. "We'll make it. We'll all make it."

Taylor nodded, understanding his meaning.

"Philip, drink this," Marilee urged gently.

The cool spring water eased the scratchy fibers in his throat, and he swallowed each sip gratefully. Lying back against his pillows again, he sighed and looked at Taylor.

"How's Spring Haven? How are our people and the crops?"

Taylor glowed as she answered, "Saul is managing quite well. We've lost a few more slaves and the army takes a great deal more than we can really afford to send with them with so many of our own mouths to feed. But she stands tall and firm as always, Philip."

"When the war is over, when we can put all this behind us, Taylor, we'll all go home to her again. She'll go on being the great plantation our father built. Bellmans don't quit, not even when war and Yankees come against us. Bellmans know what they want and fight to gain it and keep it. And Taylor," he added more softly, "you'll always have a home at Spring Haven, for as long as you want."

368

Absentmindedly, Taylor nodded. She had only half-heard his final sentence. Her thoughts were stuck on what he had said about Bellmans, about knowing what they wanted and fighting for it. She knew what she wanted—*who* she wanted. She had realized it while lying in the long grasses at Spring Haven, but only now did she know what she must do about it. Somehow, when the war was over, she would find him. She would search the world over if necessary, but she would find him. Never again would she marry because she was told to or because she felt cornered or because society said she must. Somewhere out there was the man, the only man, who held her heart. And find him she must.

Chapter 34

Wisps of curly black hair clung about her face. Her sweat-soaked bodice was plastered uncomfortably against her skin, chafing under her arms. Taylor held the dying boy's hand, and she wished desperately that the continuous thunder of guns and cannon would stop, if only for a moment, so that he might die in peace.

It was a useless wish. Even if they stopped, silence would not be theirs. The yard was filled with tired, hungry, wounded men, many of them groaning in pain. An ambulance stood at the gate, and Philip was helping the attendent carry the more severely injured men to the wagon. His face was drawn and haggard, no different from the other soldiers around her, or her own, she supposed. They were all tired and hungry. Marilee was carrying a pail of water and ladling out drinks to lifted cups.

"Ma'am," Taylor heard someone call to Marilee. "Do ya have even a bite o' bread for this hyar lad? He's doin' right poorly."

"I'm sorry. I'm so sorry," Marilee whispered to him.

Mima sat in the shade of the porch. At her feet was an unusually quiet Brenetta, her eyes wide at the grim spectacle. In Mima's arms lay three-week-old Philip Bellman, Jr.

The soldier's hand stiffened, and Taylor's eyes returned to him. His eyes grew wide in pain and terror. He groaned, the sound grating at her insides. Suddenly, the glazing of death covered his vision and she knew he was gone. Taylor freed her fingers from his death grip and then covered his face with a torn handkerchief before moving on to another.

Each day when she awoke, she prayed Philip would take them away from Atlanta. As Sherman pushed closer and closer, family after family had fled, but Philip had steadfastly remained.

"We'll be needed here," he would tell the women. "It's all we can do for the Confederacy now."

Each day, as May had led to June and June to July, more and more wounded had poured into Atlanta. Taylor hadn't been to the hospital in over a month. She was too busy nursing the wounded that filled the rooms of the Mason home. Now, even the yard was filled with them.

A hand caught at her skirt as she moved by a

man propped against an old oak.

"Ma'am?"

She turned a weary glance downward. "Yes?" she sighed.

"Sorry to trouble you, ma'am. I know you're worn ragged. But . . . I'm sorry if I seem rude, but I thought I recognized your voice when you were speaking to that soldier a moment ago."

Taylor looked more closely at the grimy and, she now realized, blind man. His face was gaunt and his hair was thinning, but there was something familiar about him . . .

"I'm sorry," she said. "I don't . . ."

His hands inched up the tree as he stood up.

"Mrs. Stone, isn't it?"

"Yes. Yes, that's me, but I . . ."

"Adair, ma'am. Richard Adair."

"Lieutenant Adair?" she asked in amazement.

He held out a hand in the direction of her voice, and she accepted it, holding it firmly.

"How are you, Mrs. Stone?"

"I . . . I'm fine, thank you." She nearly asked him how he was, but she stopped herself just in time as she looked into his vacant eyes.

"Mrs. Stone, I know it's not really proper, but it would mean a great deal to me if you would call me Richard."

She squeezed his fingers. "Of course, Richard. What do our polite little customs have to do with anything around us anymore? I am surprised that you remembered my voice, though."

"Ma'am, believe it or not, there's not a thing

that could make me forget your voice or your lovely face. Not as long as I live."

"How very kind of you, Lieutenant Adair . . . I mean, Richard," she said softly. "Please, I know you're weary. Do sit back down."

He obeyed her, again inching his fingers along the tree bark.

"Could I bring you a drink of water? I wish . . . I'm sorry there's nothing . . ."

"I know, Mrs. Stone. There's not much food left anywhere anymore. Leastwise, none worth eating. But I would take some of that water."

Taylor looked about for Marilee, but she was nowhere in sight. The water pail sat alone on the porch, Mima and the children having left their posts. Marilee had probably taken little Philip inside to nurse him, she decided.

"Excuse me, Richard. I'll get your water for you."

She moved as hastily as was possible across the yard toward the house. When she reached the first step of the porch, she looked back upon the depressing and frightening scene. Would it never stop? she wondered, suddenly covering her ears against the persistent din. She remained thus for several moments before forcing herself to drop her hands and turn to the bucket. She discovered that the water pail was empty and called for Ellie to refill it. While she waited she dropped into the rocker, closing her eyes.

"God help us," Philip sighed as his hand rested on her shoulder. She hadn't heard his approach.

Not opening her eyes, she asked him, "When will it be over, Philip?"

"I don't know. I just don't know, Taylor. Now that the newspapers have left Atlanta, it's hard to get reliable information. They're fighting no more than nine or ten miles away now, but so far our men are holding them off. With Joe Johnston gone . . ."

"Miz Stone, here's the water," Ellie called.

Opening her eyes, Taylor pushed herself out of the chair. She looked at Philip's tired face and knew in a flash that he would be ill with the fever again soon.

"Let's go home, Philip," she urged.

He shook his head. "Not while I can do anything at all to help."

Holding her skirt up, Taylor went down the steps. She knew it would be useless to argue with him.

"Come along, Ellie," she said and began to weave her way back through the men.

Richard Adair waited patiently where she had left him. If he had learned anything in the agonizing spring and summer of 1864, it was patience. And in the days since that sudden flash of light and torturous burning had plunged him into darkness, he had learned to trust many strangers.

But *she* was no stranger. He hadn't lied to her. Her face, her voice, even her tears were as clear to him as if it were just yesterday that he had seen her. He had lived with her memory so long now, it was hard to believe he had only met her once, for a brief moment, while he delivered the message that she was a widow. He knew nothing about her, but for some reason, she had become the brightness that kept him going. Through the cold winter, through the dusty retreats, through the rain and mud and fear and death, he had thought of her. He had envied her husband, dead for eight months now, whatever time he had spent with her. He would die happy himself if only once more he could see her face, if he could hold her in his arms and kiss her lovely lips.

He sighed deeply, ignoring the gnawing hunger that clawed at his ribs and the searing needles that still pricked at his eyes. He knew his wish was foolish, but sometimes it helped to dream, sometimes . . .

"Richard?"

He was so very still, his eyes looking blank and unseeing, that she thought he was dead. When he shifted at the sound of her voice, she relaxed.

"Here's your water. I've sent Ellie to find something for you to eat."

"I'm sure you can't spare it, Mrs. Stone. I'll be off to the hospital soon, and they'll have something to feed me there." They both knew better. "But thanks anyway."

He held the cup with both hands and drank thirstily. Finished, he handed the cup back to her.

"Would you like some more? There's plenty of water."

He shook his head. "Mrs. Stone, if you would

see if someone is going my way, I think I'll go to the hospital."

"I'd be glad to help," a young man volunteered. His arm was held in a body sling.

He helped Richard to his feet and then tipped his ragged cap to Taylor, waiting as they said their goodbyes.

"Thank you, Mrs. Stone. Perhaps someday we'll meet again," Richard Adair said.

"I hope so, Richard," Taylor replied as she walked with them toward the street. "And I hope you get well quickly. Goodbye, Richard."

She stood at the picket fence, watching the two men slowly make their way down the street. They turned a corner and vanished from sight. Suddenly, a shrill squeal filled the air, followed by an explosion several blocks away. For an instant, everything was unbelievably quiet. Then the air seemed to be filled with screaming, crashing shells. Atlanta was besieged!

Taylor saw a flash of light and then watched the building crumble where seconds before Richard Adair and his young assistant had been. There was no time to wonder about them, however, as another shell crashed into the Howard home across the street. Taylor wheeled and raced to the house, meeting a white-faced Marilee at the door.

"Where's Philip?" Taylor cried.

"He went upstairs. I think he's sick again."

"Get everyone into the cellar," Taylor ordered as she ran up the stairs. "Don't waste any time."

Just as she had feared, she found Philip

shivering under several blankets. A shell whistled to earth outside the bedroom window, blowing away an old shed.

"Philip! Philip, get up!" she yelled above the noise.

Outside, the streets were filled with screaming people running in all directions in their efforts to avoid Sherman's onslaught.

Half pulling, half pushing, Taylor managed to get the delirious Philip down the stairs. Once in the cellar, they made a bed for him on old crates and wrapped him in his blankets. Marilee huddled nearby while Taylor held a frightened Brenetta tightly against her breast. She had no idea how long the terror rained upon Atlanta. It seemed like forever.

When at last she dared ascend the steps, she found an awed silence blanketing the city. Dusk was spreading over the devastation, and one by one, the shocked survivors ventured forth from their hiding places. Taylor stood on the porch of the once beautiful house on the once beautiful street in the once bustling city and shivered despite the heat of summer. Brenetta, exhausted, slept in her arms; Marilee stood at her side.

"We're leaving, Marilee," Taylor said breathlessly. "I'm not staying any longer. We'll not wait for Philip to get better. In the morning, we'll put him in the wagon with whatever food we have and go to Spring Haven."

"But, Taylor, we don't know where the armies might be. We . . . ."

377

"It doesn't matter," Taylor cried, feeling the hysteria rising inside her. "Is it better to wait here to be struck by a shell? No! I'll take my chances out there. It couldn't be worse than here. It couldn't!"

Marilee surveyed the potholed street, the mangled buildings, the fires, and nodded. "No, I don't suppose it could be worse," she answered. But silently she wondered if it just *might* be worse.

Chapter 35

Despite Taylor's determination, they were hampered in their departure for several days. The shelling had resumed after a brief respite and continued, seemingly without ceasing, through the next two days. During this time, McPherson and his Union army seized Decatur, cutting the railroad to Virginia and ending any hope of possible reinforcements. Hood evacuated his outer defense lines and withdrew into Atlanta's fortifications. On the third day after the shelling began, a truce was called to bury the dead.

Amid the lull, housewives ventured forth to stock up on provisions in anticipation of the siege. Taylor was among them. She had left the others to load the ramshackle wagon while she and Ellie sought food for their journey. She came home with little. There were no vegetables or dairy products to be found. Flour was going for three hundred dollars a barrel, sugar for fifteen dollars a pound. Any meat found was already turning and would be foul in a short time. Somehow, they would have to get by on the hominy and corn until they reached Spring Haven.

It was already late afternoon when they closed the door on the large white house and started south on Peachtree Street. Philip dozed fitfully in the shade of the driver's seat with Marilee seated beside him holding the baby. Mima sat grimly atop some bedding, a firm hold on adventuresome Brenetta. Ellie was riding beside Josh, trembling with fear. Taylor walked beside the wagon, feeling the need to work off some of her anxieties. How was she to get these people safely home?

She rested her hand lightly on the hip of Heathcliff, the big-barreled horse pulling the wagon. At least she didn't have a horse to worry about. Although the sad wagon was all that remained to them for transportation, the carriage having been donated to the Confederacy and the buggy stolen, Josh's skill at concealing horses had preserved them this hardy animal for just this time of need. He was an ugly brute of questionable heritage, but his heart was even greater than his size and he seemed to have suffered little from the scant and poor feed of recent days.

As they turned onto Decatur Street in the midst of town, Taylor's thoughts returned to the journey ahead of them. With Decatur in the hands of the enemy and Union soldiers blocking everything to the north of Atlanta, it seemed the only possible choice was to go south before cutting across to the east, skirting the Union army, and then maneuvering back north, perhaps along the river. The real danger in Taylor's mind would be the crossing of the railway. She knew it was the railroads as much as the factories that had drawn Sherman to Atlanta, and she was uncertain just how heavily guarded the tracks would be. But they would do it. Somehow, they would do it.

At last they began to leave Atlanta behind them—but not the crowds. The road leading toward Jonesboro and points farther south was filled with other families seeking to escape before Sherman resumed his shelling. There was no friendly chatter between families as there would have been in other times. There were only grim looks meeting grim looks as they plodded silently away from homes, families, and friends.

Near evening, Taylor's wagon came to a halt beside a buggy in obvious distress. A broken wheel caused the rig to career dangerously to one side. A well-dressed woman was seated on a log with her back to the road, while the gentleman, equally well-dressed, worked to replace the wheel. Taylor, by this time riding beside Josh, told him to assist the man; then she climbed down and walked over to the woman.

"Excuse me, ma'am. Could we be of some help to . . ." She choked on her words as Lizabeth Reed turned to meet her gaze.

"Taylor Bellman, as I live and breathe."

Lizabeth was dressed in a gown of fine blue linen, and Taylor would have sworn she was wearing rouge on her cheeks. Her hair was covered by a perky matching blue bonnet, ill-suited to her angular, sharp-featured face.

Lizabeth's eyes quickly took in Taylor's shabby dress and the dilapidated wagon holding the rest of the family before she said, "So you're running too. Papa was terribly upset that we were leaving. He fairly yelled at Jeffrey and me. Called Jeff terrible names, too."

She stood up, smoothing her skirt over several crackling petticoats. Taylor couldn't help but wonder how she could afford such luxury.

"Of course, you know my husband, Jeff Stone," Lizabeth said as someone stepped up behind Taylor. "Jeff, you remember Taylor Bellman."

The shock of Lizabeth's words had little time to register before a greater jolt hit her. A wave of cold terror washed over her as she looked into evil dark eyes topped by bushy eyebrows, the familiar thin cigar gripped by yellow teeth.

"Jackson!" she whispered in horror.

He smiled wickedly. "Sorry, ma'am. The name's Stone, just like the Mrs. said. Right nice of you t'lend me your nigga to fix the wheel."

Taylor stepped cautiously away from him, remembering with a shudder the feel of a gun held against her ribs when last they met. Her eyes darted to Lizabeth. Dear heavens, she thought.

Lizabeth really thinks he's Jeffrey.

"Somethin' wrong, Miz Bellman? That is what my wife called ya, ain't it?"

"No. Yes. I mean, no. I'm fine. I believe I'll go back to my wagon. I'm sure Josh will have you ready in no time. Goodbye, Lizabeth, Mr . . . Stone."

Icy fingers of fear prodded at her back as she hurried to the wagon. She saw Marilee's and Mima's faces and knew at once that they too had recognized Matt Jackson and were as frightened as she was. She sat stiffly on her seat, her eyes urging Josh to hurry and finish. She stifled the desire to hail passing wagons to wait with them as the day waned. An eternity later, Josh completed his task and returned to the wagon, followed closely by Matt and Lizabeth. Matt's hand rested on Taylor's thigh as he smiled up at her.

"Thanks agin, Miz Bellman. It was right nice to meet up with you agin. Are you going to Jonesboro by any chance? Perhaps we could travel together."

"No! We're going to Spr—I mean, no, we're not going to Jonesboro."

His hand tightened unpleasantly on her leg. "I'm sure we'll meet agin some other time then, Miz Bellman. I promise I'll think of some way to repay you for your kindness. And I assure you I'm lookin' forward to it."

"Goodbye, Lizabeth. Let's go, Josh," she offered, her composure cracking.

The reins snapped smartly against Heathcliff's back in response to her command, and the wagon jerked quickly away from the pair.

"Oh, Taylor. To think we should ever have seen that man again! With Lizabeth Reed, too. And us so helpless," Marilee cried when they were out of hearing distance.

Taylor shuddered again. "I know, Marilee. To think that Lizabeth has made that odious murderer into her Jeffrey. I feel ill at the thought. Why, Jeffrey was the gentlest of souls. And he doesn't even resemble . . ."

"Mama. Hungry," Brenetta interjected loudly.

"I think everyone could use something to eat," Taylor answered as she pulled Brenetta onto her lap. "Do you know a place for us to stop for the night, Josh? Someplace away from the main road?" Unspoken, but understood, was the wish to avoid further contact with Jackson and Lizabeth.

"Yes'm. Our road's jus' up hyar a mite further. We'll find us a restin' place 'fore dark," he assured her.

It helped her to know that Josh was so familiar with the roads around Atlanta. She knew she could trust him not to get them lost. Taylor also knew that he would still look to her to make all the decisions, and the responsibility weighed heavily upon her.

They made their camp in a grove of trees, eating stale bread and hardtack before crawling wearily into their beds. Taylor feared her worries

384

and responsibilities would hold sleep at bay, but exhaustion was the victor and a dreamless slumber held her in its grip throughout the night.

The morning promised another hot day before them. They ate sparingly of the hominy Mima prepared over a crude fire before reloading the wagon and pulling out. The road they were traveling was deeply rutted from the early summer rains and the going was slow. They had an added worry when Philip took a turn for the worse. He thrashed wildly about his corner of the wagon, mumbling incoherently, flailing his arms through the air. Taylor and Marilee took turns nursing him the best they could, leaving Mima to care for the children.

By noon of that second day, they had reached the railroad tracks. Josh left them well hidden in the trees and went forward on foot to scout out any problems or dangers. He returned a short time later with a smile on his face.

"Ain't no problems hyar, Missy. I seen some Reb so'diers jus' the tother side. Cap'an said t'come on across."

Taylor pushed her straggling hair away from her eyes. Her arms ached from holding Brenetta, and she wished dearly for a good meal. She stiffened her back against the renewed jiggle of the wagon as they proceeded out into the open.

A small band of Confederate soldiers, their butternut uniforms hardly more than rags on their backs, were camped near a muddy stream. She felt their eyes upon her as the wagon approached, and she returned the gaze, her eyes flicking from one face to another. They all seemed to look alike now, she thought. Young and old, tall and short, they were all tired and hungry, beaten but not surrendering. Taylor tried to smile at them, tried to share a little hope in this sea of despair, hope that she didn't feel either.

The captain stepped up beside the wagon as Josh pulled the horse to a halt. "Afternoon, ma'am," he said politely, a gentle Virginia drawl in his voice. "Uncle here tells me you're headin' north?"

"Yes, Captain. Our plantation is on the Oconee River, northwest of Athens. Will we have trouble reaching it?"

He looked at the inhabitants in the back of the wagon—the aging negress, the woman and tiny baby, and the sick man—before answering. "Hard to tell, ma'am. Things should be safe between here and Athens. North of there I couldn't say. The Yankees have Atlanta pretty well surrounded now and have spread out from there. How far and how many is not something I know. If you keep to the river and away from the main roads, you might be better off." He paused thoughtfully. "If you don't mind me sayin' so, ma'am, I think you'd be wiser to head south."

Taylor lifted her eyes toward where she knew Spring Haven to be. "Thank you, Captain. I'm sure we'll make it home just fine."

"Yes, ma'am. I'm sure you will. God willin'."

The afternoon sun beat down on them unmercifully, yet they pushed on. After leaving behind the band of Confederate soldiers, they hadn't seen another soul. They had passed several seemingly deserted farm houses, but it wasn't until evening that they came upon a plantation. The manor house was small and genteel, and they were met on the porch by a spry, equally genteel woman of inestimable years. She welcomed them with the southern hospitality of yesteryears. Quickly, she sent an ancient black servant to prepare a room for Philip and some food for her hungry visitors before ushering them into the parlor. Their hostess kept up a friendly chatter, negating the necessity for any response from her tired guests. It wasn't long before they were all dining on corn and potatoes, the old mistress apologizing for the meager meal. To Taylor, the food seemed a banquet.

At last, they were taken to their rooms. After the day's jouncing, the beds were a touch of heaven. Taylor collapsed into a deep sleep as soon as her head touched the pillow.

Chapter 36

During the night, Philip's fever abated. He was surprised upon awakening to find himself in a strange bedroom quite some distance from where he last remembered closing his eyes. Taylor felt the weight of responsibility lighten as she sat beside him, feeding him his breakfast. He was still very weak, but his mind was active and he could take charge of everything now. He would be himself in another day or two.

"I know you would scold me if you had the strength, Philip, but it's too late now. We had to get Marilee and the children away from the shells, and there was nothing any of us could do anymore in Atlanta." His eyes bespoke his agreement, and she smiled gratefully. "Here now. Finish eating this so we can be off. With luck, we might be able to reach home by dark."

They left behind their gracious hostess with regret, promising they would see her again when the war was over. Their spirits lifted with each hour as they began to recognize more and more landmarks. By early afternoon they had reached the Palackee River, not more than ten miles from Dorcet Hall.

Taylor sat on the bank, dangling her feet in the cool water. Everything was so peaceful. The fear that had dogged her since the first shell fell seemed to float away on the current. She felt certain that no Yankees would be near her sanctuary. They would all arrive safely at Spring Haven and find all as she had left it. Her stomach growled uncomfortably, reminding her that she shouldn't dawdle. They still had to cross the river before they could be on their way home.

Josh found a spot where the wagon could ford the river safely, and at four o'clock that afternoon, Heathcliff pulled them away from the river and through Dorcet Hall lands. They stopped briefly in front of the blackened ruins of the once proud home. Taylor felt a moment of wistfulness, thinking back to the three years she had lived here. Poor David. It had meant so much to him, and he had watched it disappear into ashes.

"Let's go on," she said to the others who had been waiting silently. "We're nearly home."

Too tired to speak, they rode on in silence. Heathcliff's head drooped forward as he leaned into the harness. Philip was sleeping again, and Marilee was nursing the baby. Even Brenetta was napping.

"Miss Taylor," Josh said suddenly. "I don't think this hyar horse is goin' no further today."

Surprised out of her daydreams, Taylor looked at the animal with new awareness. He was heavily lathered and was favoring his right front leg. Josh was right. He could go no farther. She felt her heart drop. They were so *close.* An hour or so more and they would be there.

"All right, Josh," she said, looking around her. "There's an old cabin just around the next bend, I think. We'll stay there tonight and go on in the morning."

Everyone but Philip climbed out of the wagon to lighten the load, and Taylor led the way toward the old shack. It was little changed since the cold stormy night she had spent in it with Brent. As Taylor peeked inside, she half expected to hear his voice speaking her name. He felt so very near, so very real to her. She shook herself. It was no good thinking about Brent. He was hundreds of miles away—if not dead. Memories did no one any good. They only tormented a person's soul.

"Mima, please see what you can do to straighten this up a little bit," she said briskly. "Josh, we'll need a fire for cooking. Ellie, you help Mima, and Miss Marilee and I'll get Philip onto that cot."

Before long, Mima had whisked away the dirt and cobwebs and was cooking a stew of herbs and corn. Philip was sitting up on his cot, his back against the wall, holding his young son while

Marilee helped Taylor with the bedding. They had opened the tiny window and the door, hoping to bring some relief to the stifling heat inside the cabin which was compounded by the cook fire. Later, their stomachs at least partially satisfied, one by one they each found their way to their beds. All except Taylor.

She was filled with a restlessness that would not be induced to sleep, no matter how tired her body was. Regardless of her efforts, Brent's presence in this room could not be ignored. Added to that was the knowledge that they were little more than an hour from the safe arms of Spring Haven.

Quietly, she slipped outside. Heathcliff was munching happily near the wagon where Josh was sleeping. The sky was clear and stars twinkled at her through the canopy of trees as a soft blanket of moonlight spread over her. The song of the river called to her, and she followed the melody until she found a felled tree. She sat upon it and stared at the rushing water, the night lights glittering in the current. If we were all strong and healthy, she thought, we could have walked to Spring Haven by this time. But Philip was not strong enough, nor were the others either.

She was ashamed of the irritation she felt toward them all. Perhaps, she thought, cooling off would help me relax. Quickly, she unbuttoned her dress and let it fall to her feet. She removed her shoes and, dressed only in her slip, stepped carefully into the sparkling water. She leaned against a boulder near the bank and splashed her arms and neck and face with the refreshing liquid. She wished desperately that she could wash her hair but knew it had better wait until she was home.

Feeling one hundred percent better, her slip dripping and clinging to her body, she stepped out onto the bank. As she reached for her dress, she heard the snapping of a twig in the shadows. She froze, listening for something more and hoping there would be only silence. A man chuckled.

"Good ears, ma'am."

She twirled around, holding her dress against her bosom. "Who's there?" she hissed.

One by one, the blue uniformed men stepped out from the trees, their faces grotesque in the light of the moon filtering through the trees.

"God help me," she whispered, stepping back from them. *Yankees!*

"No reason to look so scared, ma'am. We don't mean you no harm. None of us have two heads and we don't eat little children."

The voice was clear and friendly. She wanted with all her might to believe what he said, to believe she would be allowed to go. The speaker stepped away from the others. He was a small, squarely built man of about forty. He removed his hat as he approached her.

"Where's your home, ma'am?"

Home. Dear Lord, the children, Marilee, Philip.

"I—I've c—come from Atlanta," she stuttered. "I—I have no home around here. I'm—I'm just trying to g—get away from the Yanke—from the fighting."

"Where's your horse?"

"I . . . he went lame. I don't have one now." *Please don't let them take the horse,* she thought, her mind racing madly. She had to get Philip, everyone, home. She had to have Heathcliff. "I'm on foot," she lied.

"Best come with me, ma'am. Can't have you wandering about the countryside." He took her upper arm with strong but gentle fingers. "You'll have to stay with us till we have things scouted out."

She held herself stiffly, raising her chin to its most noble height. "Would you at least allow me to *clothe* myself?"

Flustered, he mumbled, "Of course."

"Then please have the decency to have *them* turn their backs," she said with a withering look at the group of men. "And you too," she added.

"Men, turn around," he ordered.

When she glared at him for not joining them, he shrugged, "Sorry, ma'am. Can't have you slipping away 'cause I was too polite."

She stared at him hotly, but it did no good. She gave up and turned her back to him. She knew the dress would be as wet and nearly as revealing as her slip in no time, but she would feel a little more protected. Her fingers worked unsteadily at her buttons on the bodice of her dress. Shoes on, she found her arm once more held in a firm grip.

"This way, ma'am."

Quietly, they filed in among the trees, and she found she was quickly disoriented in the darkness. Suddenly, the trees parted and they came upon a small camp. Several men looked up as she was guided over to a campfire.

"Colonel back yet?" her captor asked someone.

"Not yet."

"If you'll sit over here, ma'am, I'll get you some coffee. I think you'll be comfortable till the colonel shows up."

"Thank you," she said rigidly, avoiding the admiring stares of the men around her.

It was an old, battered cup he placed in her hand moments later, but to her amazement, it was *real* coffee—with sugar in it! Despite herself, she drank it with relish and wished there was more. Angry at her mental slip, she looked around in search of a means of escape. A few of the men had already retired to their bedrolls. Others were grouped around the fires, engrossed in conversation. Perhaps, if she waited long enough, she would find a moment when no one was keeping watch over her.

She thought the time was about to come when a tall soldier strode over and sat down beside her. To her captor, he said, "Relax for a while, Sergeant. I'll watch over the lady."

The man at her side was handsome with bold blue eyes and blond hair. His smile was sure and friendly, and Taylor thought she might be able to convince him to help her. She turned a tremulous smile up at him.

394

"Sir, do you know what they intend to do with me?"

His confident grin widened. "Don't worry, ma'am. The colonel doesn't allow his men to rape and plunder."

She was taken back by his candor but pressed on. "Is it really necessary that I be held here? I've nothing to tell your colonel. All I want is . . . is to get away from the fighting." She shivered, hoping it would gain his sympathy.

"Here, ma'am. You're taking a chill. Wrap up in this blanket." He pulled it snugly about her shoulders.

An idea springing to her mind, she said in as helpless a voice as she could muster, "Perhaps if I could walk around a bit, I would warm up."

"Yes, perhaps you might," he agreed, his smile broadening. "Sergeant, the lady needs to move around a bit to warm up. I'll go along and keep an eye on her."

Taylor saw the sergeant frown, but he nodded. The tall soldier took her arm and tucked it in his elbow. Slowly, they strolled away from the campfires and into the waiting night. Her mind was working swiftly, trying to devise a way to free herself from her escort. He had fallen into her trap so easily, she was certain she could think of something soon to outsmart him.

"Where are you from . . . oh, my. I don't know what to call you."

"My name's Pierce, ma'am. Private Pierce. I'm from Ohio."

"Ohio. I've never been there. I'm sure it's very lovely."

"Not nearly as lovely as you, ma'am."

Perhaps this was the way to trick him. If she could gain his affections, maybe he would release her or, at least, he might become careless in his watch.

"Why, Mr. Pierce," she said in her coyest southern drawl, "how very sweet of you to say so. And you, sir, show the falseness we've been hearing about Yankee manners."

He halted abruptly, his hand tightening on her arm. "Quaint little rebel, aren't you?"

Taylor tried to release her arm but was unsuccessful. She felt the first tentacles of fear inching about her heart. How far had they walked from the camp?

"Whatever do you mean, Mr. Pierce?" she asked, trying to see his face.

He laughed. "I mean, my dear little one, that you thought to tempt this dumb Yankee with your charms so that you could escape. And perhaps I'll let you do just that . . . after I've sampled those same charms more fully."

His lips were hard upon hers as he pulled her against him. She struggled, pushing against his chest with both her hands, but it only seemed to delight him. He laughed again as he clasped her wrists in his left hand, and with his right, he began to methodically unbutton her dress.

"Please, Mr. Pierce, don't!"

She felt him smile as he proceeded undaunted.

Carefully, he inched her bodice from her shoulders. The whiteness of her slip seemed to glow in the night, her breasts rising and falling quickly with each short breath. Again he caught her up to him, his lips punishing, probing hers.

"Relax, ma'am. Enjoy. You'll be free to go home soon enough."

She whimpered as he pressed her against a tree, his hand fondling her breast, his breath hot on her face.

"Pierce, I may hang you for this."

The angry words, hurled through the darkness, brought an immediate response from her attacker. He released her, whirling quickly away from her, his body at attention. Taylor pulled her dress back around her but found that her legs were shaking too hard to be able to move away from the tree that braced her back.

"Sergeant, take this man back to camp and place him under guard."

"Yes, sir, Colonel."

Her heart pounded in her ears as her assailant was led away. She waited for the officer's next move, too weary and frightened to think of escaping anymore. She just wished he would hurry up and do whatever it was he was going to do. Then she heard him stepping forward and finally she could make out his silhouette between the trees.

"I do apologize, ma'am, for the behavior of my men."

She gasped, the sound a tiny cry on the air.

"Ma'am, are you . . ."

"Brent?" she whispered.

Nothing. No reply. No movement. Nothing. The earth stopped revolving as she waited. And suddenly he was there, just inches away from her.

"It can't be," he said. "Is it really you? Taylor?"

He wrapped her carefully in his arms, his face buried in her hair. He murmured words of love but she was beyond hearing. She was here in his arms and nothing else mattered. The ugliness of the past few minutes vanished as if they had never been. There was only now. There was only Brent.

With a sweeping motion, he gathered her up and carried her out of the dense trees. There, he set her on the ground and sank down beside her. Taking her jaw in his fingers, he tipped her head toward the moonlight. She felt him studying her face. His fingers traced her lips, her cheekbones, her eyebrows, her ears, her chin, her throat, her shoulders. She waited breathlessly as he examined her, loving his touch.

"I had hoped," he whispered. "I wanted to see you, but I . . ."

He kissed her, and she was lost. She remembered lying with him in their bed at Spring Haven, one night after another. They had vowed their love to one another and were wed in their hearts, making them one forever.

"Oh, Brent," she sighed as he released her. "I was such a fool. There's so much I need to tell you."

"I know. But perhaps it shouldn't be said. You

398

... you're married to Jeffrey and you aren't free to be with me. We'll have to forget this ever happened. But let me hold you a little longer."

Her face against his chest, she told him, "Jeffrey's dead. Since last December."

"I'm sorry, Taylor. I know you cared for him."

She looked up at him now. "Yes, I loved him . . . but never like I love you. Oh, Brent, I was such a fool. I thought you had lied to me so I refused to go with you. Then, when I discovered I was going to have your baby and Jeffrey wanted to marry me, it seemed the right thing to do. But I only made everything worse. Much worse."

She stopped. He was staring at her so oddly that she expected something terrible to happen. His hands tightened on her shoulders.

"You had my baby?"

Her lilting laughter burst forth uncontrolled. Never had she seen him look quite like this, his mouth gaping and his eyes wide with wonder.

He shook her. "Tell me again. You had a baby? Our baby?"

Sobered, she replied, "You have a beautiful daughter. Brenetta Lattimer." She knew his question and answered it. "We let it be thought she was David's. Jeffrey knew the truth all along. He loved her, Brent . . . and he loved me. He was always so good to us."

"I owe him a lot I see. Now it's too late to ever thank him. I'm sorry, Taylor."

Taylor snuggled against him again. "Let's forget it, Brent. For this moment, for tonight, let's forget all the unhappiness. Let's forget it all except that we've found each other once again."

He kissed her again, a slow, loving kiss that began to grow in urgency as they fell back amid the forest lawn. She surrendered to it, willing, desiring for him to continue, to never stop loving her, kissing her, again. But he did stop. She felt herself gasping for air as he pushed himself away.

"If we don't go back soon, they'll come looking for us." He pulled her to her feet, picking needles from her hair. "Straighten youself, Mrs. Stone, or we'll have some explaining to do."

"Indeed, Mr. Lattimer, I imagine *you* already have some explaining to do."

She clung to his arm as they approached the camp. Sarge and Pierce were seated near a fire with three or four others. The camp had grown with the addition of Colonel Lattimer's staff and aides, and several more campfires were blazing away. The sergeant and the others rose as Brent and Taylor neared them. Pierce looked at her warily, noting the colonel's possessive hand on her arm.

"Gentlemen, may I introduce Mrs. Stone, who, by coincidence, happens to be my *stepmother.*"

Several flabbergasted gazes were turned upon her. Pierce's eyes fell hopelessly. He was doomed! Taylor felt a stab of guilt for leading him on. Then she remembered his laughter as she begged him to leave her alone, and the feeling was squelched. She hoped he would be flogged.

"Sergeant, I want you and a few men to escort Mrs. Stone safely to her home."

"Tonight, sir?"

Taylor pressed his forearm. "Brent, I . . . I can't go home tonight. I'm afraid I lied to your men.

I'm not alone."

He looked at her closely, a slight frown on his brow.

"Philip and Marilee and the children. They're in the cabin by the river. It was too late to go on tonight and the horse went lame."

"The cabin by... Ah, the cabin. Yes, I remember," he said softly.

"I think it best I return alone. Brent, Philip is ... he *is* still a Confederate soldier, although he's too ill to serve any longer."

"I'm sorry, Taylor. I can't allow that. The area is filled with both Union men and stragglers from the Confederate army. You'll be much safer with an escort."

"Whatever you think is best," she agreed, willing to trust him with her life once again.

A horse was brought forward for her, and she felt herself being lifted into the saddle. Looking down into Brent's beloved face, she asked, "Will I see you again soon?"

"As soon as I'm able, I'll come ... with a chaplain," he whispered for her ears only. "Until then, my love, be careful. I'll be with you soon."

His eyes caressed her in his farewell as her horse was led away from him. She held that look within her heart, tucking it away to sustain her until he came for her.

Chapter 37

She could hear Marilee softly calling her name as they neared the cabin.

"Sergeant, please allow me to go forward alone. I promise there won't be any trouble, but I think I should prepare my family for you."

He helped her down from her mount and stood aside as she walked by him.

"Marilee, here I am. No, I'm all right, dear. Please come inside."

Several concerned faces turned to her as she closed the door. She looked from Marilee to Philip to Mima and then back again before beginning. "I'm sorry I worried all of you. I was restless and took a walk. I . . ." She paused, inhaling deeply. "I ran into Yankee soldiers."

Marilee gasped, "No!"

Philip's jaw twitched.

"They did me no harm," she hurried to assure them, again shifting her eyes from one party to the next. "It was their colonel who saw to my safety. Colonel Brent Lattimer."

"Brent Lattimer!" Philip ejaculated.

"Philip, he sent me back with men to take us to Spring Haven. He says the area is firmly in Union hands and it could be dangerous for us without his aid. Please, Philip, let's go with them peacefully."

He glared at her angrily. "You would have us seen with these men? Taylor, we both know the Yankees are the victors and that the darkies will go free, but you and I still have to live here among our neighbors and friends. Would you have us seem to be Union sympathizers?"

She stepped over to the cot, knelt down, leaning on his knees with her arms, and looked up into his face. "Philip, I love the South. No one loves her more than I do. I've helped fight this war every way I could. I've bound broken, bleeding bodies; I've worked until I dropped; I've lost two husbands. I've been a true Confederate, even when I questioned the reasons for the war, even when I knew it was lost. But, Philip, there's something you don't know. I love Brent Lattimer. It doesn't matter to me whether he's a Confederate or a Yankee. I love him, and I intend to marry him. Before the war is even over if possible." His thigh tightened under her touch. She continued in a near whisper, tears filling her eyes as she begged him to understand. "Philip, Brenetta is his child. I love him."

Taylor hid her face in his lap. She couldn't bear to look into the shock and disdain written in his eyes a moment longer. She felt Marilee's arm go around her as she knelt beside Taylor.

"Taylor dear, don't cry. Of course, Philip understands. He knows that love crosses all borders. *Don't you, Philip?*" Marilee looked meaningfully at her husband.

He returned her gaze, the struggle within him a mighty one. Finally, he touched Taylor's shoulder. "We'll go, Taylor. I won't make trouble for you. But you must allow me time to get used to what you've just told me."

"Oh, Philip. Thank you!" she cried, throwing her arms around his neck and kissing him soundly.

A sharp rap at the door brought renewed anxiety to the inhabitants.

"Mrs. Stone?"

Taylor opened the door calmly, her face still streaked with tears. "Yes, Sergeant. You may come in."

"We've harnessed our horse to your wagon, ma'am. If it's possible, we'd like to move out. We've got to get back to camp before daylight." His eyes met with Philip's. "I apologize, sir, for moving your family during the night."

"No need, Sergeant," Philip replied formally. "I understand the necessity." He struggled to his feet. "Marilee. Taylor. Get the children."

The journey through the early morning crepuscule had an unreal quality. They moved silently, the wagon preceded and followed by Union soldiers, eyes and ears alert to any danger. Taylor thought of how well fed each of these men looked, how their uniforms and boots fit them, and in what good condition their horses were. In contrast, she remembered the Confederate soldiers they had seen only yesterday, or was it the day before that? Those men had been clothed in rags, hardly anything that could be called uniforms. They were lucky if they had boots three sizes too big or even a size too small. She doubted any had a pair made to fit. They were a hungry army, fighting on sheer grit and stubbornness. The South had been predestined to lose, she thought now, but she was proud to be a Southerner, nonetheless. They had fought for something they believed in—or at least thought they believed in—and had fought heroically against awesome odds.

Funny, she thought. She felt no animosity toward these men in blue. Was it because they were Brent's men or was it simply because she knew they were just men doing their job? Just men who happened to live in the North. Men who would have fought as hard for the South if they had been born and raised there. She looked up at the stars overhead. So much fighting was left before it would all be over. So many more men to die before the guns would be silent. And then what? There would still be so much hate to be healed. Could the South forget or forgive? Could other Southerners look upon the Yankees and understand that these men were not the enemy any longer? She thought not and it saddened her.

The scars of war would fester for many years after the final shot was fired.

Spring Haven. She stood bravely against the dawn, her columns raised proudly before her. Taylor strained forward as if it would hurry the horse up the drive. They had made it. They were safe. They were home. Before anyone could assist her from her perch on the driver's seat, Taylor had jumped to the ground and was racing up the steps.

"Susan! Saul!" she cried, flinging open the door. Her voice echoed through the empty rooms. She waited, suddenly fearing they were gone, that they had accepted their freedom and departed. Her heart fell. In a flash, she remembered thinking upon her last trip to Atlanta that Spring Haven would see tragedy before long. Had something terrible . . .

A candle appeared in the hallway.

"Missy, be that you?"

"Susan. Yes, it's me. It's all of us," she answered, relieved. "Philip and Marilee and the children and Mima and Josh. We're all home."

Susan stood before her, peering around her to the wagon and the soldiers.

"It's all right, Susan. They brought us here."

Susan looked doubtful but was silent. Handing Taylor the candle, she went out to help the others down from the wagon. The sergeant dismounted and stood at the base of the steps.

"We'll be on our way now, Mrs. Stone. I hope all goes well for you."

"Thank you, Sergeant," she answered and

watched them ride away. As they disappeared from sight, she turned and entered the house, asking, "Where is everyone, Susan? It's so quiet."

"Gone, Missy. They's all gone."

"Everyone gone?"

"All but me, Missy."

"Even Saul?" Taylor asked in disbelief.

"Saul passed over, Miss Taylor. Las' week it was."

She felt shaken. Saul dead? "What happened, Susan?" she asked as they climbed the stairs.

" 'Twas awful, Missy. Some ol' fiel' darky, he argued wid Saul, sayin' he gettin' out now dat the Yankees was here 'n' he was takin' what food he wanted. Pushed Saul down dem steps out front. Wasn't nothin' nobody could do fo' him. He gone when he hit da bottom."

Saul gone. So tragedy had struck as she had feared. He had never known the freedom she had given him. He had chosen to stand by her. Dear Saul. He had pulled her through some bad times.

Taylor opened the door to her room. Nothing was changed. She smiled wearily at the old servant. "You've managed well on your own, Susan. We're very grateful."

"What you 'spectin'?" she fussed. "Dis bein' my home 'n' all."

The sun was shedding its first rays as Taylor sank into her bed and slept.

Chapter 38

She waited for him.

Each morning she looked down the oak-lined drive hoping to see him riding toward her. Each night she went to bed disappointed. She knew he would come when he could, but the waiting was hard. As much as she had hated the work at the hospitals, seeing the hungry, tattered soldiers, and hearing the shrieking shells, she wished she was as busy as she had been in Atlanta. She needed something to occupy her time. Josh and Philip spent long hours hunting and fishing, trying to feed the family; Mima and Susan cleaned and cooked, but Taylor felt at loose ends. There was only the waiting—so she waited.

They heard nothing from their neighbors. It was as if everyone was in hiding. They saw no more Yankees, but they knew they were all

around. An unreal calm hung over the countryside as if it too was waiting with Taylor.

Day followed day, the heat of August burning
down on the once fruitful fields. The planters, the
tenders, the harvesters were gone. The acres of
Spring Haven cried out for attention, but there
was no one left to answer their call. The men and
women of the Bellman household, servants included, did the best they could, but they were too
few and too inexperienced to make any real
difference. And still he didn't come.

Marilee waited patiently, holding little Phil in
her lap, while Philip completed his check of the
riggings.

"You're sure you won't join us, Taylor?" he
asked again. "We'll only stay a few days. What
difference could it make?"

"No, thank you, Philip. I'll just wait here. You
two go along and enjoy yourselves. You can tell
me all about it when you get back. Marilee, give
my love to your father."

"I will. See you soon."

Taylor watched as the old wagon jounced down
the drive, thinking of how excited Marilee was.
Just last night they had learned that the Reverend Stone had returned to Bellville from Virginia.
He had sent a young slave to learn if Marilee was
here or still in Atlanta. Marilee had promptly
decided that her family was going to visit her
father in town without delay. The Reverend Stone
hadn't even seen his grandson yet. Despite
Marilee's pleading and Philip's encouragement,
Taylor had declined the invitation to accompany

them. She just couldn't take the chance of being gone when he came.

"Well, Brenetta," she said to her daughter who was standing beside her, her tiny hand inside Taylor's. "What shall we find to do with ourselves today?"

"Ride!"

Taylor swung her up into her arms. "Sorry, Netta. The horse went bye-bye with Uncle Philip. Shall we hunt for rabbits?"

"Rabbits. Rabbits," Brenetta squealed her approval.

Of course, she didn't know that when they found a rabbit in one of Josh's traps—which wasn't very often—it became part of her supper. They were soft and wiggly and fun to find. That was all her little sixteen-month-old brain understood. They tramped around the fields and gardens for nearly two hours without success, finally returning home tired and hungry. Brenetta was fed and whisked off to bed without complaint, leaving Taylor to her own devices. Feeling a little sleepy herself, she nestled into the wicker swing on the veranda and closed her eyes.

"Miss Taylor! Miss Taylor!"

Josh was running pell-mell across the yard, waving his arms frantically over his head as he called to her. He came to a screeching halt at the foot of the steps, his breath coming in ragged gulps.

"Miss Taylor," he gasped. "They's took Atlanta."

"Josh, what are you talking about?"

"The Yanks done moved into Atlanta, Miss

Taylor."

So, she thought, it's happened at last.

"Where did you hear it, Josh?" Taylor asked him.

"Zeb from Rosewood tol' me. He heared it from da Madsens' girl's darky who come from dere las' night. 'Scuse me, Miss Taylor, but I tol' Zeb I'd carry da news t'Oak Lawn straight way."

"Go on then, Josh. Folks ought to know, though it shouldn't surprise anyone."

He was off and running before her sentence was out of her mouth. She returned to her seat in the swing, wondering what would happen next. Would the soldiers come to plunder and burn, or would they be overlooked? Now that Atlanta was theirs, would they head for Augusta or Savannah or Andersonville?

She didn't have long to ponder the questions. Upon the heels of Josh's departure, eight Union soldiers thundered up the drive. For a moment, she was frozen with fear. She wasn't ready for it yet. Philip wasn't even here to help her. Then she recognized him riding at the front of the column. All else forgotten, she was up and running to meet him. He vaulted from his still-moving horse and caught her in his arms, twirling her around in the air, both of them laughing from sheer joy. They heard a polite cough, and Brent turned her to face a handsome, red-bearded man who had dismounted more sedately nearby.

"Taylor, may I introduce you to our chaplain, Captain James."

"My pleasure, madam," Captain James said with a sharp click of the heels and a bow, his hat swept through the air with superb style.

Eyes wide, she replied, "And mine, Captain."

"Taylor, Captain James has come to marry us. If you'll have me, that is. I . . . I'll have to leave again in the morning. Atlanta has fallen and there's much to be done. Will you, Taylor? Will you marry me today?"

His rush of words sent her emotions into another whirl, but she didn't have to think about her answer. She had thought of nothing else for too many days.

"Of course I'll marry you, Brent Lattimer."

Suddenly, she remembered the other men who had ridden in with Brent. They too had dismounted and were waiting with sheepish smiles on their faces.

"Gentlemen," she said with as much composure as she could summon, "if you'll put your horses up in the stables, I'll see to some refreshments for you." She took Brent's arm and pulled him along toward the house. "Will they be staying the night too?" she asked, wondering what she would find to feed them all.

"No, love. We'll have this night to ourselves." His voice was low and intimate, and she felt shivers of delight running up and down her spine.

Looking up at him through her thick lashes, a sudden shyness possessing her, she said softly, "I love you."

He smiled, his eyes doing the speaking for him.

"You wait here, Brent, and I'll have Mima prepare something for you and your friends."

"Fine, Taylor. And one more thing."

"Yes?"

412

"After you've seen to our refreshments, go find something suitable for a bride to wear. You're about to become Mrs. Brent Lattimer. And I don't intend to dawdle either."

A sparkle lit her eyes. "Yes, sir," she laughed, throwing him a cocky salute before sprinting inside.

Dressed in a dated, somewhat school-girlish gown of pink tulle over satin, the great belled skirt looking very different without the hoops, Taylor sat in front of her mirror brushing her hair. She was daydreaming at the moment, her thoughts carrying her back over five years to her first wedding. She pictured how she had looked in the old lace and satin wedding gown. She was sorry that Brent had never seen her in it, that he hadn't been the bridegroom waiting for her at the end of that aisle so very long ago.

She returned to the present, eyeing herself critically in the looking glass. She was no longer the silly child who had wed David Lattimer. She had been widowed twice, borne a child and lived through war and hardship. Now, at twenty-two, she was about to embark into the one relationship she knew she had been born to find. She could hardly believe it was happening.

Mima entered quietly, Brenetta in her arms. "Missy, the gempmen been fed what we got and Mr. Brent is waitin' fo' you to'join 'em."

Butterflies fluttered crazily in her stomach as she turned from the mirror. "Brenetta looks very pretty, Mima. Thank you," she said as she took the little one into her lap.

"Now, Miss Taylor, you'll have dat dress all

crumpled holdin' dat babe."

"Never mind, Mima. This is an important day for Netta too, even if she doesn't know it."

Brenetta smiled at her mother, feeling the excitement around her. She, too, was dressed in pink, the material cut from an old dress of Taylor's. Her curly black hair, thick and unruly like her mother's, was tied back in a pretty pink bow.

"Well, darling. It's time you met your daddy."

Taylor walked down the curved staircase, her nervousness growing with each step. Before opening the door, she pushed the draperies at the window aside. Brent stood near his men in the shade of the oak trees, plate in hand. Carefully, she put Brenetta on her feet and smoothed both their dresses. Taking the small, trusting hand in her own, they walked outside onto the veranda and waited.

Brent turned and saw them standing there, visions in pink. Suddenly, his palms felt sweaty and his knees were weak. He was about to meet his daughter, his very own daughter.

"Hold this," he said absently, handing his plate to the chaplain.

Slowly, he approached them, his eyes fixed upon the little girl standing beside her mother. Six weeks before, he hadn't even known he was a father. Now he was facing a fetching little miss with the curly black hair of her mother and dancing, mischievous golden eyes, so very like his own and so very startling with her raven hair. Brenetta returned his gaze, her youthful curiosity alerted.

414

She was amazing. She was beautiful. She was his very own daughter. He felt his heart nearly burst with love.

Moments later, Taylor watched as Brent walked away, carrying Brenetta. She sighed as her nervousness vanished, and she sat down in the wicker swing to await their return. Brenetta had accepted his arms around her as if she had always known him, and Brent was obviously the proud father. Closing her eyes, she sent up a silent prayer of thanks for Brent's return, for the promise of a whole family and a lasting, happy marriage.

Brenetta's giggles brought Taylor's eyes open again. She caught a glimpse of Brent dashing through the trees, Brenetta on his back. Her legs grasped his sides and her arms gripped his neck. She squealed in delight as her "horsey" spun and raced in the other direction. At last they came trotting back toward the house. Brenetta's eyes were wide with excitement, and she clung to her new friend, reluctant for the fun to stop.

"I think," Brent panted, "that we're going to get along famously."

Taylor grinned. "I think so too."

"Let's get married, Mrs. Stone."

"With pleasure, Mr. Lattimer."

Chapter 39

The buzz of bees and chirping of birds were their orchestra, and the tree branches were their bridal canopy. Taylor looked up into Brent's handsome face and was oblivious to the witnesses at her wedding—to Mima's and Susan's tear-streaked faces, to Brenetta's wondering chatter, to Josh's satisfied grin, or to the six uniformed strangers gathered around them. To her, there was only Captain James speaking very wonderful words and Brent repeating them as he held her hand tenderly.

"I, Brent, take thee, Taylor . . ."

A tear slipped down her cheek, her vision blurred by the unshed others as he spoke gently to her.

"I, Taylor, take thee, Brent . . "

Her heart thundered in her ears as she echoed

him.

"By the power vested in me by the United States Government and the laws of God, I hereby pronounce you man and wife."

His arms encircled her. He drew her to him, his look serious, almost frightening in its intensity. She waited, not daring even to draw a breath.

"I love you, Taylor Lattimer," he said softly. "I'll always love you."

Her body was inflamed by his love as his lips claimed hers. She felt her knees weaken and buckle, but his arms held her steady. As his mouth released her, she opened her eyes in awe, not wanting to speak, to spoil the moment.

"Mrs. Lattimer, I'm going to like being married to you."

A cheer went up from the men, and Taylor felt herself blush, the heat rising from her heaving breasts up to her hairline. Feeling self-conscious and even a little foolish, she turned to the chaplain.

"Captain James, would you and the others join us in a toast? I'm afraid all we have is a little Madeira but we would like you to partake with us."

"Thank you, madam. We would be pleased. And might I be the first to congratulate you and Colonel Lattimer and to wish you a long and happy life together."

"Thank you, sir," she said, blushing again as Brent kissed her neck.

Brent took his arm from around her waist and

shook the chaplain's hand. "Thanks, John. You'll never know . . "

"Ah, but I think I do."

Brent laughed. "Come, let's pour the wine."

The formality of the Union soldiers had dispersed, and there was much hand-shaking and back-slapping. One at a time, they each took Taylor's hand and kissed it, wishing her much happiness and good fortune. Her head was swimming from the introductions and all the outrageous compliments paid to her and her adorable daughter. Taylor was certain they must all have guessed that Brenetta was Brent's child, but everyone tactfully referred to her as her first husband's child and she continued the charade.

As the sun fell behind the tree tops, they took their leave. Captain James shook Brent's hand heartily as they stood on the veranda.

"You're a lucky man, Colonel Lattimer. Don't forget it."

"Not likely, Captain James."

"Mrs. Lattimer," he said as he took her hand, "make sure he takes good care of you. You're one of a kind, I think."

"Thank you, Captain," Taylor replied softly. "You're most kind. I'm sure you know it's really I who am the lucky one."

He shook his red beard, his smile broad and honest. "Perhaps I should just say you deserve each other," he said with a laugh as he turned back to Brent. "We'll return in the morning, sir, with the rest of the men."

He saluted smartly and turned, but not before Taylor caught his merry wink at Brent. She felt the warmth returning to her cheeks as he swung into the saddle and the seven men galloped down the drive and out of sight.

"Shall we say goodnight to Brenetta, Mrs. Lattimer?" Brent asked her.

Arm in arm, they climbed the staircase. Mima had already fed and changed Brenetta into her nightgown, and the little girl was curled tightly into a ball under her covers. Sleep had overtaken her quickly after the excitement-filled day. They stood in the dimly lit room, holding hands, and watching her sleep.

Brent's fingers tightened on Taylor's. "Thank you," he said simply.

"Thank *you*, darling," she replied.

Brent leaned forward, kissing the mop of hair and tucking the blanket snugly under her chin.

"She's a miracle," he whispered.

They tiptoed from the room as if they had been doing it together for months. His arm around her waist, he guided her down the stairs and into the west drawing room.

"I asked Susan to prepare us something special for dinner," he said. "While we're waiting, Mrs. Lattimer, I believe this waltz belongs to me."

He bowed gravely to her in the empty, silent room. Caught up in the drama, Taylor curtsied in return.

"Do you hear the music, my dear?" he asked.

"Yes, Brent. It's lovely."

Expertly, he guided her about the room, a few pine knots providing the only illumination in the room. Her eyes and his were locked in an embrace of their own as the couple twirled around the room, lost in their thoughts, the gloaming adding a dreamlike quality to the drawing room. Yes, she *could* hear the music. It was a song of joy being played in her heart.

When he stopped, she felt her heart beating madly in her chest, not from the dancing but from his very nearness.

"Marse Lattimer? If'n you're ready, you can have your dinner," Mima said from the doorway.

"Thank you, Mima." He extended his elbow to Taylor. "Shall we, my dear?"

The dining room was lit by one lone candle centered between two place settings. The flame flickered as Brent pulled out her chair, the light shimmering on the crystal and china, Spring Haven's best. He sat down across from her, a loving smile caressing her face. Suddenly she could smell something she hadn't smelled in ages. Susan entered carrying a platter upon which was a large ham surrounded by potatoes. Behind her came Josh with the gravy and corn, and behind him was Mima with rolls and butter.

"Brent, where on earth?"

"Would I have my bride hungry on our wedding night?" he asked.

"But . . . but how . . ."

"Shhh. Just enjoy it, love, and ask me how later."

Taylor thought as she ate that a bride should have little appetite on her wedding night, but this certainly wasn't true of her. Brent watched her with a self-satisfied grin as she filled her plate again. They spoke seldom, the coziness of the room bringing their souls into a communication without words. The last of the wine was poured into their glasses, and Brent lifted his toward her.

"To my wife, who has brought more joy into my life than any other man has ever known," he said, his voice low and husky.

In response, she raised her own glass. "And to my husband, who made living worthwhile and erased the battle lines between Yankee and Rebel."

The ring of the glasses clinking together amplified the very silence around them. The servants had slipped quietly away, and they were alone in a world of their own making. In unison, they rose from their chairs, their hands reaching out to each other and clasping tightly. They walked slowly from the room their eyes locked together like their hands. Taylor floated up the stairway toward her bedroom—*their* bedroom. She felt herself tremble with desire. It had been so long, so very long, since she had lain with him, drowning in his kisses, in his caresses. Her eyes glowed in anticipation.

A fire burned on the hearth. The covers had been lovingly turned back on the bed, and the perfume of rose petals filled the air. A nightgown was laid out for her across the bed. Reluctantly

421

she drew her hand away, her eyes telling him to wait. She disappeared, negligee in hand, into her dressing room to change. Her hands quivered, refusing to be hurried as she removed her dress. The nightgown was of the finest silk, a pale apple green in color. The empire style accentuated her full white breasts and clung to her trim womanly figure. She hadn't known she even owned such a gown, and then realized it must be from Brent. Nervously she removed the pins from her hair, allowing it to tumble freely about her shoulders and down her back.

His eyes held her as she stood in the doorway. She felt unable to move, caught in the ecstasy of his loving glance. She had loved him so long, and now she was his, really his. Today had fulfilled all her dreams. Tonight would fulfill her desires.

"Come here, Taylor," he whispered.

Her bare feet sunk lusciously into the rug as she stepped slowly toward him, the flickering light from the fire casting dancing shadows around the room. His touch on her shoulder was like fire itself, the burning sensation spreading throughout her body like hot lava slipping down a mountain side.

"Taylor, my love."

She was held, a willing captive, in his arms as he kissed her, the kiss at once tender and violent with emotions. Her arms went around his neck, her fingers caressing his hair, his face, his shoulders as she surrendered to him, her body moulding itself to his.

"Touchin'. Most touchin'."

Brent's body stiffened against hers as the intruder's words shattered the spell around them. With a firm motion, he pushed Taylor behind him.

"Who are you? What are you doing here?" he demanded of the man hiding in the shadows.

The stranger chuckled, and Taylor knew who it was before he stepped forward into the light from the fire. She shrank closer to Brent's back as his face became clear.

"Matt Jackson," Brent breathed.

"So you ain't forgot me neither. Right nice of you."

"Get out, Jackson."

He laughed again as he lifted a gun from his side. "Now, I can't rightly do that. I have an appointment with Miz Bellman. You 'member, don't you, Miz Bellman? I told you I'd have to repay ya for your kindness. Jus' took me a mite long t'get here, is all."

He stepped closer, the barrel of the gun glowing red with the fire's reflection. "I was most pleased t'see your weddin', but it did interfere a mite with my plans for thankin' ya for your help. Mr. Lattimer, I'm afraid you'll be tied up awhile whilst I do my thankin'." His smile left no question in Taylor's mind what his method of appreciation would be.

"Jackson," Brent growled. "You lay a hand on my wife and I'll see you dead."

The smile vanished. "Try it. I'd love to kill you, ya nigga lovin' Yankee."

423

She felt Brent's muscles tense, ready to spring into action. Her terror grew. Jackson would kill him.

"Oh, Brent, be careful," she whispered.

Jackson lifted the pistol toward Brent's chest. "Now you move away from her, or I'll blow a hole clear through you and the Mrs. too."

Brent hesitated. Jackson would do it. He would kill them both. But he couldn't let that man touch Taylor. He couldn't bear to have her defiled by that weasel. Suddenly, he lunged forward, the full force of his fury catapulting him through the air toward the recipient of his anger. For a moment he had his fingers around Jackson's throat before a crashing pain filled his head. Taylor! he thought as he sank to the floor and into a black pit of oblivion.

"Brent!" Taylor cried. She fell to her knees, gathering his bleeding head against her. The gash where the gun butt had struck him was deep, and she pressed her hand against it to stop the red flow of life from it. "Don't leave me, Brent. I love you. Please. Nothing is worth losing you. Oh, Brent, please don't die," she sobbed.

"Leave him be, Miz Bellman. You and me got business."

His fingers closing over her shoulder caused a white rage to erupt within her. Her fear forgotten, she struck at his hand where he touched her.

"Get your stinking hands off me, you murdering butcher!"

He laughed, and her anger flared uncontrollably. She was on her feet, her fists pummeling him with all the strength she possessed. Catching him by surprise, she struck him with force several times about the face and chest before he was able to grasp her hands. Roughly, he bent her arms behind her back, enjoying her yelp of pain as he pushed them an extra inch higher.

"Miz Bellman, I warn you. I like t'hear a woman cry. The less you fight me, the less I'm goin' t'hurt you."

His mouth was just inches from her face, his breath foul in her nostrils. She felt nauseous, the bile rising sickeningly in her throat.

He pulled her steadily toward the bed. Taylor tried to force her mind to retreat. If she could just shut off her thoughts, perhaps she could survive it. She closed her eyes, bracing herself. He stopped beside the bed. Holding her wrists behind her back with one hand, his other fingered the bodice material of her nightgown which was stained with Brent's blood.

"I been plannin' this moment for years," he said thickly. Then he yanked the fabric free from her body.

"You promised! You promised!"

The scream startled them both. Jackson released her hands, spinning around. Taylor pulled her tattered nightgown around her as her eyes darted open. Standing over Brent, waving Jackson's gun wildly in their direction, was Lizabeth Reed. Her hair was untidy and windblown, and her eyes glowed with an unnatural light as tears coursed down her cheeks.

"You told me you hated her. It was me you

425

wanted," she raved. "You promised you wouldn't see her again. You lied, Jeff Stone. You lied."

This is insane, Taylor thought. *None of this can really be happening. It's just too strange.*

Jackson reached his hand toward Lizabeth. "Darlin', I was just tryin' t'punish her for hurtin' you. Give me the gun, Liz."

Taylor continued to stare at them in disbelief. Only minutes before she had been wrapped safely in Brent's arms. Now he was lying on the floor, his head in a pool of his own blood, she stood holding her torn clothes over her naked body, and a murderer and rapist was trying to coax his own gun from the hands of a madwoman. *Perhaps it's me that's gone mad,* she thought.

"Come on, Liz. You know I ain't lyin' to you. Now, give me that gun."

Lizabeth cocked it. "Not before I make sure you won't ever hold her again." Slowly, she turned the gun barrel toward Taylor.

"Lizabeth, no!" Taylor cried, stepping backwards.

"I'm never going to share my husband with you, Taylor Bellman. You tried to take him once, but I won't let you win."

Never was Taylor able to piece together the minutes that followed. It remained a jumble of terror, beginning with the gun blast ripping apart the frightened silence. Much later, she was told what happened, but her memory of it was lost.

Lizabeth pointed the gun at Taylor, her insane jealously carving her face into grotesque lines. As she tightened her finger over the trigger, Brent's hands closed around her ankle, jerking her off balance. The gun fired, and as she righted herself, she saw Jackson slumping to the floor, his hands clasping his chest, his eyes staring at her.

Dropping the weapon, she rushed to him, crying, "Jeff! Jeff, I didn't mean it. It was her. She was supposed to die."

Blood trickled from his mouth as he spoke his final words. "I'm . . . not your . . . Jeff Stone . . . Name's Jack—son . . . you crazy . . . ugly . . . woman . . ."

He went limp, his eyes staring blankly up at her in accusation.

Brent, his head throbbing unmercifully, picked up the gun where Lizabeth had dropped it. Half crawling, half dragging himself, he made his way to where Taylor sat rocking on the bed, her face covered with her hands, her knees pulled up to her chin. She was crying, short, gasping sobs, and whispering his name. As he pulled her into his arms, Josh, with Mima on his heels, came barging into the room, an old rifle in his hands. Shocked at the sight before him, he halted abruptly.

Later, as Lizabeth was led away and Jackson's body was removed, Brent was still crooning to her, his arms holding her tightly against him.

"It's all right, love. Nothing can hurt us now. I love you. It's all right. I love you . . . I love you . . . I love you . . ."

Chapter 40

The Indian summer sun blazed brightly upon Spring Haven and the inhabitants. The horses swished their tails idly as they waited to begin their journey. Likewise, their blue-clad riders sat relaxed in their saddles, long used to catching their rest whenever they could. In the shade of the veranda, Brent was shaking Philip's hand while Marilee stood beside him. Taylor waited by the swing, Brenetta in her arms, steeling herself for her own farewells.

"Philip, I hope all goes well for you and Marilee. Thanks for your hospitality." He touched his bandaged head. "I know it must have been difficult for you to have so many Yankees around Spring Haven."

"You're right," Philip said honestly. "It's never easy to lose a war. But," he added, "you *are* family now, and you're welcome."

Brent gave him a formal salute. "Goodbye, Philip. Marilee, take care of that little one. I'll do what I can to guarantee Spring Haven's safety in the days ahead."

Philip nodded, finding it difficult to accept such aid but unable to deny its need, and Brent turned to the three black servants standing in the doorway, their faces a mixture of smiles and tears.

"Josh," he said, grasping the man's calloused hand. "Thanks. You've been a great help. I won't forget." To the two women, he said, "Mima. Susan. You take care of my girls for me until I can get back."

"Marse Brent, what else you thinks we gonna do?" Mima grumbled, embarrassed by his warm handshake and affectionate glance.

He laughed. "I guess you're right. You've always taken care of her and Brenetta."

He left them, his long strides carrying him quickly to his wife and daughter. He took Brenetta from Taylor's arms and kissed the child soundly on the cheek before nuzzling her tummy.

"I'm going to miss you, Sunshine. You kiss Mama for me everyday."

Mima had come up behind them. She took the little girl from him, and he offered his elbow to Taylor. They walked slowly down the steps into the morning's glow. Brent's horse stood patiently awaiting him, his gray coat sleek and shiny.

"Taylor, it won't be long. I won't let it be long."

There were tears right behind her eyes, choking off any reply. He tipped her chin up, forcing her eyes to meet his.

"We've had longer together than we thought we

would the day we got married, Taylor. We can be glad of that, can't we?"

She nodded.

"And, love, when I get back, I'm going to take you and Brenetta and we'll go away from here. I won't have them hating you for loving me . . . or for giving me Brenetta. Maybe we'll go out west, to Oregon or California." He kissed her gently. Whispering into her hair, he continued, "Wherever we go, together or apart, we'll always be happy because we'll always be one. We'll always have each other's love."

Two tears trickled down her pale cheeks. "I'm going to miss you so very much, darling," Taylor said faintly. "It hurts for you to go."

But as she looked into his eyes, she found the courage she needed to let him go and to wait for his return. He was right. His love would sustain her.

Brent swung into the saddle. Quickly, his men were alert and prepared to ride.

"Mrs. Lattimer," he said, leaning down for one final kiss. "Remember our wedding? Remember the music we heard as we waltzed around the drawing room? We'll have that song with us the rest of our lives. Taylor love, we have all our tomorrows before us."

"I hear the music, Brent," she answered, a tremulous smile on her lips. "I hear it, and it's lovely."

He kissed her quickly, then turned his horse and rode away, followed by a dozen soldiers. And her heart followed him too, soaring overhead on the wings of a song.

SPEND YOUR LEISURE MOMENTS WITH US.

Hundreds of exciting titles to choose from—something for everyone's taste in fine books: breathtaking historical romance, chilling horror, spine-tingling suspense, taut medical thrillers, involving mysteries, action-packed men's adventure and wild Westerns.

SEND FOR A FREE CATALOGUE TODAY!

Leisure Books
Attn: Customer Service Department
276 5th Avenue, New York, NY 10001